PRAISE FOR PAUL KANE

"Paul Kane is a first-rate storyteller, never failing to marry his insights into the world and its anguish with the pleasures of phrases eloquently turned."

— **Clive Barker, bestselling author of *The Hellbound Heart, Abarat, Mr. B. Gone* & *The Scarlet Gospels***

"I'm impressed by the range of Paul Kane's imagination. It seems there is no risk, no high-stakes gamble, he fears to take… Kane's foot never gets even close to the brake pedal."

— **Peter Straub, bestselling author of *Ghost Story, Mr. X, Lost Boy Lost Girl* and *In the Night Room***

"Kane finds the everyday horrors buried within us, rips them out and serves them up in these deliciously dark tales."

— **Kelley Armstrong, bestselling author of *Bitten, Haunted, Broken, Waking the Witch* and *Thirteen***

"Paul Kane is a name to watch. His work is disturbing and very creepy."

— **Tim Lebbon, *New York Times* bestselling author of *The Cabin in the Woods, Echo City* and *The Silence***

"Paul Kane has considerable writing talent which I hope he continues to develop."

— **Graham Masterton, bestselling author of *The Manitou, Descendent* and *Edgewise***

"Kane's work pulses with poison mischief."

— **Richard Christian Matheson, Hollywood scriptwriter for *The Incredible Hulk* and *Nightmares and Dreamscapes*; author of *Dystopia* and *Scars and Other Distinguishing Marks***

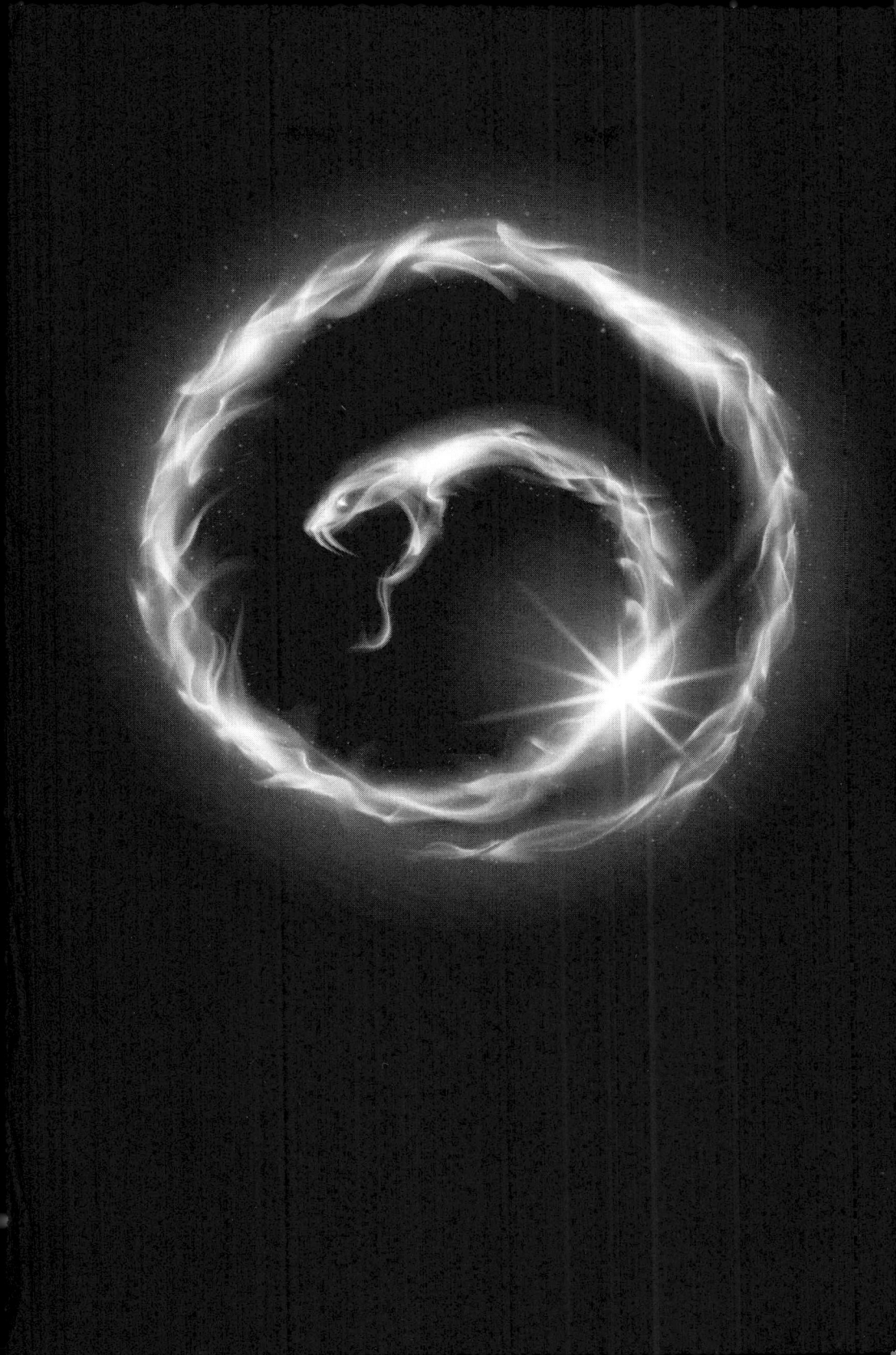

This novel remains
the copyright of the author.

BEFORE
ISBN-13: 978-1-940658-78-0
ISBN-10: 1-940658-78-0
Grey Matter Press First Trade Paperback Edition - October 2017

GREY MATTER
P R E S S

CHICAGO

Novel Website
paulkanesbefore.com

Grey Matter Press
greymatterpress.com

Grey Matter Press on Facebook
facebook.com/greymatterpress

BEFORE

PAUL KANE

FOR MY GOOD FRIEND JOHN CONNOLLY,
WHOSE KINDNESS I WILL NEVER FORGET.

BEFORE

TABLE OF CONTENTS

Here is eternal dwelling place,
Here is end of trouble,
Here is some remembrance.

—Roman grave inscription from Lamasta

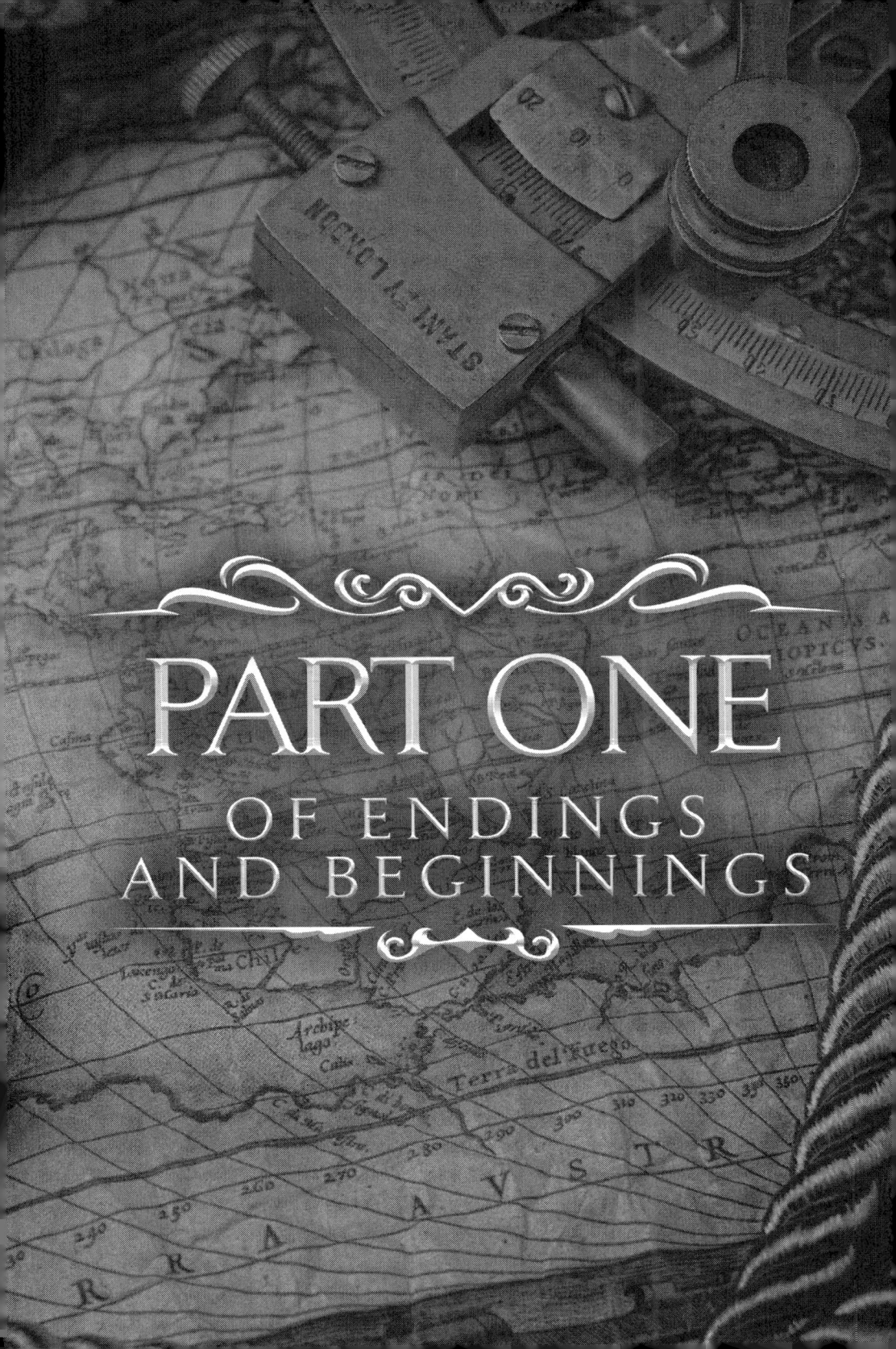

PART ONE

OF ENDINGS
AND BEGINNINGS

ONE

Wittenberg, Germany, 1970s

– i –

"You must come at once… It is most urgent."

SUMMER WAS ALMOST HERE.

And everywhere there were signs of its homecoming. Spring had done its job, revitalising foliage and flowers dulled by a severe winter. But now the show was well and truly about to begin. It was time for the warm-up man to exit stage left and let the real performers get on with their work.

The more weekends that passed, the more the annual choir of buzzing lawnmowers increased in size and volume. As the grass rose, along with the pollen count, hordes of complete strangers were suddenly sneezing and crying in unison. Insects came out of hiding, flies slipped through the gaps in open windows then spent all day trying to escape from their self-imposed prisons.

The most glaring indication, though, had to be the one hanging so high above: the central attraction in a composition of pure blues and whites. The sun was literally in its element, a burning circle of heat and light. Some said that in years to come that same sun would be the downfall of the human race, that its "friendly" rays might kill us all. But for now none of that seemed to matter. Like the ancient civilisations of before, the city's population worshipped that orb like a god, sitting out on chairs or loungers, willing their skin to turn a golden shade of brown.

Nowhere were these many suggestions of summer more apparent than in the park's gardens, its path flanked on either side by skilful arrangements of flowers. In spite of the fact it was early on a Saturday morning, the park was quite full. Teeming not only with these so-called sun-worshippers, but with those who simply wanted to stroll along and take in the scenery. It was just too nice to be stuck indoors.

A sentiment Patrick Vaughn was inclined to agree with.

"Hurry…"

For him the park was a shortcut to the place where he'd worked for the last nine months. A job that required him to be on call at weekends. He'd left his wife Marina in bed, a flick of her hand acknowledging his departure. She wasn't really a morning person and would happily snooze away till noon no matter what the weather. Patrick had kissed her on the forehead and watched her drift back into a deep sleep moments later. It always amazed him how she could do that; out like a light as soon as her head hit the pillow, while he would mull over the day's events, frequently tossing and turning for hours before falling asleep, then stirring at the slightest noise.

"It is most urgent…"

Patrick headed for the park gates. Turning right, he walked up the street, nodding a greeting to everyone he met on the way. One or two people even said *"Guten Tag"* to him.

As he passed by a house with its windows set quite low, he caught a fleeting glimpse of himself. He was painfully aware that he was losing his hair at a rapid pace, yet from this angle it looked like he owned a full head. Patrick wore a short-sleeved blue shirt, his navy tie loose around his neck and the first button undone. The sunglasses he'd been forced to wear broke up the sameness of his face, and he thought what a shame it would be to have to take them off when he arrived. For one thing they allowed him to surreptitiously observe others, something he'd been trained to do and couldn't be switched off that easily.

Now his destination wasn't far away: a special wing of the university's medical faculty. Not for the first time since he'd been summoned that morning, Patrick wondered why he'd been called out. Why Dr. Lehrer had requested his personal attendance.

Again those words drifted through his mind, "*You must come at once…*" He supposed he would find out soon enough.

– ii –

Like so many of the buildings in Wittenberg, the university was a "living" place of legend. A building where old met new, and where ideas were valued more keenly than any precious stones or metals.

The wing where Patrick worked was one of the newer additions; it had only been around for about thirty years. A clinic devoted to the study of one subject only: the mind.

He had to walk down halls that echoed with other people's memories to find it. *If only these corridors could talk*, he thought to himself, *what stories would they have to tell?* Sunlight streamed in through the windows as he made his way down a flight of steps. His sunglasses were already safely stowed away in his pocket, and now, as much as it pained him to do so, he fastened up the neck button on his collar and straightened his tie. Finally, he took out his identity card and clipped it to his shirt.

It wasn't long before he arrived at the reception desk where he was greeted by the weekend receptionist, Hilde, who had her plaited brown hair bunched up tight at the sides of her head. She was in the kind of shape professional wrestlers might only dream about achieving, which was a shame because her face was so feminine—her cheeks boasting a rosy glow. And she was as friendly as the rest of the population…if anything a little bit too friendly.

"Guten T—Good morning, Herr Doktor Vaughn," she said, patting the sides of her hair to make sure it was in place. Hilde insisted on speaking English even though his grasp of German was much better than average.

He nodded. "Hallo, Fräulein. Dr. Lehrer…Herr Doktor Lehrer called me in this morning. I don't suppose you know why?"

She leaned over the desk, elbows digging into wood that creaked with complaint. "I do not know for certain, but I think it may have to do with your patient…" She paused, trying to remember which one.

Patience, thought Patrick, *remember she only works here part-time*. "Wurfel? Ostermann?" he suggested. Hilde shook her head at each one. "Von Trapp?"

"Von… I do not believe we have a patient of that name, Herr Doktor."

The one thing they had yet to get used to about Patrick was his dry sense of humour. "My apologies, Fräulein. That was meant to be a joke."

"Ah, most amusing, Herr Doktor Vaughn," said Hilde with a completely straight face. "No, the patient is the one without a second name."

"Johann?"

"Yes, that is the patient."

Patrick frowned. "Is he all right?"

Now Hilde gave a half-smile. "Perhaps it might be best if you speak with Herr Doktor Lehrer personally. He has been waiting for you."

Patrick thanked her politely and walked off up the corridor—into the clinic wing itself.

– iii –

Ever since he could remember, Patrick Vaughn had been interested in human behaviour. In what made himself, and others, tick. Even as a child, when the school bullies were picking on a classmate, he couldn't help wondering what their home life might be like. A drunken father who beat them? An overbearing mother?

While he was still a teenager, Patrick discovered a vocation that might allow him to pursue these interests, and hopefully help people in the process. His main inspiration, like so many before him, was of course Freud. The Viennese neurologist who investigated the subconscious mind through dream analysis, childhood memories and free association, developing techniques that would come to be clumped together under one umbrella term…psychoanalysis. Patrick studied his writings and his case histories, thoroughly, coming to the conclusion that psychology and psychiatry were very closely linked. Freud was a hero figure to Patrick in some respects, and the young doctor tried as much as he could to apply his teachings to his own work when he accepted his first post in a small regional hospital in Devon.

It was around this time that he met and fell in love with Marina, who was visiting an elderly relative elsewhere in that same hospital. She got lost and asked him to show her the way, which he did…then asked for her phone number. Looking back, it was a bold move, stupid even—she might have reported him for being a nuisance. But he was glad he'd summoned up the courage, as opportunities like that only come around once in a lifetime.

Which was why when he heard of a position opening up in Wittenberg, he did everything within his power to secure it. This included asking a few favours from old tutors or more senior members of staff at his current hospital. The position was a step down from his duties there—Marina balked when he mentioned the word junior—but it afforded Patrick the chance to work with a man he'd admired for such a long time. Not quite as long as Freud…but, almost.

Doctor Andreas Lehrer was required reading when Patrick went to university. He was a living legend. His story was a tragic yet admirable one. He'd entered into the profession because of his older sister, who had suffered from depression most of her life and committed suicide at the age of twenty-five. Dedication was the key to Lehrer's success, a driving desire to help others because he'd been powerless to help his own sibling. His "fame" in certain circles was incidental as far as he was concerned. Moreover, he shunned the limelight, publicly condemning the comparisons made between him and Patrick's other hero. Patrick knew that his chances of bagging the position at Wittenberg were slim, but if he did happen to make it to the interview stage he felt confident that he could convince Lehrer to take him on. If nothing else, it meant he and Marina could spend a week away from it all in Germany while the matter was decided.

Patrick still didn't know what had swung it for him. By the grace of the gods, he'd been given his chance—an interview with Lehrer—and he completely blew it. He'd come across as a fawning simpleton, by turns a sycophantic crawler and a nervous wreck. Inconsolable afterwards, he'd almost packed their bags that night and dragged Marina to the airport to catch the next available flight back home.

Then the call came through to their lodgings notifying him he was definitely on the short list. Patrick was so shocked he nearly dropped the receiver on the floor. Why? Why had Lehrer chosen him to be on the list above the string of other, more qualified—and more coherent—psychiatrists? He was even more astonished when, after he'd returned to the clinic, he discovered that the job was his if he wanted it. *If he wanted it? Were they joking? Toying with this gullible foreigner?*

Patrick waited for the punchline, but it never came. Unlike him, Lehrer didn't make jokes. It was completely above board and Patrick was expected to start his duties as soon as all the arrangements could be made. Lehrer had obviously seen something in him at that interview. Although Patrick couldn't think what—unless it was absolute desperation. He still didn't know to this day, and was too afraid to ask the man directly. Lehrer's serious manner, not overtly cold but bordering on the rude sometimes, peering through thick milk-bottle glasses, was enough to stay Patrick's tongue. *When I get to know him a bit better,* Patrick kept telling himself, understanding full well that hardly anyone *ever* got to know Dr. Lehrer better.

He'd travelled all the way back to England with a bemused look on his face. Patrick had then dealt with the details of moving to Wittenberg, sorting out his accommodation in both countries, saying goodbye to friends and family. His father insisted he was "fraternising with the enemy," but the man belonged to a different era, and Patrick believed some things were better off left in the past. Marina had been right behind him, never once complaining at being uprooted and leaving everything she knew behind.

But that slight feeling of paranoia still hadn't worn off. Even though he was doing good work here—or so he thought—he half expected Lehrer to inform him someday that it was all over. Then he'd pack and leave Wittenberg forever. A part of him was even worried that this might be the reason for his summons today, regardless of the fact he was officially on call.

And the news that it was about Johann hadn't put his mind at ease.

"You must come at once… It is most urgent…"

Patrick had been introduced to Johann after only a week or so at the clinic. Johann had spent many years in a psychiatric institution in Berlin before being transferred into Dr. Lehrer's care. Rumour had it that the old man had been found wandering down some train tracks, his ragged clothes barely clinging to his body, his skin so filthy it took several showers and baths to scrape most of the dirt off. He was gazing out into space as he shuffled along, spittle flowing from both corners of his mouth. Childlike in his demeanor, Johann couldn't—or wouldn't—answer anyone's questions. He simply carried on staring out at something only he could see. Many treatments had been tried, including response to musical stimulus, which was how he'd come by his name. One of the doctors had noted his head bobbing when they played him Bach's *Suite No. 3 in D*—more specifically "Air on a G String." They even attempted to hypnotise him, but failed dismally to get any kind of decent feedback.

That's when Lehrer had stepped in.

To him, Johann represented a mystery. Who was this man? How had he come to be in this state? What had driven him to it? There was an intelligence behind his flickering eyes, Lehrer was certain of it. Johann was like a puppy sitting on a clifftop. He could go either way—over the edge, or back to the safety of level ground. All they had to do was coax him down from the precipice. Easier said than done.

Patrick recalled that first encounter with Johann, who'd been dressed in a pair of cream pyjamas and sitting in a wheelchair in the corner of the recreation room. Johann's chair was facing Patrick, but the man's head was lolling to one side. The first thing that struck the doctor was Johann's mane of flowing white hair. Patrick wondered what condition it had been in when they found him, what *things* had been camping out in those locks. Then Patrick's gaze dropped to those frail hands shaking in his lap, the skin loose and diaphanous.

"Johann?" Dr. Lehrer said to him. "This is Herr Doktor Vaughn."

Johann didn't move.

"Hallo, Johann," said Patrick, crouching down. The junior psychiatrist stared into the man's green eyes, where he saw a spark of acknowledgement. It was only a quick flash, but it was there. And it gave Patrick hope.

"It would appear that he likes you," said Dr. Lehrer.

The feeling was entirely mutual, and soon Lehrer's mystery became Patrick's too. Because of the interest he expressed in Johann, and because Dr. Lehrer felt that it would be mutually beneficial, the old man was added to the list of patients under Patrick's care. He never received any special treatment, and Patrick never spent any more or less time with him than he did with the others, but for some reason he felt it was important to get through to him. To bring him back from the brink.

It wasn't that Johann had a sleeping sickness, although the symptoms *were* very similar. And it wasn't that he'd been like this since birth, as a couple of his previous doctors had speculated. Something had happened that forced him to retreat from reality. Something deeply traumatic, and there was no telling exactly when it had occurred. Could have happened just before he was picked up, could have been decades ago.

But Johann still had a future, if only they could get him to face up to what had taken place in his past.

But aren't some things better left in the past…? This was different; a man's life—his very sanity—was at stake.

And since Patrick's arrival, they'd made steady progress with his recovery. He'd started off with the simple things, talking to him, trying to penetrate the defences Johann had erected. Once or twice he even looked like he was going to talk back, but he always returned to that hidden place in his mind. Then Patrick had brought out the picture-cards in an effort to re-familiarise him with the outside world. What was in the pictures didn't matter quite so much as Johann's recognition of them. A car, a house, animals… These had triggered one of the most exciting sessions yet. As Patrick was flipping through the images, Johann suddenly clutched at his chair arms and looked like he was about to cry out. Patrick immediately dropped the cards and rushed to his side.

"Johann? Johann, what is it?" he asked. But within seconds the old man had gone back to staring into space, his hands resting on the chair arms once more, shaking involuntarily.

Patrick had tried this several times since, but never got the same response again. Maybe he had been pushing Johann too hard lately, and that was the reason he'd been called out today, because his patient had had a relapse?

Patrick took the next turn on his left, which brought him to another corridor—this one with doors on either side. He counted down the ones on his right until he came to the thirteenth. *Unlucky for some*, he thought. Hopefully not for Johann…

He paused outside the door, then knocked three times on its wooden surface.

"Come," a voice said from inside. It was unmistakably Lehrer's.

Patrick opened the door and walked inside.

– iv –

Johann was in his bed, propped up with pillows behind his back and neck.

Patrick noticed that his breakfast had been tipped up and spilt all over the tray beside the bed. Next to the pool of mush were a couple of scrunched-up tissues that would ordinarily have been used to wipe Johann's mouth when feeding him, but had today been called upon to mop up the worst of the mess.

Dr. Lehrer was standing at the foot of the bed, looking directly across at Johann. His arms were folded, but every now and again he would free one hand to rub his chin, something he habitually did when nervous. Not until Patrick was fully in the room, with the door closed behind him, did Lehrer so much as glance over. And not until Patrick was by his side did the man speak.

"Herr Doktor Vaughn, there have been…developments with our friend Johann," he said quite matter-of-factly in German. Lehrer always— without exception—spoke in German.

"What…what sort of developments?"

"This morning, when the nurse came to give him his breakfast, Johann suddenly became hysterical. He began to scream and shout, and even grabbed the nurse by the arm."

"No…" Patrick began, then saw the leather restraints at each of Johann's wrists, holding him down to the bed. "I can't believe it. He's never shown any signs of violent tendencies before…has he?"

"As you say, no. But I have seen the bruises on the nurse's arm myself. She was not exactly expecting this turn of events, and was a little taken aback. Once she had regained her composure, she shouted for help, which arrived promptly." Patrick knew that the "help" Lehrer referred to was probably the orderly Carl, who could easily match Hilde in the wrestling stakes. The restraints would have been his doing, necessary more to stop Johann injuring himself than anyone else. Probably. "I was attending to another patient when the incident took place, but arrived shortly afterwards to find that Johann had calmed himself somewhat. However, it was still necessary to administer a very mild sedative."

Patrick sighed. "I don't understand any of this. I thought we were doing so well."

"Perhaps that is it. Perhaps this is directly related to your sessions with Johann."

He does *blame me, then*, thought Patrick. "Herr Doktor Lehrer, I'm sorry—"

"Patrick, Patrick…" It was the first time Dr. Lehrer had used his Christian name, a gesture usually reserved only for family members and the closest of friends. Lehrer took off his thick-lensed glasses and began to wipe them on a piece of cloth. Without these, his eyes seemed much larger—and kinder. He looked less like a living legend today, and more like a human being. "Do you not see, it is *because* you were doing so well that this has occurred."

Patrick suddenly felt rather dense. Now he knew what Lehrer was getting at. "You mean…"

"Yes, Patrick. Johann is starting to remember. He is starting to remember."

— v —

Patrick waited while Dr. Lehrer started his tape recorder up, its huge spools spinning at the flip of the switch. Then, as his superior had suggested *("Out of the two of us, he undoubtedly trusts you the most, Patrick…")*, he started to talk to Johann.

"Johann? Johann can you hear me? It's Herr… It's Doctor Vaughn. You remember…"

Was that a question or a command? A Freudian slip?

Patrick sat on a plastic seat next to the bed, one hand on Johann's arm—physical contact which might prove crucial. "What happened this morning, do you think you can tell me?"

To all intents and purposes, Johann was right back to square one: non-responsive, immobile, his eyes staring out at a point beyond Patrick. Except now he could see something more in those eyes: fear. Patrick was starting to wonder whether Lehrer had given him too much medication when Johann suddenly sat bolt upright in the bed, his restraints the only things stopping him from jumping out.

"Johann?"

Johann began to grunt, mutter and mumble. It reminded Patrick of the cavemen he'd seen in cheesy dinosaur romps, speaking in a made-up language all of their own. But it had been a while since Johann had said anything at all, and it was bound to feel strange at first.

"Mnnnmmmm amm!" he gasped.

"Take it slowly, Johann. There's no rush."

But apparently there was, because Johann shook his head. "Mmnnnno t-t-t-time."

"Well that was plain enough, even in German," said Patrick. "No time for what, Johann?"

"Bee-bee-before. No…no…mmuch time be…"

"Before," encouraged Dr. Lehrer.

Johann nodded. "Before eeet…before eet."

"You want something to eat? Is that it? Are you hungry?"

Johann shook his head violently. "Before eet, eet bee-beeegins ag-ag-again."

"Before what begins again?" said Lehrer. "What is he saying?"

"F-F-For God'ssssake, listen." Johann strained against his leather shackles. "Hee… He is gooo, he is going to come fooo… Come for me agu-agu-agu—"

"Again?" offered Patrick. Apparently this was the right answer because he wasn't corrected. "Who are you talking about, Johann? Did someone do something to you?"

"B-B-Bad."

"Something bad?"

"Heee… Hee is, he is the be-begin… And thee…theeee en…"

Lehrer stepped closer to the bed. "Who is?"

"Einf… Einf… Einf…"

Patrick and Lehrer looked at each other in puzzlement.

It was then that Johann started to cry. To begin with just a single tear ran down each of his cheeks, but more soon followed. He wept like a baby, the sorrow palpable. "Ohh, oh tho-those… *All those* people," he sobbed. "Ah… All dead… All of them… Toh-toh, tooo many… I see eet… I can seee them… Showed *meee!*"

"Johann?" Patrick climbed up to sit on the bed itself, and held Johann by his shoulders.

"N-N-Not s-strong…enough… Wh-whu-what… What have we done?"

Again, Patrick looked at Lehrer. It was obvious they were both think-ing the same thing. Johann was trying to verbalise what had happened to him, what had caused his mental collapse. It involved people dying, which wasn't uncommon. An accident? One for which Johann was responsible? There was certainly a fair amount of repressed grief below the surface. But a lot of what he was saying just didn't make any sense…yet.

Johann buried his head in Patrick's shoulder and both men were shak-en by the sobs. Moments later, he pulled away again and said: "Tuh-tuh… Tell her…"

"Who, Johann? Tell who? And tell them what?"

"Auh…or… Our fault… I-I-I… Lov…"

"Someone you loved?" asked Lehrer. "What happened to them, Jo-hann?"

"Gone." It was a single, precise word. And it chilled them both to the core.

Lehrer pressed on. "Did…did they die, Johann? Was that one of the people you mentioned?"

But Johann had moved on to another subject, or rather back to a pre-vious one. "M-n-no time. M-no tiiimme!"

"Johann," said Patrick. "Johann, listen to me. You have to trust us, there's plenty of—"

"M-nooo!" Johann roared. "Lis… *Listen* to mee! Nuh-nuh… No time left… Auh, Ai hav…m-no time. Yuh-yuh…you… You hav…have to stop it… Do-don… It can't happen again! Not again… Bru-bruh…break…." Patrick thought he wanted to rest, but then Johann finished what he was saying. "Bruh-break the cir-circ-circle!"

"I don't understand, Johann. Please, you're going to have to—"

"Eee… He is… He is the beginning. And…he…and… He…" Johann's eyes suddenly bulged as if a pressure was building inside his head. He railed against the bonds that held him, a surge running through his body like an invis-ible current. Then he slumped on the bed, his eyes rolling back in their sockets.

"Johann!" shouted Patrick. "Johann! Oh no, *Johann!*" He automati-cally went to the man's wrist for a pulse, forgetting the leather straps that were there. Quickly, he scrambled over Johann and felt the side of his neck. There was no beat. "I think he's gone into arrest."

"What?" Lehrer seemed genuinely stunned.

Patrick put one hand over the other and began pressing down on Johann's chest. "He's arrested, go get some help," he snapped in English.

Dr. Lehrer, living legend and Patrick's boss, did exactly as he was told.

Patrick continued to fight for Johann's life, compressing his chest, trying to start up his heart muscle again. He broke off and opened the old man's mouth, then placed his own lips over Johann's without a second thought. Patrick breathed life into him, hoping that some of it might take root. He felt Johann's neck again—still nothing—and began to bang on his chest. It was only after the third thump that Johann inhaled.

"Johann? Johann stay with me."

Johann opened his eyes slowly. Patrick felt at his neck again. There was a pulse now, but it was very shallow.

Then Johann whispered something to him, more coherently than anything he'd ever said to Patrick. "Let me go. There's nothing you can do. I have lived too long, and... And now finally my punishment is over."

Patrick gaped at him. Johann smiled and closed his eyes again. The doctor prepared himself to start CPR once more, then paused. Something told him to pull back, that carrying on would be futile. It went against everything he'd ever held dear, but Patrick had to let Johann go to his peace. He climbed off the bed and walked away, just as Dr. Lehrer burst in through the door with two nurses and a crash-cart.

"It's too late," Patrick told them. "Johann is dead."

– vi –

That afternoon Patrick visited a small bar he was familiar with and quietly drank one ale after another. His attempt to wipe the image of Johann's face from his mind didn't work. If anything, it made things gradually worse.

He'd never lost a patient before—he was a psychiatrist not a casualty physician—and it left him feeling... How *did* he feel? Patrick didn't really know. Cold on the inside, while out in the sunshine the temperature was rising by degrees. Upset, confused, tormented? All of these and more. The fact that he'd stood by while Johann passed away wasn't helping matters. He still didn't know why he'd done that. To let him go to a final serenity, to release him from the bondage of his own existence, such as that existence had been?

It was almost as if Johann had known he was about to die. *Nuh-nuh… No time left… Auh, Ai hav…m-no time.* And what little time he had been given he spent trying to tell them something of great importance. Important to *him* at any rate. Something about death, about endings and beginnings… The ramblings of a madman or the final glimpse of—

It hardly mattered now. Johann was no longer their concern. No longer Patrick's patient—Patrick would be lucky if he still had *any* patients after shouting at Lehrer—and no longer their responsibility.

Auh…or… Our fault… I-I-I…lov…

Who did he love? If only he'd given Patrick a name, someone to contact. A family, a son or daughter. A wife…

Marina.

Patrick looked at his watch and gulped down the last of his beer. It was time he was heading back to his own family.

He came in through the door and was greeted with an onslaught of questions. Where had he been? What had he been doing? One whiff of his breath should've told Marina that. Why didn't the clinic know where he was? The receptionist there had taken great pleasure in telling her this.

Patrick simply waved his hand, just as she'd done when he left that morning, and opened his arms wide. Right now he needed Marina more than he'd ever needed anyone in his life. He wanted to hold her and for her to hold him—which she did. She could see it in his face that he had more questions to ponder than these insignificants.

And it was too soon for answers of any kind.

But one day…

Maybe, just maybe, they would come.

Two

One year later, South-East Asia

– i –

THE HEAT WAS UNBEARABLE, THE SUN FIERCE.

Not that you could see the sun for trees. Trees so tall they seemed to stretch right up into the clouds, like Jack's beanstalk. In any normal place these might have provided some cover from the baking hot sphere above. But this was Hell on Earth, or so they said: a place where everyday rules didn't apply. Where a minute could last a whole lifetime, and you could live an entire lifetime in the space of sixty seconds.

As far as the eye could see, everything was green. It could send you a little nuts sometimes. That and the black ants, which were everywhere. And the noise: the perpetual sound of crickets rubbing their back legs together, the song of birds high up out of harm's way, and the stealthy padding of much larger beasts. If you closed your eyes and listened you could almost hear the trees breathing, their leaves creating more and more oxygen. Yet strangely there was precious little air. You could easily pass out or puke your guts up under these conditions. Dehydration was a danger if you didn't keep sipping water from your canteen and wetting your face to keep yourself awake.

If there was one thing you didn't want to be here in the jungle, it was sluggish. Every rumble in the undergrowth, every breeze stirring the brush was cause for concern. Even the ground beneath your feet was rarely your friend. Pits filled with sharpened punji sticks, covered over and camouflaged, awaited the careless like the traps our ancestors used to catch food. Or trip-wires, set so low they were almost impossible to spot.

They tried to move quietly, blend in. But this was not their territory. This was warfare on the enemy's terms, and surprise was very often their greatest weapon.

But it went on. For some poor bastards who'd pulled three tours or more this had even begun to feel like a kind of home. The land of mom's apple pie seemed so very far away. Just a dream they'd once had before waking up in this rat infested shit-hole. Their "real" lives had started when they disembarked from that plane, and a lot of them now feared returning. This place changed men. Left them numb; ate them up and spat them out. And for what?

Sergeant Grant Chester knew that he wasn't the only person who'd asked such a question. He'd seen things over here that no one should *ever* have to see, atrocities that were never reported. Soldiers skinned alive and left to hang in the treetops, the heat cooking their bodies like meat on a spit. Local women raped, their children slaughtered because they were suspected of being collaborators. Villages set alight, farmer's crops destroyed. Medics working on a platoon of infantry in the torrential rain, trying to stem the bleeding from ruined arms and legs, attempting to hold men's guts in after bullets had done their damnedest to rip them to shreds.

So *was* it all worth it? The more this war dragged on the more he was inclined to say no. Nothing was worth this—especially something that arguably wasn't their battle in the first place and was looking more and more like one they could never win. In his mind it was like a rolling snowball that had got out of control; nobody could remember who had made it, and now it was so huge that no one knew how to stop the thing. They'd tried withdrawing troops over the last couple of years and the fighting still continued. But he followed his superior's orders: obeyed the chain of command and kept his head down, as he'd been taught.

Every now and again, though, along came a mission that *did* mean something. They weren't just trudging through the wilderness for no reason this time, to scout ahead or confirm Com Sec intelligence reports. They had an honest to God purpose: to rescue US prisoners of war held captive in a village near the Cambodian border. The sergeant had heard all the stories about what they did to POWs—the Geneva Conventions meant fuck all out here—and had put himself in that situation many times. Imagined how he'd sit there in the bamboo cage, sweat flowing from his half-naked body, praying for someone—anyone—to come and rescue him. It was his greatest fear, in fact. Now he was in a position to end that nightmare for at least a dozen men.

That wasn't to say he liked how this Special Ops mission had come about. Just a few days ago they'd all been on temporary R&R, kicking back at a makeshift camp next to the beach, only a few klicks away from their current position. Most of the guys would have preferred to be in a major city like Da Nang, but there was a bar and there was music from a battered old radio playing Elvis numbers.

And there were girls.

Grant had been tempted. Jesus, in this place, who wouldn't be? One girl in particular, on a stool by the bar, had caught his eye. She wasn't like the rest, wasn't dressed in a tight silk dress to accentuate her curves, but instead wore a simple top and trousers. She seemed more...*real* than the others. Sadder, too. There was nobody waiting for him back home now, but he knew the working girls were forced into doing this to make money for their families. Some of them were barely more than seventeen, if that.

Grant had surveyed the scene, straight out of Sodom and Gomorrah. There was Little John—who, unlike his namesake, *was* the smallest member of the team—with his head buried in some girl's cleavage. And Cornball, who hailed from Iowa, was knocking back the beers like they were going to run out of supplies.

Rabbit—so-called because he once dug himself a hole during a firefight and stayed hidden until reinforcements arrived—was in the far corner smoking a "peace pipe" with the Chief. Not an actual chief but one-quarter Cherokee, or so he claimed. Grant didn't know what was in that pipe, but he had a fair idea.

Missy—short for Mississippi Max—had started up a card game with Phones the radio operator. Niles, their resident artist, was sketching in his pad between hands—having run out of space on his painted rifle—and Joe Friday, Hulk and Tailor were also gambling. Finally Wolfman—a guy so hairy it was generally agreed that some sort of lycanthropy had to be involved—and Slim were tucking into bowls of rice and raw fish with their fingers.

They were an okay bunch, all things considered, and they were a tight-knit group. Usually officers liked to maintain a reasonable distance between themselves and the troops, but Grant knew all of them well.

The last member of the team, Pope, came over and sat opposite him. Grant liked Pope, not least because he hailed from his native California.

"Joint's jumpin' tonight, Sarge," said Pope, supping on his beer.

"Yeah," Grant replied. *Eat, drink and be merry...* It was a common tactic, allowing the men to have a good time before sending them on some crappy mission from which they'd be lucky to return with both their balls still swinging between their legs.

"I notice Crowe's nowhere to be seen," Pope said. Crowe hadn't been with them that long, just a few short months. He'd been a replacement for their last lieutenant who got his throat slit supervising a listening post one night. "What d'you reckon they're cooking up for us this time?"

"I don't know, but there's definitely something in the air."

"That'll be Rabbit and Chief over there. Soldier could get high from ten miles away when they're smoking that shit."

"You know what I'm talking about."

"Yes, sir, I do. Well, I for one ain't in no hurry to find out, y'know what I mean?"

Grant nodded. He knew exactly what Pope meant. But it hadn't worked out that way at all...

The next morning at around 0900, a chopper landed in the compound. The noise woke Grant up and he looked out of the flap in his tent. He watched as a figure hopped out of the olive green helicopter. The man was average height and build, but carried himself with the confidence of a much larger person. He wore green fatigues, a beret and sunglasses. He took a long, lingering look around, sniffed the air, then strode across the compound towards Crowe's tent. The man's name was Captain Finn, as Grant later found out.

And by 0600 hours the next day, the whole outfit would be preparing to move out with him.

– ii –

Finn had brought along the fresh orders they'd been waiting for and was to oversee the entire mission himself, which would probably have put any other lieutenant's nose out of joint. But if Crowe was angry at all, he certainly hid it well.

The captain had reason to believe that up to twelve American soldiers were being held captive. He'd been given permission to take a small team out, all that could be spared at the moment. Grant's outfit was one of the closest, and it was also one of the best.

When he was called to Crowe's tent and told the details, Grant's first question was: "What about enemy numbers, sir? How many Vietcong will there be in the actual village?"

"Don't worry about Charlie. I've been assured that there's a minimal presence, Sergeant," Crowe informed him. "Plus we will have the element of surprise on *our* side for a change."

"Are you sure about that?" asked Grant.

"He's sure," came a voice from the back of the tent. Captain Finn had been sitting there the whole time, head down, never uttering a word. Now that he had, it threw Grant. His timbre was deep; it could probably be equally severe or amiable, depending on his mood. Grant could imagine him reducing a private to tears, then congratulating another for a job well done in the same breath. Finn raised his head and looked at him with a pair of deep blue eyes that matched his cool voice.

"Permission to speak freely, sir."

"I thought you *were*," said Crowe.

"Could I ask where this information originated from?"

Finn flashed his blue eyes and pointed behind Grant. He turned to see the girl from the bar at the tent flap. She was still wearing the same clothes and had that same mournful expression on her face. For the second time in as many minutes, Grant was taken aback.

Crowe beckoned her inside and she nervously obeyed. Grant and the girl regarded each other as she passed and went to stand by Captain Finn's side.

"She's a Chu Hoi?" asked Grant, figuring her to be a VC guerrilla now on their side.

"No," said Crowe. "She's just a…civilian. But she has every reason to help us. Charlie murdered her father because he refused to smuggle arms for them."

"And that makes her trustworthy?" Grant was still staring at the girl. He hadn't meant it to sound like an accusation.

"Her information has proved reliable in the past," said Finn. "And if there's even a chance of saving those men… Besides, she's putting herself in as much danger as us."

"How's that, sir?"

"Because, Sergeant Chester, Ha'ng is coming with us. She's going to lead us right *to* that village."

– iii –

Looking back, Grant was positive he was being kept in the dark about something. It was bad enough that they were about to place their lives in the hands of some young Vietnamese girl who claimed to know the whereabouts of the missing POWs. He couldn't put his finger on quite what it was, but he'd vowed to find out. If there was one thing he hated, it was secrets.

Even as they'd boarded the Bell UH-1 choppers, ready to make the insertion further inland, he'd felt uneasy—the nagging doubts more like huge, neon warning signs. At the same time he did want to free the prisoners. It was an important mission, and that was enough to fight back the demons for the time being.

So here they were. Back in the jungle.

They moved in a single line through the dense thickness, maintaining radio silence all the way. Captain Finn, Ha'ng and Lieutenant Crowe were up ahead, leading a string of helmeted soldiers behind them. Once or twice Grant looked back over his shoulder to see Hulk carrying his massive M60 on his shoulders, up and behind his neck like a peasant in the stocks. Chief, nursing a non-standard issue pump-action shotgun, was edgy. His constant glancing to the left and right was, in turn, making those in front and behind nervous as well. Grant could just about see the tip of Wolfman's M-16 waving around in the air beyond them at the very end of the line.

But regardless of Chief's jitters it was so far so good. They hadn't come across any trouble yet, and the village couldn't be that much further away, could it? Only Ha'ng knew that for sure. Small wonder his men were more keyed up than usual.

As Little John had said to him back at the compound, "We're supposed to just blindly follow a gook, Sarge?"

"Didn't seem to bother you the other night, Johnny," Pope had remarked, referring to the smaller man's dancing partner. "She was leading, wasn't she?"

Grant had sneered at Little John's use of that term, but in effect the guy was right. They *were* blindly following Ha'ng.

At that moment Grant was aware of a commotion behind him. Instinctively he turned and brought up his rifle, only to witness Joe Friday falling. Grant's first thought was that he'd been shot, except there hadn't been any gunfire. A sniper maybe? He pushed down the line and through the small crowd gathered around Joe.

"Jesus," said Tailor.

Grant still couldn't see what was wrong, but he could hear Joe crying out in pain. "What's happened?"

"Motherfucking snakebite," growled Missy.

Grant squatted down beside Joe, who was in considerable distress. "Whereabouts?"

"Hey, watch yourself," warned Pope. "Might still be around."

Tailor pointed upwards. "It fell out of the trees. Went straight for him, man."

"Joe, where did it bite you?" asked Grant, then saw the swelling on his neck. "Oh my God…" Joe was foaming at the mouth, and could hardly catch his breath.

"What's the hold-up here?" This was Crowe. Pope filled him in.

Grant took off his helmet, bent over and began to suck on Joe's neck. He felt like a vampire, only it wasn't blood filling his mouth—it was a bittersweet taste he had to spit out immediately. Grant was aware of someone bending down on the other side of Joe, and looked up to see a concerned Ha'ng. She touched his hand and shook her head. Joe was rigid and white foam covered the whole of his mouth and chin. Ha'ng was right; it was over.

"That ain't no way to go, man," said Tailor. "No way!"

"Will you shut the fuck up," Missy told him, wiping sweat from his dark brow.

Niles suddenly chimed in. "Hey, there it is!" Everyone looked over and saw a silver-brown snake sliding along the ground, heading for the undergrowth.

"No you don't, motherfucker." Missy's machete was out and he chased after the reptile. "This one's for Joe." He brought the blade down across the back of the snake, slicing it in two. "Now who's the man?" he said, hacking it again and again. "Now who's the—"

A hand grabbed his arm and held it. Missy turned to see Captain Finn. "That's enough, soldier."

For a second, Grant thought Missy was going to attack him with the machete as well. Then Finn let go of the black man's arm.

"All right people," said Crowe. "Let's break it up and get moving. We've still got a job to do."

Niles gaped at him in disbelief, resting his painted rifle on one shoulder. "Ain't you got no respect for the dead?"

"Yeah, man, what're we going to do about Joe?" asked Slim.

Lt. Crowe thought about this for a second. "Two choices: leave him and pick him up after the mission's completed, or bury him here and now... Except we haven't got time for that."

"No," said Finn. "He comes with us."

"Excuse me?" said Crowe.

"I'm...*we're* not leaving anyone behind this time. You there," Finn pointed to Hulk. "Think you can carry that man's weight as far as the village?" Hulk nodded.

And from that moment on, their attitude towards Finn seemed to change. They had respect for him now, Grant could sense it. All except Missy, who glared at him from time to time. It was obvious Finn wanted to take Joe back and give him a decent funeral in the States, but something else was also apparent from his slip of the tongue: *I'm not leaving* anyone *behind this time*. Those men being held prisoner in the village were *his* men. They had to be. That's why he was so keen to head this mission and to trust in Ha'ng's word.

Ha'ng.

Grant rose from beside Joe's body and kept his eyes on her the whole time. Somehow he knew he could trust her. His judgement might be clouded by what he'd felt when he first saw her at the bar—though God knows he'd tried to put that to one side—or maybe it had been the way she'd touched his hand, the compassion she'd shown for one of his men. Or perhaps it was something completely different?

As she rejoined the captain and lieutenant, Grant felt a sense of loss. He wanted to be up there walking with her, wanted to speak to her, find out who she was, what had happened to her father. Wanted to make those sad eyes happy again.

"Talkative sort, ain't she?" whispered Pope, but Grant ignored him. And the journey got underway again.

– iv –

Grant had been wrong about the distance between them and the village.

The troops walked for a good couple of miles more before reaching anything remotely resembling a clearing. Then, after consulting with Ha'ng, Captain Finn passed the signal back for them all to stop.

"We there, Sarge?" asked Niles from behind Grant.

"Looks that way."

Crowe motioned for Grant to come forward and specified that he wanted a three-man recon team to scope out the village. Grant chose Pope and Slim to accompany him. Crouching all the way, they split off to spy on the village from different angles. When he could see the edge of the clearing, Grant got down on the ground and crawled on his belly, watching for booby traps as he went.

He unhooked his binoculars and brought them up to his eyes. Grant could see the small village clearly. Its simplistic congregation of straw and bamboo huts was like so many he'd seen in the past. There was movement, two men wearing hats that went up to a point and green-brown, pyjama-like clothes. Each held an AK-47 rifle and had a utility belt strapped around their waists, plus a lethal-looking dagger at their hips. Vietcong soldiers.

Grant waited, and after a while saw two more VC join them. Four guards in total. But who knew how many might be in hiding? Exactly what constituted a "minimal presence?"

When he'd gathered as much information as possible, Grant returned to the platoon to find Pope and Slim already reporting back.

"Okay, time to find out where they have the POWs." Finn barked out his orders. "Grant, you take the lead. Wolfman, Tailor—you go with him and take the left flank. Cornball, Rabbit, Missy—you take the right." They split up and circled the village.

Grant glanced over as he ran towards the cover of a hut and saw Cornball mirroring his actions across the clearing. So far, so good. He drew his knife and crept closer, his heart hammering, motioning his backup to follow.

He risked a look around the side of the hut—

And came face to face with a Vietcong guerrilla.

Grant had no time to think, he acted on instinct. He plunged his knife into the soldier's chest, pushing him backwards and placing a hand over his mouth. The man shuddered and squirmed beneath him, but Grant held him down tight. Somebody slipped past on the left-hand side, and Grant looked up to see Wolfman using the butt of his rifle to bring down another VC.

Grant jumped when he felt a hand on his shoulder. It was Tailor, pointing at the man on the ground, now quite clearly dead. Grant pulled out the knife. It wasn't the first VC he'd ever dispatched, but with each kill something died inside him as well.

The three of them moved around the side of the village and came across more VC bodies. Missy, Rabbit and Cornball had also been successful. The six of them checked the huts. Looking in through windows and cautiously toeing open doors. They found no sign of anything…or anyone.

"I don't like it. Place is fucking deserted, man," said Tailor. "We should get the hell out of here."

Instead, Grant gave the all-clear signal and the rest of the squad entered the village. Captain Finn approached him first. "Status, Sergeant?"

"Nothing to report, sir. Not a goddamn thing," said Grant.

"What're you talking about? Where are the POWs?"

"You tell me."

"Maybe we ought to be asking *her* where they are," said Missy, grabbing Ha'ng's arm. "Come on, what's the fucking beef, sister?"

Ha'ng shook her head, terrified and confused. "I-I not know what happened. Americans were here, I swear."

It was the first time Grant had heard her speak. Her English was fragile, on the verge of breaking. "Leave her be," he told Missy.

"But she—"

"You heard me, I said leave her be!"

Missy released Ha'ng's arm, and she gave Grant a timid smile.

"All right," said Lieutenant Crowe. "Phones, let's call it in. This one's a washout."

Phones was about to get on the radio when there was a shout from inside one of the huts. Cornball came running out, holding his helmet. "It's Pope, sir," he said. "You'd better come quick. He's found something I think you're gonna want to see…"

— v —

That "something" turned out to be a crudely constructed trapdoor on the floor in the corner of the hut. Most of the soldiers went inside to look, all except Chief, Rabbit, Hulk and Niles, who were keeping a careful watch on the jungle.

"It was underneath all this matting and stuff," Pope said.

"Jesus, do you think the POWs are down there?" Little John asked.

"Fuckin' A!" Missy exclaimed.

"Either that or it's the opening to a set of VC underground tunnels." Wolfman put into words what everyone else was thinking.

Lt. Crowe turned to Ha'ng and asked: "Any idea what might be down there?"

She shook her head.

"So now what?" This was Slim, who was standing next to the trapdoor with his M-16 trained on it.

"Now," Crowe said, "we need someone to go down and check it out. ASAP."

Almost as one, the soldiers turned to each other and said: "Rabbit."

* * *

Rabbit was outside with Chief, staring into the jungle and wishing he could bring out the peace pipe again.

"Rabbit!" Crowe shouted from inside the hut. "Get your ass in here right now, soldier."

"Fuck," Rabbit said. "What now?"

Chief shrugged and patted him on the shoulder. "Can't be any worse than having to off two VC with your bare hands before lunch, *kemo sabe*."

"Wanna bet?" Rabbit walked over to the hut and stepped inside. His contemporaries were regarding him strangely, like he was the next Messiah. Then he saw Slim covering the trapdoor with his rifle. He began shaking his head.

"Uh-uh, no way. No fucking way," he said and tried to exit the hut. Captain Finn barred his path.

"Come on, Rabbit," Crowe said. "Holes in the ground are your speciality."

"And what the fuck would you know, *Lieutenant*? You've only been with this outfit five minutes. What gives you the right to—"

"What gives me the right is that I'm your superior officer, soldier!" Crowe's eyes narrowed. "If I order you to cut off your own dick and eat it with a fresh green salad, you will comply! And you'll love every goddamned mouthful. Do I make myself perfectly clear?"

Rabbit looked like he was going to challenge Crowe again, but nodded quietly.

Little John was told to open the door, as Pope and Grant joined Slim in his vigil. They could easily be blown sky high by a booby trap left on the door itself, but that was a risk they had to take. Luckily nothing was triggered when John lifted the lid, and no one started shooting at them from inside.

Rabbit poked his head over the lip of the void, flashlight in one hand and a pistol in the other. With one last look at his comrades, he eased himself in. Then the darkness ate him and his torch alive.

The next five or ten minutes were the longest Grant Chester could ever recall. Waiting for the loud bang of Rabbit's gun, the return fire, the screams of VC and POWs alike. But there was nothing.

Then eventually there came a noise from inside: a soft pattering and thrashing sound. Slim peered into the hole while Pope held him back with one arm. Suddenly, something—or several somethings—sprang out. Black and large they launched themselves upwards like missiles. The men guarding the door almost started shooting until Grant heard the terrified squeaking and realised they were just rats disturbed by Rabbit's activities below.

"Hold your fire," he said as the rodents scuttled away to find new hiding places.

"Wait… Listen… There's something else," said Pope, then did exactly what he'd stopped Slim from doing moments earlier. Except as *he* leant over, a hand reached up and grabbed his shirt. "*Jesus!*" He cried out and tried to wrench himself away. The others pulled him back and took hold of the hand.

"It's me… It's me!" came a muffled voice from inside, coughing from the dust and dried mud. "Rabbit."

"Well, don't just stand there," said Crowe. "Get him up!"

Rabbit looked like he'd been mining, his face and clothes covered with dirt. After they'd helped him out, he sat with his legs dangling into the cavity.

"What did you see down there?" Captain Finn asked him. "Any sign of the POWs?"

"You guys are not gonna believe it," Rabbit said. "I had to crawl quite a way inside, but when I got there… Geez, you're really not going to believe it."

"Rabbit," prompted Crowe.

"No sign of any POWs." He looked at Finn. "Sorry, Captain. But down there, right under our feet, Lieutenant, sir, is the largest motherfucking ammo dump and weapons store I've ever seen in my life."

Crowe's hand went to his brow. "What?"

"We're talking AK rifles, Chicoms, Simonovs, DP 7.62 millimetre machine guns, Tokarevs, grenades, mines, crates of ammunition. There's enough down there to supply half the VC outfits in this region."

Cornball whistled.

"Sweet mother of God," said Crowe.

Pope looked at the lieutenant. "But why wasn't it better protected?"

"Never hear of hiding things in plain sight?" Little John replied.

"I don't get this," Missy said. "I don't get this at all. We come out here on a rescue mission and find an ammo dump instead. Somethin' ain't right here."

Crowe turned to Captain Finn. "I'm inclined to agree with him, sir. What's going on?"

Captain Finn scratched his cheek. "I've no more idea than you have, Lieutenant."

"Ha'ng?" said Crowe. The young Vietnamese girl shook her head again. "Well it can't—"

The lieutenant was interrupted by someone calling his name from outside. It was Chief, backing up towards the hut itself, a worried expression on his face. He turned and took two steps—

Then his chest exploded outwards in a rain of blood, bone and muscle. Chief's expression was a mixture of surprise and acceptance, his body slumping to the ground as more bullets raked the air. Seconds later, the whole jungle lit up with flashes of gunfire.

The soldiers dropped to their knees at the sound of machine guns. Holes were punched into the sides of the hut, its straw and bamboo covering no match for the deadly projectiles.

"*Chief?*" Rabbit shouted above the noise. Crowe didn't answer.

"Niles and Hulk are still out there," Pope reminded everybody.

"If they didn't manage to find cover..." Little John said, but couldn't finish his sentence.

"Suggestions, people?" Crowe mumbled, squashed up against the floor as flat as he could get.

"Well here's one," Slim said, crawling past the lieutenant and swinging his M-16 around. He stood up and jammed the gun through a window, then depressed the trigger, firing off round after round into the jungle beyond. His platoon followed suit. Grant shoved his rifle through a hole made by VC fire, then started pumping .223 calibre bullets randomly into the green.

The enemy returned their rounds with interest, making a mockery of the hut's walls. Little John caught a spray across his shoulder and face, and stumbled backwards into the middle of the room, screaming in agony.

Crowe was shouting for Phones, but the radio operator was at other side of the hut. He bellowed the order as loud as he could. "Get hold of the choppers, we need air support and extraction ASAP!" Crowe couldn't hear Phones' reply, but watched as the man slung his backpack around and took hold of the telephone-shaped radio.

"Looks like our gook friends have come back to claim what's theirs," Pope said from the right of Grant.

"Or they motherfucking knew about us somehow!" Missy spat. "What you got to say about that, girl?" His venom was directed at Ha'ng, who was sitting with her hands over her ears, tears streaming down her face. The fact she was ignoring him angered him more. "How about we throw her out there and let her own kind deal with her?"

He got up and grabbed Ha'ng. She looked petrified, shaking as the big man from Mississippi took out his pistol. "Or we could just do her now and get it over with."

"No!" Grant said.

Missy grinned and cocked the gun—

But before he could pull the trigger, a hail of bullets tore through the hut and thumped into his back. He collapsed on top of Ha'ng.

Slim, too, caught a cluster of bullets—the force of which was so great it threw him across the hut, where he joined a dying Little John.

Grant was aware of Pope tugging on his shirtsleeve. He turned slowly and saw that most of his comrade's face was missing, replaced by a sodden red mass. The one good eye Pope had left was open wide in disbelief, begging Grant for help. Then Pope fell over sideways, his hand relinquishing its grip on Grant's shirt. He fought the urge to vomit, returning his gaze to the light display outside and slamming another magazine into the underbelly of his M-16.

"What about smashing through the back of the hut and getting out that way?" suggested Cornball.

"Worth a try," Wolfman said.

"Okay, do it!" Crowe shouted.

Cornball, Wolfman and Tailor made their way across the floor towards the back of the hut. Two of them began to hammer on the bamboo with the butts of their rifles, while the third set to work with a knife, loosening the supports.

Another soldier joined Grant in a defensive capacity. He was surprised to see Captain Finn next to him on the front ranks, but the man seemed quite at home there. The captain said nothing, he simply got on with the task. He made each shot count, and wherever he aimed, Grant noted, his fire was never returned.

"Captain?" Grant spoke up. Finn only acknowledged his question by rolling one perfectly blue eye in his direction. It was neither the time nor the place, but the sergeant had to know for sure. "Those men you—we—were looking for…"

"What of them?" Finn answered simply and sharply.

"They were yours, weren't they? *Your* men."

Now Finn did turn fully, his stare clear and precise. "Son," he said in that voice of his, the one that could be as persuasive as an insurance salesman and as lethal as a tarantula bite, "you're all my men. Every last one of you."

It seemed like a mighty peculiar answer to Grant, but at the same time it made all the sense in the world. For some reason Grant smiled, then he started firing into the brush again.

Behind him, the three men had managed to break down the back wall of the hut. Cornball put his hand to his mouth, but only got as far as, "Lieutenant Crowe—" before a vicious smattering of hot lead penetrated the hut. Cornball's body jerked around like a puppet. Wolfman and Tailor were the next to be hit. The remaining walls of the hut were given a coat of shiny red.

Now the enemy were advancing. Grant caught sight of figures emerging from the jungle, as if sensing the Americans were outnumbered. Crowe pulled himself across the floor towards Phones, obviously still trying to get through for support.

"Where the hell are those Hueys?" Crowe reached up to tap him on the shoulder and the man rolled over, revealing large craters in his chest and stomach. He gurgled something Crowe couldn't catch, then he died. Crowe looked up through the gap at the rear of the hut to see more VCs emerging.

Standing, he dropped his weapon and started furiously waving his hands in surrender. "I am Lieutenant Crowe," he shouted, "of the US—" He never got to finish his speech, the VC cutting him down in a single barrage. Crowe rolled around on the floor mouthing the words, "Gook bastards," then he reached for a grenade off his belt, pulled the pin and with his last ounce of strength tossed it in the direction of the massing enemy troops.

Now there was just Grant and Finn left. The sergeant felt like Custer making his last stand. He knew they didn't have a prayer, yet would rather die than end up like the men they'd come to save. But he was running out of ammo and soon…

Ammo.

Grant suddenly remembered the trapdoor, the ammo dump. "Captain? Captain Finn?"

"What is it?" Finn said, letting off another round. "I'm kinda busy right now." If Grant hadn't known better, he might've sworn his superior was actually getting off on this.

"The trapdoor, sir. If we can hole up in there…"

The captain grinned. "Good idea. Let's go."

They lay down a blanket of covering fire first, then made for the hatch. Grant let the captain slide in first. Next he swung his own legs in, taking one last look around him at the devastation. The bodies…

It was only now that he saw her, remembered her. Ha'ng was still trapped beneath the bulky form of Missy. He could just see her hand sticking out, fingers waving.

"Jesus!" he said. Without another thought, Grant climbed back out. He heard Finn call after him, but ignored it.

The VC had almost reached the hut, and Grant wasn't surprised to see one of their number at the shattered front door. They exchanged glances for a moment, then the VC raised his rifle at Grant's head. The sergeant closed his eyes tight, waiting for the inevitable.

And the familiar *rat-ta-tat* of machine gun fire wasn't far behind.

– vi –

Grant felt nothing. No searing hot pain, no sensation whatsoever. He was still aware of being in the hut, of being in the middle of a battle. Could still hear the noise outside, and now inside. But it seemed so very far away. *So this is death*, he thought. *It's not so bad.*

Except he wasn't quite dead yet. Someone was calling out his name. "Sarge… Sergeant Chester?"

Grant attempted to speak and found that, yes, his vocal cords *were* still working. "Hulk?"

Grant opened his eyes and saw the enormous man slipping in sideways through the hut door. He was holding the heavy M60 in his left hand and an M-16 in the other. The VC who had almost killed Grant was nowhere to be seen.

There was a noise from behind Grant. Hulk whipped his M-16 around and shot at a VC trying to clamber through the exposed area at the back of the hut.

"Hulk," said Grant. "Are you okay?"

"I'll live," he replied, grimacing. There was a tone in his voice which hinted that Niles certainly wouldn't. In fact, unless Grant was gravely mistaken, the rifle Hulk was using actually belonged to Niles. He could tell by the way he'd decorated it. Niles would never have parted with this work of art willingly.

"D'you think you can lift Missy off Ha'ng?" said Grant.

Hulk looked across and found Missy's body, then put down the M-16 for a second. He continued to fire the heavier machine gun—its cartridge belt dragged through as casings spat out the other side—while he grabbed hold of Missy's shirt and hauled the black man up with little effort.

Grant abandoned his own rifle and crawled across to Ha'ng, who was shaking in fear. When she looked up and saw his face, she stopped and reached out for him. He clasped her hands in his, pulling her towards him and the open trapdoor. It was an effort, but Ha'ng helped by kicking her legs like a swimmer transplanted to dry land. At last they made it and he instructed her to get inside. She hesitated a moment when she saw Captain Finn there waiting, but allowed herself to be lifted down. Grant climbed in, then called out for Hulk to join them.

The VCs had regrouped and were again storming the hut, overpowering Hulk. Grant didn't want to leave him there, but the decision was taken out of his hands when a VC opened fire—a killshot at point-blank range.

Grant dropped into the hole and scrambled after Ha'ng and Captain Finn. He seemed to crawl for miles in darkness before he came to a glimmer of light. There, at the end of the tunnel, was the opening Rabbit had talked about and was standing in right now, clearly having retreated here as soon as the gunfire began. Next to him were the young Vietnamese girl and the captain. Then he saw ammo. Rabbit hadn't been exaggerating when he described the place; it was like a deadly Aladdin's cave. Grant wished that he too could find a lamp amongst it all and simply spirit them away.

He came further inside, taking off his helmet, wiping the sweat and dirt from his face with one hand and drawing his automatic with the other.

"Are…" Rabbit began. "Are they all…?"

"Dead? Yes," Grant told him.

"Jesus, Mary and Joseph."

"Listen, Rabbit, is there any way out? Another tunnel maybe?"

Rabbit shook his head. "None that I've seen, Sarge."

"Could we dig one, then?"

"If we had time…and supports to stop the ground above caving in and burying us all." Rabbit sank down on the ground next to the box on which his torch was resting. "But we haven't got time, have we?"

Grant cocked an ear to the tunnel behind him. Already he could hear the VC climbing down to follow them. At least they could only travel one or two at a time. Grant took out his pistol and fired into the darkness. The warning shot seemed to work for a minute or two, but then more scrambling sounds wafted down.

Stupid… He could pick them off as they came through. There was enough ammunition in here to play that game for weeks. Thing was, they didn't have much food or water, and they didn't know whether help was on its way. Had Phones died before or after he'd patched in that call? Had he even been able to get through? If Missy's theory was correct and they were expected, then it was possible the Vietcong had cut off all radio signals at the source.

Grant looked across at Ha'ng. He'd been reluctant to trust her at first, but now he couldn't believe that she'd do such a thing.

Dirt began to shake from the ceiling; Grant looked up. More earth fell, this time accompanied by a cascade of dust.

"What the fuck?" Rabbit said.

The captain joined Grant in examining the "roof". It wasn't the most stable of ceilings to begin with, but it had chosen the worst moment ever to be giving way.

"They're going to try and dig us out," said the captain. "Right now, there's probably a group of VC directly above us with shovels."

Rabbit stood up again. "Say what?"

"You heard me."

"Oh God, oh Jesus, oh God…" Rabbit flitted from one side of the chamber to another, looking exactly like the proverbial cottontail caught in the headlights. Ha'ng watched him and bit her lip.

"How long?" asked Grant.

The Captain shrugged. "The way they can dig… Not long."

"Oh God, oh Jesus!"

As Rabbit raced past, Finn grabbed him by the arm and slapped his face. "Quit that soldier! You're a member of the United States Army. Aren't you the same soldier who dug himself in at Laos? You should be used to all this."

If anything, his past experience was making Rabbit more nervous, but that wasn't what was bothering Grant. The neon warning signs lit up again brighter than before. "How did you know about what happened to Rabbit?"

Finn turned to him and smirked. "How do you think? I read all your files before choosing you for this mission."

"You couldn't have," Grant said. "That mission was classified. Only the top brass and our outfit know what happened to Rabbit back in Laos."

"I have top level clearance."

More dirt and dust fell from above, and a piece of "roof" actually dropped behind Grant's head. Ha'ng let out a small yelp and went to him, arms outstretched, begging to be held.

"They're coming through," said Finn. "We haven't got long." He threw Rabbit to the floor and looked at Grant. "Do you know what they'll do when they capture us, Chester?"

Grant knew all right. It was his worst fear. But somehow Finn knew that, too. There was a noise from behind him and Grant was shocked to see a VC poking his head out of the tunnel opening. In all the confusion, he'd neglected his post at the entrance. In one quick movement, so fast Grant barely had time to register it, Finn had drawn his pistol and sent a bullet speeding the startled man's way. The bang was loud inside the space and caused the ceiling to shake even more. But the body now blocking the tunnel would keep others from gaining entrance…for now.

Captain Finn stepped closer to Grant, and Ha'ng hugged the sergeant tighter. It was at that moment he realised the truth. Grant raised his own gun at the captain's head.

"There never were any POWs here, were there?"

"Of course there were. As Ha'ng said—"

"Look at her, she's terrified of you. Of *you*, Finn. All those VCs out there and she's scared of you. Why is that, d'you think?"

The captain paused to consider the question, but in the end Ha'ng answered it for him: "Vietcong no kill my father."

Rabbit, who was still on the floor, said, "What's she talking about? What's going on?"

Grant couldn't answer that question. Only Finn could, and time was fast running out. "Forget about that, Sergeant. You know what has to be done."

"You're right," Grant said and pulled the trigger.

Finn dropped backwards, toppling over Rabbit and pulling the trigger of his own gun in the last spasms of death. His bullet almost hit the ammo crates encircling them.

Ha'ng buried her head in Grant's chest and wept.

"You're safe," he said, dropping his smoking pistol and stroking the back of her hair with his hand. The words were hollow. How could they be safe with the VCs digging their way inside to get to them?

There was only one true way they'd be safe, only one way to prevent the enemy from taking them captive and torturing them and…

You know what has to be done.

God forgive him, but he did.

Grant took one of the grenades from his belt. Rabbit's face contorted in horror when he grasped what the sergeant was about to do. But it was the only way. To save them all from…from a fate *worse* than death? To stop this arsenal from being used in the future to take countless lives. It was the only way.

Grant looked down at Ha'ng. She smiled her sad smile, as if she'd known this was going to happen all along. Grant pulled the pin and she placed her hands over his.

Rabbit screamed at the top of his voice, but was cut off before it could reach a crescendo.

– vii –

Now Grant Chester knew of death.

He felt it, touched it, tasted it; experienced every emotion known to man all wrapped up in one powerful bundle. And unlike the last time, above ground, when he'd thought the VC machine gun fire would finish him off, there *was* pain. So much pain it was hard to describe, not that he would ever get the chance to tell anyone.

And it lasted an eternity…

If you could live a lifetime in a minute over here, now he lived several million lifetimes of agony in the space of a millisecond. Everything around him disappeared: the bunker, Rabbit, even Ha'ng. All gone, leaving him to his own private Hell on Earth. Like Hell, there was heat—more unbearable than the hottest sun. There was also the guilt and remorse of things left undone, things you wished you *could* undo, and things you wished you'd done more of...

It wasn't insects plucking at his skin this time, but the harsh reality of oblivion. It wasn't the ground he had to be wary of but the lack of it, and the absence of *any* kind of sound. Grant could only hear the swelling of his own mind as it was stretched to the point of collapse.

Yet the trace elements of his brain could recall the last thing he'd seen as the grenade exploded; a torment the likes of which Hell could never have imagined. Grant remembered seeing Captain Finn on the floor, a bullet-hole rose blooming crimson in the centre of his forehead.

But Finn was also laughing to himself, heartily laughing when he should be…

So the final thought Grant ever had was: *How can this be? What has a dead man got to laugh* about? Nothing, as he would find out for himself soon enough. But there Finn was, laughing out loud, defying rationality. Sending Grant spiralling into madness for the last remaining moments of his existence.

The laugh followed him to this place, haunted him where no sounds could be heard. Everything he knew to be right was suddenly wrong. And now what remained of Sergeant Grant Chester's soul would endure captivity far longer than if he'd been taken prisoner by the Vietcong.

– viii –

Everything was still.

The explosion had taken out not only the village, but a section of jungle almost a mile in circumference. The crater and smoke could be seen from the air, by the single chopper now making its way across the horizon, the *thrup-thrup* of its approach increasing in volume by the inch.

Its pilot hovered above, staring at the circle through his visor. He'd intercepted the radio operator's signal, even though it had been hard to make out clearly because of all the machine gun fire—sounded like quite a party down there—and had set off for the rendezvous point immediately.

Even if he hadn't received the message, he still had orders to return. This only made things neater, and meant that his superior wouldn't have to hang around for a lift. Nevertheless the pilot who, out here, went by the name of "Blades" but was generally known as Lucas, would wait a while longer. He knew these sorts of things could take time. And he had no intention of interrupting. Lucas had no real desire to watch another reassemblage. Once had been more than enough for him, even if he did pride himself on his strong stomach.

So he watched, and he waited.

And he smiled.

* * *

On the ground the smoke was clearing. The fires were dying down.

Dust and ash fought each other for dominance over the site. But inevitably neither would be victorious. For at the core of the crater something was stirring. Tiny subatomic particles, invisible to the naked eye, were shifting about. Molecules were returning like homing pigeons to the scene of their scattering, and were sorting themselves—bonding, creating something out of nothing. Cells undergoing mitosis. Willed on by an intelligence that was yet to be housed, the miracle of life began anew.

This collection of specks began to take shape, to reform themselves—the process slow at first, then speeding up exponentially. It wasn't long before the shapes took on a recognisable appearance; not long before tubes, coils, tissues, veins and organs all fell into place like cadets on an inspection line parade. Next came the knitting together of bones, lubricated by unseen liquids, slathered with red juices; muscle upon muscle, given substance and perfect texture, tone and conformation. Crying out for nerve endings to complete the picture. Teeth and tongue appeared out of nowhere, fabricated by a craftsman with the deftest of touches. Skin swathed the structure, wrapping itself around the bloody mess of gore, giving it a more palatable facade. Empty sockets were filled with the gooey whiteness of orbs, and behind this the lenses, irises, pupils and finally corneas plopped into being. And the eyes shone with a certain blueness…

The strange thing blinked with eyelids that hadn't been there mere seconds ago.

Nails grew out of the ends of fingers and toes, hair suddenly sprouted on *almost* finished arms and legs, at the crotch—now swelling with the sight of genitalia, the skin there expanding to accommodate it—under pits, on the chest and the head.

It was a man. That is to say it had the *appearance* of a man. But this was no ordinary being. For now he looked down upon his nearly completed body, and with one wordless command encouraged his clothes to piece themselves together again in a blur of activity. Socks ravelled themselves around his feet, the leather of boots covering this immediately afterwards. Green boxer shorts appeared at his midriff, flowing down and encasing the impressive reproductive organs. Next followed the trousers and shirt, covering his nakedness—not that he would ever be embarrassed by it… And on the fatigues a name stitched itself into the material: Cpt. Finn.

The Infinity opened his mouth and let out a satisfying "*Ahhh!*"

He moved one arm, testing his work, holding out the backs of each hand, then flipping them over where lines were still being drawn across the palms. He watched the lifeline grow with interest. Then he checked each leg, lifting it and stamping it down again so that the boot made an impression on the charred soil. He walked around in a small circle, tracing the shape of the blast site. The explosion had been a good one. Very effective. And yes, he probably could have avoided being down in that hole when Sergeant Chester pulled the pin, but he would have missed all the fun.

The remaking of his corporeal form was a bothersome procedure, and there were always things he tended to miss on the first go—last time he'd forgotten to give himself a belly button, the time before that toenails. But the experience he'd just been through, being blown into a billion pieces… It had to be worth the trouble. True, it wasn't as spectacular as some he'd been involved in, but it would keep him going for a while.

Such moments made life worth living.

The Infinity gazed around at the devastation, then took in a huge breath of rank, smoky air, polluting his freshly minted lungs. There was nothing like it, nothing in the world. The smell of fear and death.

It saddened him to think that soon this particular conflict might be over. Eventually, the US would completely withdraw and the North would take over the running of the country. But what he'd done here today would fan the flames for some time, extending the war beyond its natural course. The Americans, although they'd lost one of their best teams, would take solace in the fact that they'd also accidentally destroyed one of the enemy's largest ammo dumps—so secret not even the Top Brass knew about it. *Top Brass…* The Infinity laughed softly at that. And the VC? It would only strengthen their resolve; that's why they were destined to win in the end. That's why the US should never have been here in the first place and probably wouldn't have if they'd been left to their own devices…

But that wasn't the only reason he'd come. He liked to keep his hand in, get down and dirty every now and again. The Infinity missed the old days when he spent more time doing this kind of thing than in boardrooms and corridors of power. The new global range of the world did have its advantages, but it also had its drawbacks. Manipulation of the rich, the powerful, the famous, was easy. Doing so to people like Chester, with true strength of character, now that was a real challenge.

Crowe had been a pushover, no challenge whatsoever. But Chester… he had the respect of the rest of the outfit. The Infinity had decided to earn the man's trust as a way into the squad, to use a ploy that tapped into his own fears of incarceration at the hands of the Vietcong, to use Ha'ng to confuse him even more.

It hadn't been a lie. There *had* been POWs here at one time, it was just that they'd been moved—suddenly and without warning—a month or so ago, and the village had been chosen as a temporary weapons and ammo dump. A good idea, the VC had thought at the time. They'd even keep their military presence in the area low-key to avoid drawing attention. Imagine their surprise, then, when they were informed that a group of US soldiers were heading in the direction of that village. Still, it was only one squad, only a handful of men. They could easily deal with the situation.

The Infinity laughed again. A good day's work all in all.

He held up his hand to wave at the hovering chopper above. The pilot inside the cockpit acknowledged this with a wave of his own and set the helicopter down on the charred remains of the village. The Infinity didn't move as the rotors raked the smoke and dust around him; he didn't even blink. He just waited for them to stop spinning then for Lucas to remove his helmet and climb out of the metal husk.

The pilot approached him cautiously. But he had nothing to be frightened of on this occasion. The Infinity was in good spirits and regarded him warmly, a grin still playing at his lips.

"Sir, is that you?"

"In the flesh, Lucas. In the flesh," said the entity also known as Captain Finn.

"A successful mission then?"

"For some."

"I trust you enjoyed yourself?"

The Infinity clapped him on the shoulder. "Indeed I did, Lucas. But you have a question."

Lucas looked worried, then decided to ask it anyway. "The girl?"

"The girl. Oh, Ha'ng?"

Lucas nodded.

"She's dead. Along with anything else within a mile radius."

"Yes, but—"

"She's *staying* dead, I'm afraid, Lucas. I know I promised her to you, but she has served her purpose. And she was growing altogether too wilful for her own good. Took quite a shine to one of the soldiers, too. You wouldn't have wanted soiled goods, now, would you? Someone who's...heart wasn't in it?" The Infinity knew that it didn't matter to Lucas whether Ha'ng's heart was in it or not—Lucas would probably have removed her heart anyway—but The Infinity didn't want to expel any more good energy bringing the woman back just so this man could have his way with her. There were other girls, other Ha'ngs; Lucas would never go short as long as he did as he was told.

Lucas sighed and shook his head.

"Good boy. Now let's—" The Infinity froze up completely for a beat, then started to squeeze Lucas' shoulder. Lucas cried out in alarm. The Infinity let go of the pilot and dropped to his knees. Through eyes streaming with tears, Lucas gaped at him. Had the reassemblage not taken? Had something more serious gone wrong than a misplaced belly button? It should be an easy matter for The Infinity to fix the problem.

But Lucas had never seen him in such a state. Mouth open, shaking, staring out at something terrifying. Imagine that, something scaring The Infinity! Didn't bear thinking about. Then The Infinity clasped his chest, eyes scrunching up, breath hissing out through teeth clamped shut.

Clutching his shoulder, Lucas bent down, wondering what to do.

"Sir?" Lucas ventured. The Infinity didn't so much as look up. "Sir, are you all right?" He quite obviously was not, but Lucas couldn't think of anything else to say.

Now he was holding his head, rolling it from side to side. This went on for at least half a minute. Then he fell forward, and only just managed to get a hand in front of him, to stop himself from falling into the dirt face-first. The arm quivered, but held. Lucas crept nearer, but The Infinity—who'd sensed his presence without needing to "see" it—encouraged him to back off with another hand gesture; more aggressive than the one he'd used to summon down the chopper.

Obediently, Lucas retreated.

In time, The Infinity drew up one leg and got a foot beneath him. With both of his hands on that raised knee, he pushed himself up— standing shakily, swaying from side to side like a willow in the breeze. His cerulean eyes fixed on Lucas, who was still holding his crushed shoulder. The Infinity couldn't expect him to understand. Lucas hadn't been with him the last time this had happened—hadn't even been born. There was a lot he didn't expect him to understand. And yet it would be so nice if he did.

"Sir?" Lucas asked for the third time. His nervous, worried simpering no longer appealed. The Infinity's mood had changed and he could tell that. It was safest not to say anything more.

The Infinity cocked his head. It had to happen sometime, and he should really have been expecting it. Instead it had taken him unawares again. Of all the times for it to have occurred—straight after a reassemblage when he was at his most vulnerable, if such a word could ever be used about The Infinity. Was he being toyed with himself? Was this a way of mocking *him*? It would do no good. He would seek out his quarry before the allotted time; and once he had done what must be done, then everything would change. It had all been leading up to this…

He would have his fun, his moment. He would have it all!

The Infinity began walking towards the Huey, with Lucas following well behind. When he got there, he climbed into the passenger's seat and waited. He could heal Lucas' shoulder with a click of the fingers, but The Infinity needed cheering up. So, he would make the man fly them home as he was. Each grimace, each fearful glance across, each jolt of pain would give him pleasure.

For that was The Infinity's purpose.

And his time would surely come again.

PART TWO

BITS AND PIECES

THREE

Kirkwell: Present Day

– i –

SOUNDS.

As he stirred in his sleep, the insubstantial icons of his dreamscape began to fade as surely as if they'd never existed. Soon he would remember nothing but mangled bits and pieces: the cold, stark constant of reality was drawing him back to his senses. Music that had seemed like it was coming from so far away now sounded very close indeed. It was something by Elton John.

Alex Webber resisted the urge to open his eyes as long as he could, partially cranking open one lid. He didn't care much for the brightness streaming in from the window.

"I Guess That's Why They Call it The Blues," thought Alex, listening to the tune. That was the song, though its significance was yet to dawn on him. He reached over, squinting like Popeye, and shut off the radio alarm clock before the annoying DJ could start blaring on about traffic conditions and who was having an affair according to that morning's tabloids.

Alex opened both eyes now, searching for the time. The clock on the radio alarm was a fuzzy red blur. He blinked, trying to focus, then snatched up his glasses, open and ready on the bedside table. It was just gone seven.

He groaned, praying he'd made some terrible mistake. He had set the alarm by force of habit and it was in fact the weekend. No such luck. It was definitely a Wednesday. The weekend ahead was as far in the future as the one behind was in the past. Then he noticed the date, and groaned again.

The 15th May.

"Oh God," he mumbled, laying down again. His naked back connected with someone's forearm. The body beside him was warm; it felt nice. He rolled over and saw a face on the pillow. Beverly was lovely, even with her auburn hair all tangled up like that. If anything, this only enhanced her natural beauty. She looked just the same as when he'd first met her. Back then their whole lives were stretching out ahead of them, shared dreams and ambitions. Now the only dreams they had were the ones that visited them in the night, and they hardly ever talked about those.

He didn't know whether it was because he was still waking up, or that he was feeling particularly nostalgic—who could blame him considering the date—but he felt an uncontrollable urge to kiss her. So he did, planting his lips on her neck, then her cheek. She smiled, and for a second Alex thought there might be hope. But as he came to kiss her on the lips, Beverly pulled her head away. She presented him with *her* back and immediately cooled his half-hearted ardour.

"Happy birthday, Alex," he sighed to himself.

It was a sad situation he'd found himself in. Although they still shared a bed and a surname, the Webbers grew more distant by the day. Could Alex identify a turning point, a single day, week or month when things had changed? No—it had been more subtle than that. They both had demanding jobs, that was true, but if something was worth the effort you fought for it, didn't you? It also didn't help that they'd been trying for kids for such a long time. There was nothing wrong with either of them, they'd had all the tests—that's what made it so frustrating. It was a vicious circle: they got angry and upset because they couldn't conceive, and this in turn decreased their chances of ever having a baby. If you weren't having sex anymore you most definitely *would not* get a baby. It was cause and effect.

But if Alex was totally honest, it was probably a good thing. A baby might have solved their problems for a while, papered over the cracks. But they'd begin to show through eventually, and then what? Perhaps everything really did happen for a reason.

The silence in the bedroom was suddenly broken by the telephone ringing. The rechargeable cordless was on the bedside table; Alex swung over and picked it up, depressing the SPEAK button.

"Hello?" he said. "Oh hi, Mum. Thanks, yeah…"

Snorting to herself, Beverly pulled back the covers and got out of bed. Alex watched her put on a silk dressing gown, feeling next to nothing now at seeing her naked. His wife wandered out of the room, yawning, and closed the door behind her.

"What? No, that was just Bev getting up. What's that, how are things?" Alex paused, trying to think of a satisfactory answer. "They're…okay… really. Don't worry, Mum, everything's just fine."

– ii –

A shower and shave later, and Alex readied himself for the breakfast ritual. He had thought that Beverly might make the effort for his birthday, but was clearly wrong. She'd bought him a card, but it was the standard fare—didn't even have husband on it—which contained an equally impersonal legend inside: "It's your Birthday!" and a hastily scribbled "To Alexander, from Beverly" in blue biro.

Beverly was at the table, toying with a semi-eaten bowl of Shredded Wheat in between sips of black coffee. There was nothing put out for Alex. He shoved a couple of slices of bread into the toaster and waited for them to pop up, then covered them with butter and marmalade. The water in the kettle from Beverly's coffee was now only lukewarm, so he poured himself a glass of orange from the fridge.

"What did your mother have to say for herself?" asked Beverly as Alex sat down opposite. She wouldn't stay there long; already Alex could see her fidgeting, as if being in his proximity—and awake—was too much to bear.

Alex took a bite of his toast before answering. "Well, *after* she'd wished me happy birthday, she reminded me about the small matter of a dinner we both have to attend tonight at Zino's."

"Oh. That."

"It *is* my birthday, Bev."

That was it. Beverly rose from the table, taking her cereal and coffee and placing them on the kitchen counter. "Don't give me that, Alex. I know you too well."

Do you? he wondered. *Do you really? There was once a time when I thought I knew* you. *Inside out, back to front.*

"You hate birthdays, always have done. And you particularly hate a fuss being made, although your family insists on doing just that every year."

Regarding this subject she happened to be right. The only thing birthdays were good for was reminding you that you that middle age was on the horizon; all right, practically here. Like Christmas, they were for the young, those who couldn't see past the next day, let alone the next year or decade.

"I know, I know," said Alex. "But it makes Mum happy and that's the main thing."

"Of course," sniped Beverly.

"So?"

His wife turned to face him, leaning up against a cupboard. "Yes? What?"

"So are we going to be okay tonight?" She knew what Alex meant. Beverly might not have made the effort this morning, but he was hoping she'd play along tonight. If only for old time's sake.

"Why shouldn't we be?" Her hard face softened for a second. "Look, we'll go and *try* to enjoy ourselves. Take our mind off things."

"Thanks," Alex told her. "I really appreciate it, Bev." His old mum had no idea how serious the rift was between them. She'd already endured the heartache of three divorces with her other son, and Alex wasn't about to put her through more grief until there wasn't any other choice (after all, they did still share a bed…for now).

Beverly shrugged as though it was no big deal for her, and really it wasn't. A bit of play-acting, some making nice. She could fight back the dejection and unease for a couple of hours.

Alex ate the rest of his toast and washed it down with the juice. He pulled a face, suspecting the orange might be off. Some of that stuff in the fridge had been there ages. But there was nothing he could do about it now. Almost time he wasn't here.

He rose from the table and put his pots in the sink, telling a scowling Beverly he'd do them later. He wasn't surprised when he heard his wife adding her own dishes to the mix, then running the tap.

"I said I'd do them when I get in," he repeated, but she pretended to ignore him. "Right, then," he called out as he headed for the corridor and the door to their flat. "I'm off."

"Have a nice day, *dear*," she shouted after him.

Alex winced and picked up his bag, keys and jacket. Out on the small landing he stood, cocked back his head and took in a deep breath. In some ways it was good to be out of that atmosphere, out of the place that no longer really seemed like home. Alex jogged down the few steps that led to the door on the side of the building, which in turn took him down more steps to the ground. Theirs was the top flat of a two-flat house conversion and this was their own private entrance. It meant that they hardly ever saw the other couple downstairs, but that seemed to suit everyone just fine.

Once outside he discovered that the sun was just as hot as it was bright. Almost, but not quite, summer weather. He walked to his white Almera, parked in a small concrete rectangle that was for the flats' occupants and visitors only, then slung his bag and coat inside. Beverly's metallic green Renault Scénic was tucked up alongside his vehicle, just as she had been in bed an hour earlier.

He started the engine, backed the Almera out of its space and, as he turned to look one final time at the house, saw Beverly standing on their small balcony, next to the flower boxes on the rail. She wasn't aware that Alex was watching, otherwise she wouldn't have stood there so long. But he knew that in spite of her bravado, she shared much of his own sadness and regret at the gradual breakdown of their union.

— iii —

The drive in to work wasn't particularly pleasant. Hold-ups were the norm rather than the exception in this part of town. Congestion, that was supposed to be alleviated by various government schemes and brainwaves, was getting worse. Every other day Alex came across incidents of road rage, and the building heat would only make tempers flare more.

Inevitably, Alex found himself in one of these snarl-ups only five minutes into his drive. Bored, he turned on the radio and twiddled with the dial for a bit. But after he found nothing but clones of the breakfast station from earlier, Alex slipped in a CD to pass the time. The unique and gravelly voice of Bono blared out from the speakers at him, declaring that he still hadn't found what he was looking for.

"Join the club, pal," Alex muttered.

He listened to the first few tracks on that album, but snapped it off when "With or Without You" came on. He just couldn't handle that kind of raw emotion this morning.

Next he found himself opening his bag and flicking through some of the student essays inside. Alex Webber had been a college tutor only slightly longer than he'd been married to Beverly, landing the job after a year of teacher training.

But whenever he recalled his very first classes he cringed. The nerves, stumbling around for words, voice croaky and dry, unable to deal with the talking in class. Christ, he could hardly blame the kids; his first lectures weren't exactly riveting. Thankfully he found his feet and liked to think from that point onwards he'd become quite good at his job.

Alex had been fortunate in his chosen subject too. He'd always had a very keen interest in cinema and television and, over the years, this had somehow seeped into his work. Although he studied English, his course at university allowed him to do one or two modules in Film Studies. He learnt about camera angles, direction, production, how they put both movies and TV shows together. Alex always insisted that this information would come in useful one day, might even lead to a job in the entertainment industry behind the scenes.

And while it hadn't exactly earned him a director's job, it had come in quite handy when the colleges were looking for someone to teach the relatively new subject areas of film and media. Naturally some still looked upon them as little more than entertainment: a poor cousin to art & design. But anyone who could sit through an Eisenstein or Bergman, or even a John Ford picture and not see the artistic value were *looking* but not really *seeing*.

Class sizes grew over time, as A Level and AS Levels were introduced, and it was heartening for Alex to see the enthusiasm with which the students tackled this subject. Even the class he had today, who were taking this as a theory option for their Art and Design Course, had put so much effort into their work.

The latest essays he had here were all about their favourite films. Alex thumbed through some of the titles again. Many were Hollywood-based but this was only to be expected; these were kids of the multiplex generation. But he'd also been quite surprised by some of the choices. *King Kong* was in there—the original, not the Jackson remake—spotlighting Fay Wray's contribution to women's liberation, *Henry V* and even *The Seventh Seal*.

The traffic started to move again, so Alex put the essays back down and drove forwards. He knew he wouldn't get very far before he had to stop again, but it was nice to be on the move: he hated standing still. And if he concentrated really hard he could imagine *himself* in a movie—a road movie perhaps, set in Arizona, with nothing but stretches of empty lanes ahead where he could open up the car and let rip.

It was a nice fantasy.

A few minutes later, the car was held up again as more traffic poured out of a side street to clog up the main road.

— **iv** —

Alex eventually arrived at just gone nine. Parking was the usual nightmare, with all the campus slots filled. He ended up having to use the students' car park, which did still have a few valuable spaces.

He got out, leaving his jacket where it was but remembering to grab the essays. Alex locked the car and ran across the yard. Hindered by an uninteresting design, the principal college building had been around for at least a century or more and was definitely showing its age. The orange-brown brickwork was crumbling in places, dark cracks appearing where the mortar had come loose and fallen away. The main entrance was a huge archway which looked ridiculous on a building this plain, while the rest of the access points were simple rectangles with varnished doors.

Attached to this building were more modern structures, carved out of glass and concrete, looking like younger, fitter predators about to pounce on the old facility and finish it off. Alex had heard that the extortionate quote to renovate the central building and fix its increasingly unreliable roof might finally sound its death knell. Far more cost effective, they said, to just tear the whole lot down and erect something that would need less maintenance. Somewhere that wouldn't be freezing cold in winter even when the heating was on, and didn't let water in when it rained.

Alex was indifferent to the plight of the old college. The past didn't concern him as much as the future…about what was happening in the world and about what might happen in years to come. He worried about this generation—the one he taught. People were always on a downer when it came to the "youth of today;" it didn't matter what era you were in. But he could only speak from experience, and the kids that he taught were great. They deserved to grow up in a world where terrorism and the threat of global Armageddon wasn't constantly hanging over their heads, even if they did spend far too much of their time on their mobiles.

The lesson Alex was teaching this morning was in one of the new leech-like buildings, but the shortcut to the lecture and screening theatre was through the old college. He passed over the archway's threshold, hurrying along the corridor in an effort not to be even later.

As he ran, he heard someone calling out his name. Alex turned to see a figure at one of the classroom doors. Somebody who did place more stock in the past than him: Alex's friend James Nolan. Liverpool-born and London-raised, James had started at the college about seven or eight years after Alex, but it seemed fitting that he was now based in this block. There wasn't much about archaeology and history the guy didn't know. He plucked dates and data out of the ether like some people quote football scores. It could get quite annoying sometimes and they'd long since struck a deal. If he didn't do the whole Indiana Jones thing, then Alex wouldn't bore him with segmental breakdowns of movies.

"Thought it was you dashing past. Late again?" said James.

Alex backtracked to join him. "Traffic."

"I've been telling you for ages, get a bike." James' pride and joy was his new Apollo with eighteen speed gears. Cycling had been the only way to get around London when he was down there and he'd kept up the habit in Kirkwell. Environmentally friendly, he argued, and it cut out all the jams.

"If it's a Harley I might be interested."

"Somehow I can't see you on one of those monsters."

"Me neither."

"Now a Zimmer frame maybe." James smiled.

"Watch it—I'm not over the hill quite yet."

"How old is it this year, or have you stopped counting?"

"You're on very dangerous ground, Nolan."

James looked back inside at the class, then said, "Seriously, I've got your card in here somewhere…"

"Give it to me later. I've really got to go, mate."

"Time for a drink after work?" James asked.

"Er…I'm supposed to be going out later; family get-together." Alex pulled a face. "But I can do lunchtime if you're up for it?"

James thought about this. "Well, I have got a class this afternoon…"

"It's nearly the end of term, James. Live dangerously."

"Okay, why the hell not. You only live once, don't you?"

"Course."

"I'll meet you at the gate at 12:15," said his friend.

Alex signalled his acknowledgement with a *Prisoner*-style salute and then set off running again. He sprinted across The Plaza to C-Block, to the lecture theatre and cinema.

— v —

By the time he arrived, almost ten past nine, most of his class were already in their places: bunched close to the front on the flip-down seats. He scanned them quickly, in the main happy, cheery faces, chatting about everything from what they did last night to the drawbacks of local student accommodation. Those who weren't on their phones, that was. All turned when Alex walked in.

As with his other classes, he'd had got to know these characters well over the course of the year. He knew who were the jokers, the hard graft-ers, the promising hopefuls who would probably make it into higher ed-ucation—and those who wouldn't. They also knew *him*, and he liked to think that they enjoyed his classes. This morning, for example, after they'd gone through the essays, he was going to give a quick talk on the importance of colour in film, then show clips from movies like *The Wizard of Oz*, *The Red Shoes* and *Peeping Tom*. This afternoon there was also a cinema club screening of Fellini's *La Dolce Vita* for those with free periods. It wasn't compulsory that they attend—in fact a lot of them had work they should be getting on with—but Alex hoped a few of might pop along.

"Hi everyone," said Alex, nodding. "Sorry I'm late. Hope you've had a good week so far."

This met with an undecided reaction from the audience. The end of the year was rapidly approaching; it was make or break time. Most of them needed high grades to ascend to the next level of their education and they had exhibitions on their minds. Those specialising in fine art, sculpture and design had to choose their best work; those taking photography and film-making modules had to polish up prints or put together final cuts of their short films.

"Good, good. Cheer up, David, it can't be that bad." Alex smiled across at David Blake who looked like someone had just told him the summer holidays had been cancelled.

"You haven't seen my bank statement," replied David.

Alex nodded again, taking his point. The poor kid was probably living off vapours and that was *before* he even got to university.

But no matter how much pressure was building, at least he could take one weight off their minds. "Well, I have with me this morning something that might brighten up your day. I've marked the essays for this part of the theory module."

The class moaned.

"Hey, hey," said Alex, flapping his hands to calm them down. "Don't worry, they were fine. Better than fine, in fact. I was really impressed. Some of them were of a similar standard to my regular media and film students."

One or two of them raised their eyebrows, others were more cautiously optimistic.

"Some were actually better." This caused one or two gasps. "So, without any further ado, I'll let you have them back. Claire, could you take yours and hand the rest round, please." Alex gave the pile of essays to Claire Phillips, the blonde-haired girl sitting on the edge of the bottom row. He watched as she rifled through the folders and found the one with her name on it. Alex felt a warm glow inside as she beamed at the mark. This was why he carried on, why he'd got into teaching.

For a good few moments Claire was in dreamland, just staring at the grade. The student next to her, Vince Oglethorpe, had to gently tap her before she passed on the pile. The essays went round, and it was the same result every time: a grin or sigh of relief, followed by a comparison of marks. It was the best birthday present they could have given him. There was nothing but chatter for a while, and for the first time that morning Alex felt happy.

Then it happened.

It only lasted a fraction of a second, the briefest of flashes, but it seemed to play in slow motion. One student at the back, Timothy Brailes, reached over to grab the pile of essays from Geena Lane in front. As he did so, his face changed. It darkened considerably, like a time-lapsed make-up sequence. But it was also ageing: wrinkles appearing on the now leathery skin. Tim's brown hair turned grey, then white, tied back by a headband that hadn't been there before. Red marks were spreading down his cheeks. Tim looked at Alex with eyes that were not his own, jet-black instead of hazel.

Alex's mouth opened wide. He gaped back in disbelief. From somewhere he could hear singing. No, not singing: chanting.

"Wha…" said Alex.

He felt around behind him for a chair. Alex took his eyes off Tim for a second, and when he turned back everything had righted itself. Tim's face was normal again. He was sitting holding his essay, staring across at his tutor.

Alex found that chair and collapsed into it. He removed his glasses and pinched his nose.

"Are you all right?" Alex looked up and saw a blurred Claire Phillips approaching. "You don't look so good."

He put his glasses back on. "I'm fine, Claire. Just felt a little woozy for a second."

"You should watch that," shouted Vince. "My uncle used to have these dizzy spells all the time. They found him dead in front of his TV one morning."

"Thanks for that, Vince," Alex said.

"Do you want me to fetch anyone?" Claire asked.

"No, no. I just had a bit of a funny turn that's all. Probably overworking—marking all of your essays." Alex managed an unconvincing smile, and she smiled back just as falsely.

He looked past her at Tim again. *What just happened?* thought Alex. *Nothing, that's what. Nothing happened.* It might have been that dodgy juice at breakfast. But he'd feel sick, wouldn't he? And apart from being a little confused and embarrassed, he *was* fine.

Maybe it was just his age… He sighed.

Whatever the reason, Alex assured her: "I just need a minute, thanks Claire. Just give me a minute."

– vi –

The students gladly gave Alex his minute, and more besides. Once he'd composed himself, he felt much better. Alex didn't dwell too much on what he'd seen, and certainly didn't mention it to the other students. When he felt up to it, he got on with the morning's lesson as scheduled. By the end of the session he'd almost forgotten about the incident, or at least put it to one side.

He had other things to think about—and look forward to. Like the drink at lunch. Alex knew that he'd feel so much better after that.

But at the gate he didn't find James at all.

Alex found his older brother waiting for him instead.

– vii –

There was Steve, lolling against one of the posts, eyeing up the young female students as they drifted past on their way to lunch at the café down the road. One or two even gave him a glance back, flicking their hair and smiling. Steve had always been the better looking of the pair and the years had definitely been kind to him. He still appeared the same as he had done in his twenties, more or less; the face of an angel. Pity he didn't have the personality to match.

Whereas Alex had always tried to do the right thing, Steve had gone out of his way to do exactly the opposite. Growing up, he'd been the one in all the trouble—part of gangs that sprayed graffiti or shoplifted, before moving on to bigger and badder things. Breaking into cars, petty theft… After a string of warnings from the police, he'd notched up his first conviction at the age of fifteen. Luckily his sentence, which should have been served at a young offenders' institute, had been a suspended one. Alex thought that would put him off crime for life. No such luck; it only made him smarter about it, more careful about getting caught.

When he was seventeen, Steve moved out of home. Or, to put it more accurately, their father told him to leave. Though nothing was ever said, Alex got the impression that the family blamed Steve for the terminal stroke that came later.

Since that day Alex and his mother had heard from Steve infrequently, and usually only when he wanted money. He'd been married three times—to Tina, Natasha and Fran—but hadn't invited Alex or their mother to the weddings. The marriages hadn't lasted long enough to produce kids, as Steve continued to work his way through most of the female population of Britain. Apparently he'd had several jobs during the course of his adult lifetime, including working in a bookies, barman at various pubs and clubs, and warehouse packer. Most, or all, of these were probably a front for some kind of illegal dealings. Lord alone knew what he was up to these days. And Alex had no idea what he was doing waiting for him at the gates of the college, a grin on his face so wide you could post letters through the slot.

Steve gave him a wave, as if it only been the previous week when he saw him last, not two years ago.

"Alex, bro! How goes life as a college professor?" His voice and patter, like his face, were utterly charming.

"Hardly a professor, Steve." Alex tipped his head. "Long time no see."

"Yep, I know. But I couldn't miss…" Steve brought a card out of his jacket pocket. "*Ta-da!* My little brother's birthday."

"Why not? You missed it last year, *and* the year before that." Relenting,

Alex took the card and opened it. There was a woman in stockings and suspenders on the front and a dirty limerick inside. "I'm touched."

"What can I say?" He grinned again. "So, how's your day been?"

"I've had better…" Alex rubbed his head. "Right, let's get on with it, shall we? What are you after this time, as if I couldn't guess?"

"What do you mean?" said Steve in all innocence.

"Cash, a place to hide—sorry, I mean stay. Or is it both? After last time you'll be very lucky."

"I know—and I said I was sorry." Steve placed his hand on his chest. "Is that really what you think of me, Alex? That I'd only come back when I wanted something?"

"Well…" Alex *was* beginning to wonder. There was something different about Steve he couldn't quite put his finger on. "So that's not why you're here?"

"Course not. I'm here because it's your birthday, yeah?"

Alex studied his face. He appeared to be telling the truth, but you could never really be sure with Steve. "Look, I'm supposed to be meeting someone for a drink—"

"Really? Is Beverly aware of this? Mind you, with some of that talent around," Steve nodded at a passing girl, "I can't say I blame you."

Bad joke, Steve. Really bad. "It's a colleague from work, I think you met him once briefly. James."

"Well, that's even worse, bruv. Beverly *must* be informed immediately."

Alex moaned. "Steve, will you shut up about Beverly."

Steve put his hand on his brother's shoulder. "Hey, is something wrong between you guys?"

"It's a little late to be doing the concerned brother bit, isn't it, Steve?"

"Hey now, I always looked after you when we were kids."

Alex laughed. "Looked after me? You were hardly ever around, and even when you were you'd always get me into bother."

"Like when?"

"Like that time you and your moronic mates made me crawl through the gap in the scrap yard fence and undo the lock. Then you all ran off and left me when the owner's Alsatian came on the scene. I barely managed to get out of there in one piece."

"Oh yeah," said Steve scratching his chin. "I'd forgotten about that.

Christ, you've got a good memory, Alex. Anything else you want to hold against me?"

"How long have you got?"

Steve looked genuinely hurt. "Believe it or not, you're my little brother and I just wanted to see you. I thought today would be as good a day as any; a good excuse if you like. Seems I was wrong." He took his hand away and made as if to walk off, but Alex took his arm this time.

"Hold on."

"Alex?" This was James' voice. Alex had been so caught up in the conversation he hadn't noticed the other tutor's arrival. "Is everything okay?"

"James." Alex stepped back to allow his brother and his best friend to see each other. "You remember Steve?"

"Ah, yes." James knew a little bit about Steve; Alex had given him the edited highlights after his last flying visit. Steve stuck his hand out and waited for James to accept it, which he did finally.

"Nice to see you again, Jimmy," said Steve, effecting his most charming smile.

"Right," said James. "So…?"

Alex shrugged. "Steve, I don't suppose you want to join us, do you?"

The man smiled again, making up for James' frown. "Alex, bruv, I thought you were never going to ask."

– viii –

The closest pub to the college was the White Swan, a homely place just shy of town that had been run by the same family for generations. It was close enough to walk, but Steve insisted on taking them in his battered Capri.

James offered to pay for the sandwiches and the drinks—even Steve's—so while he was at the bar arranging it all, the two brothers claimed a table for themselves next to the window.

"I still can't believe you're here," said Alex as they sat themselves down.

"Well, I am."

"So, what are you doing these days then? Still hanging around with the usual crowd?"

Steve leaned back in his chair. "Not exactly… I tend to keep my head down nowadays. I've gone straight."

Now this Alex *really* didn't believe. His brother, going straight? Had to be a gag. But Steve's mouth wasn't even twitching. "You're not serious?"

"Why do you keep asking me that? Of course I am. Do you know *why* I've not been in touch these past couple of years? Why I missed your birthdays?"

"I assumed it was because you were too busy getting up to no good."

"That was the old Steve. No, I've been in the nick."

"What?" Alex craned his head forward. "Prison?"

"I believe that's what they call it in college, Prof."

"But…how? I mean why?"

"I was caught 'getting up to no good.'"

"It wasn't——"

"Drugs?" said Steve, way ahead of him. "You know I don't touch anything to do with that shit, Alex. Not personally anyway. Never have done."

Alex knew nothing of the kind. While it was true that his brother had always steered clear of drugs in the past, that didn't mean to say on his travels he hadn't dabbled every now and again. "So what was it then?"

"I took the heat for a GBH rap. Some of my 'friends' wanted one of their customers shaken up, so they sent along a bruiser to do the hard work and me to explain a few things to him about the protection racket."

"Oh, Steve," said Alex, disgusted at the matter-of-fact way he'd described it.

"Nothing too brutal, just a broken arm and a few fractured ribs," replied Steve, as if that made everything all right. "Unfortunately, his wife called the cops out, didn't she? They arrested us. The muscle got off and I pleaded guilty—not that I had much choice in the matter, if you follow me. I was getting pressure from the boys in blue to give up my boss or my sentence would increase, and getting pressure from my boss to take a dive, or I'd be diving permanently off the prison rooftop. Not a pretty situation, Alexander."

"But one you got yourself into," Alex pointed out.

"I realise that. I've had a lot of time to think in that place, you know?"

"I can imagine."

"Oh, believe me, you can't. Three men to a cell, having to piss and crap in front of them in a small plastic bucket every day. Having to listen to the constant crying of the prisoners who couldn't handle it in there... and night-time was the worst. Do you know, there were thirty-five suicide attempts while I was in there. *Thirty-five*, Alex! And some of them were successful as well. I didn't know whether to feel sorry for the poor bastards or be envious of them."

Alex leaned on his hand. "So why didn't you get in touch? I could have visited or something."

Steve shook his head. "Do you think I wanted you to see me in a place like that? I do have some self-respect. Besides, how long would it be before Mum got wind of where I was? You never were very good at keeping secrets from her. None of us were. Not even Dad."

"What's that supposed to mean?"

"Forget it."

"No, I—"

James joined Alex and Steve and set the tray of drinks down on the table. "One bitter," he said, placing the foaming glass next to Alex. "One lager." This went to Steve. "And mine's a half." The drinks shared out, James put the tray by the side of the table and sat down next to Alex. "Food won't be long."

Alex and James took a sip of their drinks, Steve gulped a quarter of his pint.

"So, Steve," began the history teacher, his voice even. "What have you been up to since last time you were here? Anything interesting..."

Steve and Alex exchanged glances.

"Oh, you know, this and that, Jimmy," Steve answered at last. "This and that."

* * *

During the course of lunch the subject returned to Alex and Beverly, after Steve enquired about James' marital status.

"Oh, I'm currently single," James told him, somewhat uncomfortable about the admission.

"The bachelor life, eh?" said Steve.

"I've...I've just had bad luck with my choice of women," explained James.

"Haven't we all, mate. And it's when they start to choose *you* that all the trouble starts."

"The last… Well, it didn't quite work out."

"You're not alone," said Steve, breaking off the end of his ham sandwich and shoving it into his mouth. "Women, right? Still, my brother here's showing us all how to do it. How long have you and Bev been together now, Alexander? And still going strong. I guess you just know instinctively when it's the right girl."

"Yes," said James. "I suppose you do."

Alex narrowed his eyes. All things considered, he liked his brother—or was "like" too strong a word?—but sometimes the man just didn't know when to shut up.

"That's quite some achievement in my book," said Steve. "Yep, I've got to hand it to you that—"

"Perhaps you should leave it, Steve," said James, noting Alex's discomfort.

Steve Webber looked from James to Alex, then back again. "I knew it. There *is* something wrong, isn't there? I'm sorry, Alex. I didn't mean to—"

"No, you never do."

Steve shrugged. "So you're going through a bit of a rough patch. Who doesn't?"

"*You* for a start," said Alex. "You're never been married long enough to go through any kind of patch."

"Hey, below the belt, bruv. You think just because none of my marriages lasted very long that I didn't go through this kind of stuff? Well you're wrong, okay? Dead wrong. I have feelings too."

"Come on, Steve, you've always been the same. You never think about the consequences of anything."

"Is that right?"

"Look, can we just drop the subject?" said Alex.

"Oh, so you can talk about it with James here—who seems to know all about everything—but not to your own brother. I see."

"You haven't exactly been around much lately, remember?"

Steve breathed in deeply. "Okay, sorry. I deserved that. I just don't like to see things going wrong for you. There's been too much of that in our family already."

"Speaking of family," said James, trying to change the subject. "I expect that's why you're here, Steve?"

He looked bewildered.

"For the get-together tonight. Sounds as if it's going to be—" Alex silenced him a stare.

"Ah, the famous birthday ritual," said Steve. "They still doing that one? I would've thought you'd have grown out of ice cream and jelly by now."

Jealousy. That's what it all comes down to in the end, thought Alex. They'd never lavished the same kind of attention on Steve as they had on Alex—and it obviously still rankled. The birthday parties every year for Alex and his mates were a particular bone of contention. What Steve didn't seem to realise, though, was that if they'd invited all of *his* friends around for a party the Webbers would've been lucky if their house was still standing afterwards.

"It's at Zino's, actually," said Alex.

"Italian, eh?"

Alex nodded.

"Nice. Okay, I hope you have a good time. Give my regards to the clan, won't you?"

"Look, don't be like that, Steve. Listen, if you want to maybe come along I can ring Mum up—"

"You're kidding, aren't you?"

Steve was right. Bad idea. It would be a massacre if he went along.

"Don't worry about it," said Steve, glancing at his watch. "Hey, is that the time? I should really be going. People to see, places to be." He got up and left his half-eaten sandwich, but finished off the lager in a couple of gulps. "You two need a lift back?"

"It's not far," said James.

"Right."

"Steve," said Alex, "listen—"

"Here," Steve reached into his pocket and produced a tatty piece of paper. "That's my new number and address. I don't know how long I'll be there, but, well…I figure somebody ought to have it, y'know? Happy birthday, bruv." Then he was gone, striding out of the pub. Alex got up to go after him, but thought better of it. What was the point? Maybe he was a reformed character, but there was just too much history between them—between Steve and the whole family—to simply start from scratch. Too much damage had already been done.

"I'm sorry," said James. "I just assumed."

"It's all right. Really." Alex put the paper in with Steve's birthday card.

"That reminds me," said James. He reached under the table and produced another card. "Like the man said, happy birthday, Alex!"

Alex opened it up. Unlike Steve's, this was a much more conventional design: complete with a painted picture of a man fishing on his own. He opened it up and read what James had written, "Hope you have a fantastic day".

"Thanks, James," said Alex, although he couldn't help wondering exactly when his *fantastic* day was going to begin.

FOUR

– i –

ZINO'S WAS IN THE HEART OF GRIFFIELD, the nearest city to Kirkwell.

It was even more difficult to reach than Alex's college, especially at night. Dual carriageways, ring roads, roundabouts. And then there was the parking. A night's stay in a multi-storey could set you back a small fortune, provided you could find one that had any vacancies.

Not willing to face another crawl through the traffic to get home, Alex left work early—he didn't have any actual taught lessons and he'd seen *La Dolce Vita* at least a dozen times. As anticipated, the drive *out* of town was marginally better as the rush hour traffic was still in its infancy.

Beverly was not yet home from her job at the public relations firm, so he took advantage of the quiet to have a quick lay on the couch. Not that he was able to rest. He wasn't specifically thinking about the events of the last five or six hours but they kept coming back to him: Tim, his lunch with Steve and James…

To counter this, he decided to water the plants out on the balcony; they'd had precious little moisture lately with all this dry weather.

Given the opportunity Alex would have loved a place with a huge garden so he could grow blooms to his heart's content; maybe even build a summerhouse. The shared one they had here was tiny and overgrown, neither of the couples wishing to take responsibility for it. Beverly, in particular, didn't see the need for gardens: they took up so much time… She was right about that, he supposed. It was one thing to grow plants in a window box, it was another to take care of a whole lawn full of flora and fauna.

His boxes were enough for now. Alex mixed a little Baby Bio plant food into the water and went around each box in turn, though he knew he couldn't put off doing his work much longer. He was pushing himself too hard, but there were always more essays to mark, more reports to fill in, more tedious paperwork.

Still, it was almost the summer and at least he could look forward to a break from actually going in to the college. He hadn't even thought about booking a proper holiday that year; there just hadn't been the right moment to discuss it with Beverly. And was there even any point?

Alex shut these thoughts out as he spread his work on the living room table. He buckled down to it quickly, and carried on until he heard Beverly turn her key in the lock.

Under her arm she had a brown paper bag full of bread and milk from the nearby Mini-mart. She walked into the living room, took one look at Alex and his papers, then wandered off into the kitchen without saying a word.

Alex prayed they could pull this off tonight. If they did, there should be some sort of award on offer, like an Oscar or BAFTA. It would take actors the calibre of Anthony Hopkins and Meryl Streep at this rate.

They started getting ready at about half-five; the table was booked for eight. Beverly had a shower first, then Alex. Once upon a time they might have showered together but those days were long gone. After getting out from under the spray, he walked through to the bedroom towelling himself off. When Beverly came in from the living room, wearing her silk robe, a glass of wine in her hand—it looked like he was driving then—Alex felt a sudden urge to cover up his nakedness with the towel, regardless of the fact she'd seen it all many times before. It didn't seem right somehow, not when she was acting like a complete stranger.

Beverly, on the other hand, had no such qualms. She removed the robe and started putting on her underwear, almost as if he wasn't even there. Again, he felt nothing when he watched her. There was no denying that Beverly was an extremely attractive woman still; you'd have to be blind *and* stupid to refute that. But for Alex there had to be a mutual connection before he was turned on. He'd never viewed women as pieces of meat like some men do. Like his brother did. This morning, half-asleep and aroused by her physical presence, he'd allowed himself to pretend—just like he did when he thought of the future. But as soon as she'd woken up all those illusions had been shattered; gone, like his dreams.

Alex felt awkward, like he needed to fill the aching silence with something. If only to make his wife acknowledge his presence. "I saw Steve today."

Beverly, now on the edge of the bed, putting on a pair of black tights, stopped what she was doing and looked up. "Steve?"

"Yeah, I know. He was waiting at the college gates this lunchtime."

Beverly continued rolling the nylon up her left leg. "And what did *he* want?" She stopped again suddenly. "I hope you didn't tell him he could stay here again. Not after the last time!"

"No, of course I didn't." Alex had no wish for a repeat performance of that. Though he'd promised to stay only for a few days, he ended up stopping for over a month. If Beverly had thought Alex leaving pots in the sink was untidy, then Steve could probably have won the gold medal for Britain. Fast food containers began to dominate the landscape of their living room; pizza and Chinese takeaway boxes, burger wrappers and chicken buckets. In fact all Steve seemed to do was vegetate on the sofa eating rubbish. He'd caused more than a few rows between Beverly and Alex, and the final straw came when those blokes showed up looking for him. Beverly had told Steve to get out herself after that.

"Good," she said. "The man is a lecherous, obnoxious slob."

"But he *is* my brother, Beverly."

She shrugged and carried on wrestling with the tights, slipping her right foot into the other leg and standing up. "So what *did* he want?" Beverly said eventually.

"I'm not really sure. I don't think he wanted anything, just to see me on my birthday. He gave me a card, and his new number." Alex pointed to the card lying flat on the dresser.

"Good for you." She turned and regarded him coolly. "Look, Alex, he always wants *something*. I don't suppose he came to give back some of the money he owes? Or to say sorry?"

"He said that already. I don't think he wanted anything this time. He told me he's turned over a new leaf."

"*Ha!*" sniped Beverly. "That'll be the day."

"He's been in prison, Bev. I think it really shook him up."

That made her pause briefly. Then she said: "Best place for him if you ask me." She finished pulling up the tights and went over to the dresser. Her eyes brushed the card briefly, then she opened one of the drawers and fished out a dark chemise. Anybody would have thought she was dressing for a funeral, not a birthday dinner.

Alex chewed on his lip. "He seemed pretty concerned about *us*."

Beverly didn't reply.

And he's not the only one, Alex thought to himself.

They finished getting ready in silence, Beverly plumping for her little black dress and Alex donning his grey suit and tie. His wife had downed another glass and a half of wine so there was no way Alex would let her behind the wheel. It was going to be some birthday if he couldn't even have a few drinks to celebrate. He felt like just staying in the flat on his own and getting absolutely smashed out of his skull. But perhaps it was for the best; he did have work tomorrow, and if Beverly had started as she meant to carry on then it would be her who paid the price in the morning, not him.

He did take Beverly's Scénic, though, because it was smaller and easier to park. She had no objections, and if she did she wasn't saying anything about it to him; wasn't saying anything at all. The only time throughout the whole journey when she came close to opening her mouth was when a driver cut him up, almost catching their front end.

"Jesus," exclaimed Alex. "What a lunatic."

He looked across at Beverly, who was staring back at him with daggers in her eyes. He knew what she'd be thinking, that if she were driving things like that would never happen; Beverly had no blind spots apparently. Well maybe if she hadn't been downing the wine…

By the skin of their teeth they penetrated the city's defences by 7:25. Now all that remained was to find that holy grail of a parking spot. The sides of the road were packed. Alex tried a couple of open-air car parks but they were both full. Finally, at the second multi-storey they tried, and on the very top level, he found a spot barely big enough to accommodate the car: trapped between a 4x4 on one side and an enormous BMW on the other. It was a tight squeeze and there was only room on one side to get out. Always the gentleman, he ensured this was Beverly's side, scrambling over the seats to join her.

She almost laughed when his hand slipped and he nearly fell out, but regained her composure in seconds. She couldn't allow herself to have fun; to be the old Beverly anymore. It would have been worth a pratfall just to see that again.

It was by no means dark outside, the days lengthening as the summer approached, so it felt like they were emerging from a cavern when they stepped out into the street. It was also quite close, but Beverly was wearing a short jacket in anticipation of colder weather later.

Zino's may have been in the heart of the city, but the multi-storey was not. It was a ten minute walk, and Alex couldn't help thinking that a small restaurant in town would have been much better. Why make such a fuss? No wonder Steve resented it. But Alex was doing this for his mum; if she wanted a big get-together, it seemed mean to spoil things. She was so proud of him—the first one in their family to ever really do something with his life, according to her.

At last, after walking what seemed like miles, they came upon the restaurant, which had a massive glass front and a gold painted sign across the top.

Alex had only ever been here once before, for a work's leaving party a long time ago. From what he recalled it had a fairly spacious layout, but he could see through the window that the décor had altered significantly. Gone were the chequered tablecloths and curtains. The more traditional Italian look had been abandoned in favour of an up-market style with a heavy emphasis on maroon.

At the door, Alex paused and asked Beverly: "Are you ready?"

She cast him a stern look and replied: "Are you?"

Neither of them had any choice. Beverly plastered a false smile on her face, Alex did the same. And they walked into the restaurant hand in hand.

– ii –

They were met by an attentive olive-skinned man with a moustache, wearing a maroon waiter's outfit, complete with black bow tie.

"Ello, sir and madam, and welcome to Zino's," he said in an accent so thick he could have served it up as a sauce on one of the dishes. "I 'ope you have a reservation?"

And if we don't then we're screwed, thought Alex. "Er…the Webber party?"

"Ah yes, the Webbers. Follow me." Alex wondered if that accent was put on. Surely no self-respecting Italian would speak in such a stereotypical way. The bloke had probably been born and bred in Croydon.

The moustached man led them down a small flight of steps. The interior was as big as Alex remembered, and it was full. Every side table, main table and even the smaller two-seaters—lovers' tables—were taken.

This explains why all the car parks are jam-packed. Everyone's having dinner at Zino's!

"The Webber party is over there. They are expecting you," their usher told them.

"I *should* hope so," said Beverly. "He's the reason they're here!" She nodded at Alex and the man grinned weakly, revealing a row of teeth as crooked as his laboured accent.

"Would you like me to take your coat?" he asked Beverly.

"Thank you, but I'll keep it with me for now."

He nodded and retreated, gliding backwards with practised ease. When he was gone, they looked over again in the direction he'd indicated. There, by the fire exit at the rear of the restaurant, was a much bigger table than the ones at the front. Around it sat a group of people Alex recognised instantly, with a white-haired woman in the middle. His mother caught sight of the couple first and started waving, much to the chagrin of the other diners.

"Well, here we go," said Beverly, fixing her smile firmly on.

They made their way through the busy restaurant, weaving around and in between tables. The first person to greet Alex was his Uncle Gerry. His late father's brother bore an uncanny resemblance to the man and for Alex it was always like meeting a ghost. But when he started talking there could be no mistaking Gerald for Bernard. The two were at opposite ends of the scale; Gerry more than made up for Bernard's lack of humour. If Alex's father had been here tonight, he'd be sat in the corner with a sour face complaining about the prices.

"Alex, it's been too long," said Gerry, clapping his arms around the tutor and hugging him tight.

"Uncle Gerry," Alex wheezed. "How're you doing?"

"I'm well, very well! Happy birthday, son."

The pair separated, allowing the others to come and say hello. Next was cousin Kevin, who enveloped Alex's hand in his own, pumping it like he was jacking up one of his cars at the garage. Kevin's wife, Lisa, gave Alex a peck on the cheek and wished him many happy returns. Gerry's other half, Aunty Joan, also gave him a kiss, ruffling his hair like she used to do when he was a kid. His other aunty, or rather *Aunt* Sylvia—his mother's sister—was more restrained. Her husband, conspicuous by his absence, was very well off and she imagined herself as the lady of the manor at home.

Lastly, there was Sylvia's daughter, his other cousin Judy. Growing up, Judy had been a plain girl, but all of a sudden at the age of eighteen she'd blossomed into quite the most stunningly gorgeous woman Alex had ever seen. Still only in her twenties, she was now happily pursuing a modelling career and there was even talk of TV or film work. He'd made her promise to invite him on set if that ever happened.

As they said hello to Beverly, her enthusiasm flagging already, Alex went over and gave his mother a big kiss and hug. It had only been a couple of weeks since he'd visited, but it was nice to see her again. Alex had always been close to his mum, always felt a bond there that could never be broken. He thought again about Steve and felt guilty. Alex contemplated telling her that he'd seen his brother today, but now was neither the time nor the place.

"Hello, Mum."

"Happy birthday, my Alexander," said the white-haired woman, the love practically spilling from her eyes.

"Thanks for this, but you know it really wouldn't have mattered."

"Nonsense. You're worth it. Every bit of it."

The preamble over with, they made space for Alex and Beverly next to Mrs. Webber senior, then his family started handing him birthday gifts and cards. He wasn't expecting a present from his mother, the dinner was enough. But, as usual, she wanted to spoil him rotten and so had bought a specially engraved watch—*To Alexander, my sunshine.*

"Mum, you really shouldn't have. This is too much," said Alex.

Uncle Gerry leaned across the table and whistled. "Nice looking time-piece, son."

"He's my boy." Alex thought she was going to say *only* boy. "And if I want to spoil him, I will."

"You do right, Mabel. You've turned out a lovely lad there," said Joan. "Good-looking, smart, a college tutor…" Alex could see his mum's chest puffing out with each word—it was one thing for her to brag about him, but so much better if someone else did it.

"Joan," said Uncle Gerry, nudging his wife. "You're making the poor man blush."

Alex was aware of his flushed face, but it wasn't really from embarrassment. It was even hotter in the restaurant than it was outside, and the suit didn't help. Beverly had removed her jacket and placed it on the back of her chair, leaving her arms and shoulders bare.

"So what did the lovely Beverly buy you, Alex?" asked Kevin. "Or is she saving her present till later?" This immediately drew looks of disdain from Kevin's wife, Aunt Sylvia and Alex's mum. Judy put her hand up to her mouth to hide the grin.

Beverly and Alex swapped tense looks. Both their minds were racing, trying to figure a way out of the situation. Admit that she'd not bothered this year? That would really give them something to talk about. Go with the joke and pretend that they couldn't wait to get home so they could jump on each other? Or just say nothing?

In the event, they both spoke together. "Bev bought me a gardening book," said Alex, at the exact same time Beverly said: "I bought him a new pair of shoes." They made hardly any sense overlapping, and repeated their lines again, separately.

"Two presents?" said Kevin. "Lucky man. And a third to come!" This time Lisa kicked him under the table.

Handled that pretty well, considering, thought Alex, thanking his lucky stars that Lisa and Kevin were providing the floor show. But then he turned to see his mum's face. Steve had been right about one thing this afternoon, you could never pull the wool over her eyes. It was one thing to fob her off over the phone, but seeing Bev and him together, the way they acted—literally—was another. Sherlock Holmes and Poirot had nothing on his mum when there was a mystery at hand.

"Right, then," said Gerry clapping his hands together. "I don't know about you lot but I'm starving. Now where's that funny little waiter gone?"

– iii –

The rest of the party had been studying the menu for some time while they waited, so everyone had their orders in mind. The birthday "boy" and his bride had to make their minds up more quickly, or they'd be eating the dessert after the others had all gone home.

Alex decided on the *insalata primaverile* for starters, followed by *spaghetti aglio, olio e peperoncino*, and for afters he chose Amaretto ice cream. Beverly went for the tomato and rucola salad, the *pollo al limone*, and the mango sorbet.

They weren't served by the man at the door, but a rather attractive young Italian who spoke with hardly a trace of an accent. As he went around the table taking the orders, he kept one eye on Judy, who was flirting with him the whole time. He offered to fetch them the wine list but Gerry just told him to bring a couple of bottles of each colour for now. When the man had left the table, Lisa seized her opportunity for revenge and commented: "Now that's what I call an Italian stallion!" Judy giggled, but Kevin was far from happy.

The dishes arrived and they started eating. Conversation flowed like the wine—with only drivers Alex and Lisa watching what they drank. The others, quite sensibly, were going home in taxis. The group talked about everything from the government and the state of the world today, to the chances of United in the cup. Inevitably the talking overlapped, as the older generation began reminiscing. Alex even thought he heard Gerry say, "I can remember when all this area was fields." Which was peculiar because as far as Alex knew this city had been around long before Gerry was even born.

Then came the next awkward bit. Judy asked how Kevin and Lisa's children were. The couple had three kids—Sean aged seven, Joanna four, and a toddler called Freddy who was only two—all at home with the babysitter tonight.

"She's great with them," said Lisa. "Melanie's going to make a really terrific mum herself one day."

Alex could see Beverly flinching at the baby talk. With each sentence he could feel the pressure building.

"And of course it won't be long before Freddy starts nursery," Lisa was saying. She broke off from her *trota salmonata ai finocchi* to fish her mobile out of her handbag, which had baby pictures on it. They were all practically the same. It was as if they had to capture every single second of the kid's existence.

"I can remember when the other two started, you know. We had a bit of trouble with them at first, because they didn't want to leave us, but they soon settled in and made friends. Didn't they, Kevin?"

"Hmmm?" Kevin was busy tackling his plate of *maccheroni al gratin*.

She elbowed him to get his attention. Alex wondered absently if there was a part of his cousin that hadn't been poked, kicked or jabbed over the years. "I said they soon settled in at nursery and made friends."

"Who did?" This earned Kevin another blow to the arm.

"Sean and Jo, of course."

"Oh yeah...they soon settled in." Kevin returned to the dish he was eating, examining it with as much care as the engine of a broken-down car.

Lisa turned back to Judy, still looking at the photos.

"Did I tell you that Sean's now practising for the end-of-term school play?"

Of course you haven't told her, Lisa, Alex moaned inwardly. *You haven't seen her since Christmas.* Or had it been the summer barbeque last year? Either way, Judy had remained happily oblivious to little Sean's thespian leanings. She shook her head, probably beginning to regret she'd ever started this conversation.

"No? Well he is. Now what's it called again?" Lisa nudged her husband for support once more. "Kevin, what's it called?"

"Er...*maccheroni*....something or other, I think."

"Not the food. Sean's school play."

"Oh, right." Kevin thought about this for a long time, then said: "I don't know."

She rolled her eyes and mouthed the word, "Men," then patted Alex on the arm to show she meant no offence.

"Pirate...Pirates..." she murmured to herself.

"*The Pirates of Penzance*?" offered Alex cheekily, knowing full well that the Gilbert and Sullivan operetta would be well beyond the grasp of seven- and eight-year-olds.

Lisa laughed at this. "No, silly. It's got pirates in the title somewhere though. Anyway, we're..." She looked at Kevin. "*I'm* helping him with his lines at the moment. I mean, he's only got a couple but it's there isn't it? And they'll be videoing it as well, you know."

"They're really great pictures," said Judy, handing the phone back.

"So what about you, love? Do you ever see yourself settling down and starting a family someday?" asked Lisa.

Judy was taken aback by the question, but couldn't help smiling. "I've not really thought about it. Too busy with my work and everything at the moment. I...I suppose one day..."

"She's too young to be thinking about all that nonsense," chipped in her mother, who'd kept one ear on their conversation.

Sylvia probably still thinks Judy's a virgin, mulled Alex. There wasn't much chance of that these days when you looked like Judy. Men were probably lining up around the block.

"Oh, yes," said Lisa, nodding her head. "I just meant someday, that's all. When she's found a nice fella."

Sylvia gave a shrill laugh at this. "And where is she going to find one of those?"

"There are still some out there—at least I hope so. They're not all after one thing."

"Even if they are, they're not going to get it. Are they, Judy?" said Sylvia, confirming Alex's theory.

"No, mother," she replied.

"I mean look at me and Kevin," said Lisa, holding themselves up as shining examples of marriage and parenthood. "Or Alex and Beverly..."

Oh no.

Beverly tightened her grip on her fork and smiled through clenched teeth.

Here it comes.

"So when are we going to hear the patter of tiny feet in your household?" asked Lisa. "You don't want to leave it too late, you know."

Easy, Beverly. Don't lose it now...

"We're…we're still trying, Lisa," Alex got in first.

"That's the best part," said Kevin, tearing himself away from his exploration of Italian cuisine. "The *trying.*" He winked at Beverly and winced as Lisa jabbed him in the side with her finger.

Beverly was coiled up now, like a snake waiting to strike. This was going to turn nasty if they weren't careful.

"I mean, I know work is important," Lisa continued unabated, "and I know more and more women are pushing it back. But you've got to think of your biological clock, Bev. You've got to—"

"Lisa, how's your brother doing these days? Is he still in the haulage business?" asked Alex.

Kevin laughed. "I think that's what they call changing the subject. Not very subtle."

"Take no notice, Alex. My brother's doing fine, thanks for asking. He went through a bit of a bad patch but…" Alex tuned out the rest of it as he didn't really care. Bev was winding down, getting on with her dinner. The tension was abating. He let out a relieved sigh.

The back of his throat began to itch when he sucked air back in.

Alex coughed, breathed in again.

It was still there, and now he could feel it in his sinuses. An acrid smell… A clogging, poisonous smell.

Was it his imagination or was it getting even hotter, stifling?

He coughed again. It was smoke, that's what he could smell. That's what was settling on his chest. Alex looked around, not thinking twice about ignoring his cousin's wife. She hardly seemed to notice anyway, so caught up in her story about Gary and his haulage yard.

There.

A few tables away was an overweight man planted opposite a petite brunette. He had his hand under the table and there was definitely smoke rising from his fingers, in spite of the fact there was a smoking ban in public places. What the hell was he playing at? Obviously too much effort to waddle outside! Though the smoke didn't appear to be carrying far, it had to be the source of the irritation.

Alex coughed again, and reached over for his glass of water. He didn't want to cause a scene, but had a good mind to go over himself and tell that chump to put whatever he was smoking out...or maybe call a waiter to report—

Alex looked over again. The glass of water fell from his hand.

In the time it'd taken to pick up the drink, the overweight man had somehow caught fire. His clothes were alight, burning brightly with flames of flickering orange, red and yellow. *What on earth did he expect?* thought Alex. *The stupid…*

The man rose, beating at the fire with his hands—hands that were now alight themselves, heat feeding off his skin. His face, too, was slowly being consumed by a ball of flames—rising steadily, engulfing his features, bubbling the flesh like a hot pool of mud. The man looked straight at Alex—and screamed.

"Jesus Christ!" Alex said.

His glass hit the ground and shattered loudly.

He wanted to move; wanted to help. But all he could do was watch as the man was totally engulfed in fire. And it was spreading. Along the floor, up the wall and the curtains. Transforming maroon into bright, burning red.

Alex looked left and right for a fire extinguisher. He couldn't see one anywhere.

The fat man's dining companion was the next victim, the flames fanning out and fusing her purple dress to her body. She wailed, staggering from the table, but only made it a couple of yards before falling. By that time she'd spread the fire, like a runner passing on a baton, infecting the next table: a party of four. They didn't stand a chance. But something else was happening to them as well. In spite of everything, Alex noticed the clothes they were wearing. Even through the lapping and leaping tongues of fire, he could see that those were no longer suits the men had on. No longer expensive designer-label gear. Now they wore strange outfits—tunics, baggy trousers with boots—and they had long, curly hair. The women's dresses were low-cut, the skirts caught back to reveal underskirts beneath.

He shook his head; none of that was important. What mattered was the fire, the diners being burnt away right in front of him. A wall of thick, inescapable heat heading in their direction. He couldn't do much for the others, but he could try to get his own family to safety. There was a fire exit back here somewhere, he'd seen it.

"Quick! Come on," he shouted, clambering to his feet and very nearly falling across the table lengthways. He grabbed Beverly's hand. *Don't look back*, he told himself. *Don't look at what's happening behind you.* He didn't need to, he could hear the screams of pain and despair, could still feel the smoke in his throat, in his lungs… *Just head for that fire door!*

"Come on, we've got to get out of here!"

Beverly resisted, pulling him back. "Alex, what're you doing?"

"Come on, we have to—" He let go of her hand. The people sat at the table were all gawking at him, mouths open. Beyond them, the other diners in the restaurant were doing the same. All had stopped eating and were looking in Alex's direction. The restaurant itself was untouched—no flames, no sign of any upset. Not one curtain had been singed. No blackened walls or crinkled wallpaper. The overweight man had no cigarette, no smuggled cigar. His dinner companion was no longer alight, no longer on the floor—but sitting opposite him, looking across at Alex: the moron who had just interrupted everyone's dinner with his shouting.

The moron who hadn't wanted to cause a scene.

Alex frowned. He couldn't work it out. One minute this place had been a raging inferno and the next—

"Alex?" Beverly was frowning. "Alex, what on earth are you doing? Sit down."

"I…" He could think of nothing to say in explanation. There *was* no explanation.

"It can't be going that badly, can it?" joked Kevin.

Gerry laughed, attempting to break up the tension. "Don't worry," he said, turning to the other diners. "It's just his birthday. I think he was frightened we'd all give him the bumps."

One or two of them seemed to accept this, though the majority kept staring.

"Where did you think you were dashing off to like that?" asked Aunty Joan as he came back round to his chair.

"Yeah," said Kevin. "Where was the fire, Alex?"

– iv –

On the walk back to their car, Alex could feel Beverly's eyes on him every step of the way. In the end he stopped dead in his tracks and said: "What?"

Though it was dark by now and the only light source available was from the streetlamps overhead, he could see that she wasn't looking at him with her usual frosty glare. There was something else—the same thing he'd seen in his mother's eyes. It was concern.

Nothing much had been said about what had happened back there. In fact everybody had pretty much got on with their meals as if it had never even occurred. It was how people dealt with most things in their lives, by dismissing them. But now they were alone…

"I'm still waiting for an explanation," Beverly said.

"About what?"

She tutted. "About why you freaked out back there in the restaurant. Why you grabbed me and tried to manhandle me towards the fire exit."

Fire exit. *Fire.* The word alone brought back those images, the burning diners who were not really burning at all. The flames climbing up the walls and spreading out over the ceiling… Reaching out, reaching towards him.

"It was nothing."

Beverly folded her arms. "Don't give me that rubbish. We've been to-gether too long, Alexander. Just because we're not as…" She thought about what the most appropriate word might be and came up with: "not as close as we used to be, doesn't mean I can't tell when something's wrong."

"So what do *you* care anyway?"

"Don't be childish, Alex."

"Oh, I'm being childish now, am I? That's rich coming from someone who does nothing but sulk."

"You're avoiding the issue."

"Seems we spend most of our time doing that."

Beverly ignored the jibe. "If you don't want to tell me, that's fine."

Alex let out a breath. "What do you *want* me to say? The truth is I don't know what happened, okay? I had some kind of panic attack maybe…"

She tilted her head. "You haven't had one of those in a long time."

"I know… It was nothing, really. I'm fine. You can go back to hating me like before."

"Oh, Alex, I don't…" She shook her head, then hung it and carried on walking, leaving him behind. He stood there for a little while, watching her go. Wishing she could have finished that sentence, and said more besides. Wishing things were different. Wishing he hadn't just seen the things he'd seen.

But if wishes were horses he'd have a stable full of prime thoroughbreds by now.

He looked at his new watch; it was just gone half-past ten. In an hour and a half's time it wouldn't be his birthday anymore. Just another day like all the rest. In a way he was glad—he'd be pleased to put this one behind him. But what then? It was what might come next that was the frightening thing. And Alex had the weirdest feeling *everything* was about to change.

Soon nothing would ever be the same again, and he couldn't do a damned thing about it.

He pulled up his collar, the air turning deceptively chilly. And he followed his wife along the unusually quiet city street.

FIVE

Amsterdam

– i –

THE ROOM HE'D HIRED was grotty and hopelessly overpriced.

But it would do.

And the man who ran the place knew how to keep his mouth shut.

"Room 205, Mr. Peck," a sweaty Van Dijk had told him from behind the smeared glass of his hotel counter, handing over the key to the room and smiling his gold-toothed smile: one of the reasons he now remained behind a toughened pane. There had been rumours that visitors in the past, probably high on any number of narcotics that were freely available here, had tried to separate Van Dijk from his prized dental possessions, little realising that he always kept a baseball bat behind the counter for just such eventualities.

Van Dijk leered at Peck as the older man led his companion upstairs. "Have a nice time," he called after them.

Peck had *acquired* the woman in a bar in the Red Light District. Her name was April, like the month just past. Their eyes locked across a crowded room, and before Peck knew it she was wending her way towards him. It was quite obvious she was a *hoertjes*—so the deal had been struck there and then. He would pay a considerable amount for just a couple of hours' fun.

April was about five foot six with short-cropped bleached-blonde hair and chestnut eyes. She had dimples that formed at each cheek when she smiled. They looked to Peck like the holes a skewer might make if it was rammed through her face at speed.

He liked the thought of that.

She was dressed in a shiny pink top that plunged down low and revealed the not inconsiderable valley of her cleavage. And the black miniskirt she wore rode up when she sat on the high stool in front of him at the bar.

"I've not seen you in this place before," she'd said, her accent jarring and not as seductive as she probably imagined.

"No," said Peck. "I've been here a while on business, but this is the first opportunity I've had to…let my hair down." She laughed at this because Peck had a flowing head of hair; red in the light from the bar it was actually almost silver and had been since his late forties. By his suit it was obvious he had money, or was at least well-connected. And he knew *she* liked the thought of that.

After he'd bought her a few drinks to soften her up, Peck suggested they go somewhere more private. His place? she'd asked. No, he'd replied. There were…complications.

"You're married then?"

"In a manner of speaking."

"I don't see a ring."

"No. But it's there all the same. Believe me."

Peck told her he had somewhere in mind. He didn't mention he'd used it before, preferring to let her think she was his first. How far from the truth that was. But it happened. Husbands tiring of wives that were growing fatter and more obnoxious by the day, nagging and demanding instead of satisfying. April would swallow that—and a lot more besides, Peck warranted. When all was said and done, there was really only one thing she wanted. His situation didn't interest her in the slightest.

He'd driven her here in his roadster. "Why so far away?" she wanted to know. "Why not?" Did it really matter where they went?

He got the impression that maybe she'd been expecting a high-class affair. Somewhere expensive. Somewhere that *looked* more expensive (actually Van Dijk charged quite a bit for his silence).

She also asked him what was in his briefcase. Diamonds perhaps, or bonds? He shook his head. "It *is* something for you, though. Something you'll like." April smiled. A bonus; this was her lucky day. Or maybe it was full of kinky underwear or something, maybe that's why his wife didn't understand him. And that kind of thing really would cost extra.

Peck found the room without any difficulty. Like the owner and his hotel it was, put simply, a festering, clammy hole. April turned her nose up at the smell, but he knew the thought of all that money changing hands would soon overcome this. She could put up with a bit of a stink, and probably doubted he'd last more than an hour at his age…

Oh, she had absolutely no idea.

* * *

The tatty curtains hanging from the window were being blown inwards by the breeze. They looked like dishevelled ghosts who'd seen better days—once white, now filthy with dirt. The carpet wasn't much better, caked with the debris of many an encounter in this room. There were stains even April would've had trouble identifying. At least the bedding looked like it had been changed. If that had been in the same state as the curtains and carpet, April would have turned around there and then and said, "Fuck the money, mister. I'm not catching bugs for anyone!"

Fortunately—or unfortunately depending how you looked at it—that didn't happen. April stayed. She walked further into the room, not hearing the click as Peck locked the door. Privacy was assured here, but you could never be too careful. Next he went over and put the briefcase down on the far side of bed, before shutting the window. The glass in them was made from the same stuff as Van Dijk's cabin downstairs. It wouldn't break or shatter, and had one other thing in its favour: it was soundproof.

Peck sat on the edge of the bed and grinned up at April. It changed his whole appearance. That grin twisted his face, contorting it into something else. Then it was back to normal again. The face of an older man, but by no means an ugly man. She'd had worse, she'd had uglier. Who knows, she might even enjoy this.

"Well?" said Peck.

April cocked her head sideways. "Well…? Oh, I see. Do you want me to, you know, make it sexy?" she asked.

Peck nodded. "If you like."

"Okay." April began to weave this way and that; waggled her hips, gyrating to imaginary music. She danced to the beat, squatting—not easy in her skirt—and bending, thrusting out her breasts. She sashayed towards Peck and sat on his lap: grinding, making him hard.

Then she rose again, teasing, leaving him wanting more. April undid the zip on the side of her skirt, easing it over her hips and letting it drop to the ground where she quickly kicked it towards the bed; the less contact between her clothes and the carpet, the better. She wore nothing underneath—there was little point in her line of work. Peck reached out and caught the skirt, though, then held it in his hands, stroking it as he watched her undo the one button at the base of her pink top. It flapped open easily, but she turned away, looking over her shoulder. Denying him the sight of her yet.

"Turn around," he suggested.

She wagged a finger, playing with him.

"I said *turn around*." More of an order.

April nodded. She was making him frustrated now, which was not a good thing. She wanted him to enjoy his time with her; a matter of professional pride. April pirouetted and Peck's face changed again. She'd never seen anyone so happy, and this in turn made *her* happy. Happy to pull wide her top, baring her breasts for him. And why not? She was proud of them after all. The best assets she had.

"Oh yes," said Peck. "You're perfect, you're so..."

She smiled at this, those two dimples appearing again. They reminded him of what he had to do. Peck put down the skirt and rose. As he walked over to April, she felt an urgent need to back away, but fought it. Shrugging off the pink top, she threw that over onto the bed as well.

Then Peck was standing in front of her, examining her body. He scrutinised every inch. "Magnificent," he said.

April, shaking for some unknown reason, took hold of his hand. She lifted it and placed it on her right breast. Even before she'd taken her own hand away, he was squeezing the flesh, cupping its weight in his palm, thumbing the nipple and forcing her to take in a sharp breath.

He kissed her. Softly at first, then more urgently. April responded in kind, closing her eyes. Now they were moving together towards the bed. He was laying her down and withdrawing.

She opened her eyes.

Peck was taking off his jacket and placing it on a hard-backed chair by the window, the only other piece of furniture in the room. He loosened his tie. Getting ready. She inched herself back on the bed. Next would come the trousers, then... But Peck was rolling up his sleeves. April frowned. Was he intending to keep his clothes on then, or at least his shirt? Why wasn't he undoing his trousers as he walked towards the bed again? Maybe he wanted her to do it for him. Do...other things while she was at it.

"April?"

"Yes."

"Do you know that you are very beautiful?"

She'd never considered herself to be exactly *beautiful*. She was hot, sure, or else she wouldn't get the trade. In other places you could probably get away with looking a bit worse for wear, but not here, not in a city where you couldn't move for competition. But never beautiful. April shook her head.

"Oh, but you are. To me. And I would like to make you even more so."

This was a strange kind of pillow talk. She'd had clients who wanted to talk dirty—wanted *her* to talk dirty—because it turned them on. This was something else. Still, it took all sorts...

"Would you like that?"

April shrugged. Perhaps that was what he had in the briefcase, outfits? Did he want to dress her up as a nurse, or a schoolgirl? He'd said whatever was in there was for her—but probably more for him by the sounds of things. Yes, that had to be it, because he was going for the case right now, opening it up. He lifted the lid, but she couldn't see inside from this angle.

"Now close your eyes," said Peck.

Close her eyes? If they were clothes she'd have to see them to put them on. What if they weren't outfits? What if she'd been right all along and it was some kind of fetish or bondage gear?

"Close them, April, or I can't help you become more beautiful."

April was shaking again. Peck's face reverted back to the weird one that had frightened her momentarily.

"*Close them!*" he shouted and April reluctantly did as she was told.

Peck smirked and picked up the first of the implements. It looked like something that might have been used in mediaeval days to perform rudimentary operations. Badly. It had a curving blade, a half-moon shape.

He brought the steel up to his face and licked the flat side.

It was at this point that the mobile phone went off inside his jacket pocket.

– ii –

April opened an eye, saw the thing in his hand, and screamed.

Peck moved with a speed and precision that did not tally with his years. In seconds, he'd dropped the blade back in the case and dived over the bed. But April was too fast for him. She rolled off the edge, dropping to the floor with a thump. She didn't care about what was on the carpet anymore, wasn't worried about her skin touching the material, let alone her clothes. Now it was an escape route. This whole deal had gone so badly wrong.

April crawled furiously along the floor. She was almost at the door, *almost*. She wasn't thinking about what would happen when she got there, where she could go when she got outside—so far from anywhere, and naked. She didn't even know that the door was locked. None of this mattered anyway, because she never made it.

April felt a hand around her calf, squeezing. It pulled one of her legs out from under her and she collapsed face down on the carpet. She yelled again as his weight descended on her, pinning her to the ground face down.

"You can scream all you like," said Peck. "There's nobody around to hear you. I paid for this whole floor. It's completely empty… And even if it weren't, do you really think anyone would take any notice in a place like this?" He had a point there. April shut up, not wanting to give her captor a reason to kill her so quickly.

The phone was still ringing, the annoying sound of the mobile in his jacket. Peck grabbed April's hands and brought them round behind her back. Holding them together with his own left hand, he reached into his trouser pocket with his right. After rummaging for a few moments, he tied her wrists with some kind of twine.

Peck rose, grabbing April by the arm. He dragged her back to the bed and slung her down. "Don't fucking move," he told her.

She slumped back on top of her skirt, next to the briefcase.

Peck went over to the chair, keeping one eye on April all the time. He slid a hand into his inside pocket and pulled out the phone, pressing a button.

"Yes, this had better be good." April saw his expression alter yet again. She hadn't seen this one before. Nice, angry, ugly—yes. But not fear. Peck's tone of voice changed too, from authoritative and ruthless to cowardly and weak. For a split second she considered shouting out for help on the off chance that whoever was on the other end would provide it. But they wouldn't be able to do so quickly enough, not before Peck had had time to… They were probably in on it anyway, she reasoned, or at least knew what Peck was about.

"Oh, hell-hello. It's you." Peck listened to what the voice was saying. April could hear it, but couldn't make out what it was saying. "I thought you didn't need me anymore toni—" Peck turned from her, pacing up and down with the phone, momentarily forgetting she was even in the room.

She seized her chance. Slowly, carefully, she eased herself sideways. With long fingertips—the same fingertips that could drive a man wild with ecstasy—she pulled at the end of the curved medical instrument propped up inside the case. April only needed access to the sharpened edge.

"But I was just in the middle of something…" Peck was telling his mystery caller. "Or at least about to start."

April worked nervously on the twine, petrified that at any minute Peck would turn and catch her. But he didn't. He was completely engrossed in the conversation. The more he talked, the more she gained a sense that this was some kind of superior. Was there a whole gang of these killers operating in the city? For all she knew the man in the glass booth downstairs—the one with the gold teeth—was involved as well.

She felt part of the twine give. This encouraged her and she rubbed up against the blade faster, though not so fast as to draw attention to herself.

"Yes, that. So what is…" Peck paused and nodded his head, even though the person at the other end of the phone couldn't see him. "Yes. But…"

Twang! The twine split. April hadn't cut through the string completely but it was now loose enough for her to free one hand. She lifted herself up on the bed, grabbing the blade by its handle.

"No, I understand. It *has* been a long wait. No, no. I'm not arguing with you. I wouldn't do… That's right." Pecked sighed. "It's just, well… You know… I thought I could have some time to myself. Yes, yes. Okay. So where are you right—"

Peck turned just as April ran at him with the weapon, instinctively sensing someone behind him. He leaned back, narrowly avoiding the swathe April was cutting, and stumbled into the chair.

She swung again, not giving him any time to come to his senses. The blade hit home and embedded itself in Peck's upper arm. He cried out, blood gushing over the steel and colouring it bright red. April added to his pain by yanking out the blade. More blood came now and Peck dropped the phone.

April raised the weapon a final time, fully intending to sink it in this bastard's head. But she stopped. Maybe it was the fact that she'd never taken a life before, not even in self-defence, and she didn't want to start now—even though Peck deserved it. Or maybe it was because she could actually hear the voice on the other end of the phone.

It said: "Right now? Right now I'm outside in the corridor, and I'm going to huff and puff and blow my way in."

– iii –

The call girl froze, digesting the information. And it was this pause that saved Peck's life.

Behind her the locked door bowed inwards, then exploded, shattering and splintering into a thousand pieces with an almighty crack. Some of the shards found a new home in April's skin, burying themselves deep like bee-stings. It was her turn to shout in confusion and distress, but still she held on to her only means of defence. Peck, shielded from most of the blast by April, simply sat on the chair, breathing heavily and clutching his wounded arm.

April finally looked at the entrance.

There, in the frame, stood a man holding a mobile phone. He too was dressed in a suit, though it was a much more casual affair than Peck's: sports jacket and trousers—all creams and browns which went well together. He wasn't that tall, but his presence was a commanding one. When he entered a room, even if he hadn't just blown the door off its hinges, you noticed. And, if you had any sense, you backed off.

"Hello," said the man, putting away his phone. He fixed her with his perfectly blue eyes. "I'm looking for an associate of mine." Then he stepped over the remains of the door. "Ah, there he is."

April wasn't quite sure what to do next. Her eyes, her brain, had processed the events of the last few moments, but her common sense was telling her it was impossible. The only thing she knew for certain was that this guy was with Peck, and that meant he was her enemy.

She made up her mind. April ran at him with her scythe raised high, hoping to God he'd get out of the way and let her pass.

"Don't," whispered Peck, but she barely heard him.

The man wasn't moving, didn't seem bothered in the least by this threat. He raised his finger, and April's advance was suddenly halted. It wasn't that he'd stopped her, more she'd decided to stop herself.

The man smiled. "April. It is April, isn't it?" he said.

"How… How do you know my name?"

"I know many things. For instance, I know how, when you were a little girl, your uncle used to take you on those trips in his car. Your parents thought you were going to visit the zoo or the fair, but we both know what really happened, don't we?"

Jesus, thought April. *How is he doing this?*

She nodded.

"And you remember how that used to make you feel—like you were nothing, like you were an object. Something he could pick up and use whenever he felt like it. Not a person at all. Never a person, April. It made you sick to the stomach, didn't it?"

I've had worse…I've had uglier…

"The words he used to say to you—they made you feel like dirt, like you didn't want to carry on anymore. But you did. Even though you thought about ending it all, even had the bottle of pills in your hand once when you were thirteen. A bottle of sleeping pills the doctor had given your mother, your poor mother…"

April was lowering the blade, her arm suddenly heavy. Tears were welling, making it hard to see the man clearly.

"And you vowed to make something of yourself, to prove it to *him*. That's why you ran away from home, isn't it? Not just to get away but to show him you were your own person."

April could see a mental image of her uncle, his slobbering jowls, the beard that tickled so much when he—

"But it didn't work out so well, did it? Not at first. Starving, hungry, living rough on the streets."

"I've..." April said. "I've done all right."

"Oh, financially you've had a splendid career. And wasn't it fortunate that you were found by that madame in the *Rossebuurt*, who fashioned you in her own image, made you into something she wanted you to be. Something you loathe because, really, deep down, it reminds you of him, doesn't it? Of what he made you feel like. You became what he always said you would. A self-fulfilling prophecy."

"No," April said, but she couldn't deny it. His words rang so true they might have been her own. They came from deep within her, fished out by this "man". She'd managed to convince herself over the years that she was in charge of her own destiny, that she was moving away from her past. Even bought her own place with her earnings. When all along she'd been the unwitting product of it.

"Aren't there times even now when you see his face, if you're with a client? When you see that does it bring it all back? Or do you block it out? You try, don't you? But you can't help thinking that your whole life has been a monumental waste, and when you're alone you still think about ending it all."

"No."

"Yes. So why fight so hard today? Why do you resist? Because of the pain? It doesn't last long, I assure you. You never know, you might even enjoy it." The man smiled again. "And then, oh April, then comes the sweetness of oblivion. Like just before you were born. Nothing but stillness. No need to eat, sleep, shit or fuck. None of that. It means nothing there. I promise you, it's glorious. See?" He lowered his finger and pointed towards her. April suddenly realised that she'd brought the blade back up again. This time it was at her throat. She was holding it there, hand quivering. "Your head says no, no, no. But your heart says yes, yes, *yes!*" For this last bit he effected the voice she used to fake all her orgasms.

"I… No…"

"Go on, April." His tones were so seductive, the words made so much sense. It would be nice to leave all this behind, to not think about things anymore, not have to bury the secrets of the past so that they didn't hurt her.

So, with one quick movement, she drew the blade across her throat. It did hurt, of that there *was* no denying, but she knew it wouldn't last long. The man in front of her had promised. Except he was laughing; laughing as she choked, as she panicked. As she began to regret her decision after all…if it had even been hers to make.

April dropped the bloodied instrument, bringing both of her hands up to her open throat. It hurt. Oh, God, it hurt so much! She fell to her knees, and she could still hear the man's cackling. It would haunt April the final few moments of her life—and beyond.

She tried to speak, but couldn't. He was enjoying this, enjoying her torment. It was already lasting far longer than he'd said. What else had he lied about? The oblivion afterwards? The eternal peace?

She'd find out soon enough.

And with that, she collapsed onto the carpet, leaving her own contribution to the collection of stains it boasted.

– iv –

The Infinity stopped laughing. It was over.

He glanced down at the dead, naked form of April. "I've said it before but I'll say it again, Lucas. You certainly have good taste when it comes to choosing your prey."

Lucas Peck scowled and held his arm. He was not particularly happy. If The Infinity had the time to do that to April, then surely it wouldn't have hurt for him to have practised his art.

He felt like someone who'd spent hours preparing a magnificent dinner, only to have it snatched away and eaten at the last moment.

"Now, I know what you're thinking…" The connotation of the words made The Infinity chuckle again. "But she was about to kill you, Lucas. If I hadn't intervened… Well, I shudder to think what might have happened."

"But if you hadn't rung in the first—" Lucas checked himself. He was so angry that he'd momentarily forgotten who he was talking to, if that was possible.

"Yes, I distracted you. I'm sorry." Such apologies did not come often from The Infinity's lips, and Lucas knew it was far from genuine. But it was comforting to hear all the same. It meant he was in good humour and not about to finish the job April had started. "But you're not as young as you once were."

And what would The Infinity know about youth? He still looked exactly the same as the first time Lucas had seen him. Every single detail; not a wrinkle nor grey hair.

"You've seen better days," said The Infinity, bluntly.

Lucas also knew that *he* could restore him to his former glory if he so desired. Could shave off the years. He had the power, but preferred instead to watch him age this way, even if he had slowed it somewhat. Again his anger rose up. "So why do you keep me around, if I'm so useless?" Now that was a truly dangerous question. It might make The Infinity wonder about this himself.

"Why? Why do I keep you around?" He stepped over the cooling body of April. "Because… Because I've grown used to it."

It was the closest thing to a compliment The Infinity had ever given him. But he would still blast Lucas out of existence as soon as look at him if he stepped out of line.

"I would hate to find you like this one day." The Infinity pointed to the corpse.

A handful of people were gathering at the open doorway, no doubt attracted by The Infinity's explosive entrance, heard throughout the hotel. There were a couple more *hoertjes* and their clients. All of them had dressed quickly, men buttoning up shirts incorrectly, women putting on skirts back-to-front. Hands went to mouths when they saw the blood, shrieks pending.

"Excuse me for a moment," said The Infinity, turning. He waved his hand. "What are you all staring at? There's nothing to see. Absolutely nothing." As soon as his boss had said the words, Peck knew they would realise that there *was* nothing here after all. The body on the floor had been just a trick of the light, the blood an imagined thing. Nobody had blown a door off its hinges, so there was little reason to stick around. The group dispersed. The Infinity's power of persuasion only really worked this well on the weak-minded, but nevertheless it was a handy ability to possess.

"There. Now, where were we?"

"You were telling me how much you like having me around," said Peck.

"Was I? We'll discuss the matter more fully later." The Infinity grinned to himself. He passed his hand over Peck's arm, sealing up the wound. But as a reminder of the incident, and the lesson Peck needed to learn, he would let the pain linger for a while yet. "Right now we have arrangements to make."

"So you were serious then? About leaving straight away?"

"Of course."

"But after all this time, all this searching… How can you possibly be sure?"

Peck wished that he hadn't reminded The Infinity of his lengthy pursuit. It had been going on for decades and he'd still come up with nothing. "Because," The Infinity said, "I have started to tune in. The signal is a little stronger now, Lucas. And I know the general area. As the days pass it will become easier. These signals will lead me to my quarry. And then… And then…" He deliberately left off the end of his sentence.

"All right," said Peck.

"So you see, the sooner we depart, the sooner we can end this once and for all." He hoped. Oh, how The Infinity *hoped*…

He helped Peck up and the man retrieved his scythe. Lucas wiped it on one of the curtains, then returned it to the case. He put on his jacket, stooping to pick up his phone. "What about her?"

"What *about* her?"

Peck sighed. "That is not beauty, you know."

"Isn't it?" The Infinity looked down at April. "Not your idea of it, Lucas."

"I could have made her so beautiful."

"I know. But we have to be on our way." The Infinity shepherded Lucas Peck out of the room and to the stairs. They descended, with Peck glancing over his shoulder the whole time.

When they arrived on the ground floor, Van Dijk shouted at them from behind his glass booth. "Hey, what the hell's been going on up there? Sounding like fucking World War Three."

"Hardly," said The Infinity.

"So, did you gentlemen have a good time then?"

"It was agreeable. But there is a slight mess up there, Mr. Van Dijk. I wonder if you could see to it for us." The Infinity pulled out a roll of notes from his inside pocket. "This should cover any inconvenience. And your next dental bill."

Van Dijk snatched the money from under the slit at the bottom of the glass screen. He counted it and nodded. "If you're ever in the neighbourhood again, gentlemen, you know you can count on me."

Peck left the building without saying a word, and The Infinity followed. "I doubt we'll be bothering you in the future, Mr. Van Dijk," he said dryly. "But we'll bear your offer in mind." Then they were both gone, leaving Van Dijk to venture upstairs and discover exactly what kind of mess they'd created.

Six

Kirkwell: Playing Fields

— **i** —

THE SUNDAY MORNING RITUAL.

Every week grown men sacrificed here. Sacrificed their lie-ins, their peace and quiet at home—more often than not, they would get into rows when they returned—and sometimes even their personal dignity, just to relive their lost youth.

They might tell you they did it to keep fit, neglecting to mention the post-match visit to the pub, or because they enjoyed the game and the camaraderie. All very good reasons, but not the real one. Each and every man on that field, from the age of twenty-five to fifty-five, was using the game as an excuse to time travel. A way of recalling past summers and winters at school, the glories of triumphs, the devastation of defeats. Of someday making it into the big leagues and living the superstar lifestyles of their footballing heroes.

And even though in their heads they were thirteen again, there would be a price to pay later in terms of aches and pains, pulled muscles and twisted calves.

But right now the only thing that mattered was winning.

Alex gazed out over the green expanse from his defender's position. All the action was being played out at the other end of the field, but his contact lenses allowed him to see it perfectly. Blue and white strips clashed. He was left, along with his fellow defender Mick Elliot, to mill around by the goal. The scattered supporters on either side were doing their best to look interested, but it was hardly what you'd call Wembley. No stands, no capacity crowd. These were just friends, family and relations standing behind the fading white lines that marked the boundaries of the pitch.

No need to call out the riot police quite yet, thought Alex.

Some of the players' kids were shouting enthusiastically, but the adults just didn't have the energy. The most they could muster were apathetic grunts when the ball came anywhere near a goal; it didn't matter which one. You could hardly blame them. Not when the score was 0-0 and they were well into the second half.

At one time Beverly would have been in that crowd, cheering his side on loudly. Whenever the ball came into his possession she'd jump up and down, shouting "Pass!" and "Shoot!" with pride. It was a different tale now. On this sunny and unseasonably warm Sunday in May she was still in bed. She couldn't care less what he was doing, who he was doing it with, or even why.

The concern she'd expressed the other night had soon vanished along with all the many happy returns. She'd been worried for a few hours, frightened that the panic attacks he'd experienced in his youth and when he first started teaching might be returning. Worried, more likely, that her behaviour might have something to do with it. She still had no idea about what he'd seen—or *thought* he'd seen. The real cause of his attack.

Alex had tried not to think about it, just like he'd tried not to think about Tim Brailes. Nothing had happened since, except a couple of fitful nights' sleep. But it kept nagging him. The whole thing had probably been brought on by stress. It had been a rough few months at work and at home. He should really have taken the rest of the week off, but it was a busy time; he had responsibilities. He'd taken it as easy as he could, had proper breaks, not ones where he had his nose in some marking or paperwork. And while he had devoted part of yesterday to work, he'd also made time to watch an old Western on TV while Beverly went out shopping.

Now today he was doing something more physical to take his mind off things. Or he would be if ever the players came back up his end. In one sense it was good; it meant his was the better team. But it left Alex and Mick with nothing to do, which gave him more time to think.

Alex knew that he'd also frightened his mum last Wednesday. She'd rung three times since then, asking him what was wrong.

"No, honestly, I'm fine," he'd said yesterday. "I keep telling you… Beverly? She's out. Yes, she does go out a lot… It's okay. No, I'm not overdoing it, don't worry." She did fuss sometimes. But on this occasion Alex couldn't really blame her.

"Al!" He hated it when Mick called him that—made him sound like a used car salesman from the Bronx.

"What?"

"Heads up. They're coming our way."

He'd been so preoccupied he hadn't noticed the tide suddenly turning. The opposing team now had possession of the ball. One very tall midfielder in blue was leaving players from both sides behind.

Mick turned to the goalie. "Get ready, Nev."

Neville Preston who, in contrast to the lanky midfielder, looked like a lift had landed on his head, squatted down even more, and started moving from side to side like a crab.

Alex braced himself as the tall player rapidly covered the metres between them.

Right, Alex told himself. *I'm ready. Ready for anything…*

But he wasn't. Not for this.

The gang of footballers running after the midfielder drew closer together. They now resembled more of a rugby scrum. There was something wrong with their shirts and shorts, though. They seemed dirtier than they had a second ago. In fact—

All the men racing towards Alex and Mick were wearing what looked like furs.

Alex blinked, but the scene didn't just evaporate like some desert mirage. If anything it brought them into sharper focus.

Something fast and white moved into his line of vision, coming from the sidelines of the pitch where the spectators should have been. Then another from the opposite side, this time a patchy grey colour.

They were horses…with riders.

"Oh my God…Mick!" shouted Alex, wrenching his head sideways. "Mick can you see—"

But Mick wasn't Mick anymore. In spite of the heat, he too sported a thick blanket of fur around his shoulders, a leather strap holding it in place; and he wore a metal helmet that glinted in the light. Alex looked him up and down, trying to take in what he was seeing. The fur came right down past his waist, and his legs were still bare, but in place of his usual footwear were tough, knee-high leather boots.

"Mick? Christ, what's—"

Mick snarled. Alex could see the ragged teeth poking out from behind the long beard he'd suddenly sprouted. Then Mick threw back his furs and brought up an enormous sword. If the helmet's metal glinted, then the glare from the sword was blinding. It looked so heavy Alex wondered how Mick could even hold it upright.

"What…"

The man who used to be Mick ignored him. Growling again, he charged up the field to meet the advancing player with the ball. It was complete and utter madness.

Alex gaped in disbelief as "Mick" charged the footballer. The tall midfielder was changing as well, organically growing fur and leggings, but still dribbling the ball as Mick swung his sword. One blow was all it took and the player's head was cleanly separated from his shoulders. Now there were two balls on the pitch and Mick booted the wrong one: the one with eyes, a nose and a mouth.

The man's body keeled over and landed on the grass, redness spilling out of its neck. Mick stood beside his kill. He made no effort to run, just waited there for the charging tidal wave of arms and fur and flashing metal to meet him on the kick-off spot. He fought valiantly, swinging the cumbersome sword left and right. Alex saw hands, parts of legs and other appendages flying into the air, accompanied by huge sprays of blood: crimson geysers shooting into the sky and raining down on the battling rabble.

Then suddenly it was over. Mick was ripped limb from limb by the sheer force of numbers. He disappeared beneath a stampede of feet. The army looked towards their next goal. Literally. Somewhere along the line, two teams had melded into one aggressive, warring band, rampaging up the field.

The mottled grey horse broke away and stampeded ahead of the group. Its mount looked like some kind of animal, fur flapping behind him, features distorted. Rider and steed curved round and sped by Alex, sword drawn, heading for Neville.

The goalkeeper didn't stand a chance.

Neville's eyes widened as the blade went right through him, knocking him backwards into his own nets. The string held him up like a tangled puppet, arms and legs caught in the square holes, blood staining his green goalie shirt.

Alex turned back to the approaching horde that now covered most of the pitch. They were almost upon him.

"Help me!" he cried out to anybody who'd listen. "Please, won't somebody—"

Pandemonium. There was no other way to describe it.

Alex had no time to run—only brace for impact. The first of the men rammed into him, knocking Alex to the floor. He saw their faces up close, the hatred in them. He smelt their stink, their bad breath, saw flashes of plaid...

They were real.

As real as the ground he was standing on—the ground he *had been* standing on. As real as the sky above, the sensation of floating. As real as the pain he felt when he eventually landed, his back and shoulders connecting with the hard, flat turf.

An explosion of breath escaped, emptying all the air in his lungs. For a second or two he lay dazed. He saw shapes, huge shapes, leaning in.

Then he remembered the men; remembered the swords, and waited for them to plunge. For hooves and booted feet to trample him.

Thankfully, before that could happen, he blacked out.

– ii –

He was aware of a dream landscape he'd visited quite often of late, ever since his birthday.

Ah, so now it made sense. He was asleep, still dreaming... That's why all the football players had changed into sword-wielding warriors. He'd been sleeping. Perhaps even since last Wednesday? Some dreams are so real, so vivid, you can't tell the difference between them and real life…and they can last a long, long time.

That would certainly explain a few things.

It was strange here, secure and yet… He wasn't alone. There were others all around him, behind him, that he couldn't quite see. Whenever he turned to look at them, they shifted position, moved to the right or left, or sneaked around the back. He couldn't get a fix on any of them, but felt as if he knew each and every one.

And there was another figure. This one he *could* see, or at least sense. It wasn't all that clear: just a weak, indistinct outline, but again he recognised it. Alex looked around at the bright circular world he was now in, like a bubble cut off from existence.

"Where am I?" he asked the figure.

There was no reply. Were they just as confused? Just as…lost? If only he could see more clearly, discern a face. Then he might be able to—

It was growing darker inside the circle. Was night falling? *Could* night fall in dreams? Alex supposed anything was possible. But would he remember this when he woke up?

Darker still. And now Alex was worried.

There was a reason for the gloom. Something else was here with him. Something bad.

"Go. Go now," said a voice, a single penetrating voice in the darkness. It was so soft and lyrical he wanted to stay and listen to it. But Alex knew the advice was sound. "Go now. Hurry… You must leave!"

The only trouble was he had no idea how. There were no doors, no windows inside the circle. No escape hatches or ragged holes to climb through. Absolutely no way out.

"Leave before he finds you!" The voice was terrified.

But then this wasn't a physical place. If you wanted to escape from a dream, leave it behind you, then all you really needed to do was…

– iii –

Alex woke up.

His eyes flickered and he heard more voices, not nearly as smooth as the one back in that strange place. These were real, human voices.

"He's coming to."

"Told you so."

"Look, stand back. Give him some air."

For a moment he thought his contact lenses might have fallen out because everything was blurred—but not in the same way as the dream, even now fading from his memory. Then he realised it was simply because his eyes were watering.

"…don't know what he was doing standing there in the first place, just standing in the way of—"

"He was defending, you moron. That's what he's supposed to do. Defend."

"Yeah, but he didn't even try to tackle or anything, didn't even go for the ball. He just—"

"Alex? Alex can you hear me?" There was a head hoving into view above him. *You're on the floor, remember? It's was where you fell when those men—*

Alex struggled to get up, the sudden recall panicking him.

"Get away from me."

"Hold him," snapped the man who'd been leaning over. "Alex. Alex, take it easy. It's Gareth."

Alex stopped struggling and focused on the face. He did remember. Gareth Shaw, their team's answer to a physio. He'd done a few first-aid courses, even trained as a nurse once, but hadn't passed the exams.

"You're all right." Gareth didn't look convinced. "You just took a bit of a knock." He waved some digits in Alex's face. "How many fingers am I holding up?"

Alex followed them with his lazy eyes. "Three."

"Right first time."

"…him why he was shouting for help…" This voice came from the other side of Gareth. It was unmistakably Mick's. Alex craned his neck around, desperate to confirm the man was alive. Yes, there he was—beardless and furless—and Neville too. Both were fine.

"He kept asking what was happening…and that was *before* the fall," said Mick.

Alex rubbed his head, ran his hands over his eyes.

"Do you think you can stand up?" asked Gareth.

"I'll…I'll try." Now his own voice sounded funny—echoing, like there was nothing inside his head. No brain, no skull, just an empty, circular…

With the help of several men, they hoisted him up. Alex's legs buckled and he almost fell head first onto the grass. "Whoa there," said the tall midfielder, catching him. Alex stared up at his head—now firmly back in position—and pointed.

"He's in no fit state to be doing anything," Gareth told them. "Here, let's help him back to the dressing rooms."

These were actually the cricket pavilions, which doubled up during the football season. They carried Alex inside and sat him on the first available chair. Mick gave him a drink of water, but Alex's hand was shaking too much to hold it.

"So what do we do now?" asked Neville.

"Might be best if I run him down to Casualty, just to be on the safe side," said Gareth. "Where are his things?"

Someone scouted round for Alex's bag and belongings, and came back with them moments later. It was agreed that the game should carry on—there wasn't that much of it left to play anyway—and substitute Mark Oldham would go on in place of Alex.

The same men helped Alex back out of the pavilion again, and into Gareth's Sierra, laying him on the back seat. As they turned to walk away, the physio called them back.

"Do you think somebody could let me know what the final score is?" he asked.

– iv –

Kirkwell General on a Sunday lunchtime.

It was hard to know which was worse: the Saturday night rush due to drink; the doctors and nurses having to patch up the walking wounded from countless pub brawls; or the weekend DIY brigade, people who'd watched far too many home improvement shows for their own good. There were all kinds of examples here today, from sawing accidents to hammer blows and nail gun wounds.

Then came the sporting injuries. Golfers, tennis players, fitness fanatics. As the day wore on the department would steadily fill up with these. People who never exercised during the week and tried to make up for it now. People like Alex.

Before they'd joined the motley group of assembled extras from *M*A*S*H*, Gareth had called his girlfriend on his mobile to let her know he probably wouldn't be home in time to eat.

"There's really no need…for all this," Alex mumbled from the back of the car.

"I'll be the judge of that," said Gareth. "Besides, her sister's coming over today so I'll take any excuse I can get."

"Gareth—"

"Look, it really is best to get you checked out properly. Bangs on the head are funny things."

"Yeah," said Alex. "Funny… But I'm okay now." He was still saying this as Gareth helped him out of the car.

"Easy does it," said the physio, swinging Alex's arm over his shoulder. He was a slight build, but much stronger than he looked. Once inside the Casualty Department, Gareth eased Alex onto a chair then scanned the room for help. "We shouldn't have to wait too long," he told his friend. "Head injury, you see."

Gareth registered them, talking to the man behind the desk, and pointed back towards Alex. The next thing he knew a nurse was asking Alex to step through to the back. This drew some vicious looks from some of the people who'd been there ages.

Alex was armed into a bay, with Gareth following behind, explaining that he was "in the profession." The nurse told Alex to get on the bed before she stepped out, drawing the curtains with a swish. It was now that Gareth suggested phoning home.

"Won't…"

"Beverly," prompted Alex.

"Right. Won't Beverly be worried about you?"

"I doubt it."

Gareth raised an eyebrow. "Oh, it's like that, is it? Even so…"

"I don't want you to ring," said Alex, a little too brusquely.

"Fair enough. But we don't know how long we'll be stuck here."

As it turned out they didn't have to wait long before a doctor arrived, although the only way to tell was by the stethoscope dangling from his neck. Alex thought that all doctors wore white coats—which showed how many times he'd been in a hospital recently. He also assumed most of them were over the age of consent. This bloke was so young and acne-riddled he could easily have been one of Alex's students.

"Hi, I'm Doctor Goddard. And you are…"

"His name's Alex Webber," said Gareth.

"I see, and what's the matter with Mr. Webber? Has he lost his voice?" Regardless of his years, this doctor had the pompous attitude of a physician twice his age. Gareth bristled at the remark.

"I…" began Alex.

"Yes?"

"I was playing football."

"Obviously," said the doctor, nodding at the T-shirt and shorts Alex was wearing. "Took a bit of a tumble, did we?"

"He was defending and…well, some of the players ran into him. Knocked him over. He banged his head and lost consciousness for a while," Gareth said, braving the doctor's sarcasm.

"How long?"

"At least a couple of minutes."

"I see," the doctor said. He took out a pocket torch and flashed it in Alex's eyes, checking for dilation, signs of bleeding into the brain. Next he clicked his fingers at either side of Alex's head, testing his reaction to the noise.

"And how do you feel now, Mr. Webber? Any ringing in your ears? Any dizziness, nausea?"

"I do feel sort of weak still." *Keep your mouth shut about what you saw*, Alex told himself. *It wasn't real. I know it happened before the fall, but it wasn't real, none of it…* It seemed real, said the voice of contradiction in his head. You thought it *was* real; thought you were going to be cut into small pieces, hacked to bits like Mick… *Except Mick's fine, isn't he? You saw him for yourself. Neville too…*

"Hmmm," said the doctor, trying to make his mind up about something. "If you'd only been out for say half a minute, a minute tops, I'd probably clear you right here and now. It's obvious you've been shaken up by your experience—" He looked over at Gareth when he said this as if it was somehow his fault. "But that ought to pass. To err on the side of caution, though, you've been booked in for a scan."

"A scan!" said Alex. *This was more to cover their own backs than anything*, he thought, in case he sued for negligence later. "Is that really necessary?"

"Well now, that all depends." The doctor stared unblinkingly at Alex. "On what we find when it's over. If there's nothing wrong with you, it's been a monumental waste of time and our funds—but at least you know you're not going to have a brain haemorrhage in the middle of the high street. If, on the other hand, we do find something, then at least we'll know, won't we? And we can do something about it. In that particular scenario I'd say it was very necessary indeed, wouldn't you?"

Alex may not have cared for his bedside manner, but at least this doctor was bothered whether he lived or died. What was there to rush back home for anyway?

"Now, is there anyone we should get in touch with?" the doctor asked.

Gareth shifted about from foot to foot. "There's his wife."

Alex glowered at him. Gareth shrugged apologetically.

But the more he thought about it, the more he realised somebody ought to be here. And there was no way he was putting his mother through this; she'd be half out of her mind.

"Good, we'll get someone to contact your wife, Mr. Webber." The doctor parted the curtains and disappeared like a magician at the end of his act.

Alex wondered how much longer this performance was going to go on. And whether or not it would be the final curtain for him before too long.

– v –

Imagine being inside a coffin.

That's the closest thing Alex could compare it to. After another lengthy wait, during which time Beverly arrived, Alex was made to change into a surgical gown and wheeled to the lift on his trolley. At the same time, Gareth received a text telling him that their team had lost 1-0. Mark Oldham had scored an own goal.

"It's because of that stupid game he's here in the first place," Beverly told Gareth. "I've always said he shouldn't be involved."

"Beverly, it wasn't—" Alex cut in.

"You shouldn't be out there doing that kind of thing at your age!"

"Thanks a bunch."

"You know what I mean."

"Look," said Gareth, "I'll get off. Hope it all goes okay."

Alex nodded. "Thanks, I appreciate it."

"Anytime." Gareth gave them a wave and was on his way.

It embarrassed him when they rowed in public, but at least Beverly had come. And, just like before, he could tell deep down she was worried. You couldn't live with someone for so long and not know what they were feeling. She might be more of a stranger these days but she was never a total mystery.

Beverly stepped inside the lift next to him. She stood and looked at the porter, at the doors, at the reflective ceiling; anywhere but at Alex. She knew full well that her eyes would give her away. He wanted to say something, to hold her hand and squeeze it tight. It could have been because he was scared, or really needed her to tell him it was all right between them again. They'd spent so many nights with only inches separating them, yet they were miles apart in other ways. But was it really too late? If they'd been alone, maybe he would've actually reached out for that hand.

The lift reached his floor. Alex was wheeled up and down corridors until it felt like he'd wind up back where they started. Round and round in circles forever more. Alex was torn between a feeling of impatience, wanting to get it over with, and not wanting to get there at all.

But inevitably he did.

That's when they put him in the coffin. Beverly waited just outside. He could see her through the glass window talking to one of the men who operated the great machine. There weren't many around; they'd told him there was only a skeleton staff on, as Diagnostic Imaging was generally only used for emergencies on Sunday. Great.

The scanner itself was like something out of Kubrick's *2001*: a white cylindrical tube with a long stretcher sticking out like a tongue. They strapped his head to this platform, reassuring him that everything was going to be fine.

Then he was swallowed up by the technology.

"Just try to remain calm," said the voice of the technician outside.

Lights flashed and there were beeping and drumming noises.

Alex couldn't see what was happening to him, but he'd watched plenty of medical programmes in the past. Wasn't this the bit where those beams of light, or whatever, passed over you? And didn't he remember reading somewhere that a scanner like this was basically a huge electromagnet? It was enough to scare anyone.

Time passed slowly, and for someone who liked to remain active this was torment. Even downstairs, he'd had magazines to read, Gareth to talk to.

But now there was nothing to do but remain still and quiet.

And wait...

– vi –

The waiting didn't end when the scan was over.

Alex was taken back to A&E so they could monitor his vital signs—just till they ruled out any brain problems. But it wasn't long before he was left alone again, while Beverly went to find a coffee machine. She'd parted the curtains slightly and, propped up by pillows, he could see out and down the corridor. There were multiple sets of large rectangular windows going all the way down, flooding the place with light; it was even brighter than the MRI room.

Alex saw movement. It wasn't that unusual—he'd seen visitors, nurses, doctors and porters going past while he'd been stuck here. But there was something different about this person. Alex squinted, thankful that his contacts were still in place. He could see now that it was female, so probably a nurse. But her uniform wasn't like any nurse's outfit he'd ever seen. It was light pink, long and flowing, almost like a gown. Around the woman's waist was what appeared to be a thick, satin sash, tied in a butterfly bow at the back. She walked slowly, taking dainty steps in slippers like a ballerina would wear.

Alex stared as the light caught the side of her face.

And that face was ashen.

Not a nurse, a patient, he thought. *A really sick one too. And she's wearing a robe, one of those fancy ones that Beverly wears. Bit much for a hospital, though…*

He sat up in the bed. Now he could see the reason for her white face. It wasn't that she was ill. She was wearing make-up. Her face was white because it had been painted, like a mime or a clown. Except it made her look beautiful instead of ridiculous. Along with the white, a certain amount of pale blusher had been applied to the cheeks. Her lips were painted crimson, though not in the way women would wear lipstick for a night on the town. It didn't fully cover her lips and made them appear smaller than they actually were. Her eyes were outlined in black, drawing attention to this one aspect of her face more than any other. The eyes of a spectre—oval and piercing, yet never cold. Over each a wafer-thin eyebrow had been painted. In opposition to her face, her hair was as black as coal, high and taken back—a bun held in place by strategically placed sticks.

Alex had been so captivated that he hadn't seen the changes taking place around her. The corridor was transforming, walls now paper thin and made of squares. The large windows were shrinking. There were paper mobiles hanging from the ceiling, and Alex could hear the distinctive sound of wind chimes.

Nothing else existed; only the woman and the diorama around her. She turned and looked right at him, as though she'd only just realised she was being observed. For the longest of moments, she held his gaze. It was a very unusual experience, and he felt sure she could see into his very soul. Then she batted her eyelids, reached down into her robes and pulled something out. At first he thought it might be a weapon of some kind—long and thin, she handled it with the skill of a professional. But when she opened it up, Alex could see it was nothing more than a paper fan, which she flapped in front of her face, covering everything but those penetrating eyes. They communicated a hint of embarrassment, but also playfulness.

A body blocked his view. "Mr. Webber?"

Alex scrambled to look around the man, but couldn't see a thing. By the time this new arrival had stepped into the cubicle, the corridor behind was totally empty.

"Mr. Webber? Are you all right?"

Alex shook his head, still gazing out into the hallway.

"Mr. Webber?" The speaker raised his voice slightly. Only now did it register with Alex. He was aware that his mouth was open, that he must look like an idiot. It was something he was getting used to.

The man talking to him was an Indian doctor, who actually had taken the trouble to wear a white coat.

"I…I'm sorry…"

The physician glanced back over his shoulder. "What were you looking at just now?" he asked.

There was movement again in the corridor and Alex held his breath. He wouldn't have to explain, he could *show* the man. The woman was back, she was—

A nurse came round the corner, chart in hand.

Alex let out the breath. "Nothing… I just thought I saw someone I knew."

The doctor nodded thoughtfully.

"An old friend," added Alex unnecessarily.

"What's that about an old friend?" Beverly pulled the curtain and stepped inside.

"Er…" He needed to change the subject quickly. "Thought you were going for coffee?"

"Machine was out of order."

"Beverly this is Doctor…" Alex realised that he had no idea who this was.

"His name's Dr. Nidra, Alex. The consultant neurologist."

"We met outside," explained Nidra. "As I was telling your wife…" Beverly flinched at the word. "I've been put in charge of your case."

"Right. So what's…"

"I'll put you out of your misery straight away, and tell you that we couldn't find any abnormalities in your scan. I've examined the results myself and everything seems perfectly normal."

"Seems?"

Nidra smiled. "It *is*. Sorry, doctor's get-out clause."

"So there are no tumours, there's no bleeding?"

"No, no, nothing like that."

Both Beverly and Alex sighed with relief, though she quickly composed herself.

No, don't let the mask slip, Bev, whatever you do. Don't let your feelings show. Just pretend we never had anything together; that you never really loved me at all.

"You haven't passed out again since you had your fall. There's been no dizziness or sickness. You're still a little unsteady on your feet, but this will soon pass," Nidra continued, oblivious of the silent interplay between the pair. "To be quite frank with you, Mr. Webber, I'm more concerned about what your wife has been telling me."

Alex turned back to look sharply at the doctor. "Oh? And what *exactly* has she been saying?"

Before Nidra could utter another word, Beverly cut in. "I told him about the other night. Your birthday."

"Jesus, Bev. What did you do that for?"

"Mr. Webber, please. I'm only here to help you," insisted Nidra.

Alex looked doubtful. "What did she tell you?"

"That you had some sort of anxiety attack. That it wasn't the first time you've had them."

Alex snorted. "It's been years. And the thing in the restaurant, it wasn't…" His words tailed off into nothing. Alex was frightened of digging an even deeper pit for himself.

"Wasn't what?" Nidra asked. "Wasn't the same as the ones you've experienced before?"

"No. Look, when I was at university I'd sometimes get a bit stressed if it was exam time or whatever—"

"Oh come on, Alex. A bit stressed? You told me you were throwing up for an hour before your finals," Beverly reminded him.

"Yes. But I still passed, didn't I?"

"That's hardly the point."

"No, the point is I got over all that at uni. I was a different person back then."

"What about when you first started work?"

"All right, so I was nervous. But that was just—"

"Just, just, just," snapped Beverly.

"Mr. and Mrs. Webber," Nidra said, flapping his hands like a man bringing a plane in to land. "This isn't helping anyone. Just going round in circles."

Going round in...

The couple clammed up and faced front. "Thank you. Now, I have to ask, Mr. Webber, have you been under any pressure lately? At work maybe? I understand you're a lecturer. That must be quite demanding?"

"Sometimes," admitted Alex.

"Oh please," said Beverly, folding her arms. "Doctor, he's working all the time."

"I'm surprised you noticed."

"Please," said Nidra. Beverly tapped her fingers on her arm. "Go on, Mr. Webber."

"I can't deny my workload *has* increased," Alex told him, leaving a gap for Beverly to interrupt. She didn't. "But that just comes with the territory. I don't like to let my students down."

The doctor rubbed his chin. "And there's a fair amount of paperwork, I imagine?"

"Yes, you'd imagine right."

"What about...other things? Any pressure outside of work?"

Alex said nothing, he didn't have to. Five minutes in a confined space with them was enough to paint a very clear picture of their marriage.

"Mr. Webber," said Nidra, giving up on an answer. "I'm going to ask you something now and I want you to be honest with me. Will you do that?"

Oh, I'll be honest, doc. I'm seeing things. Really weird shit. I'd love to blame it on flashbacks but I've never done a drug in my life. And when I dream... What happens? If only I could remember. So what's the diagnosis? I'm crazy, right? Grade A lunatic. It's the funny farm for you, Webber. One way ticket; you're never coming out again as long as you live.

Alex nodded. "I'll try."

Nidra didn't seem very happy with this non-committal reply, but accepted it.

"Did you have another one of these attacks while you were out there playing football this morning? Is that why you were knocked over?"

"I wasn't paying attention," said Alex.

"Like you weren't paying attention when I came into the cubicle?"

"That was different. I thought I saw—"

"Somebody you knew, yes you said. These panic attacks and lapses of concentration… If they're not physical, they could be symptomatic of something else that's happening."

"Like what?" asked Alex, who'd already diagnosed himself.

He expected the doctor to declare him mad, but Nidra just said: "Stress can affect us in some strange ways, Mr. Webber. We each of us react differently to it. Some people thrive on it, others—"

"Lose it?"

"My gracious no. I wouldn't put it like that. I suppose some people do allow things to get on top of them to that extent, but you're nowhere near… Have you thought about taking any time off perhaps? I know it's difficult but…"

"Difficult? It's impossible at the moment. The end of the year's coming up, I've got marking and—"

"Well, you're certainly going to have to take a few days off this week, Mr. Webber, if only to get over the fall."

"But you just said I was okay."

"You are, but I'd still recommend complete rest for at least a couple of days."

"It's just that—"

Nidra held up a finger. "Doctor's orders. I'm sure no matter how much they need you at work they'll cope, Mr. Webber. Nobody is indispensable."

"Cheers."

"I didn't mean it like that." He looked to Beverly for support, but found none. "Mr. Webber, have you ever thought about…talking to someone regarding your problems?"

"You mean like a shrink? Sorry doctor, I don't—"

"I was thinking more like counselling, actually."

"You're wasting your time, Doctor Nidra." Beverly just couldn't hold her silence any longer. "He'll never agree to it. Alexander hates anything like that; hates opening up and talking about things."

"I'm not the only one," growled Alex. "When was the last time you ever properly talked about anything?"

"All right, all right," Nidra cut in, not prepared to listen to another marital disagreement. "I quite understand, and obviously I can't make you do anything, Mr. Webber. But if you ever change your mind…"

"So that's it then? I can just go?"

"Certainly, this isn't a prison. But if you feel at all light-headed or sick, or if you have another one of your…*episodes*, come back straight away."

"Right, okay." Alex held out his hand. "Thank you, doctor. I *am* grateful for what you've done."

Nidra accepted his hand and shook it. "Not to mention more than a little relieved, I suspect. But you're welcome, Mr. Webber. It's what we're here for."

Beverly took her turn thanking the doctor and apologised for their behaviour.

"Again," said Doctor Nidra as he left them in the cubicle, "you're most welcome." And he quietly wished them all the luck in the world, probably because over the coming days, weeks and months, they were going to need it.

SEVEN

Holden Airport, England

– i –

IT WAS STRANGE TO BE BACK AGAIN.

How long had it been since they'd set foot on British soil? Ten, fifteen years? Maybe more. To The Infinity time had little meaning. But Lucas Peck remembered vividly the months they'd spent in this country, the things they'd done. The memories comforted and excited him, as he waited with their suitcases piled high on a trolley. He wondered if that little place in Soho was still there. Probably not. Even if it was, it would surely be under new management now. Shame. Still, if he had any time to… kill…he might visit the old neighbourhood. *If.*

The Infinity had got his blinkers on and the scent was very much in his nostrils.

Peck had seen that look; seen it if he happened to noticed himself in the mirror just before… Anticipation, expectation, determination. Desperate, but not wanting to rush. Peck was glad he was here to witness this, to play his small part. He'd been pissed off about missing out on April, but The Infinity had promised him more opportunities to practise his talents. To complete his own search. He was a craftsman and he had created so much beauty. But there was still more to accomplish.

He had never quite managed his masterpiece, the perfection all artists seek. The magnum opus they would be remembered for. Maybe Ha'ng would have provided the raw material, or April? He would never know. But Peck didn't hold a grudge against The Infinity for denying him. He wouldn't dare. So his search went on, during this excursion and perhaps beyond.

Strangely their quests had become entwined. And both had brought them back here. To the land of rain and the Royal family, town versus country, pounds and pence, youth culture and multi-culture. Official politics and behind the scenes intrigue, class divides and refugees. It was good to see that the events they'd set in motion on their last stay were still running their course, like clockwork. This was a society steeped in disorder and chaos; it always had been. The aristocratic stiff upper-lip was all pretence, even when the Empire had actually stood for something other than a footnote in an encyclopaedia.

Actually, returning would be more like a pleasure trip if there wasn't such serious work to be done.

But they hadn't known they were coming to England until the very last minute. The Infinity knew the general area, but as Peck had come to realise over the years this was hardly a precise science. Consequently, they'd wasted a lot of time looking around France: specifically the Paris region.

His master seemed so sure it was the place where their hunt would begin in earnest. They'd driven around in a hired car, The Infinity concentrating, retreating into himself as Peck had seen him do so many times. Almost there…almost. So imagine Peck's surprise when it was announced that this wasn't their final destination after all. When it came to their quarry, things were often a little…clouded. Places, people, anyone or anything directly connected with this endeavor were hard to focus on, hard to read apparently.

But an unexpected influx of information—and suddenly a new destination. They would be flying over to England.

"England? But I thought you said—"

"I know what I said!" The Infinity barked. "But I was…" He would never admit to being wrong about anything, so the word that followed was: "Mistaken. Momentarily." Not for the first time during this search.

"And you're certain this time?"

"Don't question me, Lucas. It's really not your place."

"I'm sorry."

Peck should have known better; The Infinity was not in the best of moods when he realised he could have simply hopped over the ocean from Amsterdam. France had taken him so far out of the way… Lucas just hoped that he *was* right this time, because with each new disappointment—particularly at this stage—The Infinity grew more and more aggravated.

He'd watched the man through the rear-view mirror as they'd driven back to the hotel. "It's no use trying to hide," The Infinity was whispering to nobody in particular. "I can see you, I can sense you."

It hadn't taken them too long to pack and drive over to the private airfield at Dieppe. There was no need to phone ahead, as everything would be taken care of when they arrived. Peck's pilot's license was still spotlessly clean—The Infinity made sure he held on to it when much younger men weren't even *allowed* to fly—so he would be the one who ferried them across.

The private jet was comfortable, and the flight had been uneventful, save for a slight spot of turbulence. Lucas Peck never worried about things like that when he was with The Infinity. And spirits seemed to lighten now that they were on the move again.

So here they were. In England again. At the airport. They'd landed a little over twenty minutes ago and had their passports checked. The woman on duty looked them over, eyes flitting from the photos to the men in front of her. Lucas had aged considerably since the picture had been taken. The Infinity's, on the other hand, looked exactly like him; suspiciously so, in fact. The photo was quite obviously years old, but he hadn't changed one bit: the hair was the same, the nose, those blue eyes… She let it pass; some people simply aged better than others, especially in this era of the plastic surgeon's knife.

"Thank you, Mr. Finn, Mr. Peck. Everything seems to be in order," she told them.

All that remained was to go through customs and have their luggage checked. This was the part Lucas really hated. It always made his heart pump faster, his hands grow clammy. Silly, he knew, but he couldn't help it.

Several uniformed officers were waiting. There was the obligatory metal detector, the conveyor belt and the X-ray machine, but no queue this early in the morning. Lucas wheeled the cases up and a big bearded man took the trolley from him, immediately passing it to a colleague for inspection.

"Gentlemen," he said with a voice so rough it could have sanded wood. "Are you here on business or pleasure?"

"A little of both," said The Infinity.

"And do you have anything to declare before we carry on?"

"Oh, I shouldn't think so."

"All right, if you'd just step this way, removing any metallic objects you might have in your possession."

Lucas took off his watch, his rings and dug out a set of keys from his pocket. The Infinity did nothing.

"Now if you'd just walk through the detector, sir." The bearded man put a hand on Lucas' back to guide him. The hand was strong, he could feel that. Lucas passed through without triggering a beep. He looked to his right as he did so, at the other officers examining the cases. This was where it always got interesting.

They were coming to his…special case. The one in which he kept his equipment. It was locked, naturally—only a combination of numbers stood between the customs officer and a selection of the deadliest and sharpest weapons outside of a slasher movie. The officer shook the case.

"Please," said Lucas. "Be careful with that."

"What do you have in there?" asked the officer holding it, regarding Lucas over the top of a pair of reading glasses.

"Just…just some items I use in my hobby."

"Your hobby?"

"Yes, I'm…I'm an artist."

The officer frowned. "Artist? So what's making all that clanking, your brushes?"

"No," said Lucas. "I'm more of a sculptor than a painter."

"Heavy," observed the man, shaking the case again.

"Yes."

He shrugged and put the case on the conveyor belt, sending it through the X-ray machine. The man put his glasses on straight and stared at the screen. Right now it was throwing out an image of cutting instruments: curved, ridged and deadly. Hooked and flat, lethal and sharp. The stuff of nightmares.

Any moment now, thought Lucas, *he'll shout out to the bearded man, tell him to grab me.* He tensed himself.

But that never happened. It hadn't happened in all the other countries they'd visited and it wasn't about to happen now. Lucas had no idea what the fellow was seeing on his monitor, but it wasn't the contents of that case. The man was nodding, satisfied, and let the luggage pass through with his approval.

"Sir," said the bearded officer, holding out his hand for The Infinity to walk through the metal detector. When the smaller man refused to budge, the officer put a hand on his back to move him. It was like pushing against a brick wall. Puzzled, he tried again. Still the man wouldn't shift. Then, without warning, The Infinity took a step. The officer dropped to the floor. The Infinity looked over his shoulder at the burly man and tutted.

As the officer picked himself up and dusted down his uniform, The Infinity walked through the metal detector. He set if off almost immediately, the machine vibrating with a loud *Peeeeeeeep*.

A third officer, this one squat but no less well built than his bearded colleague, emerged and asked The Infinity to remove any metal objects.

"I'm not carrying any," said The Infinity, and sighed.

The squat man ran a hand-held detector over him; this too let off a high-pitched *Peeeeeeeep*, though not in any specific area. A search was then deemed necessary, but this yielded nothing. The Infinity had been telling the truth: he didn't have any metal items about his person.

"Do you have any…surgical implants, fillings?"

The Infinity shook his head.

"Jesus, look at this!" exclaimed the glasses-wearing officer from behind his desk. In front of him was another piece of their luggage: The Infinity's briefcase. This one hadn't been locked. Nobody could see from this angle what was inside, but by the shocked expression on the officer's face it wasn't what he'd been expecting.

"I'm tired of this," said The Infinity, his blue eyes flashing fiercely. He pointed at the officer behind the desk. "Close the case. There's nothing in there that shouldn't be."

Glasses man shook his head as if he couldn't believe what he was hearing. Then he took another look inside, and nodded. "Sorry guys, false alarm," he said with a laugh. He closed it and sent it through on the conveyor belt.

"But you still need to—" began the squat man.

"I do not have any metallic objects on me. No guns, no knives, no watches, no pens. You will let me by right now, and we'll say no more about it."

Lucas studied the man. For a second it seemed like he was going to disobey The Infinity, that his mind wasn't as weak as that. But then he nodded obediently and smiled. "Yes, of course. I'm sorry for the inconvenience. Please, collect your luggage."

"Thank you," said The Infinity.

If he'd been a puppy, the man's tail would have started wagging. Conversely the bearded man on the other side was staring at The Infinity as though he wanted to murder him—a guard dog, with a vicious temperament. Lucas was pleased that there hadn't been any scenes today. He just wanted to get out of here; no fuss, no bother. He loaded the cases back onto their trolley and started pushing them away from customs. The Infinity followed close behind.

"Oh wait," shouted the glasses-wearing man.

The Infinity halted. Lucas Peck copied him. They both turned at the same time, Peck's heartbeat increasing again. The tension was building; Lucas knew that any little thing might set The Infinity off.

"Yes?" asked the man himself.

"I just wanted to say…welcome to England."

Lucas expelled a loud breath. "Thanks," he called back.

"Hope you enjoy your stay."

A corner of The Infinity's lip curled. "Yes, I'm hoping so as well…"

– ii –

Alex Webber stared out of the window of his flat.

He'd been sitting like that for hours, gazing out and watching the world go by without him. It was as if someone had pressed a pause button during the movie of his life. He felt disconnected from the rest of reality, had done ever since Sunday.

The things he had seen last week he could dismiss, but not what had happened at the match, in the hospital—and since. He'd grudgingly taken the time off as the doctor insisted and the college, though hardly overjoyed, had understood. He was glad that he had now, because it felt like he was falling to pieces. And he didn't want to do that in front of his students.

The first twenty-four hours had been okay. He'd been restless and had gone over what he'd seen time and again. Trying to make sense of something that very clearly made no sense at all. But he hadn't *seen* anything else. That particular treat was waiting for him when he went to bed and Beverly put the lights out.

Alex had tried to get to sleep, but unlike Beverly he couldn't just switch off. At some point he heard a grunting noise coming from the corner of the room. Alex sat up, trying to trace the source of the sound. Everything was black. He felt like he was trapped. Inside something. Cocooned. Like he had been in the MRI scanner. But then he noted a red-orange flickering on the bedroom walls. They were uneven, like rock, and the faint light cast shadows and illuminated shapes. He reached for his glasses and saw peculiar markings on the wall. In the middle of the floor was a dead animal, half eaten. A figure lunged at him from the darkness—big and feral, holding a flaming torch. Alex caught a glimpse of its face and screamed...

When Beverly turned on the light it all vanished, just like the woman back at the hospital, just like those men on the playing field. He'd told her he was having a nightmare—which she accepted—but couldn't hide behind that line in the daytime. Not when the kitchen turned into a marshland and he heard the distinct crack of gunfire while he was crossing the living room, distant explosions causing him to duck behind the couch for cover. Not when Beverly's chopping of vegetables on a board in the kitchen suddenly became the sound of a much louder blade falling and embedding itself in wood, followed by the roar of a large crowd of people. Not when he was seeing ghost faces at every turn, figures that appeared and then disappeared randomly. Alex was never alone in the flat, even when Beverly was at work. There were always the others to keep him company. His home didn't belong to him anymore. It belonged to intruders who brought with them bits of their own realities to merge with his.

Alex's episodes, as Nidra had referred to them, were becoming more frequent, not helped by a lack of sleep. He'd spent the previous night on the couch, a sheet curled around him like a toga, jumping at every creak of the floorboards, every car alarm, every loud TV set or siren. He couldn't concentrate on anything—no films, no books. In the end he found it safest to just gaze out of the window, placing himself into a sort of trance. It hadn't gone unnoticed, and Alex knew that when Beverly started rearranging her PR clients, things must be pretty bad.

Not even the lunchtime visit from James helped. He'd heard through the college grapevine that Alex was off sick. Something about injuring himself at a football match. What he hadn't expected was to find his friend like this, an unshaven recluse: confused, bewildered, dressed in jogging bottoms and T-shirt, with bags under his eyes.

"Alex, mate, what *have* you been doing to yourself?"

He stared at James, unable to tell at first if the man was even real, reaching out and touching him to make sure. Once he'd ascertained that it was his friend, Alex finally spoke, insisting there was nothing wrong, that all was fine.

"You're far from fine. What did they say at the hospital?"

Alex grinned. "Gave me the all-clear."

"Are you sure?"

"*Of course* I'm sure!" he snapped, then apologised. "I'm sorry. I'm... I've just got some things to sort out right now."

"So I see. Is there anything I can do? I mean, is it anything to do with..."

"Beverly, you mean? No...No, I don't think so."

"Can't have helped though. Then there's that bloody place," he said, referring to the college. "They work us too hard there. And you work yourself too hard."

Alex wanted to tell him, let him know that this had nothing to do with Beverly or teaching—at least he didn't think so. It was something else, something...

"If you want to talk about it at all..."

"Thanks," said Alex. "But really, there's nothing to talk about. Honest."

"Okay," said James, his frown speaking volumes.

But nobody could do a damned thing to help; it was up to him. The scan had shown there was nothing physically wrong, so it was just a matter of getting his head together. Of willing himself better. He could do it, he was strong enough.

Except the things he saw were much stronger. He had no control over them. They came when he was least expecting them, blindsiding him. Fantasy was crossing over into the real world.

And it was just a matter of time before something gave.

– iii –

Breaking point came late Thursday afternoon.

Beverly was dropping to sleep on the sofa after another fitful night, when she was woken abruptly by a series of ear-splitting cries coming from the bathroom. She ran down the corridor, only to find that the door was locked. They never used to do this, back when they felt comfortable in each other's company, but it had become a habit now for them to re-spect each other's privacy. Just one more barrier between them.

She banged hard for him to let her in.

"Alex? Alex, what's happening in there?" Her voice cracked as she called through the wood.

There was no response, except the horrendous screams.

"*Alex!* Open this door, right now!" Beverly fought with the handle, hoping it would somehow give. But it didn't. Her eyes darted left and right, looking for something she could bash the lock with. She settled on a heavy brass plant-holder. Beverly removed the aspidistra, another one of Alex's beloved plants, and struck the handle with the bucket-shaped container. The door jarred, but the lock still held. Her second attempt was more successful, and the simple bolt gave way on the other side.

The door swung inwards. Beverly dropped the plant-holder.

There was Alex, spread-eagled on the floor of the bathroom, shaking. As she took a step towards him, he bucked and screamed in pain.

"No, please… Stop… Not again…" The cords on his neck stood proud and his back arched. Beverly stood frozen to the spot, her hand raised to her mouth. She could see the red welts around his wrists, marks on his bare arms: deep cuts, some bruises.

He slumped again, exhausted. Alex shook his head. Then he looked up at her with tears in his eyes, really seeing her for the first time. "What's happening to me?" he breathed.

Beverly said nothing. She didn't answer him because she couldn't. All she could do was stand there as he asked her again.

"What's happening to me?"

– iv –

Dr. Goddard had seen a variety of patients that day.

It had started with a mother who'd brought her daughter in because she was having an allergic reaction to something. The rash on her stomach and shoulders looked angry and he knew she was frightened it was meningitis. A few simple questions later and they'd determined that a new, cheaper brand of washing powder was to blame and cream was administered.

Then he'd had to get tough with a red-faced, out of breath fifty-year-old who was heading for a coronary if he didn't cut out the binge drinking and fast food. "I just don't have the time to eat healthily, doctor," the man had told him.

"Then. You. Are. Going. To. Die. Mr. Shippam! Is that not registering with you? The pains in your chest are just nature's way of warning you."

As he was leaving the cubicle, he heard the man mouth under his breath: "Jumped up, wet behind the ears… What does he know?"

I know quite a bit, Goddard thought to himself. *Like not to buy you a birthday card next year if you don't get your head out of your arse!*

The next case, where the patient came limping in on crutches, turned out to be nothing more than a routine twisting of the ankle. The young woman had been running to catch a train because she had a meeting in Liverpool that afternoon. "For God's sake could you get a move on," she said to Goddard. "I've already been waiting ages. I have a very important presentation to give."

Goddard sucked in air through his teeth. "I'm sorry, that'll have to wait. You might even need to have an X-ray."

"Oh, for Christ's sake!" said the patient, attempting to get off the bed again. "I'll call in at the local supermarket and get a pack of peas to put on it!"

She'd barely made it out into the corridor before she was back.

He had to stop and wonder what was wrong with these people. Half of the things they came in with were either self-inflicted or could be treated very easily by their own GP. What a waste of everyone's time! What he wouldn't give for something to break up the monotony.

Goddard had been treating an ear infection when the paramedics answered his prayers. And he wished he'd kept his thoughts to himself. The Accident and Emergency Department was suddenly filled with shouts and screams.

"What in the name of—" He handed the drops to the nurse assisting him and tore back the curtains. "Who's making all that noise?"

Then he saw. A man on a stretcher being wheeled in, thrashing about. They'd had to strap him down because of his violent jerking, head snapping from side to side. He noted that they'd tried to treat his arms, which were bleeding, but somewhere along the line the pads they'd used had been ripped off.

"He was okay until he got here," said the male paramedic pushing him. "Then he suddenly started ranting and raving."

"He has cuts to the upper arms and bruises. Wife's outside. She says he was on his own when he got them so possibly self-inflicted," chipped in his female partner. "Name's—"

"Webber," Goddard finished for her, approaching the trolley. "Yes, we've met before. Very recently as it happens."

He tried saying the man's name a couple of times, but it seemed Mr. Webber wasn't here with the rest of them. His eyes were distant, but full of terror. "Keeeeep away!" he shouted.

"Okay, get him into the end bay," said Goddard. "We'll fix him up and take it from there." But it was quite obvious that the wounds on his arms were the least of anyone's concerns.

He'd need help with this one. But thankfully he knew who to call.

PART THREE
THE SEARCH

EIGHT

Kirkwell General: Psychiatric Department

– i –

THE PAST COULD DO SO MUCH DAMAGE.

Events and situations beyond anyone's control could ruin lives, scar people emotionally, cripple them forever. And nothing was more damaging or harder to come to terms with than the loss of a loved one. Mrs. Rosy Wilkes was now in her mid-sixties. Her husband, Alfred, had passed away almost a decade ago. Brain aneurysm. There was nothing anybody could do. He'd arrived home from work at five forty-five on a Monday evening. His dinner was on the table, the same as always, sausages and mash. Rosy asked him how his day had been at the bakery.

"Fine, love," he'd replied, kissing her softly on the cheek.

Then he collapsed in the hallway and died. No warning. No struggle. It was simply as if his body had decided it didn't want to carry him around anymore. Alfred had never taken a day's sick leave in his life, and on his last check-up with the local doctor he'd been declared "fit as an ox." Although, as they were quick to point out during the inquest, it would have been impossible for them to detect a weakness like that. It wasn't as if Alfred had the most taxing job in the world. Most of his duties involved simply supervising the production of loaves and rolls. It was a job he loved, and he got on well with the people who worked there; which was why every single one of them turned up to pay their respects.

Rosy had tried to rouse her husband, believing he had fainted. It was warm weather for the time of year, even at night. But when she got no response she rang for help immediately. The ambulance men arrived and found her kneeling, cradling her husband's head on her lap. She was telling him everything was going to be all right, that the medics would do whatever it was that they did to bring people around again.

They explained to her that he was gone, but even when they covered his face with a blanket, Alfred's death still didn't sink in. She rode with them in the ambulance back to Kirkwell General, promising them he'd wake up any minute and wonder what all the fuss was about. Even when the doctors talked to her, she wouldn't accept it, kept repeating that they'd made a mistake.

Rosy's only daughter, Jane, dealt with all the arrangements Not because Rosy was so upset, but because she couldn't understand why they were talking about putting Alfred in a wooden casket and lowering him into the ground. At the funeral, she said nothing. It couldn't really be *her* Alfred in the casket. How on earth would he be able to breathe in there? At the wake she listened as friends and family told her what a lovely man Alfred had *been*, what a doting father. She'd nodded and said, "Yes, he *is*." All the time wondering why everyone was suffering from the mass delusion that Alfred was dead.

After the funeral, Jane moved back home for a while, just to keep Rosy company. But as the weeks passed, she became increasingly worried about her mother. Jane had lost Alfred too, but Rosy just didn't seem to be coping with the fact he was gone. Often she'd walk into the kitchen or the living room and find her mother talking to him, having one-way conversations as if he was there in front of her.

"I've bought some of those fish cakes you like so much, Alf. Thought we could have them tonight. No, don't worry about the price, they were on special offer. Yes, I know, sweetheart. I know."

Jane tried telling her this wasn't healthy; she had to let go and move on. She was still relatively young, maybe some day she might even meet someone to share her life with again. Not to replace Alfred, no one could ever do that, but perhaps ease the pain a little. Rosy stared at her as if she were deranged. Why would she want anyone else when she had Alfred? He was her one true soulmate. He was everything to her.

Eventually it got too much, especially when Jane discovered Rosy had started cooking meals for him as well; washing his clothes and dressing up the pillows at night with his pyjamas so she could snuggle up next to him.

That's when she'd been forced to seek professional help.

Rosy had been placed in the care of Kirkwell General's head psychiatrist at the time, Dr. Sylvester Thorpe. But he got no further convincing Rosy than her daughter. Rumour had it that Thorpe's methods were heavy hand-ed and produced sporadic results. He was of the opinion she projected a mental image of Alfred, recalling memories of him and playing them back to herself; tricking herself that he was still alive. Thorpe had forced her to visit his grave as a last resort, but Rosy saw only what she wanted to see.

All his efforts failing, Thorpe turned to drugs for the answer. He'd tried various combinations over the years, but nothing seemed to work. They just doped Rosy, reducing her quality of life. Jane complained about her mother's treatment and Rosy was referred to a new psychiatrist, while Thorpe moved to a hospital in London.

So the first contact Dr. Ellen Hayward had with Rosy Wilkes was five years ago, when she took over some of Thorpe's cases. Jane had been unsure at first, but once she saw them together she knew there might still be hope. Dr. Hayward was nothing like Thorpe. When she smiled it was genuine, her grey eyes anything but cold, her pretty face framed by dark blonde ringlets. She talked to Rosy like she was a human being, spent hours simply listening to her stories. To some it might have seemed like Hayward was indulging her, but as she explained to Jane, "The only way I can help your mother is if I can get her to confide in me. Then we can start to think about confronting what's happened. I won't lie to you, it will take time. But we're already making steady progress."

It was a question of trust. And over the months, the psychiatrist gained that from Rosy. Enough to take her back to that ill-fated night, to re-live it with her. They pieced it together bit by bit: the cooling of Alfred's skin as she held him, the medics feeling for a pulse in the neck, the lifeless expression.

When the tears finally came, it was like they'd broken down a gigantic dam. Ellen held her for at least an hour, stroking Rosy's hair. As hard as it was to get Rosy to grieve, Ellen still knew that the hardest road of all lay ahead of them. Now the woman had to get used to life without Alfred. Do what she'd been putting off for so long. Remember the past but not live in it, looking to an uncertain future and being brave enough to accept what it brought. But Rosy wasn't alone. She had some wonderful friends, a loving family, Jane.

And she had Ellen.

Today, during her outpatient's appointment, they had talked about that future. About Rosy's planned day-trip at the weekend with an over-sixties group. A real milestone.

"You do think I'm ready for this, don't you?" Rosy asked as she sat in the comfortable chair opposite Ellen.

"Do *you* think you're ready?"

Rosy looked at a point on the carpet, then slowly raised her head. "Yes. Yes, I believe I am."

Ellen smiled. "Then so do I. One step at a time, Rosy. It's how we've always played it."

"Thank you, Ellen."

Their time was almost up, but before the silver-haired lady left she asked the psychiatrist another question. One she'd never raised before.

"Do you believe that there's only one person out there for us all, Ellen? Just one perfect somebody who knows us inside out, even before..." Rosy shook her head. "Listen to me, rabbiting on again. I've taken up enough of your time."

Ellen opened her mouth and closed it again. Was Rosy thinking ahead, about possibly meeting someone else? Or did she just want Ellen to confirm that you only got one chance, one shot and that was it?

"I...I honestly don't know, and that's the truth. What you had with Alfred, it was so special it makes me want to believe. But I also think there are lots of special people in this world, and if we're only meant to be with one of them... Those are pretty big odds don't you think?"

"Makes me feel sorry for all those who never find theirs," Rosy replied, a sad tinge to her voice.

Ellen smiled again. "Come on, let's go and see Jane. She'll be waiting." She helped Rosy to the door and opened it. Jane was sat in the waiting area on one of the plastic orange chairs, scanning an out-of-date magazine.

"Here we go," said Ellen. "Now you take care, okay?"

Rosy patted her arm. "I will, dear."

"Thanks, Doctor," said Jane, who still couldn't bring herself to call Ellen by her first name.

As the psychiatrist watched them go, Rosy's question nagged at her. It wasn't as if it hadn't crossed her mind during their sessions. The way she'd talked about her husband, like he was the only man who'd ever existed—he *had been* as far as Rosy was concerned. Fate put him in her way at the tender age of seventeen and they'd just known. But providence could also be cruel; it could take back what it gave. Ellen had been telling the truth when she said she wanted to believe, but there was also a part of her that hoped Rosy was wrong. Because if you could only love someone like that once...

Well, the pain that came with that knowledge would be far worse than anything Rosy had ever encountered.

– ii –

The phone was ringing before she set foot back in the office.

She picked it up, waiting as the call was connected. "Hello?"

"Ellen?"

At first she didn't recognise the voice. Then it came to her. "Hi, Stuart."

"Hi. Sorry to bother you."

Ellen transferred the phone to her other ear and came around the side of her desk. "It's no bother, what can I do for you?"

"I think it could be the other way around. Got a patient here you might be interested in seeing. Came in screaming blue murder. Possible self-inflicted wounds. He was non-responsive at first, but he's settled down a bit now and claims there's nothing wrong with him."

"You notified the on-call psych team?" she asked.

"Thought you might want to have a look at him personally. Could be an interesting one."

"Go on."

Goddard explained that the patient had been in last weekend having suffered a blackout.

"Who saw him?"

"Dr. Nidra."

"Ah, Vikram. And you've got his notes there?"

"Mr. Webber was given a scan and they found no abnormalities. This has got to be your territory, Ellen."

She looked at her watch. "I was just about to do my rounds, Stuart."

"It's your call, I just thought you might want first dibs. Sounds right up your street."

"Okay, okay… Give me about fifteen minutes and I'll be right with you."

"Cheers," said Goddard and hung up.

– iii –

Goddard met her at the bottom of the stairs, near the entrance to A&E.

He could often appear conceited, and oozed self-confidence, although Ellen knew that was often only a front, hiding insecurity beneath. But he cared about people, even if he sometimes had a funny way of showing it. That made him okay as far as she was concerned. He also had an eye for spotting the more unusual cases and usually gave her the heads up when anything interesting appeared.

She raised a hand in greeting and Goddard returned the gesture. "Right, so what's the story, Stuart?"

He fell into line beside her as soon as she hit the bottom of the steps, explaining in more detail about what had happened last weekend and what Dr. Nidra had to say. "He actually recommended a counsellor at the time, thought there might be stress involved, but apparently Webber didn't seem too keen."

Ellen clicked her tongue. People were wary when it came to counsellors, psychologists and psychiatrists. She was used to it. They still had this old-fashioned idea that therapists would strap you down and electroshock you till your fillings flew out.

"Do we have any idea what happened to him today—why he was in such a state?"

"Wife says he's not been himself recently. Not been sleeping, edgy. He does have a bit of a history of panic attacks apparently. She's through there." Goddard pointed to an auburn-haired woman sat on a chair, biting her lip.

She had a natural beauty, which was just as well because she wasn't wearing much make-up, and her hair looked like it had only been given a cursory brush. The navy blouse and black trousers didn't really match the time of year, and it crossed Ellen's mind that she was unconsciously reflecting how she felt through her choice of clothes.

The woman studied Ellen too. When she finally smiled, it was weak, and she stood when both doctors approached.

"Mrs. Webber," said Goddard. "This is Dr. Hayward."

"You're a psychiatrist, aren't you?" said the woman immediately. She obviously wasn't too bad at reading people herself.

Ellen nodded and held out her hand. "Dr. Goddard thought I should take a look at your husband."

She shook Ellen's hand just once, then let it go. "What's going to happen to him?"

"I can't really say without taking a look. You told Dr. Goddard you were concerned he might hurt himself again?"

When the woman swallowed, it was with some difficulty. She was trying to keep her composure, but behind the hard veneer was totally vulnerable. "I didn't know what to do."

"And he has a history of panic attacks?"

"Nothing like this. I…"

"Take your time," said Ellen. "It's okay."

Mrs. Webber shook her head. "No, no it's not. You didn't see his face when… He was screaming, Dr. Hayward—"

"Ellen," she told her. "Call me Ellen."

She looked the psychiatrist in the eye. "I think he's been seeing things."

"What kind of things?"

"How in God's name should I know?" snapped Beverly, then regained her composure. "I'm sorry, it's been a rough day."

"Understandable. You're worried about your husband."

"I'm worried about *both* of us," said Beverly.

Was the woman being selfish, or was she scared? Ellen hesitated before asking her next question. "Has your husband harmed you in any way, Mrs. Webber?"

"*No!*" Beverly said abruptly, then added: "He hasn't harmed me, but…"

"You think that he might?"

"No, that's not what I meant… I don't know… When it happened at night he said it was a dream and he hadn't really woken up, but… When the…when it starts, it's as though he's watching people who aren't there, Doctor. Even listening to them. He's tried to hide it from me, but…"

Ellen immediately thought of Rosy and the conversations she'd had with her dead husband. He wasn't really there and yet had been as real to Rosy as her daughter or Ellen.

"I see." Ellen looked at Dr. Goddard. "Where is he now?"

"In the end cubicle. Two male nurses are with him."

"Okay," she turned back to Mrs. Webber. "I think I'll take a look at Mr. Webber now."

"Alex," said Beverly. "His name is Alex."

— iv —

Alex Webber was sitting up in bed.

He flinched when the curtain was drawn, but relaxed when he saw who it was.

"Dr. Goddard, look, I keep telling you there's no need for—" He stopped when he saw his new visitor. Ellen caught his gaze briefly, before he had time to look away again. Like his wife outside, she knew he had a fair idea who she was. And she didn't expect him to welcome her with open arms.

Alex Webber was dressed in very casual clothing—sweatpants, tracksuit top with a hood—yet his behaviour was anything but relaxed.

"Would you mind," she said to the two nurses who'd been keeping guard. They looked at Goddard, and he eventually nodded. They exited, leaving a wide gap in the curtain in case they were needed.

Ellen covered the distance between them slowly, carefully. "Hello, Mr. Webber… Alex," she said softly.

This time when his eyes found hers they locked on. "I shouldn't be here," he said. There was no malice in the words, just certainty. "And I'm *not* dangerous."

She looked at the bandages on his arms. "How did that happen?"

He didn't answer.

Ellen had seen self-abuse cases before. Had treated men and women who cut and burned themselves, sometimes because they were so disgusted with who they were they craved punishment. But she wasn't getting that from him. Maybe it was the only thing he could control in his life, when to hurt himself?

"This looks worse than it is," Alex assured her.

"And how does it look?" she asked him.

Alex offered Goddard a pleading look, but found no ally.

"This will work a whole lot better if you talk to me," she said. "My name's Ellen Hayward."

"And you're here to cart me off to the funny farm, right?"

"I'm here to help you," she stated.

"Then let me go. I'm okay now."

Ellen shook her head. "Not until we've figured this out. Not until you tell me what happened to your arms, what happened when they brought you in."

"I…I panicked. I don't like hospitals," said Alex.

Goddard folded his arms. "Strange, you weren't screaming the place down last Sunday when you came in."

Alex had no answer for that.

"Your wife's very worried," Ellen told him.

"Is she?"

"Yes."

"She shouldn't be."

"Are you sure about that?"

Alex shut up again.

This is slow going, thought Ellen. *But then Rome wasn't built in a day.*

"You're going to have to talk about it sometime."

She waited for the answer, but he was now staring past her; out into the hall…

Through the gap in the curtain Alex saw a patient being pushed past on a trolley; a wooden trolley.

A wooden cart.

Somewhere a bell was ringing. Not a telephone, but a real bell. There was a dead body on the back of that cart. Its skin was grey-white—what bits could be seen beneath the hard, angry-looking boils and swellings.

What the hell were they doing bringing him in here?

In the distance Alex could see houses. It was as if an entire wall had dropped away like a flimsy movie set façade, revealing the reality behind it. The houses were made from wood too, their doors painted with red crosses.

He gave a start when the corpse suddenly moved. It let out a loud groan and began to sit upright. Rolling off, it fell heavily to the ground. Then it disappeared from view for long moments, during which Dr. Hayward, continued to talk to him.

"Your wife seems to think that you might be experiencing some sort of delusions. Perhaps imagining things that aren't really there."

Almost as soon as she'd said it, the grey-green figure rose up behind her: its eyes glassy and white, mouth wide and black as a void. It let out a pitiful moan.

Alex's attention shifted from the shape to Goddard, expecting him to notice it at any moment and react. But he didn't, he just rocked backwards and forwards on his heels. "You can't see…? Look!" he said, pointing.

Ellen looked behind her, right at the figure. "What?" she asked.

"It's… You really can't see it?"

She turned back, frowning. Alex was hitching up the bed, desperate to get away from the diseased creature. "You're seeing something right now, aren't you?"

Alex closed his eyes, willing it away. If he just wished hard enough, when he opened them again it would be gone. It was only in his head—it wasn't really here. *Keep it together, keep it together,* he told himself, breathing erratically.

"Alex? Alex?" Hayward's voice.

He opened his eyes and the half-dead man was now centimetres away. That was it. Alex let out another cry and scrambled out of the bed. Goddard grabbed him before he could get far, wrapping his arms around the patient. "Some help in here!" he called.

The two male nurses returned and Goddard ordered a sedative to be administered. "This is as far as we go down here," he said to Hayward then, withdrawing and letting them get on with their job. "He can't keep disturbing the other patients like this. I think the ball's well and truly in your court now, don't you?"

Hayward watched as the injection was given in a bruised right arm.

"No… Wait…" Alex began, but everything was already growing fuzzy as he slumped on the bed.

"Yes," he heard Hayward said, the decision already made. "Yes, I think probably it is."

— v —

"You're keeping him, aren't you?" said Beverly Webber. She'd risen from her chair in the visitor's lounge when Ellen entered, and now her eyes were attempting to find somewhere to settle. Like a butterfly, her gaze landed on the doctor's face, then the walls, then the door.

"I think that would be for the best," Ellen told her.

Beverly bit the side of her bottom lip. "Where's he going to end up, on a ward?"

"I'm trying to arrange a room for the time being. It might take some doing, but…" Ellen held out a hand for her to sit again. Beverly lowered herself back down into the cushioned seat, but still perched on the end as if ready to spring up again at any moment. The doctor sat next to her on a spare seat, hands clasped together.

"So it's serious then?" asked Beverly, giving the answer to her own question once more.

Ellen dodged the issue. "We're… I'm going to do all I can for him, Mrs. Webber. But I'll need some help."

Beverly looked horrified. "What kind of help?"

"I need you to tell me anything you can about Alex. What might have triggered this kind of behaviour."

"I…" Beverly started, then snapped her mouth shut.

"It's okay, I totally understand. I wouldn't want to share my private life with a complete stranger either," Ellen said. "But if I'm going to do this I need to know all about your husband, everything you can possibly think of that might help me."

Beverly nodded. And then she began.

– vi –

Dr. Ellen Hayward gazed in through the window of the room.

Alex Webber was on the bed, head turned to one side. He looked asleep but she knew it was the drugs. He wasn't technically sleeping, it was more like unconsciousness. Total blackout. At least he was getting some sort of rest. From her lengthy chat with Beverly Webber, Ellen guessed that sleep had been in short supply at their household over the past week. She'd told her about her husband's overworking and dedication to the job, all about his panic attacks when he was younger—but nothing that could explain his sudden hallucinations, delusions, whatever you wanted to call them. From Beverly she'd also gained a sense of who this man was, and although it was obvious that the woman no longer cared about her husband in the way she once had, the fact he was a decent man came across loud and clear. For all that, the psychiatrist still had a sense that she was holding something back. It could just have been that guarded way she had about her, but it felt like she was hiding things, being economical with the truth.

Ellen had thought about pushing the issue of the current state of their relationship, but now really wasn't the time or the place. Just as it wasn't the right time to talk to Alex again. Much better to wait until tomorrow.

She watched him through the circular safety glass. Studying him.

"Managed it then," said a voice behind her.

Ellen's heart leapt into her mouth. She whirled and saw Stuart Goddard.

"Sorry," he said, "didn't mean to startle you."

Ellen's hand was on her chest. "You didn't," she lied, controlling her breathing. "What do you mean 'managed it'?"

"Got him a room."

"Pulled a few strings," she told him. "Wasn't easy, especially at this short notice."

"Well, if anyone could sort it… So, how's he doing?" Goddard peered into the room.

"He's…resting," Ellen said, mirroring his actions.

"That was quite a conflab you had with the wife. Find out anything interesting?"

"Never heard of doctor-patient confidentiality?" Goddard glanced across and she flashed a quick smile.

"Come on, if it wasn't for me you wouldn't even have got the shout," he protested.

"For which you have my undying thanks, Stuart."

"I'd rather know what she said."

"You were right, if that's any comfort. I think this one *is* going to be interesting."

"Right. I can see I'm not going to get anything out of you, am I?"

Ellen shook her head. "Uh-huh."

"Where is she now?"

"I sent her home. Nothing more she can do here tonight. She's coming back tomorrow."

"It is getting late I suppose," said Goddard. "You fancy a drink or a bite to eat?"

Ellen knew it wouldn't mean anything, not with Stuart, but she declined anyway. "Going to hang around a while here."

Goddard nodded as if he'd been expecting that answer. Everyone knew Ellen practically lived in this place. "Okay, but don't be surprised if I check in again."

"Be my guest," she said.

Goddard wandered back up the corridor as silently as he'd drifted down it. Ellen only watched him for a couple of seconds before switching her attention back to Alex, lost again in her own thoughts.

Just like her patient.

– vii –

Jubilee Gardens, South Bank

London hadn't really changed since the last time they were here. Yet in a lot of ways it had changed *so* much. Walking through Leicester Square earlier, the crowds had seemed bigger. There were so many more people wandering around shops, sat outside cafes, waiting to see films in the huge cinema. Lucas had slowed down to watch the street artists at work, drawing caricatures, doing paintings. The creative process had always fascinated him—pencil lines on paper, brush strokes across canvas…knife into flesh.

Tourists posed on deckchairs, eagerly awaiting the finished products. One couple sat together, mugging for a man wearing a cap. Their happy, smiling faces were captured in a series of quick, bold lines. But Lucas only had eyes for the woman. His intense scrutiny drew some attention—before The Infinity dragged him away. They had been traipsing through the city all day long, riding on an underground packed with commuters, sweaty bodies pressed up against them. Well, against Lucas. For some reason they always gave The Infinity a wide birth.

It was France all over again. No real sense of direction, nothing to go on.

Now it was growing dark. They'd ended up coming full circle, back to Big Ben and the Houses of Parliament—The Infinity remembering fondly his last visit and the wheels he'd set in motion. Crossing the bridge that overlooked the Thames… To stand in the shadow of the Eye, a huge landmark built to mark the Millennium. All over the city, lights were coming on. They lit up the London skyline. "Though I have seen it brighter," The Infinity said to him. "A long time ago."

He told Lucas he needed to be alone for a while. The Eye was closing for the evening, but The Infinity was granted the last ride of the day. The machine cranked up and Lucas lost sight of him from below; The Infinity a tiny flea in the capsule holding him. He knew that to The Infinity the people down here would look the same. But then didn't they always? Even when he was on the ground with them.

Lucas waited patiently when the Eye paused at the top. The view must have been incredible—twenty-five miles in each direction. Many Londoners had become regular users, he was told by staff: getting married, having birthday parties, even conducting business meetings up there. The Infinity was doing something altogether different. Something Lucas couldn't possibly understand even if he tried. And so he waited.

When The Infinity finally descended, he got out of the cab and turned to Lucas. "We are to head northwards," he said. "That is where we will find what we're looking for."

"North?"

"Yes. I was starting to lose the thread, Lucas. Something was blocking me, but now it's beginning to clear. With each mile we travel we are closer all the time."

Closer, yes, but to what?

The Infinity walked away, issuing instructions over his shoulder as he went. Lucas trod in his footsteps taking note. Soon they would be on the move again, for the last time he hoped. Then maybe everything would finally be revealed.

And he would at last be told what this was *really* all about.

NINE

– i –

AGAIN HE WAS AWARE OF VAGUE IMAGES—a dreamscape—but he was under so deep that he couldn't recall a thing when he resurfaced, except leaving the blackness behind. It was light, he could see that through his eyelids. There was no music this morning, though. Rolling over, he expected there to be a warm, naked body lying next to him. But he felt nothing except the coldness of clean linen. His hand glided over it, reaching up until it found a pillow. Memories flooded back all at once—bizarre, fleeting pictures of a figure at the side of his bed. Of a wooden cart and the smell of death.

Alex opened his eyes, but again everything was blurred. He squinted though it did no good; that hadn't worked since he was twelve and they'd diagnosed his short-sightedness. His hand went instinctively to the bedside table, but it wasn't there. Not on the right side anyway. The room was different too; smaller. He wasn't at home. Which could only mean one thing.

He sat up in the bed. Looking down, he saw that he had pyjamas on. Not the ones that he wore in the winter sometimes when it got cold. These were of a plain, loose variety—standard issue. Alex panicked. He looked to the left and right, and it was then he noticed the buzzer hanging down. Alex hesitated before pressing it, not certain he wanted to let anybody know he'd woken up. But he pressed it all the same, and kept pressing until a smudged figure came into the room.

It was big, he could see that even without his glasses. But when the person spoke it was with a friendly voice. A male voice. "Hello there. You must be Alex."

"Where the hell am I?" he asked.

"Would you like something to eat?" the voice enquired, ignoring his question.

"No, I'd like to know where the bloody hell I am."

"You're at Kirkwell General," the man told him. "My name's Ben, I'm one of the nurses."

"I'd like to go now," said Alex. "Could someone fetch me my clothes?"

"I'm afraid that's not possible. Not until Dr. Hayward's been to see you."

Dr. Hayward. "Ellen Hayward," said Alex, remembering the name. "She's the one who put me in here, isn't she?"

"I think it's best if I let her know you're awake."

"Yes. You do that," he said. "You do that."

The nurse departed.

While he was waiting the notion occurred to him that he could just open the door, get out of this room, make a break for it. But how far would he get without his clothes or glasses? He didn't have time anyway, because someone else was standing in the doorway now. Smaller than the first person, they came inside, and Alex could just about discern an outstretched arm.

"Thought you might be needing these," said an altogether different voice. One he recognised from the day before.

There was a hand holding his and Alex's natural reaction was to pull away. Then something was forced into his palm, something with thin metallic edges and two flat circles. The foreign hand let go, allowing him to put his glasses on.

Dr. Ellen Hayward came into focus, her face framed by dark blonde ringlets.

"The nurse on duty kept them safe for you last night."

"Thanks," he said, though there was very little of it in his tone. "Where's the other one? Ben?"

"He's nearby."

"Just in case," said Alex.

Ellen pulled up a chair and sat down. She was wearing a purple short-sleeved blouse and dark trousers. Clipped to the breast pocket of the blouse was her ID card; the photo wasn't good. "How are you feeling today?"

"How am I feeling?" Alex let out a pained laugh. "How do you think I'm feeling? I wake up to find that I'm in a strange room, in a hospital. That I've been doped up to the eyeballs—"

"Just something to help you sleep," Ellen interrupted.

"Yeah, I'm sure."

"It's true."

Alex pointed at her. "You had no right to do that."

She held his stern gaze. "Tell me what I was *supposed* to do."

"I..." Alex found that nothing was forthcoming. "I don't know."

"You were shouting and screaming in an A&E department, you came in with cuts and bruises on your arms."

"So that's it then, fit me up for a straitjacket, lock me away with all the other fruitcakes."

"That's not a word I like to hear," she said. "There'll be no straitjackets, and nobody's locked you away, Alex."

He pursed his lips. "But I'm not free to leave, am I?"

"Do you even want to, before we've got to the bottom of this?"

"Have I been sectioned, doctor?"

She rubbed the top of her head and sighed. "You're looking at me like I'm the enemy here. I'm not. Trust me."

"Trust you? I don't even *know* you."

"Then get to know me," she said. "All I want is to find out what's wrong with you, so I can put it right."

There was silence for a few moments, then he said: "Shouldn't I be on a couch or something?"

The corners of Ellen's mouth rose slightly. "Would that make you happier?"

"No."

"Then it's a good job I haven't got one."

"So, what now?" Alex wriggled about. "Tell you all about my childhood, so I can get out of here."

Without missing a beat, Ellen came back with, "If you think that's relevant. Personally I'd rather hear about what happened yesterday. About what's been happening to you recently."

Alex retreated into silence again.

"Look, you're an intelligent man. You must be, you're a college lecturer."

He frowned, trying to work out how she knew that. Then he remembered they'd taken his details last weekend. Nothing more, nothing less— no mind reading. "You've done your homework," Alex said. "No pun intended."

"It's my job. Just like it's yours to find out about your students when they first come to you."

"You know, when you train as a teacher you're taught about all this psychology stuff. Students are 'Reflectionists' and 'Activists'; the schools of learning are all about Behaviourism and Humanism. But in my opinion students are people. And teaching... That comes down to instinct."

Ellen raised an eyebrow. "You think it's any different here? Patients are people, Alex, not case studies and stereotypes. I'm not going to force you to tell me anything, that's not my style. But I am here to help. You should believe that if you don't believe anything else. You want to get better, get back to your teaching. I want that too. I know you must be scared—"

"Scared?" Alex broke in. "That doesn't even begin to cover it. Until a week and a half ago everything was okay." *Was it? Was it really? Your marriage was falling apart, you were lying to cover it up and you were under stress at work. You call that okay? Better than it is at the moment—that's for damned sure.* "Now..."

"Now, what? Tell me."

"Now I'm falling apart at the seams, is that what you want to hear?"

Ellen shook her head. "I just want you to tell me what happened." She shifted her position so that she was leaning more towards Alex. "Let's start with yesterday when you came in. What spooked you so much?"

"You wouldn't believe me if I told you. Then again you might. Maybe that would be worse."

"Try me."

Alex exhaled. "You really will think I've lost it if I say 'I see dead people.'"

"Dead people? What do you mean?" She was frowning now.

"Obviously not a film buff, are you?"

"Not really," she confessed.

"All right…I saw *something*. There was someone standing next to you. I thought they were dead but they weren't."

"Hold on, hold on. Was this somebody you know, someone you've lost recently?"

"Never seen them before in my life. Never want to again."

Ellen pondered this new information. "What did they look like?"

"Terrible. Sick. Sores all over them. I've never seen anything like it." He didn't mention the fact that they'd just rolled off a wooden cart, or that an entire village had appeared in the A&E department.

"And it's not the first time you've seen something like this, is it?" Ellen craned her head.

"You've been talking to Beverly."

"I had a brief word with your wife last night, yes."

"What did she tell you?"

"That you've been suffering from anxiety, that you've been overdoing it at work."

"You all make that sound like it's unusual. Goddard and the Indian doctor I saw last weekend…"

"Dr. Nidra," she informed him.

He nodded. "Most of the bloody country is overworking, doctor. Haven't you ever pulled a few late nights?"

She shifted her weight in the chair, sitting back. "We're not here to talk about me."

"Kept your husband or boyfriend waiting while you attended to an emergen—"

"*Alex*," she said. "Has this happened before? Have you seen other things?"

He couldn't dodge the issue any longer. She already knew the answer. "Yes," he admitted.

Ellen gave a small nod of thanks. "You said that everything was okay until a week and a half ago. So what changed?"

"I…" Alex dried up.

"What happened?" She waited for him to say something. When he didn't Ellen added: "Please. We have to start somewhere."

Alex gripped the sheets. "I thought I saw something at work."

"What kind of something?"

"One of my students. His face... It's hard to describe."

"Okay. Take it slowly. Just tell me what you saw. Everything's going to be all right, Alex. I promise."

Why that reassured him, he had no idea, but it did. "It was my first class of the morning, a week last Wednesday. I hadn't slept very well the night before, maybe that had something to do with it..."

"Go on," she said softly.

"This student, Timothy Brailes, his face just seemed to change—right in front of my eyes."

"In what way?"

"One second it was him, the next it wasn't. His face was older, more tanned. He had grey hair." Alex twisted the sheets in his grasp. "Jesus, listen to this. Do you see what I mean? It doesn't make sense."

Ellen neither agreed nor disagreed. "What else can you remember about the face?"

"It happened really quickly. I'm not even sure if..."

"It might help," Ellen told him.

Alex closed his eyes, dredging up the image. When he opened them again he said, "There was a headband. And the face was painted, marks down each side of the nose. But the weirdest thing was..." He paused once more and Ellen thought she'd have to prompt him, but he started up again of his own accord. "I think I recognised that face. As quick as it was, I think I knew that person from somewhere."

"So it could have been a memory," Ellen mused. "Someone you met once?"

"I...I don't think so. I would have remembered meeting someone like *that*. At least I think I would."

"Then perhaps you saw the face somewhere else. Maybe it was second-hand?"

"Maybe."

"What happened next?"

"Nothing. I mean... Well, Tim's face went back to normal. Like I said, it happened really quickly. I didn't think too much about it until..."

"Until the next time," Ellen stated.

Alex nodded. She listened as he told her in fits and starts about his birthday dinner, about the fire that never really existed, about his bizarre behaviour in the restaurant. "Which I'm sure Beverly filled you in about."

"You've never been in a fire like that yourself?"

"No, never."

"Or maybe you have and you've just blocked it out?" Ellen caught herself. "Sorry, thinking out loud. Occupational habit."

"I think I would remember."

"Not necessarily. The mind is a selective thing."

"Oh, come on," said Alex. "You're telling me that I've been in a fire and suppressed it?"

Ellen shrugged. "I don't have the answers. But somewhere in there," she pointed to his head, "you do. Now, you say this fire was happening all around you."

"It was as real as anything I've ever experienced. Well, it seemed real at the time."

"So the people in the restaurant were on fire?"

"Sort of." Alex let go of the sheet to scratch his cheek. "They weren't exactly the people in the restaurant. They were…other people. They looked different."

Ellen was puzzled. "Like Timothy?"

"No. They were dressed differently."

"How do you mean?"

"More…more old-fashioned, I suppose you'd say."

"Old-fashioned?"

"Yes. Look, I told you before this doesn't make any sense."

"Oh, it does. Everything always makes sense eventually, Alex. It's just that we can't see it yet."

"Great," he moaned.

"Let me ask you this, did you have one of these…lapses before you banged your head last Sunday at the football match?"

"Is that what we're calling them, now? Not episodes; lapses?"

"For want of a better word."

"Momentary lapses of reason, right? Like in the Pink Floyd song… Let me guess, not a music fan either."

Ellen didn't bite. "I'm right, aren't I? You did see something."

A tip of the head was the only confirmation he'd give.

"What happened that time?"

"All right," said Alex, "if you really want to know...the players on the pitch all turned into rampaging lunatics with swords and horses."

"Horses!" Ellen couldn't keep the disbelief out of her voice.

"You heard me. And one of the blokes was beheaded. What's the matter? Changed your mind about that straitjacket?"

Ellen didn't contradict him this time.

"It's gets worse. I haven't told you about the white-faced woman in the hospital. And the other night I saw this figure in a cave, an honest to God cave! How about that? It was dark and there was a fire—only not like the one in the restaurant. Whatever I saw was using it to keep warm. Warm, for Christ's sake! It's got to be eighty degrees outside at night!"

"Alex, listen to me," Ellen leant forward, she was about to reach out a hand but withdrew it. "We can sort this out, nothing's as bad as it seems."

"Isn't it? Judging by the last couple of weeks of my life, it's worse."

Ellen's eyebrows stooped. "Is that why you hurt yourself yesterday, Alex? Because things were getting too much?"

"You still don't get it, do you? I didn't hurt myself, I didn't do that to *myself.*"

"No, no of course not."

Alex was trembling. "Don't you understand? I was being tortured. I was being bloody well tortured!"

– ii –

"Excuse me?" said Ellen, but she'd heard it right the first time.

Alex took off his glasses and rubbed an eye with the back of his hand. "I know how it sounds," he said, voice catching in his throat. "But I swear to you that's what was happening. I could hear Beverly banging on our bathroom door to be let in, but couldn't open it. I was...somewhere else, with stone walls."

"Being tortured."

"Right. There were chains, and I could see those bastards as plain as day. Felt it as they took my arms and..." Alex couldn't go on. Tears were welling in his eyes. He wiped them away quickly before replacing his glasses. "Now, you said it yourself, Doctor—"

"We're not standing on ceremony. Call me Ellen."

There was a hesitation before he repeated her name, then another before he finished what he was saying. "I'm a pretty level-headed sort of guy. I'm not prone to delusions, or lapses, or whatever the hell you want to call these things."

"Nobody ever is," she told him. "It's not something you can prevent or predict. And it can happen to anybody—that's the first thing to get straight—triggered by anything. What we have to try and figure out is why this is happening to you, and why now."

"So what's the next step?" Alex asked her.

"The next step is you telling me again what happened, from a week last Wednesday onwards. Everything you can remember, okay? No matter how it sounds."

"But—"

Ellen wagged a finger. "I'm not here to judge you, Alex. I've told you that, I'm here to help. All right?"

Alex nodded. "All right."

So he told her his story.

* * *

They talked for what seemed like hours.

Alex explained about the things he'd seen, everything he could remember, down to colours and even smells. Ellen never once criticised or patronised. She was nothing but encouraging and supportive, which in turn made Alex open up more. When they were finally finished, she got up and sat beside him on the bed.

"Now you know everything," Alex said.

Ellen smiled. "I wouldn't go that far. I know what's happened to you in the short term, but that's just the start."

"So what's your gut reaction? What do you think might be causing this? Why am I flipping out?"

"Again, another term we don't like to hear, Alex."

"You know what I mean."

Ellen drew in a breath. "I do have one theory, but I'm not sure whether—"

"Please, Doctor…" She gave him a stern look. "*Ellen*."

"Okay, you teach film studies, right?"

"Yes, like I said, and some media. Why?"

"Films and television. It's a form of escapism, isn't it?"

Alex tapped his leg with his fingers. "It can be."

"As you probably guessed, I don't get a chance to watch either very much. My work tends to get in the way."

Alex nodded, not really following the turn of the conversation.

"But I'll bet you've seen your share, haven't you?" She pointed at Alex again. It wasn't a threatening action, merely marking him out as the subject of her statement.

"Yes, but I don't see what—"

"How many films and TV programmes would you say you've watched in your time, Alex?"

"I couldn't narrow it down. A lot."

"Comedy, romance, action, science fiction, horror…"

"I still don't—"

"Historical?"

Now he understood where she was going. "You're not trying to say that these things I'm seeing are related to films or TV shows I've watched?"

"Not exactly." Ellen brought her knee up and rested it on the mattress. "I think they could be the external manifestation of something that's much more deep-rooted. Sometimes when we go through traumatic events our mind can't cope and we bury things, so deep we don't even know they're present ourselves. What if you've buried something in the past, Alex, and what if these filmic images are your mind's way of trying to get you to deal with it. The fire, the swords, the torture. You've got to admit, that's quite strong stuff."

"Jesus," whispered Alex.

"I mean, what are our memories after all but little film shows inside our own heads? You can close your eyes anytime you want and run a home movie from your life. And some people are so familiar with scenes from films and television they can quote them line for line."

Alex said nothing, but there were certain favourite scenes he knew inside out. Everyone had them, it's just that he probably had more than most. "I can't believe this. So indirectly it's my job, my hobby, that's doing this to me?"

"I didn't say that. Those images were only your mind's way of dealing with something else. If you'd been a vet, you might have started to see talking animals or snatches of operations performed in the past."

"That makes me feel so much better," said Alex, barely concealing his sarcasm.

"It wasn't meant to," Ellen informed him. "Look, the real breakthrough will come when we find out what you're hiding from yourself. Only then can we start to get you back to the old Alex Webber."

"I take it we're not talking some quick fix here, are we?"

"I wish I could say, but these things take as long as they take."

"But college—" he started.

"Is going to have to manage without you." The way she said this left no room for argument.

Alex looked down. "That's if they want me back anyway after this gets out."

There were no words of comfort this time, just a change of subject. "It's past lunchtime," she said. "Get something to eat and we'll talk later."

"After lunch?"

"After I've seen some of my other patients." She smiled. "Later." Ellen got up and walked to the door.

Alex watched her linger there just a moment longer.

"It *will* all be okay, you know," she promised him again.

Then she was gone.

– iii –

She felt almost physically sick returning to this place.

After taking a ticket at the gate, Beverly drove around the car park, trying to find a space for her Scénic, and finally discovered one not too far from the hospital's main entrance. She reached over to the back seat and picked up the carrier bag: just a handful of necessities like toothpaste, toothbrush and a comb. She gripped the top of the bag tightly, gaping out through the windscreen at the large building. The central section was only three storeys high but wide at the same time, with connecting corridors branching off like octopus legs. Small patches of grass scattered around the car park tried their hardest to give the impression of rural tranquillity, but it did nothing to alleviate Beverly's dread.

As she got out and walked towards the main entrance, her insides were churning. She'd managed to get some sleep last night—nervous exhaustion more than anything—but still felt drained. Her legs were heavy and it took a long time to get to her destination. Beverly almost stepped into the path of a Mini that was backing out, which earned her an evil look from the driver.

Screw you! Try going through everything I've been through the last few days and still know whether you're on your head or your feet. Just try that and see how it feels!

That was unfair. For all she knew the driver had a dying relative in the hospital. Then again, maybe it was only something as simple as an in-growing toenail. What Alex was suffering from they couldn't even identify; couldn't run tests on. Beverly kept seeing him in the bathroom, arms covered in blood, staring up at her pleadingly. She ran the scene in the restaurant through her mind over and over; the night when he thought she'd been asleep but he'd been shaking because he'd seen something in their bedroom.

And she just knew something else had happened in A&E yesterday, could see it in Dr. Hayward's eyes, hear it in the tone of her voice. Something serious enough for them to detain Alex.

The double doors opened and she found herself in a much larger space than the casualty waiting room. There was a queue of people at reception so she joined them. Dr. Hayward had told her that Alex would be staying in the psychiatric department, but she wasn't entirely sure how to find it. Or even whether she wanted to.

Glancing nervously from side to side, she gripped the bag even tighter, almost putting holes in the plastic. Was she ready for this?

It might have been better just to ring.

Beverly gave a small shake of her head. No, she was here now.

She was here and she would be strong.

– iv –

He had to be strong.

They weren't really there. Just figments of his imagination.

Alex had asked to go for a walk after lunch—an unappetising plate of boil-in-the-bag fish and new potatoes, as sterile as the hospital that served it. Ben had checked with Ellen, who'd agreed, on the proviso that he didn't wander too far. So Alex was escorted down the corridor, flanked by Ben and another large nurse whose nametag read: CLIFF. Alex's room was one of only a few that were private and, as they walked further, he saw that there were wings just like any other hospital ward. To all intents and purposes these patients might have been admitted with any number of ordinary illnesses, instead of the disorders he knew they specialised in here.

"Not what you were expecting to see, huh?" asked Ben.

Alex shook his head. "I didn't really know what to expect." But that was a lie. He'd been anticipating a scene right out of *One Flew Over the Cuckoo's Nest*.

"We do good work here," Ben assured him. "Don't we, Cliff?"

"Yeah," said Cliff. "It's all good."

"What's down there?" Alex enquired. Another corridor branched off to their right.

"That's the rec room. I'll take you when Dr. Hayward gives you the okay. But you've had a busy day today."

Alex wasn't sure if you could describe his day as busy, all he'd been doing was talking. "Can I just have a quick look?" he asked.

Ben looked at Cliff, who shrugged.

"I don't know…"

"Please," said Alex. "I've been cooped up for hours in that room."

The nurse's eyes softened. "Okay, but just a quick peek. Then we get you back again."

They took him down to the Recreation Room, and Alex could see the edge of a pool table through the glass. The noise of a TV was also plain, and he heard the distinctive voices of Laurel and Hardy. When he pulled up alongside the room, he saw patients inside, playing board games and cards. A couple were watching the black-and-white film on a television bolted to an armature in the corner. It was a little like the students' rec room at college, only smaller and minus the darts board, for obvious reasons. The people were much older too, and most were wearing housecoats. By far the youngest was a man with tousled hair and a pool cue in his right hand. He sank two balls before looking up and flashing Alex a grin.

Alex was through the door and into the rec room before Ben or Cliff could stop him. And the pool guy was already making his way over.

"New face?" he asked the nurses.

"For the time being," Alex told him.

"That's what they all say," the man told him seriously, before breaking into another smirk. "I'm Sam."

"Alex." He instinctively held out his hand, but the young man didn't take it.

"I'm…I'm sorry. I don't," said Sam, his only explanation. Alex could see him counting the fingers on his left hand with his thumb.

"It's okay."

"So, how do you like the place?" Sam asked.

Alex glanced around the room. "Not quite as bad as I first thought," he admitted.

"You under Ellen?"

"Sorry?"

"You being treated by Dr. Hayward?" Sam elaborated.

Alex nodded.

"Thought you might be, you hear things on the grapevine. She's one of the good guys, Ellen." Sam was hopping from foot to foot. "So what you in for?"

"Sam," scolded Ben.

"Only being curious."

Alex looked up at the nurse as if to say it was all right. "I've not been feeling myself lately."

"That's a shame," said Sam. "Everyone should feel themselves every now and again."

In spite of himself, Alex laughed.

"Now that's more like it." Sam beamed. "You fancy a game of pool, Alex?"

Ben stepped in. "He can't right—"

"Ah, go on, Ben."

"You have to watch this one," the nurse explained. "Bit of a hustler, aren't you Sam?"

But Alex's attention had drifted. Over to the TV, where Laurel and Hardy—dressed in Foreign Legion garb—were traipsing through the desert. There was a big, round sun blazing down on them, baking hot. Sand was everywhere, as far as the eye could see. Drifting down dunes, roll upon roll, pouring...

Pouring out of the TV.

Alex gaped as the sand flowed from the screen to puddle on the floor. It turned yellow as it spilled out into the real world, glistening and golden. He snapped his eyes shut and opened them again quickly. Everything was back to normal. The sand was back inside the television.

"...fan, are we?"

Alex turned back to Sam. "What?"

"Those two? Are you a fan?"

"Er... No... I just thought..."

"Are you okay?" asked Sam. Except it wasn't Sam anymore. His skin was darkening and the robe he wore was shrinking. The pool cue he leant on was more like a staff, and his arms were exposed to the beating sun. Alex looked down and saw the sand; it was all over the rec room floor. The tables where patients had been playing their games were expanding. Market stalls were appearing, sacks underneath them, while various baskets of fruit and vegetables were on display above: an explosion of reds, greens and purples. Canvases held in place by four poles at each leg of the stalls shielded the produce from a fierce sun. And manning them were traders, stripped to the waist—some selling fowls strung up by their necks, and beside these hares; others offering earthenware jugs and bowls. They wore what looked like linen skirts, with sandals on their feet.

Stay strong, he told himself. *It's all an illusion. This isn't happening. Ellen told you that. Just hang in there and you'll snap out of it, like you have done before. Oh, please God let me snap out of this!*

There was a hand on his shoulder and he spun round, only to see that Ben and Cliff had changed too. Their eyes were dark, encircled with black marks, almost like eyeliner. The coverings on their heads were a square shape at the front, with flaps that hung down at the sides—again, offering some protection against the sun. Cliff wore a beaded necklace as well, with a symbol of a cat's head in the middle. The man that had been Ben grumbled something at Alex in a language he didn't understand. Alex tore away from his grip, dodging past him and heading for where he thought the door should be—where now there were only bleached cream buildings and pointed shapes on the horizon.

Alex was aware he was being chased. Although some part of him knew the men following were just psychiatric nurses, another quick glance over his shoulder suggested they were different people entirely—with knives drawn, ready to attack. He also had difficulty thinking of this as a corridor anymore. It was definitely some part of a town or city complex.

Alex faced front and saw a woman holding a basket of fruit. A cream band held her straight, ebony hair in place and two large circular earrings hung down on either side of her head. She shouted something in that same language, but it was too late to avoid her. Alex ran headlong into the woman, scattering her fruit everywhere. They both tumbled to the ground.

The men caught up and grabbed him by the shoulders.

"Get off me!" shouted Alex as they dragged him back. Then he called out to the woman, "They've got knives!" just before he felt the blade of one digging into his arm.

It was at this moment that the desert scene dissolved, like a scene change in the theatre. He blinked once, twice, then saw the woman in front of him for who she really was—a staff nurse who'd been carrying a bundle of files.

One or two patients had come down from the wards to see what all the fuss was about and were gawking at him. Alex stopped kicking. Ben and Cliff held him tightly. "It's okay, I'm all right," he argued, but his words didn't count for much. A needle was already in his arm, where the blade had been, and its contents were soon inside him. He was dragged backwards, past Sam and a few of his rec room friends who'd trailed them out. "I'm all right," he repeated, slurring his words.

Then he saw her, through a haze, at the other end of the corridor.

He saw his wife standing with Ellen Hayward, saw her put a hand to her mouth and disappear completely from view—the doctor not far behind.

"Beverly," he mouthed. But it was much too late.

The blackness had taken him again.

— v —

The petrol gauge of the Scénic was screaming at her to refill.

Beverly Webber pulled in to the first station she came across on her way home. Absently, automatically, she manoeuvred the car alongside the pumps, popped open the covering that hid the petrol cap, and climbed out. As she pushed the nozzle in the hole and squeezed the trigger, her mind was elsewhere. Back there, talking to Dr. Hayward and then standing, watching the disturbance in the corridor. It was hard to tell who'd been more shocked, wife or doctor.

She'd been half expecting bad news, but to actually see something like that for herself… It had answered her question at least. Was she ready? Definitely not.

"So what now?" she'd asked Ellen Hayward before departing.

"We're going to let him sleep this one off again. I have been making progress, I assure you. In fact only this morning we—"

"Progress? You call that progress!" she'd cried out. The conversation hadn't lasted much longer.

Beverly lowered her head, studying a spot on the concrete, a drip of petrol that had splashed there; a small, dark spot. What if all this was down to her? Had she really caused it? *No!* Alex had been under pressure at work as well, all these new rules and regulations, the amount of paperwork he had to do to satisfy his heads of department. End of term exams and exhibitions were coming up. That must have had something to do with his…the word rattled around inside her skull: breakdown. Her fingers squeezed the trigger harder.

It was just like when he'd been a student himself. Except it wasn't, was it? Nothing like that at all. Those had been nerves, Alex had always been one to get wound up about things—so his mother said. His mother! How was Beverly going to tell *her* about all this? The situation was bad enough without that matriarch flapping around the place.

She was bound to blame Beverly once she found out the truth. That their relationship had been a façade for some time. Sometimes it was better to bite the bullet and come clean, as things had a habit of catching up with you. And when they did, oh when they did...

The trigger jerked and clicked in her hand and Beverly almost dropped it. She released the pressure and pulled out the nozzle, the tank full. *If only you could do that with life*, she thought. *Empty out all the bad things, get rid of worries and heartaches and pain, then refill it with happiness. Drive off and make a fresh start with miles of new road stretching out ahead of you.*

At the pay kiosk, she fumbled with her purse, counting out bills as impatient customers jostled for position behind her.

"You're a fiver short," muttered the panda-eyed teenager serving her, lip-ring glistening as she spoke.

"I...I'm sorry," said Beverly. "I thought that was a ten." She counted out five pound coins, nearly dropping them on the floor. "Sorry," Beverly repeated before beating a hasty retreat to the car.

The door clicked behind her: a sanctuary of sorts. She closed her eyes and leaned back against the headrest. For a second everything was still and Beverly drifted away, forgot who and where she was. The blare of a car horn soon shattered the peace. She checked her mirror to see a man in a red Mazda thumping his steering wheel. Beverly started her engine, ground the gears before finding first and pulled away from the pumps. As she guided the car out of the forecourt she saw the man standing next to his car, tapping a finger to his temple and pulling a face.

She could imagine what he was thinking: dizzy cow, probably PMT. Beverly waited for the next gap in the traffic, then left the scene behind. Her foot pressed hard on the accelerator, doing thirty, forty, fifty. Her mind was racing like the Scénic, full of so many emotions she couldn't keep track. Full of so many images of Alex, of their life together. She'd loved him once. How could she be so cold? At the next crossroads a car tried to beat her, the driver changing his mind and braking just in time. Beverly jammed on her own brakes, swerving around him, avoiding a collision by inches. Up ahead there was a turning for a small estate and Beverly took it, tears already welling in her eyes.

Finding a quiet street, tucked away next to what might laughably be described as a playing field, she parked her car. She couldn't hold it back any longer. Every bit of anxiety, every ounce of frustration and confusion broke free in a deluge of sobs. Beverly thought it would never end, that she would just cry herself out of existence and disappear in a puff of dehydration and steam. But it did. She took control again and wiped her face with a hanky.

For a few seconds more she stared out of the window at the field. Then she reached into her handbag and took out her mobile. She'd switched it off as soon she entered the hospital, so she depressed the ON button and held it in. A welcoming chime greeted her, followed by a series of beeps as she entered a set of numbers. Placing the phone to her ear, she heard it ring out several times before someone answered.

"Hi," said Beverly. "It's me again. I need to see you."

She listened to the other speaker, then answered, "Yes, I know what I said. Look, I've changed my mind. I know, but it's been difficult for me too. You have no idea. Please…I don't want to talk about what's happened, I just need to see you. I… I need to be with you right now. Can we meet up?"

The voice on the other end of the line said something.

"Thanks," Beverly breathed into the mouthpiece. "I'll see you there."

– **vi** –

The key took some turning before the lock gave way.

Not surprising; it had probably forgotten what its function was in life. She hadn't been back home for a few nights, and had only really returned tonight to get fresh clothes, check that the place hadn't been completely ransacked. Ellen flicked on the light, mouthing a silent thanks that it hadn't.

Clutching the pile of mail she'd picked up from her box, Ellen walked in and shut the door behind her. The flat was cold, in spite of the warmness of this May night. It hit her like a blast from an opened tomb, making her shiver. If she'd believed in the notion of places having feelings she might have wondered whether she'd hurt them. She hardly spent any time at home, so why would it feel cosy? Then she remembered she'd left the air conditioning on; just set it too high, that's all. Nevertheless, the notion remained with her as she made her way into the hall and dumped her post on the table. The corridor looked lost and lonely—like it was crying out for people to walk through it. One would have to do. The red light of her answering machine was flashing. Even that had an accusatory tone to it.

Where have you been? Look, there are messages for you. People have been trying to get hold of you. And were you here to answer them? No, you bloody weren't.

"I'm sorry, okay?" said Ellen, instantly feeling foolish. *Physician heal thyself.*

If only it were that easy.

It wasn't even as if there would be anything important waiting. Ellen shrugged off her coat and played the messages back as if to prove her point. "Mrs. Hayward," said a voice in broken electronic English, "you have been selected to enter our prize draw with a chance to—"

"Missus? I don't think so," she said to herself, skipping to the next message. "Ellen, it's Mum and Dad." This was more chirpy, the woman sounded ecstatic. "Just to let you know we're having a wonderful time. Currently parked up in Barbados, though how the Captain backed the liner into that small space I'll never know." Ellen's mother tittered in her girlish I've-never-taken-responsibility-for-anything-in-my-life-and-don't-intend-to-start-now way. "The meter must be doing somersaults. Hold on, your father just wants a quick word..."

The next voice was deeper, though only just. "Hi El, you really should get yourself on one of these trips, you know. Do you the world of good to get away from it all for a while, do some travelling. You should see our tans! And as for what it does for the libido..." Ellen could hear her mother giggling in the background. *Too much information, Dad!*

Her mother returned to the phone. "Your father's right, and the amount of eligible young men on the boat...ship...oh whatever you call it... Anyway, have to love you and leave you, sweetheart. We've been invited out for drinks with a couple we met last night. Don't go working too hard at that hospital. Talk soon, bye!"

"Bye, Mum," said Ellen. If they could only hear themselves sometimes. Ellen loved her parents, but they really did only think about themselves. It had been the same thing growing up; bundling Ellen off to the all-girls boarding school so they could pretend they were still in their teens. They never changed. Still, she ought to be grateful they'd even bothered to ring. And no, the irony wasn't lost on her that it was usually the other way around, parents grumbling because their kids didn't keep in touch.

But they always had to have a dig, didn't they? She could just imagine the eligible men her mother was talking about: playboys with more money than sense, who thought with their penises so that they wouldn't have to disturb that other—more dormant—organ inside their heads. Even if she *was* interested, they'd run a mile as soon as she told them what she did for a living.

There was a beep and the next message played. Ellen listened to the hiss of static and an audible breathing sound, then the machine clicked off. Biting her lip, she played it again. Ellen bent, as if expecting to hear something different this time, but the message was exactly the same. Silence, then a sigh as the receiver was replaced. Twice more she played it, and Ellen closed her eyes each time, letting the sound wash over her. The cold noise of nothing, the fizz of a telephone line. Then what? A sigh?

His sigh.

No… Ellen shook her head. It was a wrong number, just someone who'd made a mistake, misdialled. So why listen to the entire greeting on her answer phone and leave a message, such as it was? But that message said more than the others combined. She picked up the phone, praying nobody had called after it. She dialled 1471 only to be told that the last person to ring had done so at nine o'clock the previous night; they had also withheld their number. Now she knew for certain…almost.

How did she feel? Scared, or more than a little glad? Could she even put into words the mixture of emotions that triggered inside her? *Tell me what's going through your mind.* That's what she'd say to a patient. But when it came to her own life, Ellen was hardly qualified to give advice.

She needed a drink. Ellen backed away from the phone, hardly able to take her eyes off the thing, daring it to ring again. *What, at this time of night? Hardly likely. And what if it does, Ellen? What are you going to do then? Answer it, talk to him?*

Ellen continued to back down the corridor, only turning when she was at the kitchen door. Even then she twisted her head around, eyes focused on the cream slim-tone. Ellen opened the door and turned on the light, keeping it ajar.

Was she hoping it would ring again? Why? *Ellen, you can't go back*, she told herself. *It's impossible. How can you ever forget? How can you ever forgive?*

Without knowing it, she found she'd taken a glass out of the cupboard and had already filled it with white wine from the fridge. She stared out through the hall as she sipped at the liquid, leaning back on a countertop.

"Damn you, Graham," she said quietly to herself. Just when she was getting on with her life again, just when she was beginning to get through the day without seeing his face at least once. Without flashing back to times long gone: good and bad. That was the curse of having a photographic memory. It was good for storing facts, but it also stored memories like digital images on a computer. Snapshots so vivid she could see every detail, every glint in his eye, every smile. Glimpses of yesterday blurred with today. And the moving ones were the worst, like home videos repeating themselves on a loop. "What are our memories after all but little film shows screened inside our own heads," she'd said to Alex Webber, knowing the implication of those words. In these she could even experience the sounds, tastes and smells.

Out walking in the countryside on a summer's day, a light breeze caressing her face. Laughter as they'd sought shelter from the sun under an enormous chestnut tree and she tickled Graham in just the right places; that spot on his back in particular. Murmurs as he drew her in close and their lips touched, so soft and warm, his hands in Ellen's hair. The scent of his aftershave blended with his sweat from the walk and she was lost in the moment...

The time they got caught in a shower on the way back from the cinema. Neither of them had umbrellas, and Graham had taken off his coat, holding it over her until they could hail a taxi. Ellen wrapping her arms around his waist, pressing herself up to his strong, hard body so he could hold the coat over both of them. There was something about the rain that night; the way it pounded on the pavement and bounced off cars made her feel alive. Then back home—their home—getting out of their dripping wet clothes as fast as they could, falling into the big double bed, naked. They'd made love as the thunder and lightning performed their own coupling outside. Energised by the forces of nature, they'd held each other as the sky's rumblings grew more distant. "Night, Angel," he'd said to her, kissing her on the forehead. She'd mumbled something back, before falling into that deep, easy sleep of contentment…

Painting the living room of their rented house together, getting more on themselves than the walls. Graham in his T-shirt and scruffy old jeans, her in dungarees, music playing in the background. "You've missed a spot," he'd said, coming over to admire her handiwork on the skirting boards. "Where?" she'd asked. And he'd touched the end of her nose with his brush, leaving a dab of pastel green behind. She'd pulled a face of mock annoyance which she could only hold for a few seconds before bursting into fits of giggles, then racing after Graham with her paint pot, threatening to tip it over his head…

These images and more returned, though she fought hard against them. But along with these came memories of the split. About the night she discovered who he really was. It had only taken one slip to uncover the truth, one lie that backfired. The best friend who'd been covering for him had a serious car accident and was rushed into the hospital where she was working at the time. Word got around and she'd dashed down to casualty, expecting to find Graham there too—in Christ knew what kind of state. Ellen could feel tears breaking free as she'd pushed her way into the room where the friend was being treated. Seeing Dave's face, swollen and cut, blood everywhere.

"What happened?" Ellen demanded as two of the nurses tried to usher her outside. "Is he going to be all right?" It took some time for them to calm her down enough to explain. Dave had been broadsided by drunk driver, way over the limit. When she'd asked where Graham was, they looked blank. Dave had been the only person in the car at the time of the accident. Ellen's initial relief—at the thought that Graham was all right— soon gave way to confusion. So where was he? Why had Dave been on his own when the accident happened? They were supposed to be heading to the gym together. Ellen had gone outside to try Graham's mobile; it was switched off. She debated leaving him a message, but for some reason stopped herself.

She stayed to see if Dave came round, but he was taken away for emergency surgery. His family arrived not long afterwards and Ellen went home; she only knew Dave through Graham and felt like an intruder. On the drive back, those questions still nagged her about what had happened.

If there had been a change of plans then surely Graham would have let her know.

Ellen waited on the couch for at least an hour before Graham let himself in. He was surprised to see the lights on, and her sitting there when she was usually still at work. But he was even more stunned by the strange look on her face. Her initial reaction was to go over and throw her arms around him, tell him how much she loved him and how glad she was that he hadn't been in that wreck. Instead, she asked him how his session at the gym had been.

"Fine. You know, usual kind of thing."

"Have a good workout?"

"Yeah, not bad. Ellen, are you okay? You're not ill, are you?"

Ill? She was sick to the pit of her stomach, but she had to know. "And how's Dave?"

Ellen saw him look away, before answering. "He's fine."

Wrong! He was about as far from fine as you could get. She closed her eyes and opened them very slowly. "Graham, there was an accident tonight."

He came over and sat down beside her, taking up her hand. "Oh my God, Angel." How that pet name stung her now. "Are you hurt?"

Are you hurt? It was a good question. Physically, she was fine, but emotionally...

"Dave's in hospital. He's been in a car crash." Ellen studied his face, saw it change. Saw the concern for his best friend, but also the realisation that she knew.

Ellen pulled her hand away. She didn't ask where he'd been, what he'd been doing. She'd seen enough cases of this to know what followed next. She didn't need to be told the tawdry details, not right now—didn't think she could handle them. So Ellen rose, went to the bedroom and packed a small case.

When she returned he was still sitting on the couch, hand to his mouth. "He's having emergency surgery," she told Graham. "You'd probably better get down there."

He looked up at her, saying nothing; he just gave a small nod. Then she left, driving to a hotel and checking in. Ellen waited until she was alone in her room before crying again, and didn't stop till morning. It was the single worst night she'd ever endured. She berated herself for not spotting the clues, even with her training. They say that love is blind, but Ellen thought she must have had both her eyes poked out not to see the signs. The flowers he'd bought, the recent meals at restaurants. She just thought he was being romantic, rekindling the spark—which had never, as far as she was concerned, faded. Now she knew he was doing it to ease his own conscience.

And the questions; oh Lord, the questions. Who was she? What did she look like, what did she have that Ellen didn't? Could she have done anything to prevent it from happening? They were stupid and pointless, designed to drive her mad. But they came anyway, and she couldn't provide the answers.

I don't have the answers...

The days and weeks that followed satisfied some of these, but not all. She arranged for one of her colleagues to take over her patients for a while and made enquiries about Dave, who pulled through his surgery, but would need months of physiotherapy to properly recover.

Graham sent texts and left voicemails on her phone, telling her that it had meant nothing, that *she* was the one he loved and always would. That it had been a mistake, he'd been weak and he thought the absolute world of her.

"For the love of... Ellen, you *are* my world!" he said in one emotional message. She'd almost caved. Missing him, she returned to their home, only to see an unfamiliar car parked on the road outside. Hanging back she'd spotted the woman emerging moments later. Tall, with black hair reaching down her back, she had a statuesque beauty about her Ellen couldn't hope to compete with. Graham had trotted after her, holding out a diaphanous scarf she'd left inside. He gave her a swift peck on the cheek, before waving her off. Ellen had turned the car around and vowed only to return when she was positive no one was around. And then only to collect the rest of her belongings.

Later, Graham swore that he was telling the woman it was over; and yes, the pair had parted company not long after Ellen split with him. But she could never be sure. That was the hardest part. This man, whom she'd invested so much trust and love in, had betrayed it all so casually. He'd broken them apart in a way that couldn't possibly be mended. There were times when she'd lie awake at night and wonder if she ought to give him another chance. It was the uncertainty that always held her back. The fear he might put her through this terrible pain again. He'd left her with no choice but to walk away. To cut him out of her life completely.

Her father had said, "At least there were no kids involved." Her mother had said, "Plenty more where he came from." But were there? What if Rosy Wilkes was right? What if there was only one person you were meant to be with? Had Graham messed up their one, true chance of happiness?

Ellen swallowed the rest of her wine, wiping away a tear with the edge of her finger. She'd moved out of the area, got another job in another hospital. But look, he was still very much on her mind. And she was obviously still very much on his, especially at this time of year.

It only took one thing to set everything off again. One call… That wasn't good, wasn't constructive.

Ellen shook her head, composing herself. So what if he was trying to get back in touch? There was no going back. Time to move on and let go. Leave the past behind where it belonged. She walked into the living room, turning on a lamp. In the subdued light she slumped on the couch and poured herself another glass of wine, which she drained much quicker than the last.

Move on and let go. You could say it over and over again, but the memories, those snapshots, those home videos… If only she could erase them, or even control them.

Ellen curled up her legs, tucking them tightly beneath her, making herself small. *Classic childlike retreat into oneself. Next thing you know, you'll be in the foetal position, Ellen.*

The wine was taking effect though, and combined with the tiredness and crying it made Ellen's eyelids as heavy as lead.

She was aware of drifting into unconsciousness, but couldn't really do anything about it. Except relinquish the final bit of control she did have left.

And pray she wouldn't dream.

He returned to the dream place again. To the circle.

Alex felt that same sense of security he always experienced here. This was where he belonged. It was a gut instinct, more powerful than anything he'd ever known. The figures were here again, too. Peculiar, transient shapes, nebulous—like the circle itself. Neither real nor unreal. This time he was determined to find out who they were.

He flitted from one to the other, followed them, reached out his hand, clasped shoulder after shoulder. Trying to twist the figures around. They would always evaporate almost as soon as he touched them, dispersing into the ether. He caught glimpses though, faint outlines of faces just before they vanished. They were somehow familiar to him, like this place. He knew all this, it was just…out of reach. His hand snatched at another figure and clawed only empty space.

Empty, until another person appeared. The outline was more defined. Alex saw a shape forming.

"Where am I?" it asked, just like before.

"I don't know," replied Alex.

"Who are you?"

"Who are *you*?" Alex countered.

"I…I don't remember."

Alex closed the gap between them, still unable to see a face or even most of this figure's body.

"Help me," said the voice.

"How?"

"By remembering. By helping *me* to remember."

"Remember what? Who you are? I don't understand." Alex reached out and suddenly there were hands in front of him. They linked with his, fitting perfectly and he did remember something. He remembered holding these hands. The touch of them, the feel of the skin. For this person was perfectly solid, flesh and blood, or as close as you got in a dream.

"You *have* to remember," the voice repeated with some urgency. "Before it's too late. Before—"

Light in the circle was dimming. It was as if a huge shadow had been cast over the arena, and in a way Alex knew it had. A shadow was falling; a shadow given form.

"Go, run. Get away from this place!" shouted the figure.

"Why? Why are you so frightened? What's going to happen?"

"Run!" It let go of him, wrenched its hands away. Alex snatched at them but it was already too late. "Run, before he finds you," said the voice, growing fainter.

The shadows inside the circle were lengthening. Darkness was upon him. Alex looked round, searched for the shape, but couldn't find it. He wasn't alone though. There was someone—something—else here with him. Yet another figure, so different, drawing up the black, absorbing it and spreading it at the same time. Alex shivered, felt his dream-flesh prickle, his metaphysical blood turn to ice.

And he remembered what the voice had told him: *RUN*.

So he tried, but didn't get very far. At every turn there was a barrier, the edges of the circle folding in on him. He was trapped.

"What do you want from me?" shouted Alex, but it gave no response. "Leave me alone!"

But Alex knew it couldn't do that, either. Whatever this monstrosity wanted, he had it. Whatever it craved and desired, only Alex could supply.

The darkness wound itself tighter around him, the circle closing. The beast inches away from Alex. Ironically, he could see this fiend's face more clearly than he wanted to. It was human, yet at the same time it was anything but. Blue eyes shone out of that face like lasers, bathing him in the beams. It made Alex want to retch. Somehow he could see below the surface of its disguise, the mask it showed to the world. And that sight was more terrifying than anything he'd ever seen in his life. Alex saw—no, *felt*—the suffering it had inflicted. Caught flashes of people in the throes of anguish and agony more severe, more intense than anything he'd endured in his bathroom back at the flat. There were worse kinds of pain than the merely physical, and this abomination was an expert in every possible kind.

Alex sensed the pleasure this gave it. The almost orgasmic joy it experienced reflecting on the fates of these unfortunates. Billions upon billions—face layered upon face. Alex rocked with the sensations, as he was bombarded with wave after wave of misery and despair. Hopelessness and pure, undiluted evil. The thing was all this and so much more; the embodiment of sudden realisation.

As the monster drew closer still, hands reaching up in a replay of Alex's other encounter tonight, he was offered a close-up of this being's eyes. For a fraction of a second, he thought he saw what was to come. Something so horrific that the other revelations paled by comparison.

Closer, closer.

Then the beast began to smile.

– viii –

There were hands on him, gripping him, their strength incredible.

Alex fought to break free, but it was no use: he was held fast at the shoulders. And he was screaming.

Now he was being shaken, hard, violently. The creature was obviously intent on taking what it wanted by force, ripping this out of him with claw-like hands. He could feel them digging in, so hard they must surely be penetrating the skin—fingers sinking through bone and muscle. Another shake and—

Alex's eyes snapped open. The face in front of him was no longer that of the great imitator, it was one of the night nurses. He was restraining Alex, throwing him back against the bed.

"Hold him steady," he heard a female voice say. The first nurse wasn't alone.

"I'm trying," said the man pinning him down.

Alex mumbled something. He wanted to tell them not to send him back, that he was in danger, that they all were.

The male drew his head nearer. "It's okay, you were just having a bad dream."

No, not just a dream!

"There…there was something… Something was coming for me…" Alex told him. There was another sharp pain and he was feeling drowsy again. "You…you…don't…" he started but never finished.

As he fought to keep his eyes open he heard the female nurse say, "There you go, just take it easy. It was only a nightmare, and they can't hurt you. It's not like it's the end of the world or anything."

Those words followed him into oblivion.

It's not like it's the end of the world...

The end of the world.

Ten

Room 11a: Saturday

– i –

"Alex... Alex?"

He jumped when he felt the hand on his shoulder, rolling over quickly.

"Easy. Take it easy."

Ellen Hayward was close enough for him to recognise, even without his glasses. But then she pulled back and started to blur. Behind her he saw a large figure. Alex reached over for his glasses and everything came into sharp relief. Ellen, standing by the side of his bed, Ben behind her.

She took a seat and the male nurse hovered not far away. "Hi," she said.

Alex pulled a face, smacking his lips a few times.

"There's a drink of water on the side there," Ellen informed him.

He nodded and took up the plastic cup, drinking most of the liquid in a couple of gulps. Then he looked at his doctor. She was dressed in a white blouse and beige trousers today, but it was more than just her clothes that had changed. Her curly hair seemed to have less bounce and her eyes were dark, as if she'd barely slept. Alex wished he'd been given the option.

"Feel like anything to eat?"

He shook his head.

"Okay... So," said Ellen, "how are you doing?"

Alex spat some of the water back into the cup, coughing. He wiped his mouth with the back of his hand. "That's a good one," he said, voice low and reedy.

"You feel up to talking about what happened?" she continued, undaunted.

"You mean before I was put under?" Alex looked at Ben accusingly. The nurse shrugged, as if to say they'd had no choice.

"That was for your own protection."

"Just like before," Alex said.

Ellen looked over her shoulder at Ben. "The nurses didn't want you to—"

"Hurt myself? Or maybe hurt anyone else?"

There was no reply.

"Haven't you got anything better to do with your Saturday, Doctor? It is Saturday, right? I haven't lost a week of my life or anything?"

"Yes, it's Saturday," she said simply.

"You didn't answer my question."

"Right now, no, I don't have anything better to do. My time's my own today; I'm all yours. So tell me what you saw."

Alex drank the rest of the water, shaking his head. "I'm losing my mind, that's all there is to it."

"What did you see?" she prompted again, more firmly.

"You want me to tell you how the rec room turned into a desert, how there were market stalls everywhere? How Sam, him…" He jabbed a finger at Ben. "…and his mate suddenly turned into different people?"

"A market?"

"That's right, a fucking market!" he shouted.

She blinked. "Remember, I'm here to help you get through this."

"So you said. What if I *can't*…get through this?"

"Not an option, Alex." She tried to sound convincing, but the crack in her voice gave her away. "I'm told you had a rough night."

He was tempted to say, *by the looks of things I'm not the only one.* "You… you could say that."

"Care to tell me what that was about?"

Alex took a moment before answering. "I had a bad dream."

Ellen nodded. "Was it connected with your other experiences? Were you in the fire again, or being tortured?"

"Not exactly."

"Then what?"

"It was just a dream, that's all. Just a dream." This time it was his words that didn't ring true.

Ellen raised an eyebrow. "There's no such thing as 'just a dream' in my profession, Alex."

"Oh, right, I forgot," said the lecturer, laughing, "all that stuff means something, doesn't it? The subconscious and all that."

"It might," said Ellen. "I won't know unless you tell me."

"Haven't you ever just had a bad dream?"

Ellen turned away from him, head dipping. When she raised her eyes again she caught him staring at her, as if he knew he'd touched a raw nerve. "We're not here to discuss my dreams, Alex. We're here to sort this out. Now, when two of my nurses report that you've woken up screaming in the middle of the night—on top of everything else you've told me—well, call me..." Alex thought for a second she was going to say "crazy," but she continued, "...silly if you like but I think there might be a connection there, yes." Now Alex detected a tenseness that wasn't present yesterday.

He moaned softly. "I'm sorry, Doctor. Really." He meant it and hoped she could see that.

Apparently she could because the next words out of her mouth were: "I thought we'd agreed it was Ellen." Her face softened and she gave him a brief smile, forced but genuine.

"Okay, Ellen. I appreciate that you're trying to help me, and God knows I think I need it. But this is still pretty difficult for me."

"I know."

"I can't get my head around any of this. One minute I'm fine, then the next..."

"We've been through this, Alex. It's nothing to be ashamed of."

"That's easy for you to say. You think even if we stop whatever's happening, I'll be able to go back to a normal life with this hanging over me? You think Beverly and I..." He couldn't get the next words out.

"I think you think about the future too much. We have a more immediate concern here, something we need to address right now. The rest we deal with when it comes."

He had to admit she'd got a point. Except the problem wasn't that he was thinking about the future, so much as the past. Or *a* past.

"The first step is to get you better again. You're only adding more stress to the load at a time when you could do without it."

"No kidding," muttered Alex.

"So stop fighting me, tell me about your dream."

"My nightmare," he corrected. "Okay…" Alex told her what he could remember. The circle, the undefined figures, the thing with blue eyes that scared him stupid at the end. Ellen listened intently, making notes on her pad. He could see her watching for signs, on the lookout for any clues that might give something away. When he'd finished she sat there deep in thought.

Eventually she said, "Alex, have you ever had this dream…sorry, nightmare, before?"

Alex pursed his lips.

"I'll take that as a yes, shall I?"

"It wasn't quite the same as the others—"

"The others? Alex, how many times have you had it?" Ellen asked.

"Once or twice."

"And when did it start?"

There was a long pause before he answered that one. "I've only been able to remember them the last few days."

"But when did they start?"

"I think maybe longer than that, a week or so."

"Just before the first incident at college."

"Yes. But that doesn't mean… Look, there's something really familiar about the nightmare. I think I may have had it before that, or even lots of times, and maybe I couldn't remember it. I'm not the sort of person who remembers their dreams anyway."

Ellen's brow furrowed. "Okay, but you said this one was different from the one you *can* remember. How so?"

"The people there for one thing. One person in particular."

"Who?"

"I don't know who it was, but it was like the others. I couldn't make out a proper face or shape. But they were warning me about something, about the thing that was coming for me."

Ellen tapped her pen against her mouth. "Can you remember anything they said?"

"They kept asking me to help them."

"How?"

"By remembering."

Ellen stopped tapping and jotted this down on the pad.

"They said that I had to remember before it was too late."

"Remember what?"

Alex saw quick flashes of the faces in torment, those he'd seen dying in his dream, the visions that monster had shown to him.

"I've no idea," he said. "The next thing I knew they were telling me to run. They seemed more frightened of the thing coming after me than I was—and that's saying something."

"Hmm." Ellen put down her pad and pen, and got up. She paced a little, arms folded.

"What are you thinking?" he asked.

"I'm thinking that the figure might have represented you."

"Which, the one warning me or coming to get me?"

"Both maybe, but in different ways."

Alex sighed. "I don't follow."

"The warning voice might be the part of yourself you've closed off, trying to get you to remember something you've suppressed. The other one might be the damage you're causing yourself by suppressing this."

"Right," said Alex, "makes sense, I suppose."

"Whatever that is, it might also be causing the problems you're going through in the waking world. By not releasing this information to yourself, it's seeping out in other ways."

"Like the 'film clips' you mean?"

Ellen nodded.

"About that... I've been thinking and...the images, the things I'm seeing don't feel like replays of movies I've seen."

"But they could be distortions of them, like we talked about."

"I suppose. What I mean is, all right I can remember bits from movies—most people can. But when I experience these things, it's like I'm there. Does that make sense?"

"These kind of incidents can often seem incredibly real, Alex," she offered by way of defence. "I know what I'm talking about. But I still believe you're grafting these scenes onto real memories somehow. It's painful to remember something like a fire, so you have to remember it through the filter of an old movie you've seen. Mental torture you've been through manifests itself in the shape of the physical torture you went through in your bathroom. Do you see what I'm getting at?"

"I understand the concept." Alex laced his hands and played with his thumbs. "But… Oh, I can't explain what I mean. It just feels wrong, that's all. There's just so much detail."

"There can be a hell of a lot of detail in a memory, Alex." Her voice trembled and it didn't go unnoticed. She cleared her throat and spoke again. "Even a made-up one. The figure in your dream is trying to get you to remember what really happened."

He stopped twiddling his thumbs. "Before it's too late. Before the other figure gets me."

Ellen walked over to him. Ben took a few steps too, but one glance told him to hang back. "We're going to figure this out long before it comes to that." She placed a reassuring hand on his shoulder. "I promise."

– ii –

She sat with him for the next few hours.

"Now we're going to try and focus on what you've been seeing in these episodes." She'd asked him if he minded her recording their sessions, and Alex was unsure at first. "I don't want to do anything you're uncomfortable with, but it could help me—help us both—to figure this out."

Still reluctant, he'd agreed. She took out a small digital recorder and placed it on the arm of her chair. "Okay, so let's start at the beginning. With what you saw in that classroom at college. Tim's face; let's start there."

"It changed so quickly," he said, "it was hard to get a good look."

"Try and remember, Alex, it's important. Close your eyes and visualise his face."

He did as he was told, casting his mind back to that Wednesday morning. "Can you see him?"

"Yes," said Alex. He could see Tim as he was, just before he changed: the young fresh-faced kid he'd been teaching for almost a year. Quiet, often more serious than his years would suggest. Now Alex saw those features altering, saw the darkness of a shadow fall over them, the skin wrinkling.

"Describe to me what's happening," said Ellen.

"It's too fast."

"Slow it down, think about it as if it *was* a film you could just rewind and watch frame by frame."

That trick seemed to work. Alex focused on the face of a much older man now, weather-worn, skin the colour of varnished wood. There was the headband, the markings on the face, painted red and white. The eyes were dark and should have been hard, but there was a tremendous love behind them, and enormous pride. Alex watched as the old man held something up to his mouth; it looked like a long pipe of some sort. "Wait, I didn't see that before," he told Ellen.

"Stick with it. Go with the flow."

"He's smoking," said Alex. "I can see smoke…and…there's a fire. I can hear it, I can see the orange glow on his face."

"Good. What else?"

He could hear the chanting again, in low voices. Drums too this time.

"Why don't you try and pull back from the face, see what else you can picture," suggested Ellen.

Alex thought about it as the difference between an extreme close-up and a long shot. He was pulling the camera out to take in more of the scene. People dancing around a large fire, the men bare from the waist up, leggings with tassels below. The old man that had been Timothy Brailes passed his pipe along to another weathered man by his side.

"It's a celebration," said Alex. "Some sort of gathering." He looked around and saw tents, large canvas tents—a great many of them. He frowned. No, not tents. "Those are wigwams."

"Wigwams?"

"Wigwams, teepees. Whatever you call them. James would know."

Ellen asked who James was, but he'd already moved on to describe another part of the picture: a large pole with faces carved and painted on it. Alex opened his eyes, but could still see the panorama in front of him. Ellen and Ben were gone, there was only the dance and the noise from the singing, the drumming. "They're giving thanks for something."

"Perhaps it's a rain dance?" said Ben, with a light tone. He was soon silenced by Ellen.

"One word I can hear: '*Tatonka.*'"

"What does that mean?" she asked him.

"I have no idea. This is so strange, Ellen. It's like being inside a Western or something. You have no idea…"

"Can you hear anything else, see anything?"

"A name. At least I think it's a name. Something the old man is saying, I can't quite catch it… Broke…Broken Tree?"

"'Broken Tree.'" She rolled the name around on her tongue. "It definitely sounds Indian. Sorry, Native American."

"I don't think political correctness had been invented when these people were around," said Alex. He gazed at them: men, women and children. Happy, at peace with each other and the world. "They have no idea."

"What?"

"They have no idea how much danger they're in. Of what's about to happen." Alex began to breathe faster, more erratically. "No. No…"

He felt a hand on his, and the scene suddenly dissolved. Ellen was beside him on the bed.

"I've lost it. It's gone," he told her, breathing returning to normal

"That's okay. You did really well, Alex."

"There was more, I'm sure of it."

She patted his hand. "It'll come, in time."

They spent a while talking about what it might mean, about what she thought his mind was trying to tell him. "The connection with the fire is there again," she said. "And a celebration, like your birthday. I'm wondering if that might be the trigger, you know."

"What, my birthday?"

"Something connected with a birthday in the past, something that happened when you were younger perhaps? Does anything spring to mind?"

Alex shook his head and realised he'd done it much too quickly.

"Doesn't matter right now. If you've buried it so deeply you won't remember just like that. I wouldn't expect you to." She took the opportunity to ask him who James was again.

"A friend from college."

"Another lecturer?"

"Yes."

"Film studies as well?"

"Actually, he teaches history." Alex felt like he'd admitted a dirty secret. He knew she'd make more of this than she should; already he could see the cogs grinding away. "But listen, I've banned him from talking about any of that stuff around me. I can't stand it."

"Doesn't mean some of it hasn't rubbed off."

"It hasn't," he promised emphatically.

"Anyway," she said, getting up for a second time, "we'll leave it there for now. Ben, make sure he gets something to eat, will you." She wagged her finger. "No arguments."

"But can't we—"

"A little at a time, Alex. You're starting to control what you're seeing and that's a positive step. We'll pick it up again when you're stronger. We're in this together now and we're going to see it through to the end."

"Before you go, Ellen." She paused on her way to the door. "Do you think I could ring home? I'd like to try and explain to Bev, after… At least talk to her."

"Are you sure that's a good idea right now?"

He gave a shake of the head. "No, but I'd like to try."

"Okay," she said.

Alex watched her leave, taking Ben out with her. He saw them talking to each other through the glass circle in the door. Ben nodded something and she turned to walk off down the corridor.

Alex lay back on the bed, hands behind his head.

We're going to see this through to the end…

As he stared up at the ceiling he couldn't help wondering just what the end might have in store for him.

– iii –

At the Webber house the phone rang out for the longest time.

But nobody answered.

The phone went dead for a few minutes, then started to ring again. It rang seven or eight times and stopped. A few more minutes passed and it rang again; same thing, except the caller hung after a few more rings. One final, futile attempt to get through. And suddenly all was quiet.

The phone never rang again that night.

Eleven

Yazmin's Nightclub, Quarter to Midnight

– i –

The queue to enter Yazmin's stretched around the corner and down the next street. On a Saturday night there was no other place to be.

If you were in, you were *in*. If you weren't, you could spend half the night just trying to gain admittance. Two people stood between this bobbing string of bodies and their entry through the gates of paradise. They decided who made the grade, and hardly anybody argued with them.

Terence Gilligan and Francis Austin were the human equivalent of monster trucks. Wearing matching tuxedos that cost a fortune, not simply because of the designer cut, but also due to the sheer amount of material, they flanked the red metallic entranceway of the club, three steps separating them from the line of hopefuls below.

The blue and pink of the neon sign protruding from the side of Yazmin's reflected off the top of Frank's bald pate, while what remained of Terry's once lustrous head of hair had been gathered together into a ponytail that any three-year-old colt would have been proud to have hanging from its rear end. Each wore Ray-Bans, because although it was pitch black everywhere else at that time of night, it was so bright down this particular street it defied the laws of nature.

"Next," said Terry in a voice so deep you could have thrown a coin in it and made a wish. As if to labour the point, his partner beckoned the next couple in the line.

On the left was a man in an outfit that appeared to be a throwback to the eighties. His thin pencil tie was horizontally striped, while his grey polyester suit had vertical pinstripes. The effect was akin to a test card designed by a blind man. His shoes squeaked as he walked up the steps, and the mess he'd made of his hair with gel would have been enough to make any top coiffeur have a heart attack on the spot.

The woman to his right, in contrast, knew exactly how to dress for an evening out. The dark see-through lace top she wore drew attention to her most prominent features, namely her artificially enhanced breasts, crammed into a black Wonderbra that was certainly living up to its name. Both Terry and Frank were wondering how such a small garment was supporting those delicious mounds of flesh without snapping under the strain. Her leather trousers clung to every curve of her thighs and calves so tightly they might have been spray-painted on. And her boots sported heels so needle thin that simply balancing on them required training that would have put any Royal National Ballet dancer to shame.

When she flicked back her long, golden locks, she hit them with a bat of the eyelids that could have—quite literally—blown them away.

It took Terry and Frank all of ten seconds to come to their unanimous, telepathic decision. Terry waved a hand to let the lady by, while Frank stopped her escort by holding his hand up flat.

"Sorry, sir. Some other time," said Frank, whose voice was slightly more jagged than Terry's.

"But—"

"You heard him, some other time." Terry had now raised his hand and was ushering in the blonde by placing it on the small of her back.

"That's my date. You can't just—"

"Yes," said Frank, "we can."

The man made a move towards the entrance and Frank blocked his path. His date had now disappeared inside Yazmin's, without once looking back.

Frank lowered his voice, but it lost none of its serrated edge. "Look, just get lost, will you. You're causing a scene."

"You can't do this," protested the man. Either he was new to the area, didn't get out much, or just didn't value the ability to chew food very highly.

Frank took hold of him by the lapel and dragged him down the steps. At the bottom, he pushed him. The man lost his balance and fell. The line of people remained silent. No one was willing to jeopardise their chance of getting in.

As Frank started to walk away, he heard the man shout: "You're going to regret this. Look at my fucking suit!" He waved a torn sleeve in Frank's general direction. "I'll show you. I'm going to set the fucking police on you, that's what I'm going to do. You can't get away with this."

Some people just don't know when to leave it alone, thought Frank. He turned back in time to see the man take out his mobile phone. It beeped as he jabbed a number.

And suddenly Frank had snatched the phone out of the man's hand. He dropped it onto the pavement, then ground it under his heel. The phone died with a petrified whine.

"Hey!" shouted the man, scrambling to his feet. "You're going to pay for that." He grabbed Frank's arm as he was turning away.

With a groan, the doorman reached down and seized him by the collar, lifting him up into the air. "You know something?" he said, bringing the man's face closer to his. "You talk too much."

Frank brought back his enormous fist and plunged it into the man's face.

Someone in the queue let out a gasp, only to be nudged into silence. The man went down again with a startled yelp, hands covering a bloody nose and mouth. There he stayed, in the gutter. No one came to his aid, no one even uttered a word of outrage. It was just one of those things you had to turn a blind eye to if you were to stand a chance of admittance. It was his own fault, the crowd was thinking, shouldn't have made such a fuss.

Frank returned to his post. Terry nodded once to tell his comrade that was a job well done.

"Next," Terry said, after Frank had adopted his usual position at the top of the steps. Another couple approached, shaking slightly as they did so.

– ii –

"I still don't see what we need these people for."

Lucas drove their new black BMW into the parking space and set the handbrake.

"Many hands make light work," said The Infinity from the back seat. "I'm closer than I ever have been, but there is still much to be done. Contrary to what you believe, I cannot be everywhere at once, Lucas."

"You have me."

In the rear-view Lucas saw The Infinity chuckle. "There's no need for jealousy. I am enlisting their aid, that's all. You will still be in charge of the…operation. Besides, it never hurts to have a few foot soldiers on tap."

Lucas grimaced. Much as he knew his master was right, this whole business left a bad taste in his mouth. He climbed out of the car and undid the back door, holding it open. The Infinity joined him, dressed in a fine indigo suit and shirt. He adjusted the sleeves as Lucas closed the door, then strode across the lot, leaving his lackey to walk a short distance behind with the case.

"If I've learned anything in my time on this planet, Lucas, it's to be prepared. I always cover every eventuality. These people, as you call them, have a part to play in my plans—just as you do."

Lucas shut his mouth. He would only end up digging himself into a deeper pit, and he knew that one of these days he'd dig a hole so deep he wouldn't be able to get out. One that came complete with a headstone.

They arrived at an alleyway, which brought them out just opposite Yazmin's. The Infinity halted and scanned the scene. Two men at the door, a line of punters queuing…and a figure crawling around in the gutter. "I remember when the first dance halls and dens of iniquity came into existence," he said to Lucas, now on his right hand side. "Everything's changed so much. Although certain things will always stay the same, thankfully."

Lucas ran his eyes over the queue and spotted several women who would make excellent raw material for his art. He considered saying something to The Infinity, then decided against it. They were here for a single purpose and it would only enrage his master to deviate from the task in hand. There would be time for that, The Infinity had promised him. Although hadn't he promised him Ha'ng and others along the way?

"High time we introduced ourselves, don't you think?" The Infinity crossed the street. When he came to the man sprawling around on the floor, The Infinity stepped over him. Lucas skirted around the wretch, wondering who his tailor was, and how he was still in business.

They pushed in ahead of the queue, earning one or two shouts of serious annoyance. The doormen had just finished turning away two more unsuitable candidates and were surprised to see Lucas and The Infinity. For one thing neither of them had said the magic word: "Next."

"There's a queue," pointed the bald one, who looked like he'd been carved out of granite.

"So I gather," said The Infinity, without even looking at it. "We're here to see the owner, Mr. Metcalf."

The other doorman came to join his friend. "I don't think so."

"Nevertheless, we're here to see him."

The first man took a step closer to The Infinity. "What part of 'I don't think so' didn't you understand?"

The Infinity smirked. "How about the part where you are able to think at all."

Lucas set the case down on the floor and braced himself. He could see the bald bouncer grinding his teeth, his companion opening and closing his fists.

"You talk too much," rumbled baldie.

The Infinity tipped his head. "I find it helps me to communicate my meaning. In this instance, the fact that I wish to talk to your employer. Now, why don't you both stand aside."

Baldie's mouth dropped open. He probably wasn't used to being talked to like this, not unless it was his boss doing the talking…

In fact, nobody had spoken to Frank like this since he was at school—and the teacher in question still walked with a limp. For a second it threw him; but *only* for a second. What came next was a natural reaction for him, and his colleague.

But the outcome was very different to the one they'd both been expecting.

Frank brought up his hands to grab the man, but found himself stopping. He froze like the granite sculpture he resembled.

He felt Terry move forward, but then this man's older partner was behind his friend, holding a blade to his throat. "You don't want to do that," he whispered into Terry's ear. More a piece of advice than a threat.

Frank struggled, unable to move as the man in front of him reached out a hand. He plucked the sunglasses from Frank's face and dropped them on the floor. "That's better." He took one more step; the Ray-bans crushed underfoot. "Now then, Francis, let's see if we can't get rid of some of that pent-up aggression you have."

Frank's mud-coloured eyes whipped left and right. Four thoughts went through his head at the same time, which was quite an experience for him. Who was this man? How had he done this to him? How did he know Frank's name? And what was he going to do next?

Only the last question was answered.

"Would you like a trip to the circus, Francis?" said the man with the blue eyes. Frank's own eyes widened. "Come play with us, little boy."

Instantly Frank was back there, aged six, separated from his parents in the big top. He was panicking; he'd only wanted to get a better look at the lions and tigers in those cages before the performance started. Now he was lost. There were so many people here, he was never going to find his mum and dad. All he could see were brightly coloured stripes: on the tent, on poles and on lollipops the other children were holding. He scrambled over slatted seats, found himself on a sawdust floor. The little Frank, still big for his age, rolls of fat yet to become hardened muscle, was jostled this way and that.

He ended up behind the scenes, backing through a gap in the canvas. A group of feather-wearing showgirls walked past, giggling and patting each other on the arm. This was years before he knew what sexual attraction was, so they simply looked surreal to him. Next he saw Lycra-clad acrobats and the dwarves who took part in comedy routines. They were smoking and playing cards on an upturned barrel between performances. Trying not to be seen, or caught, Frank slipped under another tent flap and found himself in a darkened corridor. The walls flapped and rippled, causing him to jump. Then he saw a silhouette at the other end.

It came closer. The man was wearing that same stripy uniform—the norm here—though this one was baggy at the elbows and knees. It looked like his body was swelling at certain points. The shadows still hid his features, but when he moved forward a slit of light from outside fell on his face.

White as a ghost, almost luminescent, that visage glowed eerily in the half-light. The eyes seemed too large for the head, and sunken; black rings encircled them. His nose was long, bent in the middle and drooping. The mouth was smeared with redness, the same redness Frank had seen when he fell off his bike the year before and cut open his knee. It had so obviously been feeding on human flesh. When it opened its mouth yellow teeth glistened, in contrast to its stark albino skin.

Frank's jaw hung down as he stared at this terrifying sight. The figure moved out of the light and back into the shadows. Frank lost sight of it, then suddenly the creature was back with more of its brethren in tow. Some of their faces were half finished, noses hanging off. They were coming for him, to devour him. And those evil, evil smiles.

"Come on, little boy," they said, joking. "Come play with us."

Frank screamed and ran away, falling headlong through one of the tent walls and into the arms of the circus master. Tears were streaming down his face and he was quivering. The moustached man held the boy, tried to get him to talk about what had scared him, but Frank never did. He'd never told anyone about his experience, not his mother or father when he was reunited with them—especially not his father, who punished any little act of cowardice with a smack. But to this day he couldn't go near a circus, couldn't even look at clowns in films or on TV without breaking into a cold sweat.

And somehow *he'd* known, his opponent in the here and now. Somehow he'd plucked this memory out of his brain and was using it against him.

Frank was aware he was pissing himself, but couldn't do a thing about it. He couldn't even look at the wet patch on his trousers, the yellow liquid running down his leg and puddling on the steps. When he was finally released, he sank to his knees and cried like a widow at a funeral, the stink of urine fresh in his nostrils.

His fellow doorman observed this with shock and embarrassment. It was not just his workmate on the floor, this was his best friend. A man he'd seen take on ten men without a trace of fear; seen him headbutt, break kneecaps and generally cause grievous bodily harm to anyone who even looked at him the wrong way. Yet here he was, grovelling at this man's feet like a worm. Frank simply couldn't help it.

"Do you know," said the man dressed in indigo, "I really rather enjoyed that." He left Frank on the floor and faced Frank's colleague. The man twitched, but the blade was pressed harder to his throat. "So, Terence, do you think Mr. Metcalf might be ready to see us now?"

Terry tried to nod and the knife nicked his skin.

The man with blue eyes smiled. "Lucas, let the man go. After you," he said, then waited for Terry to open the doors of Yazmin's, while this guy Lucas picked up his case.

The people in the queue all had the same expression of puzzlement on their faces. None were sure what they'd actually witnessed, and soon it would be as much a rumour as the urban myth about the battered rat's leg in the fast food chicken meal.

But the spectacle wasn't over quite yet. Someone else was approaching the door, holding his nose and mouth. He staggered up to the weeping doorman. A disorientated Frank shied away from him, away from the stripes of his shirt and tie, from a mouth all bloody, from a crooked nose bent out of shape.

"Come on, little boy. Come play with us…"

The man brought back his foot and kicked Frank as hard as he possibly could.

– iii –

The music inside Yazmin's was ear-splitting. Lucas could feel the organs vibrating inside his body with each new pump of the techno beat. Lights flashed all around, and the dance floor was packed full of pulsating bodies—many female. Lucas scrutinised them, his eyes fixated on bare arms and legs, his imagination peeling off the few clothes these girls wore to reveal the splendours beneath. Then peeled off the skin…

"We're not here for that," The Infinity reminded him, and somehow Lucas could hear his voice perfectly.

Tearing his eyes from the dancers, Lucas trained them back on Terry. The large man was leading them through the bar area, where it looked like you had to wait at least twenty minutes to part with your money, and on to a seated area towards the rear of the club. Above them on a plinth was the DJ, a red-and-white bandanna covering his head. Around him spun a gridded light system that made it look like he was being dissected by lasers.

Lucas spotted a clump of men in the corner balanced on a slightly raised section of carpeting. The position of the seating arrangement gave them a perfect view of the entire nightclub. He could guess, without The Infinity having to tell him, that this was their target: Nick Metcalf. He was sitting in the midst of a collection of business associates and personal bodyguards. Slicked-back hair and sharp suit gave him the look of a modern predator; Lucas recognised it immediately. This man had not ended up in his position by chance.

Right now Metcalf was allowing himself a moment to survey his kingdom. All that was stopping him were the three men approaching in a triangular pattern, one of them his own.

Metcalf gestured to a henchman, a mean, needle-nosed individual who got up to deal with the situation.

"Who are these people?" he shouted above the music.

Terry shrugged. "They want to talk to Mr. Metcalf, Hamilton."

The man shook his head. "Impossible. What did you think you were doing bringing them in here?"

The Infinity walked towards him. "He did it because I asked him to."

The man looked this newcomer up and down. "Who are you?"

"It's a question that has often been asked. No reply I could give would be satisfactory. Now, kindly tell your superior I'm here to have a chat."

"Fuck off," said the man, "before you get hurt."

"I'm afraid I can't 'fuck off' until I've spoken with Nicholas Metcalf."

Lucas saw the last remaining bit of patience drain from the man's face. His hand reached into his jacket, fingers curling around something. Before he could bring it out, Lucas hefted the case, knocking him to the floor. A second bodyguard rose on their left and Lucas threw a knife, planting it in the man's shoulder.

Two more men were up, heading for The Infinity. "Terence? Would you mind…?"

The doorman looked once at The Infinity, then elbowed the charging minders out of the way. The final bodyguard tried to pull Metcalf to safety, but Lucas was already on the underling, a length of wire wrapped around his neck. The man made a few choking noises before falling unconscious at Metcalf's feet.

Metcalf took a swing at Lucas himself. It glanced off his temple, slowing him down. The club owner was all set to shout for reinforcements, but The Infinity was there waiting.

"There's no need for any of this," he told Metcalf. "I only wish to talk. I have a proposition for you."

– iv –

The back office of Yazmin's was a large, rectangular room covered in paintings. Turners, Monets, Dalis… *Either the man has good taste,* thought Lucas, *or likes people to think he has.*

Or they once belonged to someone else.

There was an oak desk at the far end, with a plush leather seat behind it. Metcalf sank down in the chair, placing a barrier between himself and the two other men. His jaw was set firm; this was clearly a man with a strong will, which explained why his master hadn't simply squeezed his brain till it popped. He reached into his pocket and Lucas tensed again.

Metcalf noted this and aimed a finger at him. "You, relax!" He took out a pack of cigars and unwrapped the cellophane. "I don't carry in my own club." As much as he tried to disguise his origins behind a considered accent, the backstreet yob in him was still fighting to get out. "How's the head?"

Lucas rubbed his temple. "Hardly even felt it."

Metcalf pulled out one of the slim cigars and lit up. He inhaled the smoke, blowing out a stream in Lucas' general direction. "Next time maybe you will."

The Infinity glanced from Lucas to his sparring partner. "Enough of this macho posturing. Metcalf—"

"*Mr.* Metcalf to you," said the owner of the club, leaning forward in his chair and pointing with the cigar this time.

The Infinity rolled his eyes. "Very well. Mr. Metcalf, as I said before we wish you to—"

"Let's get one thing straight," Metcalf interrupted, "I don't like people barging into my place, making demands. Now you got my attention and I decided to hear you out, Christ alone knows why, but that's all."

"From where I was standing it didn't look like you had a choice," Lucas said.

Metcalf's eyes turned to slits. His hand hovered over a raised red circle on his desk. "This office is soundproofed. I only have to press this button, and in seconds it'll be filled with my boys. Seconds later you'll be full of something too."

Lucas snorted. "You're the one full of something."

"Lucas, that's enough," said The Infinity.

"But—"

"I said *enough*."

Lucas caught Metcalf's nod of approval; the hired help had been put in its place. His hand pulled away from the button. "Good. Now we've got that sorted out, I'll listen to what you have to say. Something about a business proposition?"

"You could call it that." The Infinity strode through the smoke still in the air and sat down on the other side of the desk. Lucas stepped forward too, but remained standing.

"Did Charlie Granger send you?" asked Metcalf. "Because if he did, you can tell him from me—"

The Infinity held up a hand. "No, nobody has sent us. We come of our own volition."

"Your own what?"

"We don't work for anyone," Lucas clarified.

Metcalf locked eyes with him again. "So you're from out of town, then? Let me guess, London way?"

The Infinity smiled. "We...travel around a lot."

Metcalf turned his attention back to the seated man. "We talking this country, or further afield?"

"We have conducted business abroad, yes. But that's not important right now, Mr. Metcalf."

Lucas could guess what was going through the crime lord's mind.

Trying to get a handle on them. Were they troubleshooters? Or did they represent a chance to expand further overseas?

"We're looking for someone," The Infinity explained.

And now he's thinking something else entirely. Lucas watched Metcalf's hand inch towards the red button again. *He thinks we're hitmen, maybe we've even come for him or someone involved in his organisation? It would explain how we managed to get past his security, how we managed to get to* him.

"Oh yeah?"

He's starting to wonder if he's out of his depth, but he can't show it. Can't let us see how the tiniest bit of fear has crept in. But I can see it behind the bravado, Mr. Metcalf.

"Yes," said The Infinity.

"Listen, I don't want anything going down on my doorstep. You understand?"

No, you don't want to rock the boat, do you? You have things just the way you like them.

"We need your help to complete our task," The Infinity continued, ignoring him. "You have the resources and contacts in this area, you have the manpower."

"Hold on, hold on. Manpower? I haven't agreed to anything ye—"

"You will," The Infinity promised. He didn't add "one way or the other" but it was implied.

"Two men," said Metcalf—The Infinity raised an eyebrow—"waltz in here, attack my lads and tell me they need my help to find someone. You'll forgive me if I'm a bit reluctant to have any kind of association with you at all...sorry, didn't catch your name..."

"Finn. You can call me Finn."

"All right, Finn—"

"*Mr.* Finn," said The Infinity.

Metcalf conceded the point. "You don't have any credentials, Mr. Finn. You won't tell me where you come from or who you've worked with in the past..."

"If I told you I doubt you'd believe me," said The Infinity. "Not that any of it matters anymore. I'm all about the here and now, Mr. Metcalf—and the future. About what is and what shall be."

"I don't follow."

"I'm not asking you to, merely provide a little assistance. And yes, I can see your dilemma, but let me show you something that might just sweeten the pot. Lucas." The Infinity motioned for the man to hand him the case, which he did. Metcalf's fingers were almost on the buzzer. "Like you," said The Infinity before he could press it, "we do not carry, either. Guns that is."

He opened the snaps on the case and turned it around so that Metcalf could see. The case was completely white inside. Or at least that's how it looked to Metcalf. Bags and bags of white.

"Holy shit!" A moment or two later and shock gave way to joy. A broad smile spread across Metcalf's face. "You do travel around, don't you?"

That's right, thought Lucas, *and it's your fucking birthday.*

The Infinity placed the case on Metcalf's desk and pushed it towards him. "It's all pure, you can have your men check it if you like."

Metcalf stuck the cigar in the corner of his mouth and picked up one of the bags. He cradled it in both hands as if it were a baby. The powder moved around inside the clear plastic and he felt its weight. "Do you have any idea what the street value of this lot is?"

"A ballpark figure, as the Americans say."

Lucas saw Metcalf's expression change again, a frown appearing. "Wait a minute, how do I know this isn't all a set-up? I accept this and the next thing I know the filth's crawling all over me like crabs around a crotch." He paused, before adding: "How do I know *you're* not cops?"

The Infinity couldn't help laughing. "I assure you, we're not."

Something in that statement must have placated Metcalf, because he nodded—accepting the truth as if he'd just seen a signed document by the chief of police. Lucas had observed that trick far too many times to be amazed, an assurance in the tone of voice that worked on both the weak and the strong-minded alike. Metcalf turned the bag over in his hands, transferring it from one to the other and whistling as best he could out of the corner of his mouth not containing the cigar.

"So," said The Infinity, "I take it you're willing to help me." It wasn't a question.

The nightclub owner dragged his attention away from the drugs, although it pained him to do so. "This person you're looking for."

"Yes."

"What's going to happen when you find him? I mean, I assume it's a man."

Lucas leaned in, curious to hear what his boss would divulge.

The Infinity said nothing at first, then spoke quietly. "Now that, Mr. Metcalf, is something not even I know the answer to."

— v —

Ellen pored over the notes she'd made that day, stopping occasionally to refer back to those from yesterday, before writing up new ones.

She was propped up on one of the on-call doctors' single beds in the basement of G-Wing. It was a favourite haunt of hers when something was on her mind. The doctors from A&E rarely got a chance to use these beds on a Saturday night, or any other time really. So it was quiet here, a good place to think...or hide. It also had the added bonus of its own entrance and exit, leading to the car park. Ellen had spent a lot of time in here since she came to work at Kirkwell, slipping in and out unnoticed when she needed to get away from everything and clear her mind; to concentrate on a particularly difficult case. Like now.

It was two days ago that Alex Webber had been brought to this hospital, but felt like two years. It wasn't so much his condition. She'd come across bad cases of repression before and dealt with its symptoms: from severe sneezing to rashes, from continual vomiting to wetting the bed. She'd even treated a man who couldn't control his erections around older women because of a sexual encounter he'd had when he was twelve. Then there had been the cases where it had manifested itself as waking hallucinations. Patients would see things in the real world because of something they'd suppressed in their own little internal worlds. The mind was such a complex thing and they'd only just begun to delve into its mysteries, but Ellen had been confident about helping all those people. She'd managed it too, her success rate above average. Even those she hadn't been able to cure had seen some improvement over the long haul.

So why was Alex different? Regardless of what she kept telling him, why did she get the strangest feeling it would take more than this before he was well again? They had made good progress earlier, and she'd get him to do the same again tomorrow. It should be just a matter of locating the repressed memories and forcing him to remember them. Then all the fantasies would fade and he could concentrate on his own life, his *real* life as Alex Webber. Not some bizarre time-travelling tourist whose trips could come anytime, anywhere.

Before making a start on the notes, she flipped through some of the books she'd brought with her—it was how she'd learned…how she always *liked* to work—but they contained nothing she didn't already know, no new insights or sudden flashes of brilliance about his condition. On the spider diagram in front of her she'd already linked together the fire, and the fact that it was associated with celebration. She'd ringed the film connection and that his best friend taught history. It must all have played a part. Then there was the dream with the two people: one good, one evil. They had to be the opposite sides of her patient's psyche. There was also another factor, that of his partner and what was happening in their personal life.

Now she was playing back the recording and listening as Alex described what he could see. She picked up on all the nuances, so certain and at the same time like a child's voice: frightened, vulnerable. Ellen found herself idly ringing Beverly Webber's name again.

Connections. Everything was connected somehow.

All she had to do was figure it out.

Twelve

The Olympia Hotel: Room 435, Sunday

– i –

IT TOOK A CERTAIN DEGREE OF CONTROL.

The Infinity needed to be alone to properly concentrate on his meditation. That's why he'd sent Lucas Peck away to get some rest. While it was true his travelling companion would require all his energy for the coming days, The Infinity just needed to be left to his own devices for a while.

It was necessary.

Plush and luxurious, the room, this entire hotel, was a far cry from the one he'd found Lucas in not long ago—about to practise his art on the latest young lady to take his fancy. The Infinity couldn't help grinning when he thought about Peck's appetites. He understood exactly what drove the man and how to use it to his advantage. The Infinity could still remember how good the baseness of such desires felt. How the gratification of them satisfied him…for a time. Maybe that was the real reason he kept Lucas around—because he saw that element of himself in the man. Microscopic as it was, The Infinity recognised it and could relate to it. This, more than anything, was what stopped him from reducing Peck's mass to a puddle of slime.

And wasn't The Infinity's quest little more than a desire to be sated? However much he regarded himself as being beyond Lucas Peck, however much importance he attached to this search, wasn't it merely a scaling up of what Lucas did? Except it was the thrill of a much larger chase that spurred him on. A means to pursue his own agenda. His artwork wasn't produced by tearing limbs from their sockets or cutting into flesh so he could paint with the blood. The Infinity's art was practised on a much grander scale. Where Lucas focused on the finite, he focused on… well, the *infinite*. The entire human race was his paint box, not one naked girl shivering in a seedy hovel. When he created, it was with millions. A brushstroke here, a dictator rises to power in the Middle East. A splash of colour there, an experimental virus somehow finds its way onto the open market and is used by terrorists to cause havoc on the underground. It was as JFK had once said to him on the golf course, after a particularly stressful week: "Life's too short not to enjoy yourself, Finn."

Human life was, indeed, short. Not long after that, Kennedy was assassinated and there were still question marks over what had happened that day. No one really knew, except for a handful of people in the FBI who had all died in mysterious circumstances. And The Infinity. Who lived on, just as he always did. Enjoying himself.

Until the day it had begun again.

That day, standing in a crater of his own making after putting his physical form back together again, he'd felt the familiar stirrings from another part of this world. An event that might seem to those around it so minor as to be totally insignificant, but was in fact the trigger for another round of this particular game. He'd vowed there and then this time would be different. He *would* have the element of surprise, crush his prey long before there was a chance to build up resistance or formulate a plan. Long before realisation dawned and things got…complicated. So it started: slowly at first, taking months, years to pick up on even the remotest hint of the source. During that time there had been periods of frustration, irritation and…not doubt exactly, but as close as The Infinity ever experienced. He'd still carried on with his vital work, but hadn't taken as much pleasure in it as usual. Hadn't enjoyed "life" as much as JFK encouraged him to do on that sunny day in Washington so many years ago. His preoccupation with this other problem excluded all else sometimes. And although Lucas had borne the brunt of his anger on these occasions, he'd also been there to make sure that his dealings were carried out to the letter. For that The

Infinity was, not so much grateful, but more inclined to show leniency during his rages.

Though not always.

Once, he recalled, he had even come close to ending Lucas' life, so furious he had been at almost pinpointing a tiniest trace of the beacon, only to lose it again just as quickly. They had been in Ethiopia, The Infinity sitting cross-legged in the desert, Lucas on the next rise in a pitched tent. A windstorm was whipping up on the horizon and Lucas, fearing for his master's safety, had dared to call on him to seek shelter.

Concentration shattered, The Infinity rose with the storm on his back. Grains of sand flew about him but he took no notice, walking instead through the maelstrom of ochre like a figure in a snowstorm ornament. Unaffected by the elements. The Infinity would never forget the look of pure terror on Lucas' face. Peck was used to his master doing malicious things because he was bored—to take a setback out on him, or simply because he was able—but this was something else. This was pure hatred, unleashed in his direction. He could do nothing but stand there, waiting on the tracks for this particular train to hit him with more force than he could ever have imagined. The Infinity seized him, then suddenly was in his head, filling it with a thousand screaming voices so piercing they made his ears bleed. Lucas' eyes had rolled back into their sockets as his body shook. Spittle flew from his mouth, the hairs on his arms standing on end.

At the very point of death, The Infinity halted, reining the power back inside and dropping Lucas on the sandy bed beneath them. The Infinity cast his arms wide, fingers tensed, taking out what was left of his wrath on the windstorm, which dissipated instantly. He'd stood there gazing at Lucas, who was twitching on the desert floor. He had only let a fraction of his true potential loose, but it had been enough to cause serious damage. Yes, it would have been easy to bring him back even after his heart had stopped, but The Infinity knew that he wouldn't be the same. He might look like Lucas, talk like Lucas—to all intents and purposes *be* Lucas Peck—but he would no longer be the original. Something would be lost that could never be regained. The Infinity restored his health and sanity—or Peck's idea of sanity—and had even wiped the experience from his mind, leaving only the vaguest recollections like ghosts to haunt him.

Just like those tantalising snippets of the beacon haunted The Infinity.

He'd persevered though, as always, chipping away bit by bit as the years turned to decades. As slippery as soap in his grasp, it evaded him. Until now. It always became much easier once the dreams started, once a form of contact had been achieved. But he was still being obstructed. In an ideal world he would be able to home in on the source straight away, but this wasn't such a world. That was the point. As it was, his instincts had finally led him to this country, to this city. And it was time to narrow down the search parameters even further. Even Metcalf and his men couldn't cover the entire area section by section. It would take too long, and by then it might well be too late. Once the dreams started, The Infinity never knew how much time he had left. But he did know it wasn't long.

Which was why he'd retreated to this five-star sanctum, built because this pathetic city once thought it stood a chance of hosting a future Olympics rather than London. He sat crossed-legged again, not on a desert floor this time, but on silk sheets, a plump mattress supporting him. His eyes were open but they didn't see the patterned wallpaper in front of him. They bore right through it, branching out. Hardly breathing at all, The Infinity was completely aware of his own being and senses, and what they could do. He could hear the heartbeats of billions of people. They pumped rhythmically, some faster than others. He could hear their chatter as they talked, snores as they slept, moans as they made love. He could smell so many different scents, some strong and foul, some subtle but fragrant. He could taste a bitterness in his mouth, replaced almost instantly by a sugary sweetness that made him want to retch.

All this and more, but hidden amongst the rough was a diamond. He stretched out with his mind, picking up a faint impulse, comparable to a crackle of static in the ether.

Zeroing in, shutting out everything else, The Infinity followed. He allowed it to guide him, the static transforming almost into a vapour trail. He was brushed and battered in the slipstream of thought. The prey's remembrances: images flashing by so quickly they were a nonsense and would take a lot of unscrambling, even by him. He caught one, fairly recognisable. Something, some*where* he had seen before, albeit vaguely. A building. A blend of old and new. It wasn't much, but a start, and he was seeing so much more of it today than in previous sessions. The Infinity's hands clutched his knees.

The building…he could see…it was empty right now, but wasn't normally. The Infinity saw a flash of the building as it had been in the days, in the weeks, before his arrival. He saw young people. With bags. Haversacks, backpacks. Some kind of hostel?

They were laughing, joking, eating, teasing, kissing; some were even smoking, but hiding the fact. It wasn't a hostel at all, The Infinity realised with growing excitement. It was a school! The place where so many patterns were formed, where the course of a life could be altered or sent spinning off in different directions. How appropriate that he should find his prey there, of all places. In a seat of learning, in a place of future expectations. Now if only he could…

The Infinity roamed around this spirit of a memory, trying to pinpoint where he was. He could see the stone of a wall, could see the gates at the entrance. But so many, *too many*, schools looked like that. And in a city this size… What he needed was a sign. Not in the revelatory sense, but more a—

There!

The Infinity zoomed in, blew the picture up 200 percent. There was the sign near the entrance to the school. Teenagers were walking past it, through the gates. It was blurred. Damn, even at this stage he was being blocked. But no, the words were forming now. He could almost see them, read them.

He was aware of a knocking sound.

The Infinity had shielded himself from so much that this one noise took him by surprise. It jarred him out of his trance-state, ripping him away from the image of the school and the sign. An irritant, like a fly buzzing round his head. His first thought was:

Lucas.

But even as his mind formed the name, he knew that wasn't the case. It was a girl outside the door, wearing the hotel staff uniform and wheeling a trolley filled with toilet rolls and other sundry cleaning equipment. She knocked again, checking to see if anyone was in. There was no DO NOT DISTURB sign on the handle so…

A minor oversight, a major problem.

The Infinity gritted his teeth. He would have had the location were it not for this interruption. This half-wit maid banging away on his door, wanting to clean. *Clean* for fuck's sake!

She raised her hand a final time and the door opened inwards.

"Housekeep—" she started, then stopped. There was nobody on the other side of that door. Just a man, sitting on his bed, looking at her, his blue eyes filled with animosity. Before she knew what she was doing, the maid was walking stiffly forwards, leaving her trolley behind. The door slammed shut on its own.

"I'm s-s-s—" She tried to get the word "sorry" out, but failed miserably.

The Infinity climbed off the bed, and swept towards her. Consumed with loathing for this creature who had interfered with his business at just the wrong time, and half recalling appetites he had thought forgotten. How he would make this human pay!

He was so quick the sheets came with him, swirling and flapping around his person like a cape around Dracula, giving the whole scene the look of a B-movie horror film. A vampire about to claim his next victim.

Except The Infinity, now the rage was upon him, made a vampire look like something from a children's story. Snarling, he was on her.

"Life's too short not to enjoy yourself," he roared as he grabbed her by the throat.

– ii –

Something had been rifling through his thoughts.

He was aware of it on some level, the memories being pumped out like oil from the ground. But they were a mish-mash of events, faces and recollections—some not even *he* could understand. Was this, as Ellen had warned him, his conscious mind attempting to gain access to his sub-conscious? Trying to fathom out what he was hiding from himself? He'd been remembering past birthdays, especially when he was young, sifting through for one that might have been particularly traumatic. Perhaps the time Steve brought his friends back and they ended up fighting amongst themselves? He'd been blowing out the candles on his cake. Had something happened, the candles catching light to something, sparking a fire?

But his mind kept dragging him back to that wonderful birthday when he was ten. His parents had bought him a BMX and Steve had shown him how to do stunts on it. The whole family had gathered for that one, and it had been a cheerful time. He could see them all in the living room singing *Happy Birthday* to him, balloons and bunting hanging from the walls. They were all there: Uncle Gerry cracking his bad jokes, Aunty Joan helping herself to the buffet, Kevin playing with his Matchbox cars under the table, Aunt Sylvia, making excuses about why her husband had to dash off so early. His mum was clapping, and his dad was—

The thing with the blue eyes was staring at him from the corner of the room. The thing from the circle, invading this memory.

Make a wish. Make a wish!

He closed his eyes and made one. When he opened them it hadn't come true.

The room was growing black, the light blotted out, and all he could see were those blue eyes.

"Get away from me! *Get out of my head!*"

Alex shook himself awake, snapping his eyes open.

He chastised himself for dropping to sleep, but it wasn't really surprising. He'd stayed awake most of last night with these things and more on his mind. Like the fact the room had started creaking at one point and he could hear the swishing of water outside his window, even though he was miles from the coast. There were other people in the room with him, he could hear them crying, could just about see arms and legs, a tangle of bodies; some wrapped around each other for comfort. And a myriad of tiny white circles floating in the dark—eyes wide and scared. Alex had pulled up his bedsheets as the creaking of the room, the creaking of the wooden hull, grew louder. He told himself again that this wasn't really happening, it was just another trick of his rapidly disintegrating mind, but that hadn't helped. Alex rode it out, remained silent and waited for it to fade, which it did in time. The room returned to normal and he was alone again.

Now, Sunday, in broad daylight, it seemed ridiculous. But of course it wasn't. This was as serious as the difference between sanity and insanity, between him spending the next few days, weeks, in here or the rest of his life. He debated whether or not to tell Ellen when he saw her. He wanted to trust this woman, but there was still a part of him holding back. She seemed to be fighting his corner, or was she just interested in his case because it was unusual?

She's one of the good guys, Sam had said.

Right now Alex had no choice but to hope that he was right.

THIRTEEN

Yazmin's Nightclub

– i –

The club always looked very different during the day.

The heaving, thriving pleasure dome was just a memory, and now it seemed empty, sad, dejected. There was no music, nobody dancing, no couples up against walls sticking their tongues into each other's mouths and whispering drunken promises they'd regret—or forget—the next morning.

Nick Metcalf preferred it this way. He'd spend days in here alone, in his own personal Camelot. From this one central location he gave his commands and conducted his business. He didn't need to *be* anywhere else, *doing* anything else. It could all be handled from Yazmin's—named after his ex-wife, the bitch, who had also been married to its previous owner.

He'd taken the woman, taken over the nightclub and taken charge of the entire set-up, all in one fell swoop. In one swoop of a tyre iron across the back of the head to be precise. The staff had seen which way the wind was blowing and decided to back the right horse. The only horse still alive. Eddie King's time had been coming ever since Nick first walked through those nightclub doors. The old man had grown weak and people knew it; they took advantage. So when he saw Nick's style, how he handled the clientele—with charm when needed, and a heavy hand when necessary—Eddie was impressed. And Nick was taken on as manager.

It felt like home to him, the only home he'd ever really known.

Nick's mother had dragged rather than brought him up, his alcoholic excuse of a father's contribution being to pummel the boy on his return from the pub. It taught him to duck when someone was swinging for him, and when he was old enough it forced Nick to defend himself. He'd never forget that one night when his dad had come for him, hardly expecting the young Nicky to raise his own fists—let alone deliver a series of well-aimed face and body blows which left Jim Metcalf in a bloody mess on the floor.

"*Get out!*" the man had screamed at him from the floor. "Fucking get out and never come back, you little shit!"

Nick had looked to his mother, perhaps expecting her to speak up on his behalf. But she'd never done so before and wasn't about to start now. Nick did as he was told; he left and never came back. He heard a couple of years later that his father had died choking on his own vomit after passing out drunk in the toilets of *The George and Dragon*. He hardly batted an eyelid at the news.

Nick embraced a life of crime to survive. Stealing at first, petty theft mainly, then when the gangs took him in he graduated to joyriding and ram-raiding, though it didn't have such a media-friendly name in those days. It wasn't long before he had a gang of his own and was sending others out to do the hard work—although he liked to pitch in every now and again, so he didn't get rusty. The gang grew along with his reputation, until he got greedy and careless. He trod on the wrong toes, encroaching on a much bigger and harder bastard's territory.

Napoleon Naylor they called him—just not to his face. He tore Nick's operation apart and trampled on the remains. The only satisfaction Nick had got out of it was personally sending three of Naylor's boys back to him in an ambulance. But that still left Nick without much of a future in the business. So he'd drifted for a while, doing one-off jobs for the faces, people who still remembered his reputation and how he'd earned it.

Then he'd heard whispers, rumours about King and the trouble he was having holding on to the empire he'd built up. He'd been one of the most powerful bosses around when the only thing on Nick's mind had been driving his next Escort through the window of the off license in the high street. Now things had changed—for both of them—and Nick sensed an opportunity to regain some ground. Others had approached Eddie King offering to "help", but only Nick got past the front doors. Perhaps King recognised himself at that age, Nick had no idea. Or maybe those rumours about his sexuality were true and he only kept his wife Yazmin around for show. In which case, Nick had been doing both Eddie and Yazmin a favour when he screwed the former model's brains out behind the old fella's back. Perhaps he'd seen himself as some sort of father figure to Nick? The son he'd never had, because his first wife had been sterile and Yazmin was too careful to ever fall pregnant by a man she'd only wed for his money and influence.

If he'd allowed himself to trust such a figure again, Nick might have felt the same way. Might have waited until Eddie passed on the club and all that came with it when he retired. But Nick had never really been a patient person, and while it was true that he saw the place as his home now, he could still detach his emotions when it came to his surrogate parent.

He'd done the deed late one Thursday night. It hadn't been a calculated thing. Eddie had caught Nick and Yazmin at it in the office when he returned unexpectedly from a business trip. True, Nick had been thinking about arranging an accident for Eddie, but not quite yet. He would have preferred to plan things in a little more detail. But so much for that. Eddie had walked out on them, and Nick had chased after him to the car park, leaving a sobbing Yazmin half-naked on the desk. In the blackness behind the club, Nick saw Eddie opening up the door of his Jag and caught him just before he could climb inside. Nick snatched the keys out of his hand and threw him to the ground. As Eddie lay there, momentarily fazed, Nick went around to the boot of the car and opened it. The next thing he knew, the tyre iron was in his hand and Eddie was trying to crawl away. Nick brought the heavy bar down on the back of the man's skull—twice. It made a sickening noise, a thud and crack spliced together.

Nick told himself afterwards that he'd only been trying to knock the man out, so he could buy some time to think. But he'd brought that iron down so hard... Had he actually for one split second imagined that Eddie *was* his father? Was it a weird kind of revenge? It didn't matter in the end. King was dead. Long live the new king.

He'd dragged the body around and placed it in the open trunk.

Returning to the club, he found Yazmin dressed and pouring herself a large brandy from behind the bar. He took it away from her and handed her his car keys.

"W-Where's Eddie?" she'd asked. But Nick didn't answer her question.

"We're all going for a little drive," he replied, with a lethal glint in his eye.

Nick led her to his car and instructed her to follow him as he drove Eddie's Jag to a river out in the middle of nowhere. After wiping everything he'd touched with a cloth he found inside the Jag, Nick took the handbrake off and rolled the car into the water. It slid down easily and, weighted with rocks, sank like a ship capsizing in the ocean. Yazmin never asked about Eddie, and kept her mouth shut as he drove them both home.

By the time they got back it was almost light. As he pulled in, Nick noticed the red patch in the middle of the car park. He made a mental note to get one of Eddie's…correction, *his* men to clean that up as soon as possible.

Word spread quickly that Eddie King had gone missing, and spread even quicker that Nick was in charge. The police came sniffing around, but he told them he hadn't seen his boss since he left for his business trip and was just looking after things until he returned. But even as he spoke the words, he knew Edward Gilbert King was never *going* to return and he, Nicholas Metcalf, would be looking after things for a very long time to come. In the end they left him alone; there was no evidence that he was involved and the majority couldn't really care less about the whole situation. Those that could were either bought off or intimidated into submission.

His employees remained loyal to him. If they suspected any wrong-doing in the handover they didn't dare openly suggest it. Usurpers came along, but Nick dealt with them swiftly, setting an example to all that he was tightening his grip. One of the tin-pot bosses he crushed in this flamboyant display of power was Napoleon Naylor: burning down his house and shutting down his businesses within the space of a month. He'd enjoyed seeing the man grovel at his feet on the dance floor of Yazmin's, begging Nick to forgive him. Nick had smiled, said he accepted the apology, then introduced him to Hamilton, Terry and Frank, telling him that unfortunately *they* didn't.

Yazmin stayed with him too—more out of fright than anything. It was definitely fear that made her say yes to his marriage proposal. But he underestimated her quite spectacularly. Over time she collected enough evidence to sink Nick more deeply than he'd ever done to Eddie. Copies of business transactions squirreled away which would be released if anything were to happen to her. And she also knew his biggest secret, of course. It had scared her to begin with, and Yazmin knew that if she ever walked out on him she might end up going for a little swim herself sometime. But the more time she spent with Nick, the more his attitude rubbed off. Yazmin became hard and she became strong. So strong that when she announced she was leaving Nick, he could do nothing but let her go.

"I hope you burn in Hell," Yazmin told him as she packed her cases.

Nick had squinted, lighting up one of his cigars. "I'll be waiting for you there, sweetheart."

That had been a blow—not only to his ego, but also to his bank balance. It had been a bad few months.

Now, thankfully, things had turned around again. He had the pick of the women who came to the club, banging any of them whenever he felt lonely. No strings, no huge fucking payouts. And he'd just about got his little corner of the world completely sewn up. He ran the protection rackets for the entire city. There was no drug dealing without his express say so—and without a cut being paid to him. Money laundering was carried out via a host of businesses he owned. The porn and prostitute rings in the area all bowed down to him. He'd even dabbled in the property markets, buying up rented accommodation and charging the tenants a fortune or kicking them out. It still wasn't enough, though.

Which is why he'd heard out the strangers yesterday and agreed to help. Anyone who could just walk in and plant that much snort in someone's lap had to be connected. He could do very well indeed out of this deal, not only in terms of white but also through the contacts he could make. All right, so Finn wasn't exactly the most trustworthy guy he'd ever come across, but then who was Nick to judge? What mattered was that Finn had impressed him. He still didn't understand how he'd got past Frank and Terry, not to mention his personal bodyguards, but he had. And Nick was glad in a way.

There were just two things that made him nervous. One was that bloke Peck. Nick couldn't stand the man and figured it was mutual. He also got the impression it had been Finn's idea to hook up with Nick. Peck would have been happier if they'd gone solo. That made him a bit of loose cannon and a threat to whatever business relationship Nick might have with his boss. Obviously Finn could keep the man in check, he'd seen that for himself, but Nick knew there would come a time in the not too distant future when they'd lock horns again. He wondered who's side Finn would come down on then.

The second thing that worried him was this person they were looking for. Finn had told him nothing apart from he was desperate to speak to the guy. That he had important information which could prove very profitable indeed, to all of them.

"What kind of information?" Nick had pressed.

"That is not your concern," the man in the indigo suit had told him. But Nick guessed it was something to do with the drugs and how to bring more of it into the country.

Now, waiting here in the club, Nick pondered what might happen if he and Finn were to go into permanent business together. Or even if he cut Finn out of the loop completely. Deal with the source directly and—

The phone rang. In that large, empty club, the sound echoed off every single surface.

Nick walked across to the bar and picked up the receiver. "Nick Metcalf," he said.

"Metcalf, it's Lucas Peck."

Nick ground his back teeth. "Yeah?"

"Mr. Finn believes he might have a lead on where to start looking."

That was quick. Last night he didn't have a fucking clue where to begin. "Go on."

"We're going to have to cover the schools in the area."

Nick swapped the phone to his other ear. "Say that again."

"Mr. Finn has it on good authority that we'll find what we're looking for in a school."

"What is this, fucking *Jackanory*? What have schools got to do with anything?"

"We have a rough sketch of what the building looks like. It has large gates and—"

"Hold on, hold on. This Mr. Finn of yours…" Nick chose his next words very carefully. "He's not funny for young kids, is he? I don't want anything to do with that. I might be a businessman and I might dabble in certain adult areas, but I do draw the line somewhere, Peck."

There was an audible sigh at the other end of the phone. "No. It's nothing like that."

Nick nodded. "That's all right then."

"Mr. Finn would appreciate it if we could move fairly swiftly on this."

"Looking for schools?" Nick was still trying to get his head around the idea. What would that have to do with dru— "Wait," he said suddenly. "Your man isn't supplying to children either, is he?"

"No," spat Peck. Nick could almost taste the venom. "There's no time for explanations. You'll find out everything soon enough." Nick didn't like the sound of that last remark. Threat or promise, it still made him uneasy. "I'll be calling a bit later on. Round up some of your men and we can discuss how we're going to approach this."

Nobody was going to speak to him like that! "I don't take orders from you, Peck. And the next time you give me one I'll ram that fucking suitcase full of blow up your arse myself."

"An hour and a half," Peck replied, then put down the phone.

Nick held the receiver away from his ear. "Little prick," he murmured. Then, his face one big question mark, he repeated: "A school?"

– ii –

"So, are we ready to carry on with this?"

Ellen was sitting on the chair by his bed, recorder and notebook at the ready. It was getting to be a familiar routine. The only difference being Cliff was keeping watch behind her today instead of Ben.

"I don't have much choice really," said Alex.

"There's always a choice."

"Not if I want my life back the way it was."

"We did well yesterday, Alex. But there really is no rush. That's why I left it where we were. Just say if you don't feel up to it."

"I'm ready," he confirmed.

She didn't look convinced, but continued anyway. "I want you to think back to the night of your birthday, at the restaurant. What do you remember?"

"The Italian waiter was a dick."

Ellen gave a small laugh, then composed herself. "Everyone was having a good time, good meal, wine—"

"No wine," he cut in. "I was driving."

"Right, but you were having an enjoyable evening?"

"Beverly and I had been arguing."

She coughed into her hand. "I see."

"We were doing our best to cover it up. Wasn't easy." He shook his head. "I don't know why I'm telling you that. It has nothing to do with what happened."

She gave him a look of understanding. "Doesn't matter. You can tell me anything you like."

"You want to hear about what I saw, though."

"When you feel able to tell me. There was a man smoking, wasn't there? Hiding it?"

"I thought so. Large guy. I could smell smoke anyway."

"But then he changed too, just like Timothy?"

"One minute he was fine, the next he was a human fireball. Then everything altered."

"So, do the same thing you did yesterday. Focus on what you could see. Try to remember the details, play them back to yourself."

He did just that, directing the film, cutting and editing it mentally and describing what he could see to Ellen. "Suddenly he was on fire," Alex started to cough, not the embarrassed kind Ellen had given a moment before, but rough and choking. His chest began to feel tight.

"Do you want another drink of water?"

Alex held up his hand, determined to go on. "I was looking around for someone to help him. But nobody could see it; only me. It spread so fast…" He was lost in the vision again.

Ellen sat upright in the chair. "Alex? What can you see? You're not in the restaurant anymore are you?"

"No, it's not the restaurant. Everything's different. People are dressed differently."

"But where are you, can you remember?"

"I don't know. It's smaller. The walls are made of wood, there are wooden tables. People are trying to escape from the fire. Someone is shouting a name: Wendy."

"Who's Wendy, Alex?"

"I think she works here. Oh my God, no! The people, they were asleep when it happened, when someone raised the alarm. I think this is some kind of inn. They were all in bed"

"In bed?"

"Yes, the fire came in the night."

"Did…" She couldn't believe she was asking this. "Did someone set the fire, Alex?"

"I… Jesus! Help them, *somebody!*" he cried.

Ellen perched on the edge of her seat. "You stay with me, Alex. Remember you're only watching this. It's like watching one of your films."

His fingers dug into the mattress. "Christ Almighty, they're all going to die and—" Alex stiffened.

"What is it? What can you see?"

"He's there. He's watching them through the flames. I can see him."

"Who?"

"I can see those blue eyes. Jesus, he's walking through the fire." Alex fell back on the bed and started shaking.

Ellen was over there in seconds. "Alex, snap out of it—you're not there. You're only *watching* this."

He let out a terrifying scream and grabbed her. Cliff rushed across the room, but Ellen told him to stay where he was. She held Alex tight as he started to cry, head buried deep in her shoulder. She held him until she could feel his body stop shaking.

And then she held him some more.

– iii –

For a long time he lay on the bed, not moving, not saying anything. She stayed with him and, when he was ready to speak to her, she listened.

"I saw him," Alex said in a quiet voice, "the dark figure from my dream."

"That much I guessed."

"He was connected to what was happening somehow. It felt like he was looking for something."

"And the thought of that—"

"I've never been so frightened in all my life."

"I feel like I owe you an apology."

He looked blank. "Why?"

"We should have left this till some other time."

Alex sat up. "No, we shouldn't."

"Your dream self, the representation of whatever it is you're hiding, is starting to cross over into your waking world. That's my doing, and it could be dangerous."

"I just want to find out whatever it is I'm keeping from myself."

"Me too. But we have to do this more gradually," she explained. "Or we might make things worse."

"How could they possibly be any worse?" he spluttered. "I'm seeing people on fire, torture chambers and Japanese women. I'm seeing half-dead men with—"

"Complete catatonic shutdown," she informed him. "Or if your mind doesn't want to accept the truth, you may become trapped in one of these fantasies. I can't, *won't* be the cause of that."

"Ellen…" It didn't feel quite so weird this time, calling her that. "I have a terrible feeling that if I can't control all this—and soon—then that's probably going to happen anyway. Or much, much worse."

She didn't ask him what he meant, she just nodded, patted his arm, and promised they would talk more tomorrow.

– iv –

"So it's all in hand?"

Lucas Peck, standing at the threshold to The Infinity's room, told him that it was.

"And how is our new business partner?"

"Argumentative," said Lucas.

"As is to be expected."

Lucas scowled. "I really wish we didn't have to deal with him."

"If I hadn't been interrupted this morning we might not have needed to. After all this time, Lucas, I was almost there. I almost *had* the location." The Infinity tutted. "Instead we only have my—admittedly quite accurate—drawing to guide us. When is the search due to begin?"

"Tomorrow morning, first thing. Metcalf is sending out five teams with three men each and a list of the schools in and around Griffield and Kirkwell, including the underlying villages."

One of The Infinity's eyes narrowed. "Only five teams?"

"All he could spare at the moment, he says."

"I see. Well, I suppose it will have to suffice. You'll keep me informed of their progress?"

Lucas told him that he would. "So you think he's linked to this school, maybe works there?"

"I certainly don't think he's attending one, do you? Perhaps he is working there, but not necessarily as a teacher. He could be the caretaker or even one of the cleaning staff for all I know."

"Or one of the parents?" suggested Lucas.

"Exactly. Our search is not over even when we find the school; in fact it might be only just beginning, Lucas. And time is growing short. With each day that passes, he remembers a little more."

"I thought that was a good thing. I thought that would help you find him quicker?"

"While he's still unsure of who he is and what part he has to play, yes. But once he discovers his true nature… I am determined that things should go differently this time, Lucas."

"I'm sure they will," Lucas replied, having no idea what The Infinity meant.

"Yes," said his master with a sly grin. "Yes, for some reason so am I."

FOURTEEN

– i –

THE RINGING OF THE MOBILE BROKE HER DREAM.

In it she'd been a fairy tale princess in a large tower, trapped and longing for the handsome knight to come and rescue her. It was a stupid dream, one she'd been having since she'd was a little girl. But it had changed as she'd grown older, every year becoming a little bit longer, gradually revealing more and more. When she was very young she'd remained in that castle, waiting patiently, but no one ever showed. It was so lonely.

Then, one day, he'd arrived. Her hero.

He was so handsome. He'd fought the monster guarding the entrance to the tower—a horrible, scaly creature with fangs. He'd slain the beast and mounted the steps. One kiss was all it took for them to fall in love… and for a while that's where the fairy tale ended.

Then, eventually, she'd been given the next instalment—where the knight took her hand-in-hand back down the tower steps and out to freedom. But something wasn't quite right about these later dreams. The knight's face was in shadow as they descended those steps. She would keep looking across at him to catch a glimpse of that face she'd fallen in love with, and every time she'd been denied. Back up in the tower, when he'd held her in his arms, she'd felt cared for. It was as though she'd known him forever. Now here, on the stairs, she was suddenly frightened. She wasn't quite sure she knew who this was anymore—now that she couldn't see his eyes, nose, those lips she'd once kissed with such abandon.

The more steps they took, the deeper the shadows became. She recalled countless dreams about those steps; they never seemed to end. Down and down, spiralling, his grip tighter with each one they took until he was hurting her, almost crushing her hand.

Until finally, at long last, they reached the bottom, stepped out into the light.

And she saw his face again...

Her scream was piercing as she realised she was holding the hand of the scaly devil from the entranceway. Somehow her beautiful rescuer had transformed into a hideous demon, with fierce eyes and a giant tongue which lapped her face. She'd tried to push him away but it was no use, his grip was too strong.

At the very last moment, fearing that all was completely lost, a new champion had emerged to save the day. Riding up on horseback, he'd snatched her away, carried her off with him. As they rode she wrapped her arms around him, holding on tight. She risked one quick look back and saw the monster on its knees, holding out its arms for her return.

The further away they went, the less like a scaly demon it appeared.

And more like the knight she'd kissed back in the tower, now with tears in his eyes. But she was on the back of the horse, and they were going faster and faster and—

The persistent *deep-de-deep* of the ringtone forced her to leave that world and return to reality.

Beverly Webber rolled over and reached into her handbag, pressing the button automatically.

"Hello," she mumbled.

"Ah, at last. Beverly?" The voice was light but with a concerned undertone.

"Yes?" It took her a moment to recognise it, but now she wished she'd checked the number ID before speaking. "Oh, hi..."

"Beverly, thank God," said Alex's mother. "Sorry to call you on your mobile, but I've been trying you both at home all weekend; there was no answer."

Beverly pulled back the covers. She padded across the floor to the bathroom, grabbing a dressing gown as she went. "No…I…we haven't been at home."

"I know," was all she said to that. "Is Alex there? His phone's switched off."

"Er…He's…"

"Is everything all right?"

"Everything's…okay," said Beverly, slipping one arm into the towelling and shrugging it over her shoulder; it was way too big for her.

"Are you sure?"

"Look, it's a bit hard to talk right now—"

"I was ringing to see how he was. I thought he sounded a bit under the weather last time we spoke."

That's the understatement of the century. "No, he's not been too well. But he'll be better soon."

"Beverly, is there something you're not telling me? I'm his mother, I have a right to know."

"And I'm his wife," said Beverly, with more rancour than she'd intended.

There was silence at the other end.

"I know that," said the other Mrs. Webber at last. "I'm just worried about him. He's my son and I love him."

"I know, I'm sorry… I'll pass on the message, I promise. But I've really got to go."

"Beverly—"

She switched off the phone and held it out in front of her like it was going to bite. If she'd been thinking straight and not half asleep, she never would have answered it in the first place. In fact if she hadn't been checking for missed calls last night—of which there were a number—it wouldn't even have been on.

Shit! she thought. *Shit, shit, shit!*

Quietly, she returned to the bedroom and put the phone down on the bedside table. But as she straightened, she saw her wedding ring lying there, right where she'd taken it off. The band of gold shone in the morning sunlight.

And I'm his wife!

The lump on the other side of her bed stirred.

"Who was that?" came a voice from under the covers.

What a mess, she thought. *What a complete fucked up mess.*

"It doesn't matter," Beverly said. "Go back to sleep, it's still early." In seconds she could hear his laboured breathing again, deep and even.

And absently, biting her lip, she wondered if he was dreaming.

– ii –

Today was not a good day; he could feel it.

All right, they hadn't been good for some time, but today—Monday—he'd woken and it had really hit him that his life was well and truly in the toilet. The pills they'd insisted on giving him last night had made him drowsy, but he'd resisted as long as possible. The sleep, when it came, was sporadic. He could only recall the vaguest hints of the dream-place—in fact he'd fought to prevent it invading his mind. And there'd been no nightmares thankfully.

Only the one waiting for him when he opened his eyes and remembered where he was. As if freaking out twice in the hospital wasn't enough, he'd broken down in Ellen's arms during their session yesterday. He felt helpless, powerless. Everything was out of his hands.

Breakfast had come and gone, and he'd hardly touched a thing. Just couldn't stomach anything. What else was lurking in his mind ready to shock them all? Alex guessed he'd find out soon enough, but one thing he did know for sure.

Today was not a good day, not a good day at all.

– iii –

"What's the name of this place again?" asked Terry Gilligan.

Squashed behind the steering wheel of the red convertible, he looked like one of those performing monkeys taught to do tricks. In the passenger seat was Frank Austin, and the combination seemed even more ridiculous to Lucas: almost cartoon-like. The sunglasses did nothing to improve this. He'd been surprised the car even started, let alone reached thirty or forty miles an hour on the main roads. When he looked behind him as they set off, Lucas fully expected the exhaust pipe to be scraping along on the concrete, sparks flying every which way.

Frank wriggled about in his seat, reaching into the pocket of his trousers for the piece of paper he'd been given. At last, he located it.

With hands like cricket gloves, he unfolded it and attempted to read the words. "Jam…Jim…Jan…"

Lucas reached over from the back and snatched the paper. "Jennswell Secondary," he shouted. "Look for the signs for Lower Hutton on the next roundabout then turn off."

Frank showed his teeth. Lucas showed his back. Any kind of respect or even fear he'd had for this man had been shattered after Saturday night. He was big—probably the biggest man Lucas had ever come across in his entire life—but that didn't mean a thing once you'd seen him piss his pants on the steps of Yazmin's nightclub. As for Terry, he'd been like a pussycat after Lucas had pulled the knife.

He hadn't asked what The Infinity had shown Frank, but he knew it must have been something bad. It usually was.

"Why're we looking for a school anyway?" said Terry. "I don't get it."

Lucas watched the streets passing by on his left. "Why doesn't that surprise me?"

"Do you know, then?" Frank asked him. "If you're so clever."

"Yes. But it's not something Mr. Metcalf wants broadcasting."

Terry and Frank exchanged glances. "Oh yeah?" said Frank. "Tell us."

"I don't really think I should."

Frank tried to smile; it wasn't a pretty sight. In fact, thought Lucas, it was worse than seeing him wet himself. "Go on, we won't tell anybody. Will we, Terry?"

Terry shook his head. "No, you can trust us two."

"Oh I don't know…"

"Go on, why are we looking for a school?" Frank was practically begging.

"All right then, if you really must know."

"Yeah?"

"Mr. Metcalf," said Lucas, lowering his voice, "is looking for a school…"

"Looking for a school…" repeated Terry.

"Where he can stick you two dumb shits to teach you how to read and write."

It took nearly a whole minute for this to sink in, and even then Lucas could have sworn Frank was going to say: "He's not, is he?" Then he glowered and his cheeks turned crimson.

"If we hadn't been told to play nice," he said, "you'd be a dead man right now."

Lucas chortled, not just because he knew that neither of them could take him—even without The Infinity's protection, he'd be fully capable of defending himself against these two walking monoliths—but also because of the irony of the statement. Once this was over, they'd be the dead men. And Lucas? He was going to live forever.

"The roundabout is coming up. Look for the exit," he told them.

– iv –

"I can see fields. No wait, they're more like small hills. It's green with splashes of purple and pink. The skies are darkening, the sun falling in the sky, and on the horizon there are men waiting. Some on horseback, some on foot.

"They're lined up. There's going to be a battle here. More men now, coming from another direction. Jesus, it's started. No warning, nothing. They're just charging into each other. Big men with fur covering their backs, with swords twice their own size. One strikes a shield almost cracking it in two, another man's thrown from his horse. He's on the ground twisting and turning, looking up into the face of his enemy. Before he can strike an axe catches him, sending him sprawling sideways, staining his tartan red. Their piper is playing as more men descend, some running, some on horseback. They're like a wall of bodies.

"I can hear a name being shouted: Fraser. It's a warning; a large, bearded man is charging at him. They hack at each other, but finally the bigger man plunges a sword into the other's chest, so deep it comes out the other side.

"There's a shout of disbelief. Two more men attack the bearded giant, but he shrugs off their blows. There are chunks of meat still left in his beard from the last time he ate, the dried froth of ales mixed with spittle from his mouth—teeth rotten to the gum. While one of the smaller men distracts him, the other draws a knife and dodges round the back, plunging it into his side. The big man drops to his knees, as tall as the ones still standing. Then he falls over sideways.

"The fighting is raging all around. So many men dying, so much blood and carnage. But there is something else. Something… There, in the middle of this. Something is watching. It stands with the men but isn't one of them. The skies are turning red, the sun boiling behind the clouds.

"'Death itself is here,' shouts someone. I can see… There's another cry: 'Come on then, will ye! Come on then and git it over with, ya blue-eyed Dunsan bastard'!"

— v —

It wasn't a bad match.

Lucas looked from the photocopied sketch in his hand to the school entrance, then back again. The stone wall, the gates, buildings the right blend of old and new: exactly how The Infinity had described it. But there were certain details that didn't quite fit: a playground instead of a car park, the overall layout of the school. He wanted this to be the right one so badly he was *trying* to make it fit. Lucas wanted to be the person to find the school so much he was willing to overlook such things. But he knew The Infinity would recognise the difference, and he'd be less than pleased when he did.

He cursed under his breath. Looking over at the red convertible parked just down the road, Lucas shook his head. He didn't know which was worse, The Infinity's rage or the prospect of spending even more time with Tweedles Dum and Dee. As he was contemplating his options, Lucas' mobile sang out a tinny tune from his pocket. He pressed the screen and held it to his ear.

Seconds later he was switching it off and replacing it. Another team had just checked in; they'd come up empty, like the rest. Lucas was beginning to wonder whether this was all some wild goose chase. Maybe The Infinity's intuition had been off again, or *he'd* been so desperate to find what he was looking for that he'd fooled himself. Those were dangerous thoughts, but Lucas knew what all this meant to his master. And when things mean a lot to you, your judgement can easily be impaired. Even a being as powerful as The Infinity had his off-days.

None of this would be repeated to his face. Lucas would bury these doubts so far at the back of his mind The Infinity would need a lamp and a pickaxe to find them. But they were there all the same.

Lucas began the walk back to the car, kicking the odd stone on the street as he went. So was this all one big, gigantic waste of time and energy? He had no choice but to carry on with his task regardless, until they found the school or The Infinity became so impatient he decided to lash out at the nearest person. Lucas had already decided he'd be standing behind Terry or Frank when that time came.

That thought at least made him smile as he reached the car.

– vi –

"She's beautiful, the woman. Her face is so white, hair so black.

"She walks lightly, as if she's gliding on air. Tiny steps, taking her down the corridor, the walls of which are just as flimsy. I can hear the sound of wind chimes. There are birds fluttering in a cage. She's turned a corner, vanishing. Wait, I can see her again. She's inside a large room, and has joined two or three others dressed just like her. But one stands out in the middle. She carries herself differently, neck straight. She stands tall. I think the other women are handmaidens of some sort.

"I can't really understand what they're saying, it's too quick. '*Cho, Yoku.*' I got that. There are men standing nearby, their hair tied back, and they have sheathed swords by their sides. They look like guards. I… Yes, I think this is some sort of temple or even a palace. Through the window I can see a garden. Oh God, you should see the court, the *grounds* of this place. There's a lot of activity in the room, as though they're preparing for something, a gathering maybe. They're getting things ready for a visit. Someone important.

"On the wall at the far end of the room is a picture. It shows a dragon spitting fire—a red dragon with deep, blue eyes."

– vii –

He must be missing something.

About the place itself? No, the drawing had been quite accurate based on his vision. He would find his quarry there, of that he was certain. So why, out of all the schools they had searched, had they not found it yet? The Infinity paced up and down in his room. This hunt was almost over, he could feel it, could taste the flavour of victory on his tongue—so sweet and tart at the same time.

Why was it taking so long?

That, in itself, was something of a joke. After all these years, after all this waiting, at the very last stretch to be so impatient. "All good things to those who wait," he reminded himself.

Bad things, too.

He should distract himself somehow, take his mind off the agonising ticking of the clock on the wall—the hands of which seemed to be going backwards just to infuriate him. His dalliance with the hotel girl had been fun, so maybe that was the answer. Call up room service and demand another be sent. But The Infinity knew it wouldn't be the same. That had been an act of pure aggression, even revenge. Not necessarily upon the girl, because the part she played was of no great significance—wrong place, wrong time—but revenge upon the entire world, the universe and every-thing else he could think of for bothering him at such a crucial moment.

If it hadn't been for that, he would have seen the name of the school. He'd be one step closer. Now they were floundering again while his enemy continued to put the pieces together. That's what had fuelled his delicious time with the girl, doing things to her that Lucas Peck could never have conceived of, could never have accomplished and, even if The Infinity did say so himself, could never have stomached. Abuse both mental and physical, bringing her greatest fears to life—plus some she didn't even know she had. Granting her wishes and shattering them in the space of seconds. He'd tampered with her on a molecular level just for the sheer enjoyment of it. Breaking her down, reshaping her into all manner of things, rearranging and removing, replacing, ripping her apart, over and over again. One minute a bloody pulp of a thing on the floor, seeping and weeping juices from every orifice, the next strung out across the room like elastic, wrapped around chairs, tables, wardrobes, flesh so taut it should have snapped several billion times.

The worst thing of all for her was awareness. The Infinity hadn't even spared her that; he'd given her temporary knowledge, enough for her to understand what he was doing to her, and why. Enough for her to recognise her position in the great scheme of things, the equivalent of bacteria. Which, like her, could cause untold damage without even realising it.

"Now do you see," he'd asked her, "why this must be done? No good deed ever goes unpunished."

Boredom had set in after a while, though, and he'd released her from her agony.

The Infinity felt better for having set this matter straight. For every action there must be an equal and opposite reaction. It was simple cause and effect. She understood this right before her end. Which is why there would be no real purpose in doing the same thing again to someone else, even if it did take his mind off the search. He would gain little satisfaction from recreating a scene from the past. Or replaying it.

Which was, in essence, the reason why he was here. So that things could be different this time, so there would be less of a struggle. That was the plan anyway. If the school could not be located soon, then it might all be in vain. No chance of the total victory he'd dreamed about since…well, ever since he could remember.

He shook his head. No, that wasn't going to happen. It was time to finish this. The Infinity wanted to settle things once and for all.

Then nothing could stand in his way.

– viii –

"I can see the flickering of the flames on the cave walls.

"There are men here, at least I think they're men. They're speaking in grunts and groans. They're cooking something over the fire, some kind of meat. I can even smell it. I think this is where they live. One of the men is drawing something on the wall, painting with his fingers. Hold on. It's a depiction of the hunt; I can just about make it out. The big fur-covered thing they were chasing, and three of them holding spears up, running after it.

"That's what they're cooking on the fire. I can see a female over there nursing a young baby in her arms. They've stripped the fur from the animal they killed, and have used it to wrap both of them up in.

"The one painting with his fingers has stopped to pick up a rock. He's drawn a dark shape on the wall and he's filling in the eyes. It's almost finished, there it is.

"A dark shape with…bright blue eyes."

– ix –

Ellen stopped the recorder.

She was tapping her pen against her teeth, looking down at the notes she'd made after playing back the day's sessions. It was an interesting read. Based on previous episodes, Alex had recounted details about three separate and very different delusions. As with the restaurant fire, he'd expanded the scenes and was again bringing in aspects of the dreams he'd been having. She'd stopped him before he went too far, but it would have been interesting to see what he'd come up with if she hadn't.

However, the thing that kept surprising her was how vivid these recollections were. How much trouble his mind was going to so it could hide some vital truth from him. When she had a moment, she'd tap a few of those names and references into the net to see what she could come up with. As it was, she'd already spent far too much time with this one patient, neglecting the others in her care.

Ellen was just about to leave the office when her phone rang. She let the answer machine get it, but dashed back when she heard Beverly Webber's voice.

"Hello, Mrs. Webber. I'm here."

The woman sounded shocked to be suddenly talking to a human being. "Dr. Hayward?"

"You just caught me."

"Oh, right. I'll make it quick anyway, I have a client waiting."

"Okay."

A pause. "I was ringing to see…" She never finished off the sentence.

"Don't worry, he's doing all right. As a matter of fact I've been with him most of the weekend."

"Oh. And?"

"I think we're making some progress."

"That's exactly what you told me the other day," said Beverly.

"I know things looked pretty bad but—"

"If you're going to tell me that it's always darkest before the dawn, Doctor, I think I might just throw up."

"I think I'd probably join you," said Ellen. "Chirpy stock phrases are not a part of my repertoire."

"Good. I'd be lying if I said it hadn't thrown me. I've had trouble getting a handle on all of this, but…" Beverly went silent, then said, "Is he going to be all right?"

"Physically he's fine."

"That's not what I asked, Doctor. Is he going to be *all right*?"

"This isn't the sort of thing that comes with a rulebook, but yes, I believe he will."

"In the meantime what do I tell people? His mother rang this morning."

"Tell her whatever you feel comfortable with."

"I said he wasn't feeling well." It sounded like she wanted someone to confirm she'd done the right thing.

"That's not far from the truth."

"She'll want to visit him if she knows he's in hospital. You don't know what she's like. He's still her darling little boy."

"Lucky Alex," said Ellen. "Some parents don't bother at all. I think that's nice."

"You wouldn't if she was your mother-in-law."

There was an awkward pause for a few seconds until Ellen finally filled it. "You mentioned 'people.'"

"I'm sorry?"

"You said what do I tell people. Are we talking about the rest of Alex's family? His friends?"

Beverly thought for a moment. "Yes, I suppose so."

"Are they quite tightly knit?"

"He's closest to his mother, as I say. His father died when he and his brother were young."

Ellen's eyes widened. "Alex has a brother?"

"Yes, Steve," said Beverly, and left it at that.

"Mrs. Webber…Beverly? Could I ask you something?"

"What is it, Doctor?"

"Please, it's Ellen. Just Ellen."

"All right, Ellen then."

"In my profession, you pick up on things. It's not something you can help, you understand, and sometimes I wish I didn't."

"Yes?"

"This is going to sound like a very personal question, and I'll understand if you just tell me to go to hell but… Do you love your husband, Beverly?"

There was a sharp intake of breath. Ellen thought that if the woman was here in front of her, she might have slapped her in the face. "You're right, it *is* a very personal question," she said.

"Believe me, I wouldn't be asking if there wasn't a good reason. I know it sounds ridiculous coming from someone like me, but I'm the last person in the world to pry into people's private lives."

"Yes, it does." Another gap. "What makes you ask in the first place?"

"I can see you're concerned about Alex. Anyone in your position would be. But when you talk about him, when you mention his name—"

"We've both been through a lot these past couple of weeks. You know that."

"And before? How were things between you?"

"Fine," snapped Beverly. "They were fine."

"Sorry, I had to ask. I'm looking for things that might have triggered his episodes. I'm not doing this just for the sake of it."

"So what you're saying is that you think I might be responsible for what's happening? Is that it?"

"Not at all." Ellen sat down on the edge of her desk. "But if you two were going through... Listen, nobody's to blame. It's not anyone's fault. I just need to know the truth."

"Alex and I..." Beverly began, but her words tapered off again. Ellen thought she heard her sniff.

"It's okay," she said.

"No it's not."

Ellen tried a different tack. "How long have you two been together?"

"Since we were in our twenties," said Beverly.

Ellen thought of Rosy. "Long time."

"Yes."

"This might seem like a weird thing to ask, but has Alex ever had trouble sleeping?"

"Excuse me?" Of all the questions she was expecting, this was probably not one of them.

"Tossing, turning? Maybe calling anything out?"

"He hasn't slept very well recently, as I said."

"What about before that?"

"He's a worrier. If something's on his mind then he might be a bit restless. He was pretty bad when he started teaching."

"But nothing out of the ordinary?"

"No, I don't think so. Are you going to tell me what this is about?"

"It's nothing to worry over," Ellen told her. "Just some bad dreams he's been having."

She thought Beverly was going to ask her what they were, but she didn't. "I still care about him. You don't know someone for that long and not..."

Ellen nodded to herself. "I know you do. I know you do."

– x –

The last school that day. No resemblance.

It was home time and Lucas Peck sat on a wall opposite the gates—too polished and new to be those he was looking for. He let out a desperate groan. This was their last hope, St Bernadette's. He'd heard back from all the other teams, they'd turned up nothing. The Infinity was going to be pissed: *very* pissed. He stared at the sky, not really knowing what to do. Not relishing ringing his master, he thought he would just stay here for a little while. The kids were coming out, flooding through the tacky orange doors.

"Haven't seen you here before," said a voice. Lucas turned to see a man of about forty, with thinning, greying hair and small but intense chestnut eyes. He was wearing a tank-top in defiance of the heat, and there were sweat stains under the arms of his turquoise short-sleeved shirt.

Lucas grimaced. "Er…no."

"Who you waiting for?"

"Beg your pardon?"

"Which one's yours?" said the man impatiently.

"Oh, I see. None of them. I'm just looking around at schools for my son."

"New to the area, eh? Have you been to Bambridge's?"

"Yes," said Lucas.

"Chigley Grammar?"

"Yes."

"Hollingthorpe?"

"Yes."

"So which one do you think you'll settle on?"

"Not really sure." All Lucas wanted was a bit of peace before having to deliver news of his failure. The last thing he needed was small talk. If there weren't quite so many people around, he might have dragged this jerk behind one of the nearby bushes and garrotted him. Even with the crowds it was still tempting.

"Well, this one isn't so bad. My Steph's been here since she turned eleven. Taking her GCSE's next year. How old's yours then?"

"Nearly fifteen," said Lucas without even having to think about it. "His name's Ryan."

"Ah, the father and son bond. You can't beat it." He said the words as if he felt he was missing out on something. "So you moved here from...?"

"Not far. Actually we had to take him out of his previous school because he was having problems."

"Lot of it about. Bullying, was it?"

"Something like that."

The man followed Lucas' gaze, watching the children of various ages. "Course, the only problem is that Steph can't do her A-Levels here. And she wants to go to university, study to be a lawyer. A lawyer, I ask you."

Lucas nodded, not really listening.

"Sharks, all the bloody lot of 'em. Still, they're rich sharks I suppose."

Lucas' ears twitched at the word. *You have no idea what a shark is, my friend. You're standing next to one right now.*

"Anyway, it means she'll have to go to a college in Griffield or Kirkwell to do her A-Levels and—"

Lucas rounded on the man. "What did you just say?"

"She wants to become a lawyer, although I don't know what—"

"No, no, after that, about her A-Levels." Lucas had the look of someone who'd just discovered the meaning of life itself, only to forget it moments later.

Perplexed, the man said, "She's going to have to go to college, then on to university."

Lucas beamed. It wasn't just a smile, it was as if his whole face had split in two—like a grapefruit chopped in half by a cleaver. "That's it!"

"Is it?" said the man, but before he could ask what, he was distracted by something. "Oh, look, there she is."

The man's daughter had just emerged, waving to him from the gate. She looked both ways before crossing the road.

"Look, butter wouldn't melt. Don't think she has it in her, do you? That killer instinct."

Lucas scrutinised her, still smiling. She appeared older than her years, long brown hair rippling over her shoulders. Lucas found his eyes appraising her. As she came nearer, he looked more closely at her face. A face so classically beautiful it made Lucas want to cry: those perfect cheekbones, those red lips, naturally red not artificially enhanced.

"No," said Lucas. "It takes a certain kind of person. You've either got it or you haven't." *You're either the victor or the victim, the hunter or the prey. The shark…or the meat.*

"Hi, Dad," said the girl, and then to Lucas, "Hi." She smiled back at him.

"Hi, sweetheart," said the man, kissing her on the cheek.

"Hello," said Lucas.

"This is Mr… Sorry, didn't catch your name."

"Peck."

"He's thinking of sending his son here, he's about the same age as you." The girl perked up even more at hearing this. "Oh?"

"Yes, that's right. And I hear you might be going to college soon too?" She nodded.

"That's good, that's very good." *Leave it, you haven't got time for this. You haven't got time for—*

"Well, it was nice meeting you, Mr. Peck. I hope everything turns out okay with Ryan," said her father. "Maybe we'll both see you again sometime."

"Yes, I'd like that." Lucas envied the man as he put his arm around Steph and led her off towards their car. He ached to see what she was like inside, what sort of art she would inspire. The perfect masterpiece? She glanced over her shoulder once at Lucas, and he knew he would never see either of them again. Never have the answers to his questions.

But he did have the answer to a more pressing concern.

Lucas raised himself from the wall as the school bus pulled in. More children passed by his gaze, much younger: thirteen, twelve, the boys chattering about sport, the girls discussing pop bands and who was "fit" in their classes. He ignored them, focused on the task in hand.

Wondering just how he was going to broach this subject to The Infinity without it sounding like his master had made a mistake.

She'd only intended to call in. Just to call—

To see how he was doing. Pressured by the guilt trip his mother had given her on the phone, and the words of Dr. Hayward...Ellen—

Do you love your husband?

—she'd felt compelled to return.

How could she face him, though, after what she'd done? It had felt like she'd been outside of reality the past couple of days. She could forget about all this, pretend it hadn't even happened. But now it felt so real again.

She'd asked to see Ellen, but was told the doctor wasn't around.

"She hasn't checked out, but she's not in her office either," said the nurse at the desk in the psychiatric department.

Beverly peered through the glass in the double doors, down the corridor, and imagined what it must be like for Alex stuck in here with no visitors. How frightened, how lonely he must be. And suddenly, to her surprise, she'd *wanted* to see him.

"Oh, I can't allow that, I'm afraid," said the nurse.

"I only want to look in. I won't disturb him." *I don't* want *to disturb him. That's the last thing I want to do.* "You can send whoever you want with me if you like. Please, I haven't seen him in three days." *And whose fault's that?* "I'm his wife."

It was exactly what she'd told his mum that morning, and it sounded just as strange now. As Beverly spoke to the woman she fingered the wedding ring on her left hand. The receptionist sucked in some air. "I shouldn't really." Beverly gave her a pleading look. "Okay, but only for a minute. George, come over here will you?"

Beverly thanked her and accompanied the male nurse through those doors and down the hall.

When she reached his room, she changed her mind again. Suddenly she didn't want to see Alex. Not even a quick glimpse. The thought of it made her feel sick. But she'd come this far, made such a fuss about it. George—just a few yards away—was waiting patiently for her to get on with it.

Beverly walked up to the door and pressed her face against the circular glass. She saw Alex propped up in bed. Head tilted, he was facing a small portable TV on a trolley not far away. The set droned on, music blaring.

Whatever he was watching, he didn't seem to be enjoying it very much. His forehead was crumpled, bottom lip jutting out much further than the top. She recognised that face immediately, the one he wore when he was worried about a student, or had a difficult meeting at work to prepare for. It was the face he'd worn just before he met her parents for the first time, before he'd asked her to marry him. It was the face he'd worn all last week when he thought he was going completely insane.

He must have sensed her presence at the door, because he turned sharply. Beverly moved her head back, hoping he hadn't seen her. But it was too late; he was at the door before she'd made it three steps down the hall.

"Bev?" came his voice from behind her. She stopped walking, closed her eyes. "Bev, please don't go."

She screwed up her eyes, fighting the tears. Beverly choked them back somehow, before turning. "Hello, Alex," she said. "How are you feeling?"

He searched her face as if he'd find the answer to her question there. Maybe he did, because he looked down and shook his head. Alex took a step, but George was standing in his way.

Before she was even aware of what she was doing, Beverly was putting one foot in front of the other. She pushed George gently aside. Her arms were up and open, and she folded them around Alex. The weight of his head felt familiar on her shoulder; it should do, it had rested there many times. With her hands she rubbed his back, patting him. He made no effort to hold her back. It was as if he knew there was no point—this wasn't the hug of two lovers anymore. It was one of pity, of loss.

When they parted, Alex's eyes were still focused on the floor. Gradually he looked up, and she could see that he'd had less success at controlling his tears than her. "What happened to us, Bev?"

"I don't know, Alex. Honestly I don't. Sometimes things…" Beverly gave up groping for words that wouldn't come, explanations that were beyond her, and repeated: "I don't know."

"We were happy once, though."

Beverly attempted a smile. "Yes, of course we were…for a while."

"If this hadn't happened, do you think—"

"Oh, Alex," she interrupted. "Please, don't."

So he didn't.

She stroked his cheek with one of her fingers. "You're in safe hands with Dr. Hayward. You *are* going to get better."

"But you won't be there waiting for me when I get out, will you?"

Her silence said more than she ever could. "Look, I've got to go."

"Already?"

"I'll be back to visit. I still think a lot of you, you know."

"Do you?" he said.

"Yes." Beverly was pulling away from him. "I'll see you soon, okay?"

"Okay," said Alex, but she knew he didn't believe a word of it.

Beverly was about to turn, when she remembered something. "Your mum called this morning, I didn't really know what to say. She's worried about you."

"I'll...I'll give her a ring."

She nodded. Then Beverly was retracing her steps down the corridor. She didn't look back once.

If she had, she might have seen Alex's head drop again. Might have seen him go back inside his room, wiping more tears from his face.

FIFTEEN

– i –

TONIGHT HE DID REMEMBER. The combination of more pills and sheer exhaustion sent him into a deep sleep.

The circle built itself around him, a spinning strand of light. But he no longer felt safe. He was conscious of the other thing lurking just out of sight.

He also saw the faces of the ghost people a little clearer. They were more solid, hardly bearing any resemblance to the wraiths from before, passing through him, walking around him, whispers of humanity. But they were still out of reach. One of the people was a Native American.

"What are you doing in my dream?" Alex asked him. "What are you doing in my head?"

The man's expression was blank.

Another figure was materialising beside this one. He was clothed in loose-fitting trousers and a tunic, with a belt and buckle around his waist. He also wore a hat and had a moustache.

"Who are you?" Alex demanded. The man was clutching a tankard of beer in his hand, and he raised this in salute.

On the other side of the Native American, a third spectre coalesced. He was fully bearded, with much longer hair. There was leather wrapped around his wrists, and his clan's tartan made up the kilt that covered the lower half of his body. He planted his sword in front of Alex and leaned on it.

A man of Asian descent stepped forward and drew a sword of his own. He slashed it through the air in a fierce display, before replacing it in its sheath.

"What do you want with me? Why are you showing me these things?" he asked them. More spirits joined them, spreading themselves out around the circle, so that they *became* the circle. He took in face after face—some white, some black, every creed and colour represented. So many he lost count. He spun round until he made himself dizzy. "What's happening? Please, won't somebody tell me what's going on?"

None of them said anything, they just raised their fingers and pointed. At him.

He clutched his head in his hands and fell to his knees. It was all too much. "Leave me alone. Get lost, all of you. Just fucking well leave me alone!" But they didn't. Instead they tightened the circle, crowding in on him. Alex could hardly breathe. There were too many to fight, and they were so close together he didn't stand a chance of breaking through.

So he curled up on the floor, let them pile in on him, one on top of the other. Everything went black, the bodies were heavy. Alex made himself as small as he could, but still they pressed up against him, eradicating every fraction of space he had left. With the last bit of breath he had left in his lungs, he shouted: "Leave. Me. *Alone!*"

And they were gone. All the bodies, all the hands had vanished. Replaced by a single pair on his back, arms around him, squeezing him tight. Holding *him*. But it was far from unpleasant; it felt good. He felt safe again.

"You're starting to remember," whispered a voice in his ear.

"You," said Alex, twisting to see the person—the head resting on his shoulder, as he rested on theirs—but they refused to let him. Wouldn't pull away.

"Yes, me."

"Who are you?"

"I don't know. But you do."

"I don't understand."

"Help me to remember," it said.

"Are you me?" asked Alex.

"Help me to—"

"Am I you?"

"Help me. Help me!" The voice cried out, panic-stricken. The embrace tightened, and he was being squeezed so hard he felt his bones might break.

"You're…crushing…me…" he gasped, but they didn't let go. Their efforts intensified, threatening to snap Alex in two. Squirming, he succeeded in jamming one of his arms between him and this human boa constrictor, using it as a lever to push them back. Alex brought up a knee for added support, and they finally lost their grip on him. Separated, Alex and his wrestling partner fell backwards to the floor in opposite directions.

When he looked again, he saw the black figure rising.

"Hello," it said, the word little more than a rumble of thunder. "I've been looking for you."

Alex and the shadow-thing scrutinised each other. Its blue eyes twinkled. So this was the hidden part of himself, this was what he had to face to make the hallucinations go away. This was what he was so frightened of.

"Yes. And now I'm coming. Ready or not. Ready or not."

– ii –

The Infinity's eyes snapped open.

At last he had seen the face of his quarry. It wouldn't be much longer now. The Infinity lay back on the bed in the hotel room and laughed out loud.

No, it wouldn't be much longer at all.

Sixteen

Yazmin's Nightclub, Tuesday Morning

– i –

ONE BLOW, JUST ONE. It wouldn't be the first time. And then a little drive.

Nick Metcalf was thinking how easy it would be to kill him, as he watched Peck dish out the orders. His men were gathering on the dance floor, divided into their groups from the previous day. Peck had already gone through the spiel about where they were to search next. There'd been a change of plan. They weren't looking for a school anymore, they were looking for a "further or higher education establishment." Why didn't he just say university or college, for Christ's sake? Their target could be located there, at one of the matches in or around the Griffield and Kirkwell area.

"This is for definite, is it?" said needle-nosed Hamilton.

"It is," Peck guaranteed. "One of these places fits the bill, so check it against the photocopied drawing that you have. We also have a lead on who we're looking for."

Nick watched as Peck handed out more photocopies, fresh from Yazmin's machine that morning. "This is a sketch of the man we're after, so if you do happen to see him, ring in for instructions. Do not, I repeat, do not approach him on sight."

"Why, what's he gonna do to us?" said Terry, sniggering.

"Nothing, probably. But if you damage him in any way, Mr. Finn *will*."

The men exchanged glances and there were a few muttered swear words.

"You want to take that risk, Frank?" asked Peck, turning to Terry's partner. "Bearing in mind that since the last time you had a run-in with him you've needed to wear Pampers?"

Frank lowered his sunglasses and gave Peck the evil eye. Nick almost nodded for him to get stuck in. But Peck was his. When the time came, and it would, Nick would be the one to settle the score with this tosser.

"Good, so have you all got that straight? You find the location, you call in. You see this person, you call in. You need to take a shit, you call in. Got it?"

A further round of mumbles.

"I said, *got it?*"

The men offered as close to a "yes" as Peck was going to get.

Look at him. Swanning around as if he owns the place. Well, he doesn't. I do! I'm not even in business with him, *I'm in business with his boss. The organ grinder not the fucking monkey.*

"Right then, off you go," said Peck.

Nick hung back until all the men had gathered their things and were heading out before he approached this usurper. Peck was forced to acknowledge his presence when he tapped him on the shoulder.

"Yes, what can I do for you, *Mr.* Metcalf?"

"I won't lie and say that it wouldn't make me very happy if you dropped dead right here on this dance floor." The remark hardly even registered. "But, as I doubt that's going to happen, you can answer me a question, *Mr.* Peck."

"Is it the one about where babies come from?"

Nick took out a cigar and lit it. "No, it's the one about who the fuck your boss really is." He blew a stream of smoke into Peck's face, but the man refused to cough.

Once the smoke cleared, Peck answered, "You know who he is. He's the man who's just given you a small fortune in exchange for the loan of your trained—and I use that word loosely—gorillas." Peck thumbed over towards Frank and Terry, who looked up from the paper they were holding. Now both removed their sunglasses and glared at Peck.

"That might be true, but I still know fuck-all about what this is about."

"And that's the way it has to stay until Mr. Finn decides otherwise."

Nick invaded Peck's space even more. "I don't like you," he said. "I don't like the way you talk to my lads, I don't like the way you lord it about down here. And I *don't* like the way you think you're the one in charge when you're obviously not. I reckon it's about time I had another chat with Mr. Finn and straightened a few things out."

"I'm afraid that's impossible right now. But I speak for him. When you're talking to me, you're talking to him," stated Peck.

Nick prodded him with the two fingers holding the cigar. "I don't think I'm getting through to you, am I? I'm not some jumped-up little toerag, Peck. I'm Nick Fucking Metcalf. My name counts for something around here, and you'd do well to remember that."

Peck looked down at his chest, at Nick's fingers. "I will," he said when his eyes found Nick's again. "I always remember everything."

"Just make sure you do. In the meantime you tell your boss I want to have a pow-wow with him A-S-A-Fucking-P."

"I'll tell him. Now, if you'll excuse us." Peck backed up and walked around Nick, heading for the exits. "Dumb and Dumber?" he called over his shoulder. "I'll be in the car when you're ready."

Terry growled, and Frank stuck up his middle finger.

"Easy, boys," said Nick once Peck was out of earshot. "He'll get his soon enough. It's just a matter of time."

– ii –

"We don't have time for this."

"What do you mean?" Ellen sat down opposite Alex for the fourth time in as many days.

"Something's going to happen soon," he warned. It was the most agitated she'd seen him yet: palms sweaty, eyes red and sore, the colour drained from his face.

"Calm down, Alex."

"You don't understand. I saw it…him…whatever it was."

"Who?"

"You know, the dark thing. It was there again in my dream last night."

"You had another dream?" Ellen jotted something down on her pad. "And you came face-to-face with the figure that's been chasing you?"

"Yes," said Alex. "It wasn't pleasant, believe me."

"I can imagine." Ellen put her jotter down. "So tell me about it."

Alex told her the bare bones of the nightmare, but when he came to describe the shadow-thing he couldn't find the words. "I don't know, it's like I can picture it, but every time I try to focus on it the image becomes blurred. Except for those eyes. But it saw me, that I do know. It saw me and it said it was coming for me."

"Try not to panic. This could be a good thing."

"*Good?*" He couldn't believe what he was hearing.

"It must be down to the fact that you're getting the stories out. You're allowing yourself to see the characters in them, and as a consequence you're starting to see the thing that's been hidden from you all this time."

"The difference is, it can see me now, too!"

"But it could mean a turning point's been reached."

"What if I don't want to reach it?"

"You said that you wanted to know whatever it is that you've been hiding from yourself."

Alex baulked at this. "What about the catatonia, being stuck permanently in my fantasies?"

"There are things in your past I think you *need* to see. In my opinion that's what all this is about, Alex."

"It's just that it all seems so real. And when it starts to spill over into reality—"

"That's when the trouble begins," finished Ellen. "What you've got to try and hold on to is that it's *not* reality, Alex. Your dreams, and to a certain extent these experiences you're having, are a manifestation of your inner demons. There's nobody out there coming for you. No actual monster chasing you."

"I wish I could believe that."

Ellen smiled and tapped him on the knee. "You can. The only monster you have to tackle is the one inside you. God, that sounds dreadful. I didn't mean it that way."

Alex shook his head. "Don't worry, I do get it. But why do I feel like I'm running out of time?"

"If the thing in your dreams is telling you that, then it's scared you're going to uncover something important. But like I said, there really is no hurry."

"I know, I know. I just want this to be over, Ellen."

She gave a nod of understanding. "Then relax and we'll see what we can turn up today."

– iii –

The whole of the year had been leading up to this point.

Even the word "exhibition" was enough to send her into a flap. Now the actual thing was here—all her work displayed on huge red stands in the middle of C-Block's dome, her sketchbooks open at the bottom for people to flick through. She'd spent all last week and most of the weekend choosing the final line-up, finding a nice balance between the photography work she'd done and oil painting projects. There was a good contrast between the two, the black-and-white images of industrial machinery providing a counterpoint to the colourful pictures of life drawing models and portraits of family members. So she'd spent yesterday putting everything up, along with the rest of her group. But she was the only one still working on it today.

Claire Phillips adjusted the corner of one painting, tipping it and standing back so she could check if it was level. She wouldn't be happy until it was absolutely right. Stepping forward again, she returned it to its original position.

"Looks fine."

Claire spun around, blonde hair catching in the top of her dungarees. "Oww!" she said.

"Here," said Vince Oglethorpe, offering to untangle her. He unhooked the catch at her shoulder and freed the hair, then clipped her strap back up again.

"Thanks," said Claire, cheeks flushing.

Vince grinned his cheeky grin. "No problemo." He pointed over at her display. "It really does look fine, Claire. Stop bricking it."

"Easy for you to say, you sailed through your other units. I need a good grade for this if I'm going to get into my first choice uni."

"Chill," said Vince. "You'll get the grade. This stuff's amazing."

Claire's eyes opened wide. "You really think so?"

"Course, wouldn't have said it otherwise. You're really talented."

Her face reddened even more. "Thanks."

"Everyone's meeting up in town later, did you hear?"

Claire nodded.

"So?"

"So?" she repeated.

"Are you coming?" Vince smirked again.

Claire bit her lip. She really wanted to do a bit more work on her exhibition before the tutors came round and awarded marks. But this might be one of the last times she'd see everyone together. She'd worked all year, but she'd worked all year *alongside* them. That was important too.

You know what, Vince is right, it does look fine, she told herself.

"Okay, let me just grab my bag." Claire bundled her tape and stapler inside, then slung the backpack over her shoulder, consciously trying not to tangle her hair up in that, too.

As they walked through the dome towards the exit, Vince said, "Hey, you hear about Webber?"

Claire shook her head. She hadn't seen him around for a while, in fact she'd been a bit worried about him since that dizzy spell in class. She just figured he'd been busy with end of term stuff, like them.

"There's a rumour going round that he's completely flipped."

"What are you talking about?" Claire was looking at Vince and nearly tripped on a piece of carpeting.

"Had some kind of breakdown or something."

Claire punched him on the arm. "That's not funny. I like Alex, he's been really good to us."

Vince rubbed at the wound in mock protest. "I know you *like* him, Claire. Everyone knows that."

"Shut up. You shouldn't spread things like that around."

"What, the nuts thing or the 'you and him' thing?"

She glared at Vince, who held up his hands in surrender. "Look, all I know is what Geena's friend over in printmaking said. Her mum's cousin works at Kirkwell General. Reckons he's been checked into the psychiatric ward."

"Oh my God, really?"

"A year teaching us, wouldn't you be in a cracker factory?" said Vince.

Claire opened one side of the double doors and Vince pushed on the other. "Do you think it's true?"

"Dunno," he told her.

"I hope it isn't. I really like Alex."

"I know, you said." Was there a touch of jealousy there when Vince said that? If so, he'd picked a lousy time to show it. They'd be going their separate ways soon, would probably never see each other again. It was too late to be more than just good friends. Besides, Vince wasn't mature enough for her. She preferred a man who knew who he was, who'd been around a bit longer.

"I hope he's okay," Claire reiterated as they made their way to the gate.

"Yeah," said Vince.

They were both too wound up in their thoughts to notice the car across the road with three men inside. And they were halfway up the road when one of the men took out his mobile and started to talk into it, asking to speak to someone called Peck.

– iv –

"So you're in the rec room with Sam, talking…"

Ellen left Alex to pick up the thread and run with it.

"Ben's telling me what a pool hustler he is."

"That's true," said Ben, standing in the corner. "He's taken me more times than I care to remember."

Ellen smiled, then continued her questioning. "But what happened next? You were suddenly in the desert."

Alex looked like he was sucking on a lime. "There's sand everywhere. It's very hot."

"And Sam?"

"His face, his clothes…they're changing." He went on to describe the transformation.

"What about Ben and Craig?"

"They're changing as well. They're wearing these toga-like outfits, heads covered."

"Alex, where are you?"

"It looks like a market." He closed his eyes and took her through the fruits, vegetables and livestock on sale in the market, going into detail about sights, sounds and smells. "It's some kind of city, sandstone walls, and there's a big temple with pillars not far away. In the distance there are pointed shapes on the dunes."

"Why did you run, Alex?"

"I thought I was in danger."

"You thought Ben and Craig were going to hurt you?"

"They weren't Ben and Craig anymore," he corrected.

"Okay, but was that all?"

Alex considered this, then told her: "No."

"Go on."

"I feel as if something is just out of sight, just out of my line of vision. And it's coming for me. I can't explain it."

"The nightmare thing crossing over again."

"I have to get out of here!" Alex shouted.

Ellen leaned forward in her chair. "Out of the market?"

"Out of here!"

"Easy, Alex."

"Quick, hurry, we have to leave. He mustn't find me!"

"Why, what will happen?"

Alex's eyes flicked open and looked right at her. "Something terrible."

— v —

"So, are we all clear about that then?"

James Nolan took in the faces of his class, their glazed expressions telling him little. He ran a finger under his collar, loosening the tie. Damn, it was hot in here today, the sun streaming in through those massive windows. Unlike some of his fellow tutors he couldn't get away with wearing whatever he liked; it was full dress for him. The subject he taught deserved respect. Which was more than these kids were giving it.

"Come on, you lot, we've covered this a million times. Your exams are almost here, try to summon up a little bit of enthusiasm." But then why should they? They hadn't really bothered the rest of the year, and it wasn't as if this was an exciting subject. It was only history for goodness sakes. *Only* history. "I'll ask again, are we clear about the timeline of the Roman invasion of Britain?"

A few nods, and some pupils nodding off.

"Yes? Starting with Julius Caesar's first raid on southeast England, which was when... Mark Townsend?" James pointed at Mark, something they expressly told him never to do in teacher training. But in this instance it worked because Mark made an effort to rouse himself

"Er...45 BC?"

"Close," said James. "You were only a decade out. "It was 55 BC."

Mark shrugged, as if it was near enough. What was ten years here or there?

James clapped a hand to his head. "What's the matter with you lot today? I've seen more life on cheese that's gone mouldy." A few of the other learners shrugged too, creating a sort of Mexican wave effect. "This is important stuff, not just because you need it to pass your exams. It's what life's all about. You're *living* history right now. In years to come people just like you will be looking back at what we did here today and studying it. Doesn't that make you think, 'wow'?"

Apparently it didn't. The students had heard his "looking back" speech several dozen times and were less impressed with each recital. *The trouble is*, thought James, *most teenagers had no scope to see beyond the next week, month or year.* It was a medical fact. They lived in the here and now, with no conception of the future, and not much thought for the past. But James still tried his best to encourage them, even though he knew most just needed this subject so they could go on to university and study something completely different. It was the lesser of many evils, not quite as boring as English, and not nearly as complicated as Maths. His was a middle ground subject, the pin jabbed in the list with eyes closed.

Looking up at the clock and seeing that it was almost lunch, he had one last shot at it. "Look, you never know when this is going to come in handy. History has a way of repeating itself and if you know the patterns…" That was it, the big hand touched 15 and his students rose as one, packing their study notes into their bags.

They tramped past, a couple thanking him for the revision session but most eager to get out into the gorgeous summer sun, to laze about on the grass and eat their dinners or head into town.

"Good luck, everyone," James called after them, but they were gone before the last word left his lips. He shook his head and gathered his notes together. It wasn't as if he'd had to organise this class for them. They were big enough and ugly enough to sort out their own revision for the exams. And he was beginning to wonder why he had bothered. Perhaps it was more about taking his mind off things than about their grades?

Everyone had their own problems, and for a moment James wished he could swap them, wished history would repeat itself. Exams and zits he could handle.

He grabbed his leather satchel, jacket and helmet, then stepped out of the classroom before locking the door. He'd return the master key to the general office at reception, then go and have some lunch in the staff canteen—on his own. If Alex had been around then—

James caught himself just in time. Alex wasn't around, hadn't been around for nearly two weeks. He cast all thoughts of his friend from his mind, shaking off the mental images of him at home, those wild staring eyes.

He slung the jacket over his arm and held up the key. *Get on with what you're meant to be doing, James*, he told himself.

It wasn't far to the office, yet today the journey took James forever, it seemed. But on approach, the voices he heard through the open door caught his attention. There were two that he could make out, one polite but firm, the other slightly gruffer, older perhaps, though still articulate.

"…looking to speak with this man if possible," said the rougher voice.

James now heard the familiar reply of Joyce, the secretary. "I'm sorry, I don't think—"

"It is extremely important." This was the first voice again.

James questioned whether to interrupt or not, then made his decision—

more out of curiosity than anything. He knocked on the door and entered at the same time. Everyone turned in his direction, Joyce first, then the two men.

He matched voices to the faces instantly. The rougher one obviously belonged to the man with silver hair, leaning on the desk with one hand, holding out a paper with the other. The more refined voice had to belong to the gentleman by his side: younger, average height and weight, wearing an impatient half-smile.

For her part, Joyce looked like his students had done during the lesson. Eyelids struggling to keep open, face slack. *What was wrong with everyone today?*

"Hi, Joyce," said James. "Sorry to interrupt. Just returning my key."

Joyce bobbed her head. It wasn't quite a nod, but it had the potential to become one. "Thanks," she replied sluggishly.

He looked back at the men on the other side of her desk. "Is everything okay?"

The older man stood upright, still brandishing the paper in his hand. When he turned, James could see it was a drawing of a face.

"As I was just saying to this good lady," the second man told him, "we are seeking a certain individual connected with the college."

Joyce was opening and closing her mouth as if her jaw was springloaded.

There were many things about this scene that struck James as odd, not least the way these two people were acting as if it was the most normal thing in the world to walk in here and flash a drawing around like some kind of wanted poster. But the most unusual thing was the likeness on that paper. The older man, now referred to as Mr. Peck, was asked to hold it up for James.

Now his own jaw didn't seem to work properly, either. No matter how hard James tried to shut his mouth, it dropped open straight away.

"Ah…" said the average-sized man, his smile widening. "How fortuitous. Would you care to step outside with us, Mr…" He cocked his head. "…Nolan. I think we have matters to discuss."

Peck turned back to Joyce and was gazing down at her, eyes narrowing.

"Lucas! If you please," snapped the man. Then he told Joyce to go about her business, thanking her for her time.

Peck took James by the arm and escorted him back out into the corridor. The younger man followed, closing the door.

"Do you know where we can find this person?" asked Peck, pushing James up against the wall.

He said nothing, just reached for his mobile which Peck quickly batted away. There was a clattering sound as it smashed against the floor. Looking left and right up the corridor, James willed someone to walk by.

The polite man tutted. "Of course you do. You know him very well, don't you, James." He turned to look at Peck. "We're actually in the wrong building. Our Mr…Webber is based in the Art and Design department. Right up your alley, I'd say, Lucas." Now back to James, fixing him with hard, staring eyes. "But we are in luck today."

The name—Alex's name! James had no idea how this man suddenly knew it, but he had a feeling it was something to do with him, and his proximity to this individual. Just as he had done when he left the classroom, James tried to blot out all thoughts of his friend, except now it was for a completely different reason.

"Don't be shy, James. You have no secrets from me."

The historian tried to struggle, but Peck glued him to the wall. There was a whistling coming from behind, and a man in green overalls emerged from a room not far away. It was Eric Butler, one of the caretaking staff. *That's it now, he's seen you. Look! He'll go and get security and then you'll both be—*

Eric walked past them, offered a mumbled "afternoon" and continued on up the corridor.

"That's what I like to see, a man who knows his own business. And we most definitely know ours, do we not, Lucas?"

Lucas' response was to ram James hard against the wall. He dropped his belongings and let out a huge gasp of air.

"W-What do you want?" he managed.

"An address," said Peck.

"Yes," agreed the other man. "Tell us where we might find Alex Webber…and his lovely wife, Beverly."

– vi –

"But don't you think that it's all down to men and their insecurities?"

"You mean their little…shortcomings?" The woman with no lipstick on laughed herself stupid at this remark, slapping the horseshoe-shaped table in front of her.

"No, hold on. I don't think you can tar them all with the same brush here. There are some men who do try to respond to a woman's needs," said someone else off-camera.

"Most of them don't even know what a woman's needs *are*," argued the first, sat on the very end of the table.

Beverly aimed the remote at the TV and changed channels. A well-groomed newsreader was shuffling his papers, coming to the end of his report. "And finally," he said, "it looks like we might be heading for record temperatures this summer as the heatwave is set to continue into June and even July. Janine Gallagher joins us now from our weather centre to tell us what we can look forward to." Mechanically, he turned left, where there was a gigantic monitor in place. Janine, dressed in a hideously garish yellow outfit, said hello.

"Janine, what's the cause of all this?"

"Derek, I'm afraid it's all down to our old friend the ozone layer again."

Beverly lost interest and flicked over again. An advert for ice cream greeted her, the bikini-clad woman with perfect curves licking the phallic cone suggestively. After a couple of seconds Beverly switched the TV off completely.

What was the point of gawping at that thing anyway, when her mind was still tuned in to last night's station? The hospital drama that had un-folded outside Alex's room. That had to be the most painful thing she'd ever been through. Although hardly any words passed between them, they'd said all they needed to. There was just one thing now he didn't know. Or did he? That look he gave her, had he guessed what might have happened, what might *be* happening behind his back? She hoped not, if only for the sake of his recovery. She didn't want that on her conscience as well.

Beverly had picked up the phone three or four times last night when she got in; the same phone that was now unplugged at the socket, just in case. She'd almost called *him* again, but something stopped her. Perhaps the memory of Alex and the need to give their dead marriage a little bit of grieving time? Last weekend had definitely been a knee-jerk reaction to her husband being admitted. She'd needed to be held, needed an escape route.

But who was there to hold Alex? To love him?

No one. He was all on his own now. All on—

The buzzer startled her and she jumped. Her first thought was that *he'd* decided to come over. She wasn't sure how she felt about that right now. Whether she even wanted him here today. Maybe she should just ignore it and hope they'd go away. But if it was him, he'd see that her car was parked outside. He'd know she was at home.

The buzzer went again. Whoever it was they were persistent. And there was something about the urgency of the buzz that alarmed her.

Beverly went out and looked down over the balcony. She saw two cars she didn't recognise, a black BMW and a convertible with two men sitting in the front—big men wearing sunglasses. They didn't look pleasant.

The buzzer was being ferociously attacked.

Beverly didn't like the look of this. The convertible and its occupants reminded her of the people Steve had associated with in the past. But he'd promised...

She retreated into the apartment, slowly. "Crap," she said under her breath.

The buzzer stopped.

Beverly could feel her heart beating in her chest. She wanted to go to the window again and *make sure* they'd given up, but found she couldn't move. Beverly waited like that for at least five minutes.

They must have gone, surely, she thought. She was just about to move again when she heard a knock at her door, a sharp rap as urgent as the buzzer blitzing.

She jumped again.

"Mrs. Webber," someone shouted. "Please open the door."

Beverly's breathing came in short, sharp bursts.

"We only want to talk to you."

Keep quiet. Just keep quiet and they'll go away again. They don't know for sure you're in here.

"We know you're in there," said the smooth voice, ridding her of that last hope.

"What do you want?" Beverly found herself asking, nerves affecting every syllable.

"We want to talk. That's all."

She didn't believe them. People like that never *just* wanted to talk. They wanted what they were owed, usually. "He's not here. I haven't seen him."

"Who?" came the question through the door.

"Steve."

"My dear, Mrs. Webber, we aren't looking for Steve. We're friends of your husband."

Alex? Now alarm bells really were starting to go off. What connection could Alex possibly have with men like this? Her eyes found the phone, but then she remembered it was disconnected. Her mobile! Beverly re-alised she could actually move again, and did so, sideways, towards her handbag on the chair.

"If you don't go away I'm going to call the police," she warned.

"No," said the voice. "No, you're not."

Her hand was outstretched when the first thud rattled the door. In spite of herself, Beverly let out a small scream. She made a grab for the bag. Two more loud bangs came in quick succession.

She pulled out the mobile and dropped it on the floor. Turning to look where it had landed, she inadvertently kicked it under the couch. *Shit!*

Beverly bent and looked underneath; she could see the end of it, but it was just out of reach. Tongue protruding from the corner of her mouth, she rammed her shoulder up against the edge of the sofa. With her little finger she hooked the phone.

There was another loud crash and the door caved in. Beverly had a hand around the mobile, but then found her arm was stuck. She tried to switch it on as hands clamped down on her neck, hauling her up. She let out a yell as her arm was yanked free.

Beverly was pushed backwards onto the couch, and suddenly there was someone on top of her, virtually straddling her, slapping the phone out of her grasp. She screamed again, so he struck her across the face. "Be quiet."

"Lucas, Lucas," came a voice from behind the man. This was the person who had been talking to her from outside. "You're scaring the poor woman."

Her attacker, Lucas, got up and stood back, allowing her a better view of the other man. Compared with his friend, he seemed harmless enough. Except for those chillingly blue eyes. Beverly wiped her mouth with the back of her hand and saw blood there from her split lip. "You bastard," she spat at Lucas.

In reply the man did what could only be described as a reasonable Robert De Niro impression, tilting his head, half grinning, half nodding, as if to say: "What's your point?"

"Allow me to introduce myself, Beverly," said the less brutal one. "Some call me Finn. And Lucas, I believe you have already met."

"What do you want?"

"If I told you, it might just blow your mind," was his reply. "For now, I would gladly settle for a quick chat with your husband. I trust he is not at home?"

Beverly glared at him. "What do you want Alex for? Is it something Steve's—"

"Steve? *Ah!* I see what you mean and why you might think that. But no, it is between Alex and myself." He leaned in, resting his hand on the back of the couch. His face was all she could see.

"I-I don't know where he is right now," said Beverly, the loudness of her speech dropping with each word. "I could pass on a message."

Finn laughed softly. "I'm afraid that just won't do." He looked directly at her, so hard she didn't dare blink; he frowned, concentrating, then shook his head. "Why are you protecting him, Beverly?"

She considered this for a moment. "He…he's my husband."

"Oh? I see. Such loyalty would be touching if I didn't know the truth about you—that much you can't hide, the guilt is oozing from you. If I didn't know that you were such a whore, Beverly. And with Alex's—"

"Shut up. You don't know a thing."

But she searched those cold eyes and realised that he did. This Finn knew everything about her sordid romps, could describe every moan, every grunt, every thrust. She saw it now through the eyes of this stranger, saw it not as the fairy tale she'd dreamt about but as the desperate and pathetic coupling of two sweaty bodies, writhing and clinging to each other in an effort to experience pure joy. But what was worse, she saw it through the eyes of Alex: her husband. Saw the tears as he found out about what she'd done, and her trying to explain it away. And all this man could do was laugh.

He was the true monster. But there would be no knight to rescue her now.

"Tell me what I need to know, Beverly. Tell me where he is."

She groaned. It had taken this creature to show her what she'd done, how much damage she was about to cause. How much of a betrayal she'd committed. Beverly wasn't about to betray Alex again.

"Tell me."

"No!" she said, simply and with real strength this time.

Finn hung over her, as if deliberating. As if wondering whether to just plunge his hands into her head, scoop out the contents, then sort through them later. But he didn't have time for that, and somehow she knew it.

"Lucas," he said, turning to his companion. "Bring your equipment. I think it might be time to practise your art."

SEVENTEEN

Kirkwell General

– **i** –

IT WAS ALWAYS THE SAME.

Alex would lock down tight as soon as he got anywhere near the source of his trouble. When it came to describing this thing chasing him, he'd start to get agitated or upset. There was no doubt they were on the right track, and what she'd said was true, there was no rush. But Ellen had to admit as they carried on the therapy into the afternoon, that his impatience—his insistence about there being a time limit—was starting to rub off. She began to feel that same sense of urgency.

Which was why she'd decided to have one last try at getting this out of him.

Ellen asked Ben to wait outside, which he reluctantly did. "You can see everything if I need any help," she reassured him.

Once that was done, she sat down beside Alex, notepad and recorder on her lap. "Right, I want you to relax first of all," she started. "And I want you visualise the dream you had last night. Picture it in your mind's eye, take me there."

Alex looked unsure. "I…"

"Nothing's going to hurt you." She took his hand. "I promise."

He nodded and closed his eyes.

"Are you there?"

"Yes."

"Tell me what you can see."

He told her about the ghost images, faces drifting in and out of focus. Alex began to squirm. "They're all crowding in on me. I—"

"No they're not. You can make them stop. It's *your* visualisation." She waited a second or two while he settled down again. "Are you all right?"

"Yes, yes I feel safe."

"Now I want you to look around for this shadow creature you encountered last night."

His breathing quickened. "No, I don't—"

"Listen to me, Alex. If you want to control this fear you have face it again, on your terms."

"I'm scared," he told her in a quiet voice.

"I know you are, but I'm right here." She squeezed his hand. "Can you feel it in there with you?"

"Yes."

"Then you have to go to it."

"I don't. It's coming to me."

"Good, that's good Alex."

"No, trust me. It's not."

"Just hang in there a little longer. I want you to look right at this thing, just like you did last night."

"I can't!"

"Yes you can. It's okay."

"Oh God, its eyes! Those blue eyes!"

Ellen placed her other hand on top of his.

Alex showed his teeth, but said nothing.

"Calm down. It can't do anything to you."

Alex began to shiver.

"Just remember that, it can't physically harm you." *Only mentally.*

"He's coming," said Alex. "Oh sweet Jesus, he's coming." He was crying now.

"Who is he, Alex? Describe him to me."

He was shaking so hard she could feel the trembling up her arm.

"Look at him, and tell me. Look—"

"He's coming!" Alex opened his eyes again, pulled his hand free and gripped her by the wrists. The recorder and notepad almost fell. "Listen to me, we have to get out of here! He's coming, and he's coming right now!"

– ii –

The vehicles pulled into the car park, one after the other, as soon as the gate barring their way had been disabled.

They didn't bother looking for the correct spaces, just parked wherever they pleased. The convertible's doors were the first to open. Terry Gilligan and Frank Austin let their passengers out. They both gave Peck's boss a wide birth as he stood upright and smoothed down his suit. He clicked his fingers. Peck handed him the bunch of flowers they'd bought on the way over. The Infinity took a deep breath and smelt the blooms.

"Beautiful," he pronounced. "Visiting hour is upon us, gentlemen."

He walked across the grass, and Peck waved for Terry and Frank to join them. They pulled a face, but did as he requested, three more of Metcalf's men tagging along. The rest were to wait here and keep their eyes open for the man in the photocopies.

Lucas hurried to catch up with The Infinity.

"Can you sense him yet?"

"I have been able to sense him for some time. I just haven't been able to locate him. One of life's little irritations."

"But he *is* here?"

"You think Mrs. Webber might have been lying?"

Peck had a distant look in his eye for a few seconds, recalling the events back in the flat. "I doubt it."

"Then have some faith, Lucas. Have some faith."

– iii –

The main reception was busy; there was even a queue to join the queues waiting for information.

Two people, a man and a woman, sat behind a glass partition doling out advice to the sick and friends of the same.

"All we need to know is where the psychiatric department is," said Lucas.

Terry took this as a hint to stop a dark-haired nurse in her tracks. "S'cuse me, love, but where's the…"

"Psychiatric," prompted Frank.

"…Psychiatric place?"

She gave him a complex list of instructions—lefts, rights, ups and downs—that Terry didn't have a hope of following, but he thanked her all the same with: "Cheers."

"I hope someone was listening to that," he said.

Lucas nodded. The group moved further into the hospital, passing through a white corridor with paintings by a local artist on the walls. The style was somewhat crude, but the colours were vibrant and Lucas paused briefly to admire the pieces for what they were: attempts to cheer people up. Frank shuddered as they walked past a picture of a clown, its bleached white face, red nose and mouth leering at him from behind the glass.

The Infinity turned and laughed.

They were given some strange glances as they negotiated their way through the hospital, but nobody stopped them to ask what they were doing or where they were going. One look at Terry and Frank was enough to dissuade anyone. At the lifts they discovered there wasn't enough room for all of them to fit in at once, especially the largest members of the group, so they took turns. Lucas and The Infinity travelled up with an ancient-looking woman in a floral dress, accompanied by a man in jeans and a T-shirt.

The woman studied The Infinity. He offered her a civilised tip of the head in return.

It wasn't until they were two floors up that she finally spoke. "I can see you," she said.

The Infinity touched his chest.

"Yes, you."

"Then there can't be much wrong with your eyes," The Infinity replied.

"The scales have been lifted from them."

The young man, embarrassed by her outburst, explained that his gran had been to have her cataracts removed last Christmas and she was here for a check-up. "She gets confused sometimes, though," he said. "The first stages of…you know."

"I quite understand," said The Infinity

"I am *not* confused," she insisted. "I can see him clearly enough."

"And what exactly *can* you see?" The Infinity asked.

"Death."

"Really?"

"Death and destruction."

"Is that a fact?"

The young man apologised again. "She gets like this from time to time. Say sorry to the nice man." His tone was so patronising, like he was talking to a child who'd misbehaved.

"I will not!" She beckoned The Infinity closer with one crooked finger. "I know who you are."

He stooped so that he was looking directly into her cataract-free eyes. "I doubt it. But I," he whispered so that only she could hear him, "know who you are, Norma Higgins. You will not leave this hospital alive."

She shut up then, until the doors opened for her floor and, hobbling out, she rounded on him. "You'll pay for all you've done. You see if you don't."

"Gran!" snapped the lad, genuinely shocked by this remark, then repeated his apologies as the doors closed again.

Lucas looked at his master, checking for signs of irritation. He found none. The Infinity was smiling to himself, holding the flowers still tighter in his hands.

– iv –

"I don't know what comes over you sometimes," said Dolan Higgins, guiding his elderly grandmother by the arm. "What would grandpa have said, eh?"

Norma barely reacted to the mention of her late husband. "Are we going to the matinée now?"

"Yes, if you like, Gran." He shook his head and walked her down the corridor towards the sign that read: OPTHALMICS.

"We can call and pick up Sal and Harry as well."

"That's right." He had no idea what she was going on about now. One minute she was spitting fire and brimstone, the next she was planning to go to the flicks. He hated when it was his turn to take Gran anywhere. The last time they were out shopping he'd had to stop her from undressing in the middle of Marks and Spencer's.

"Come on, we've just got to go and see the doctor first and get those eyes looked at. Make sure you can see properly."

"But I can see. I see plain enough."

That's right, you could see that guy back there couldn't you? Could see him well enough to make a complete nuisance of yourself. Dolan caught himself. It wasn't his Gran's fault she was going loopy. He could remember when she used to take him shopping for stuff when he was small, and if his mum and dad were to be believed, there were one or two incidents of him taking his shorts down in stores just for the hell of it too.

"I can see. I can—" Norma Higgins suddenly stopped, refusing to budge. Dolan pulled on her arm, but couldn't get her to shift.

"Come on, Gran, we're going to be late." Dolan looked back at the old woman and he stopped too. What he saw stunned him into silence.

Norma Higgins was crying. But these were no ordinary tears. They were thick and viscous, tracking down her cheeks slowly like fat, bloated slugs. They were red—a deep, almost ruby colour. Just like her eyes had turned.

She brought her hands up to her face, touching the liquid. Norma was shaking violently, and would have collapsed had Dolan not snapped out of his stupor to catch her. He could hardly see the whites anymore in those eyes, nor any colour at all bar one. It was as though the cataracts had returned, but instead of clouding the pupils with a milky film they'd turned the orbs the colour of rotten tomatoes.

"Help!" shouted Dolan, finding his voice again. "Somebody help us!" It was a hospital for goodness sakes, not far from the eye department. Surely there was someone around who could stop his Gran's eyes from bleeding like this.

But even as the medical staff rushed to answer his appeal, Dolan knew that it was far too late.

And soon his Gran would be long past seeing anything at all.

– v –

"All right, all right, best of five."

Sam brushed the hair out of his eyes and waited for an answer. The bearded patient he knew only as Wynn—a misnomer if ever he'd heard one—slammed his cue down in defeat. "I've had enough. It's all that hopping about you do!"

"Hey, I can't help that," Sam argued.

"I reckon you do it on purpose."

"Oh, come on, where's your competitive spirit?" Sam was reaching for the triangle and dropping the hard, colourful balls inside it. He began to count them, touching the tops over and over. Even if Wynn didn't want another rematch, he'd be happy enough to play by himself. Hardly anyone wanted to play him more than once or twice anyway.

He wondered when that new guy Alex would be back. Might be a while, going by his behaviour. Ellen would have her work cut out for her there. But when he was up to it, maybe he'd feel like a few frames. Might even prove a challenge, unlike the rest. All that hopping… Just Wynn's excuse because he was crap at judging the angles.

Speaking of which, where was he going now? Sam looked up and saw Wynn was nosing out through the rec room window, face against the glass. One or two others from that end of the room had joined him.

Then the figures walked past. Sam stopped counting the pool balls.

"Who're these guys?" asked one of the patients.

"They look like something out of a Cagney flick," said Wynn.

Sam joined his friends at the glass. The seven men were walking down the corridor with purpose. Two were the size of small mountains. Three more kept to the back, like wingmen in a flying formation. But it was the two at the front who really caught Sam's attention: the man with the steely glint in his eye and the other carrying flowers.

They marched past the rec centre, barely noticing the patients inside. However, the man with the flowers did throw Sam a fleeting look, the time it takes just to turn your head then back again. Those blue eyes made the hairs on the back of his neck prickle. He started hopping from foot to foot.

"Now who do you suppose *they've* come to see?" asked Wynn.

Sam didn't have a clue, but he did know one thing; he wouldn't like to be in their shoes.

– vi –

"They're coming. Listen to me, we have to get out!"

Alex's expression was stern, his hands gripping Ellen's wrists. She looked for Ben through the circular window in the door, but he wasn't there.

"Alex, let go."

"You don't understand. We're all in danger," he insisted.

"What are you talking about?"

"Oh God, please listen to me! He's coming."

"Calm down. It's okay, really."

Alex shook his head violently. "No, there's no more time. No time."

"We have all the time in the world."

"*No!*" This was a frustrated scream.

"That's enough!" Ellen broke free and grabbed his arms.

"Have to... Have to..."

Ellen shook him. "Snap out of it, Alex."

"Have to—"

"What?"

"Break...break the cir..."

"What did you just say?"

"Break the circ—"

The last word was cut off forever, replaced by the sound of mayhem outside in the corridor.

Then, despite the fact that it was a word Ellen Hayward hated to use, everything turned crazy.

Ben was gone.

He'd disappeared, abandoning his post at the door. There was shouting coming from outside, and she heard a scream. Ellen let Alex go. He was oblivious, mumbling something she couldn't hear.

Ellen placed the recorder and pad on the bed. Getting up, she made for the door and poked her head out. The psychiatrist couldn't quite grasp what she was seeing. Down the far end of the hall was a gang of men, entering wards, kicking in doors and looking inside rooms. Several of her patients were also in the corridor, wandering backwards and forwards as if they didn't know what to do. But they all had one thing in common, they were terrified. Ben, she could see now, was not that far away, bellowing something into the intercom on the wall.

"Ben," she called out. "What in heaven's name is going on?"

He gestured for her to go inside, before racing up the corridor. She stepped back slightly, but continued to watch as the large nurse reached the men. Ellen caught only a snippet of the conversation.

Ben shouted something like: "Just what do you think you're doing?"

One of the two men at the front answered, the one not carrying flowers. He said something about the receptionist not being very helpful and taking a look around themselves. How on earth they'd gotten through the doors was anyone's guess…

She thought she heard Ben mention the police, but this didn't seem to deter any of them. In fact, that same man told him to stand aside.

Ben refused.

The man made a move to shove him out of the way, but Ben grabbed his arm and spun him around, trying to force it up his back. It was a typical restraint manoeuvre, one Ellen had seen a million times. She'd never seen anyone get out of it—until now. Faster than she had time to draw breath, the man countered Ben's spin and now had hold of the nurse's arm. He pulled it up and sideways. Ellen winced at the loud cracking of bones. Ben let out a howl of agony as his attacker pushed him to the floor.

"Good God!" said Ellen.

The men continued to search rooms and knock down doors, but something told her they wouldn't find what they were looking for in any of them.

It was then that he saw her, the one carrying the bouquet. The man with the blue eyes.

She could hardly tear her gaze away.

"They're coming. Listen to me, we have to get out! "

So penetrating, somehow searching, knowing.

"Oh God, please listen to me! He's coming."

And suddenly it was all so clear.

"We're all in danger."

The danger all too real.

More nurses were appearing behind the group, and security staff as well. The man with the flowers broke away from the pack. He started to walk towards the room.

Alex was right, there was no more time. No time to think about the whys or wherefores, no time for questions or any hope of answers. There was only one thing she could do now.

Get Alex Webber out of there.

– viii –

He was back in the room, still on the bed, eyes half closed, almost catatonic.

"Alex, we've got to go," she said quickly, echoing his own words from earlier.

He didn't reply.

Ellen picked up the digital recorder and notebook, stuffing them into her pockets, then pulled him into an upright position. With one of his arms slung over her shoulder she walked him outside.

"Come on." Ellen hauled Alex into the corridor. She almost pitched them both forwards when she saw the blue-eyed man there, metres between them.

"I've come a long way," he said, running his tongue over his bottom lip. The sight made her feel nauseous. "And I've been waiting such a long time for this moment."

Ellen tucked Alex behind her. Over the man's shoulder she could see a fight raging between hospital staff and his men.

"Look, I've even brought flowers." He proffered the spray as if expecting her to take it. When she refused, he cast them casually aside.

"Who are you?"

"You'll find out soon enough. But first." He pointed behind her with one finger. "Mr. Alex Webber, I presume."

Ellen backed up, forcing Alex to do the same.

He wagged his finger. "No. You're not going anywh—"

One of the security men broke through the ranks and hurtled headlong into the man with blue eyes, knocking him to his knees. It was totally unexpected. If he hadn't been concentrating so hard on them, there was no way he would have gone down at all.

This was their chance. "Alex, time to go!"

She ran up the corridor with her patient, away from their pursuer, towards the set of double doors that needed a security code to gain entrance. Ellen punched in the numbers and dragged Alex through.

There was a roar of anger from behind. Ellen ignored it and dragged Alex to a set of stairs. She listened for the sound of footsteps following, but there were none.

Let them try and find us now, she thought, now that she had the run of the place. She knew this part of the hospital better than she knew her own home. She should do, she spent a lot more time here. They'd find somewhere to hide and wait for the police to arrive. It sounded like a plan, and the best she could come up with on such short notice.

"Alex," said Ellen as she helped him down the steps, "what have you got us both into?"

– ix –

The Infinity stood.

The cry he had just let out had been painful to hear. But not as painful as his revenge on the security man. He tried to crawl away, using his elbows to propel himself, but The Infinity had him by the ankle. There was by no means the time to go to town on this specimen, but some sort of punishment was definitely in order. And by the time he'd thought of what to do, it was already done.

He twisted the guard around, then located the man's most dreaded fear. It was nothing spectacular, simply that of drowning—the consequence of once falling into a lake when he was young. For long minutes he'd thought that was it, thought the weeds below him were dragging him down. Although he was a strong swimmer, it had taken him far too long to surface, and even longer to recover. He'd puked his guts up on the banking, that first taste of air the sweetest thing he'd ever experienced.

Sweeter than the taste in his mouth now, of dirty water with things moving around in it. The man felt a rumbling in his stomach, a swelling. He was finding it hard to breathe as his lungs suddenly filled up with fluid. He twitched and gagged beneath The Infinity, flailing hands everywhere at once, hoping the man would throw him a lifeline. Not a chance. The Infinity dissolved his internal organs one by one, melted his bones so that they could no longer support his body. At the same time the guard was blowing up like a balloon filled with helium, bigger and bigger. His skin now just a membrane containing gallons of runny juices. The Infinity left his head alone so that he could witness his own body flop and bounce, so the guard could see exactly what was happening to him as the lack of air turned his cheeks pink, then beetroot.

His clothes split like the Incredible Hulk's, arms and legs no longer recognisable, receding back into the blimp of a body he now possessed. Wider and wider, fuller and fuller until the inevitable happened.

The popping sound wasn't as loud as The Infinity had hoped, but there was a satisfying squelch as the man exploded, splattering the walls with gore. The other guards, nurses and Metcalf's men had seen this too, breaking off from their fight to take it in. None of them had been able to look away as this poor thing struggled in the last throes of death, coating the floor with its own matter.

Nobody uttered a word. What was there to say? The medical staff turned and fled, hoping that at some point all of this would fade from their memories. And indeed it would; in time it would be like it had never even happened.

Peck came over, almost skidding on the slippery surface. He was about to ask where the woman and Webber had gone, but knew better.

"They won't get away," he assured The Infinity.

"No, they won't."

"We'll find them."

"Yes, you will."

Peck called for their men, explaining that they had another search on their hands. The people they were looking for had escaped and they were not to leave this building, otherwise—

He nodded at the mess they were standing in.

He didn't need to say any more.

— x —

It was the one place she knew she could retreat to in times of crisis, the one place that would allow her to think.

Ellen sat Alex down on the bed in the basement of G-Wing. Her first instinct was to ring for the police, but she'd left her mobile back in the office. She very rarely took it on the wards with her; it would only end up switched off. Someone would have contacted the authorities, though. She hoped. Definitely, after that display.

Her mind was reeling. She'd seen acts of violence on the wards, of course she had, but it was usually to do with the patients—not visitors... or intruders. And why Alex? What could they want with him? Ellen re-minded herself that she knew very little about this man, apart from what he'd told her. Who knew what kind of messes he was mixed up in? He appeared respectable enough, but that didn't mean a thing. People were capable of lies, as she knew all too well.

So why did she protect him? *Because he's my patient,* was the immedi-ate answer. But she'd left a whole ward full of those upstairs, crying and screaming. *The nurses and security men would protect them.* Would they? She'd seen what that older man had done to Ben.

They weren't after them. Just Alex, only Alex.

This had to be the reason Alex was blocking out his memories. She'd as-sumed that the mysterious figure was another element of his subconscious, a part of him even. But he was real. He was here, right now, in *her* hospital.

And just how do you explain the way he made you feel upstairs, Ellen? How you felt as if he was inside your head, poking around and asking too many questions. Those damned blue eyes of his burning holes into your brain.

That was just brought on by fear, by adrenalin, by—

Are you sure? Are you quite sure?

Alex moaned, opening his eyes. "Where…?"

"Where are we?" she said. "Somewhere safe, for now I think."

"What just happened?" he asked.

"I wish to God I knew. But I have a funny feeling you do," Ellen answered.

EIGHTEEN

– i –

"FIRST THINGS FIRST, ALEX… WHO ARE THOSE PEOPLE?"

He responded with a pained expression.

"Those men upstairs, terrorising my patients, beating up my nurses."

"It's all a bit…fuzzy," Alex told her.

"How did you know they were coming?" she asked, struggling to keep her voice even. "How did you know *he* was coming?"

"Who?"

"Now's not the time to be playing dumb. Yes, I can believe you've repressed a lot of things, but this is serious."

"I told you, it's all a blur. I don't know."

"They… He was here for *you*."

A look of terror replaced the confusion. "The thing from my dream."

"Not a thing; a man. Someone you know. Someone who knows you! If there's anything you want to tell me, you should do it right now before the police arrive."

"What? I don't know anything about this, Ellen. I don't know who those people are."

"Don't you?" She didn't believe a word of it.

"No…Wait a second. Oh, no. He told me he was going straight. Said he was staying away from all this stuff."

"Who did?"

"Steve. He's my—"

"Your brother, I know." Ellen folded her arms. "What's this got to do with him?"

"He…"Alex groped around for the words. "He's been in jail. He was mixed up with some nasty people at one time."

"*What?*" she cried.

"He came to see me, to try and make up I think. But he promised he was out of all that business. He said—"

"Let me get this straight, this could all be because of your brother?"

"I don't know."

She fixed him with a barrister's stare. "And when did you see him last?"

"On my birthday."

Ellen threw her arms up in the air. "The day you started having your lapses! And you didn't make the connection?" She sighed. "What was he inside for?"

Alex fell silent.

"Tell me."

"Intimidation. Look, it's not what it sounds like…"

"I'm sure it isn't!"

"He told me he was going straight. I believed him." He bowed his head.

"Perhaps someone forgot to tell his friends, Alex," she lifted his chin and looked him in the eye again. "I want you to be honest with me here, have you ever been involved with any of his dealings?"

"Christ, no! What do you take me for?"

She didn't answer him. "No incidents involving Steve, nothing ever happened in the past?"

Alex blew out a puff of air and with it came an admission. "Okay, he's crashed at our place before, and we've lent him money. Once a couple of…well, I guess you'd call them thugs, even came round the house looking for him after he'd gone. But they left when I told them Steve had moved on."

"Dammit, Alex!" He flinched at this, had never heard her raise her voice before. "You didn't think any of this was worth mentioning to me in our sessions?"

"No, I—"

"This has to be linked with your brother somehow, and the guy currently tearing my psychiatric ward to pieces. I'd stake my reputation on it."

But that still doesn't explain how he knew exactly when this guy was coming, said that little voice of doubt in her head.

"This is…" She flopped back on the bed. "I just can't take this in."

"I'm really sorry," said Alex. "It's all my fault."

"Yes." Ellen sat up. "I'd say it is. But it doesn't help my patients, does it? It doesn't help Ben. Why aren't the police here yet?"

"Maybe they are," he offered. "How would we know?"

"Maybe." *You think the police are going to get you out of this?* Her mind flashed back to the man with the blue eyes, the way he'd looked at her, the way she'd felt his "fingers" inside her skull.

"There's something you're not telling *me*, isn't there?" Alex inched forward on the bed.

A solitary shake of the head was her reply.

"There is, I can see it. Tell me."

"It's nothing."

"So tell me."

Ellen moved to get up again. "I'm going to have a look at the car park."

"Ellen?"

"Back in a sec."

Alex watched her walk away from him, out through the basement door. He was the cause of all this trouble—however indirectly—and now he'd dragged Ellen into it. What's more, he felt like he'd let her down, that some of the trust that had built up between them was now lost.

And that made him feel a hundred times worse.

– ii –

"Nothing."

Lucas mopped his brow with his handkerchief. "I don't want to hear that."

"It's a big hospital," said Hamilton.

Can't you just sniff them out with that huge fucking nose of yours? I mean, for Fuck's sake, look at the size of that thing! "They have to be around somewhere."

"If they are, they're hiding, and they're very good at it. We've checked the floors directly below and there's no sign of a bloke like the one in the picture."

"What about the woman?" Peck knew there was no point in asking this. None of them, apart from The Infinity, had got a good look at her.

"They may have split up," was Hamilton's unhelpful answer.

Lucas had considered this, but thought it unlikely. If she was Webber's doctor he doubted she'd leave him. Doctors had to sign an oath or something, didn't they? "They'll be together."

Hamilton shifted about impatiently.

"What is it?" asked Lucas.

"Er…the lads and I are a bit—"

"Yes?"

"What with all that's happened, won't be long before the old bill are here. Then we'll all be going down."

"You leave that to Mr. Finn and myself," said Lucas. "We'll handle the consequences of our little ruckus."

Hamilton didn't look convinced.

"Anyway, who got hurt but some wackos and a few nurses."

Hamilton opened his mouth. He was about to bring up the security guard's demise, Lucas could tell, but decided not to. It was as if to speak about the incident would make it real, would bring back images of something both of them knew couldn't actually have happened. But if that was the case, why did Hamilton look like he thought the same might happen to him?

"The only thing that matters now is finding the man and woman, do you understand?"

"Course."

"Gather the men and widen the search. I want you to check every inch of this place. I don't care if it takes all week." Lucas' phone went off and he answered it. He nodded sombrely, then said he would inform Mr. Finn. As he brought up the number, Lucas waved Hamilton off. "So, get on with it!"

"What if we have any more trouble?" asked Hamilton.

"You're professionals," replied Lucas Peck. "Or supposed to be. Deal with it."

He waited until Hamilton had left before talking into the receiver. "You should look out of the nearest window at the car park. I think we have a situation on our hands."

– iii –

Kirkwell General was no stranger to vehicles adorned with chequered patterns, boasting blue flashing lights and sirens that sounded like a cat's mating call. But today the vehicles weren't carrying the sick and injured, they weren't being driven by men or women in green jumpsuits who would spring out of the back with stretchers pumping oxygen into their passengers.

Today they were filled with men and women wearing navy blue, with peaked caps and walkie-talkies. Also, the lead car wasn't chequered, it was dark green—and it didn't have any blue flashing lights on its roof. But it so obviously belonged with the rest of them, and the two plain-clothes detectives who jumped out when it screeched to a halt were easily identifiable as well. It may have been their air of authority, or the fact they'd tried so hard—too hard—*not* to look as if they were policemen. Or it could have been the way they zoomed in on the other cars parked where they shouldn't have been, and the dodgy-looking men milling around not far away.

Detective Constables Collins and O'Shea had been working together for almost a year and got on well. They usually saw eye to eye and were gradually rising in the ranks, meaning that promotions could be in store soon upon passing their sergeant's exams. When this happened they'd probably be rotated out of the area to other police forces, split up so that other divisions could benefit from their talents. It would be a sad but proud day for both of them. The highlight of their careers so far was the foiling of a DVD piracy ring, the haul from which amounted to about seventy grand's worth of films on the open market. They'd received a commendation and the perk of being able to sneak the films home and watch them. The fact that they'd stopped the money falling into the hands of organised crime syndicates was an added bonus.

They'd only just got back from their lunch break when this shout had come in. Sounded like more than just your average upset, so they'd decided to bring two units along to check it out. It had been reported that several men had threatened and injured members of staff, specifically in the psychiatric ward. The hospital's limited security had tried to deal with them and failed. That's when the flag had gone up. It was interesting, and if anything heavy did go down they'd be the first CID officers on the scene. They might even make it onto regional news if they were lucky.

He didn't have to say anything, Collins clearly shared his colleague's opinion. The men near those illegally parked cars had something to do with it. They might be responsible for the aggravation—in which case they were extremely stupid for hanging around—or they might be waiting for those responsible. That meant they were loyal, but equally as stupid.

The pair waited for a few uniforms to join them, then walked over to the cars.

"You gentlemen know anything about a disturbance?" O'Shea called out.

The men, who looked like they'd gathered for a mini-gangster reunion, traded looks and scratched their heads.

"Some friends of yours causing trouble inside?" asked Collins.

Again they looked perplexed.

"Okay. Jameson, Phelps and Tucker stay here and keep an eye on these guys—we're heading insi—"

"Might I be of assistance?"

Collins and O'Shea hadn't noticed the man, hadn't heard him creep up on them either; yet here he was. This one was trickier. He didn't really have the air of a criminal about him, certainly not a petty one. And he was dressed as if he could either be this gang's boss, or the officer's chief back at the station.

"I don't know," said O'Shea. "*Might* you?"

The man smiled broadly. "I think I might."

"We've had reports of a—"

"A disturbance. Yes, I heard. An unfortunate incident, but it's all under control."

Collins sucked on his bottom lip, one of his bad habits from childhood and one of the reasons why he was still single at twenty-nine. "In what way, 'under control'?" he said at last.

"Dealt with. It was just a silly scuffle really. No need for you to waste your time, not when there are so many real crimes to be considered."

"What do you mean?" said O'Shea.

The man clasped his hands behind his back. "You boys didn't hear it from me, but the Fordham brothers are planning to hit the jewellers on Vanity Street in Griffield later today. Now, I know it's not exactly your patch, but…"

Collins was sucking on his bottom lip again.

O'Shea was tempted to join him. "How exactly did you receive this information, sir?"

"I have my sources," said the man. "So it's up to you. You can either spend the rest of the day here, looking into something so trifling you'll wonder why you were even called out in the first place. Or…"

"Or we can head off to Griffield following this juicy tip-off and end up on the front pages of this week's locals." O'Shea spouted the words like someone reading from an autocue.

Collins stopped sucking, and his bottom lip flopped out of his mouth like a slug.

"You've still got time, but only if you hurry," said the man.

Collins and O'Shea didn't need to discuss it. They began ordering their PCs back to the squad cars.

"Thank you," shouted O'Shea over his shoulder. "If only there were more vigilant people like you about."

"I try my best," said the man.

Then as quickly as they'd arrived, the police cars vanished.

And when Metcalf's men turned back to ask how Mr. Finn had just done that, they found that he had disappeared as well.

– iv –

Now that *was* weird.

Ellen Hayward pulled back from the door that connected the basement in G-Wing to the car park. Like so much she'd seen today, she didn't have any kind of explanation for what had just played out. She'd seen it clearly enough, that wasn't the problem, and although she couldn't hear what was being said, she'd recognised the look of gratitude on the faces of those two policemen as they left.

A few words with the flower man and off they'd trotted. Couldn't they see he was dangerous, didn't they know what he and his men had done up in the psychiatric department?

They should have at least gone inside and had a look around, then they would have seen for themselves.

Although she tried not to, her thoughts returned to the man and what he'd done to her. The way he'd looked at her, causing thoughts to surface that she'd buried deep down inside. The way he'd been looking for information about who she was, what she knew and about Alex. Always Alex.

What if he's done something to the police?

Ellen shook her head. No, impossible. *But look at what you can do to people, you get them to remember things with a few words.*

Not against their will, she reminded herself. Plus she couldn't do it to dozens of people all at once, and so quickly. It was as if this man was using some sort of mass hypnosis.

But that wasn't really the point. The question remained, what were they meant to do now? She'd been relying on the police to come and sort things out. But they were on their own again.

And they couldn't hide forever.

— v —

"I have to get out of here."

"If we sit tight and wait, maybe—"

"Maybe nothing. They're going to go through this place from top to bottom until they find us. He won't give up."

Ellen hated to admit it, but Alex was right. These weren't the kind of people who simply shrugged and said *c'est la vie.*

"This is ridiculous," she said. *Oh yes, more ridiculous than being able to turn back police cars with a few words? More ridiculous than a man—a patient—turning your whole life upside down within the space of a few days?*

"I have to go. I have to try and warn Beverly."

He had a point there. If these people were after Steve's family, then Alex's wife could be in danger too. "How do you propose to do that with the rest of his men out there standing guard in the car park? It's not like they're just going to let us—"

"Us?"

"I said I'd see this through, Alex, and that's what I'm going to do." Ellen wasn't sure whether she was trying to convince him or herself.

"I can't let you do that. It's me they're after and I've put you in enough danger as it is."

"You don't have a choice. We're going to figure this thing out, together."

"I'm your patient, right?"

She hesitated slightly before answering. "That's right. And I've got to at least try to report this to someone."

"So, any ideas?" he asked her.

Ellen looked around the room as if waiting for inspiration to strike. Her eyes settled on the lockers at the back. She walked over to them and opened up a door.

"What are you doing?" asked Alex.

"What people usually do in situations like these."

"What's that?"

"Something so stupid it might just work." Ellen took out a white coat. "If we can't sneak by without being seen, then we're just going to have to walk straight past them."

Alex raised his eyebrows. "I'm not so sure that's a good idea. Besides, that coat's way too big for you."

"But not for you." She tossed it over to him. "I've never worn one of those in my life, and don't intend to start now. For a little while at least, Alex, you're going to be the doctor and I'll have to be the patient."

– vi –

Alex took one last look outside before placing his glasses in his pocket. "So, you've never acted before?"

"Never," said Ellen. "You?"

Alex thought about the times he'd had to fool people that everything was okay between him and Beverly, how he'd tried to hide it when he was seeing the things he'd seen. "Not officially, but I get the general gist. And I've seen enough movies, I guess. How do I look?"

With his hair flattened with water, and no glasses, Alex looked completely different. And he'd changed not only into the white coat, but other clothes that belonged to the man he'd borrowed it from: spare shirt and trousers, pair of black trainers. From a distance, they might just get away with this. "You look…like a patient pretending to be a doctor," she offered.

He groaned. "Thanks. So which car's yours? You're going to have to point me in the general direction because I'm blind as a bat."

"You can't really miss it," Ellen informed him. "It's a Freelander."

Alex began to laugh.

"What's so funny?"

"Nothing," he said shaking his head. *I just hope you left enough room to open the doors in a hurry, that's all.* "You ready for this?"

"Are you?"

"It was your idea." But before she could say anything in retaliation, Alex opened the door. "Here we go."

They walked out into the car park side by side, Alex taking Ellen's arm. To anyone observing, it probably looked like he was leading her, not the other way around. In his free hand he was carrying her case notes, while the recorder was in the pocket of his newly acquired white coat.

Once they were out and onto the grass verge, there was no turning back.

"Are they looking?" asked Alex.

"Hold on, I don't want to make it obvious that I'm watching them. No, not—"

"What? What is it, Ellen?" He squeezed her arm.

"They've seen us." There was a tremor in her voice. "Just keep calm and keep walking. It isn't far now."

"Okay."

"Just keep walking, not much further to… Shit!"

Alex was rattled, and it had more to do with hearing Ellen swear for the first time. She was becoming more human, less and less his doctor with each passing moment. Right now she was scared. "What is it?"

"Alex, they're pointing over here. They're coming over."

"Okay, Ellen, we keep walking, ignore them for as long as we can. When you think we're close enough, we make a run for it." Alex felt her stiffen. "How far away are we?"

"Staff car park's just across the road here. Alex, they're speeding up."

The temptation was too great and he turned to look. Everything was blurred, but he could see dark shapes moving towards them. "Got your keys ready?"

Ellen's hand went to her pocket and she slid it inside. Her fingertips brushed the jagged edge of a key. "Yes." The word was barely audible.

Alex could hear the men shouting something. "When I say run, you run."

"What about you?"

"Just go fetch the car."

"Alex?"

He let go of her. "Run!"

There was a heartbeat's hesitation, but then he heard her move away and break into a sprint. Alex brought out his glasses and put them on. The ill-defined blurs were suddenly all too sharp: men—large men—lumbering across the car park. Ahead of him he heard the *plick-plick* of an alarm being disabled, a door opening.

"You! Oi, you…stop!" Some of the men had veered off to chase Ellen, which still left most of them heading towards him. The one nearest— hair cropped short, with a moustache—was holding up a piece of paper and checking Alex against it. He wasn't quite sure to begin with, then it dawned on the guy that this doctor was their man. Alex shot off in the opposite direction to Ellen's car.

He could hear the engine of the Freelander turning over, just as the men chasing Ellen reached it. Two stood in front of the vehicle and another pair slid down the side to try and open the door.

She's locked it, thought Alex, *please let her have locked it.*

The door opened easily and the men tried to grab her. *Fuck!* Alex was half twisted around, keeping one eye on the silver Freelander, another on the men coming after him. The 4x4 jerked backwards and the thugs at the side fell away. She rolled it forwards, nosing between the gap before the two men in front had a chance to close ranks again. Ellen shut the door as she drove.

Yes!

Alex shrugged one arm out of his white coat, then transferred the notebook to the other hand. He fished out the recorder then flung the coat back at the men who were after him. It caught the lead right in the face, sending him toppling over and he took another man down with him.

The Freelander pulled up alongside Alex, but he didn't have any free hands to open the door. He nearly dropped the recorder, fumbling to place it in the crook of his arm, but was finally able to stretch out and pop the handle. As he climbed in he said, "Go!"

She didn't need any encouragement, her foot was down on the pedal. They drove through a small hedge and over a triangle of grass to get to the entrance and narrow road. Alex rested his head back in the seat.

"I never want to go through anything like that again," Ellen said, letting the wheel slip through her hands at the turn.

"At least we made it."

"Oh, no." Ellen was checking the rear-view. She saw some of the men piling into two cars. "They're coming after us."

"What?"

"They're com—"

"Ellen, watch out!"

An ambulance was careering towards them on its way to A&E. Ellen switched her attention back to the road just long enough to dodge it. Alex gripped the dashboard. "I'd seen it," she lied, looking over.

Saying nothing, he manoeuvred around in the seat so he could look behind. "This is not good."

"Hold on, I think we might be in luck." The traffic system leading to the main road was controlled by lights, and they were just turning from amber to red. Ellen sped past and made a sharp left-hand turn. Alex fought against the bend to stay in his seat. The cars on the main road were just setting off as their pursuers emerged, preventing all but the lead one from coming through. A cacophony of blaring horns accompanied the Freelander and the remaining navy car dogging it.

"Now we're down to one."

"That's bad enough," said Alex. "They're bound to have mobiles."

"I'll see if I can lose him."

They moved from a 30 mph zone into a 40, and Ellen increased her speed again. The car behind copied her. They passed through a built-up area with cars parked down one side of the road. "The roundabout ahead," said Alex. "We might be able to shake him on that. It's always pretty busy with traffic coming off the dual carriageway."

Ellen nodded, shifting down the gears and pulling as far over to the right as she could. When the road widened and split off into three, she took the right lane. The blue car was still tailing them. They had to wait in a queue for a few seconds and Alex was worried that one of the men might risk climbing out and walking up to the Freelander, but then they were moving again.

"Right, choose your moment," said Alex.

"Is this a good time to tell you I hate roundabouts?"

"Who doesn't?" *Especially ones where the cars are coming round like Wacky Races*, thought Alex. They waited, Ellen creeping out bit by bit. "Okay, now!" shouted Alex.

Ellen hesitated, then stamped on the accelerator. She missed the Volvo coming round the corner by inches. "Jesus!"

"It's okay," said Alex. "It's okay."

"No it's not," she assured him, "it really *is* not. None of this is."

Leaning over the back of the seat and peering round the headrest, Alex saw that the blue car had now pushed its way onto the roundabout as well. "You could be right."

Ellen caught sight of the car in her side mirror. "What now? Drive right over the middle of the roundabout?"

"Not exactly. When I tell you to, move over to your left. Ready?" Ellen didn't answer him, so he went ahead anyway. "Now, go left."

She jerked on the wheel, sliding the Freelander over into the middle lane. For once Alex was glad to be in a bigger vehicle because it meant no one would argue with them.

"Okay, now left again. Hurry!"

Ellen just squeezed in between two other cars, then took the exit Alex was indicating. White-faced, she checked her mirror one last time. There was no sign of the blue car.

"That's it. Now we just take the next right onto this estate and we can take the back road to my place."

Ellen loosened her grip on the steering wheel, relaxing a little now they were on their own. Even if the blue car did another circuit of the round-about and followed them, they'd be long gone. Lost in the maze-like estate she was now navigating.

"I'm not so sure we ought to go there, Alex."

He sat back down again, facing front. "What?"

"There might be more of those men waiting for you."

He obviously hadn't even considered this, because he didn't know what to say. Yes, there might well be. They could be springing out of the frying pan into... But he had to go back, warn Beverly, see her in person.

"Take the next right," Alex told her, then tacked on, "please, Ellen."

Silently, she nodded and flipped her indicator.

– vii –

"You don't even need to speak," The Infinity said.

There might have been two reasons for this. One, he didn't want to hear what Lucas was going to tell him; or two, he knew already it was bad news. Either way, Lucas was glad he didn't need to talk, because it was always the messenger who paid the price.

As it was, Lucas fully expected The Infinity to throw a fit, and quite possibly do something to all of them in turn, with varying degrees of consequence. He didn't fancy the lowly foot soldiers' chances much if his master wanted to take this out on someone.

Didn't fancy his own, either.

"We're sorry, Mr. Finn," said the short-haired man with a moustache still holding up the white coat, as if he thought waving it might placate The Infinity. "We tried to stop—" His mouth continued moving but no words came out.

The Infinity was holding up a finger. "I said there was no need to speak."

Moustache man coughed, tried to croak out a word or two, but found that his larynx had stopped working.

"Do you know why you shouldn't say anything right now?"

The man tried to use hand signals, pointing to his throat to indicate that he couldn't reply.

"Because if you did, I might just be tempted to stick my hand down that useless gullet and pull you inside out."

One of the other men tapped Lucas on the shoulder and whispered something. The Infinity looked across, rage building.

Lucas attempted a nervous smile, then took out a pad and pen and wrote something down. He had no intentions of disobeying The Infinity's orders, even if it was to relate the only piece of good news they had.

"What's this, Lucas, your last will and testament?" The Infinity took the pad and read it. As his eyes passed over the words, the shadows behind them seemed to lift somewhat. "Let me know where they're going and when they get there," he said, then handed the pad back and walked off to sit in the BMW.

Lucas read back what he himself had written. That there'd been a car following Webber and the doctor as they left the hospital car park. It was the one thing that was still keeping them all alive.

When his phone rang, Lucas answered it, knowing it must be Metcalf's men in pursuit. But like the moustached man, they didn't even have to say anything. His face fell and he turned away from The Infinity's line of vision.

The car had lost them.

They were all dead men now.

– viii –

"Nice," said Ellen as they pulled into the side road that contained Alex's house.

"Glad you approve."

"Which one's yours?"

Alex pointed up to the top floor. "The people below us are on holiday. Look, Bev's car's here so she must be home."

Ellen parked the Freelander alongside Beverly's Scénic and Alex's Almera, leaving enough space for Alex to get out. "Can't see any of our boys around."

"Good," he said. "But they won't be far behind. I'm not really sure how I'm going to explain all this to her."

"No, I'm not sure I could either," Ellen admitted. "You want me to come in with you?"

"Thanks. At least then she won't think I've escaped."

They got out and walked over, Ellen following him down the path. "Oh shit," he said, patting the pocket of his loose-fitting hospital trousers. "No keys." But when he looked up the steps to the side of the house he saw the door was slightly ajar. They exchanged glances, but didn't say a word.

After creeping up the steps, Alex pushed gently on the door. It had been forced open. He stepped inside, but couldn't see anything unusual.

Ellen put a hand on his arm. "Be careful."

"Come on," he said.

They moved forwards, trying to make as little noise as possible. The inner door was also open, the lock smashed.

Alex swallowed hard.

"I don't like this," whispered Ellen, but Alex was already through the door.

"You hear that?"

Ellen cocked an ear. It sounded like crying.

Alex walked through into his hall. Everything was still, calm, peaceful—except for that noise. The weeping sound was getting louder.

"Beverly?" he called and wasn't surprised to hear the crack in his voice. "Bev, is that you?"

Something sprang out at him from the room at the side—the kitchen as far as Ellen could make out. Alex was knocked back into the wall, the figure sprawling about on top of him. A punch landed, winding Alex, but he managed to wrestle the person off and pin them down on the hall floor.

"James?"

His friend's eyes were wild, and they were filled with tears. "Alex? Is it really you?"

Alex clambered off. "Who did you think it was?"

"I-I don't know. I thought they'd... I thought it was—"

"Are you all right?" asked Ellen.

Alex didn't know if she was addressing him or James. In the end he answered for both of them. "I think so. James, what are you doing here?"

His eyes flitted from Alex to Ellen, asking them the same question. "I had to come. It's my fault."

"What is?"

"All this. I'm sorry, Alex. I tried to call. Tried to get here…"

"Okay, James, now you're scaring me. And I've had enough of that to last me a lifetime. Talk to me."

But James just started shaking his head, so hard Ellen was frightened it would fly off and roll across the floor.

Alex started to get up, intending to head through the hall. James grabbed him by the wrist. "No." He looked over pleadingly at Ellen. "You can't let him go in there. Please, for pity's sake!"

Frowning, Alex removed his friend's hand, but James stood too—forcibly trying to restrain him, arms wrapped around Alex. "James, get off me. This is my home!"

"Alex, *no!*" The crying came again and it looked like James was biting into Alex's shoulder like some kind of animal. It only made him more determined to get past. He practically had to lift the man and shove him to the side before he could unblock the route, walking past James' abandoned mountain bike. James was about to grab him again, but Ellen placed a hand on his shoulder.

"You don't understand," James said to her, turning. "He can't see this. He *can't!*"

"What? What is it you don't want him to see?"

But it was too late.

Alex was in the living room.

And it wasn't long before he was crying too.

– ix –

What he was seeing wasn't Beverly.

He couldn't match the two in his mind, couldn't connect them as being the same thing. The object hanging in front of him had Beverly's face—the face he'd gazed at a million times. The eyes he'd looked into as they'd fallen in love, as they'd slept together for the first time and all the times since. Still the same, just a little older, a hint of crow's feet at the edges.

Now a little deader. Glassy and frosted over, glaring accusingly at him.

The same face, yes. But everything else was different. Alex wasn't even sure you could describe the rest of it as a human being anymore. Parts of it, perhaps. But only that. Only…bits and pieces.

It was naked, that much he could ascertain. Stripped of all clothing and dignity, but stripped also of a distinguishable form or whole. Its arms bent impossibly back, so that the shoulders jutted out like two rockets about to launch. From bicep to wrist the skin had been sliced open, the tendons and veins pulled out and left to dangle like messy dreadlocks. Its fingers were missing—cut off, gone, God knows where.

The breasts had also been removed, but these had been given a new home—on the wall, placed symmetrically on either side of the body. Inserted where the breasts should be were handfuls of roses from Alex's window box arrangement. Her chest looked like an explosion of pure colour.

The flesh was peeled back on the belly, right up the sides, exposing its ribs which were still steaming in the heat of the room. Its guts had been pulled out, the intestines wound nonchalantly around each grey thigh. The legs had been forced wide apart, so that it looked like the figure was doing the splits. Two metal pins were holding these back, hammered into the wall, and Alex could see more splashes of colour between the legs themselves—again, flowers inserted where they would never grow organically.

The legs had been amputated—quite crudely—at the knees, the discarded extremities forming a cross in the space below it. All the toenails had been ripped off, exposing the glistening meat to the air. Blood and leaves formed a circle around the target, standing out against the cream colour of the paintwork.

How was the lump hanging there at all, apparently frozen in mid-air? It took a moment or two for this to register, but the figure was suspended by its hair, wound tightly around one of the wall lamps, which only added to the surreal vision.

The smell was awful. Already flies had gathered to investigate this abstract and they were still buzzing around the open wounds.

This wasn't Beverly. It wasn't. And yet that face! The only thing they'd left alone, as a reminder of who this had once been, or because there hadn't been time to do any more work? It wasn't important; the fact remained it was doing its job, messing with Alex's perception of what he was seeing.

He wasn't even aware that he'd fallen his knees, or that his clasped hands gave him the look of someone praying to an icon of his preferred deity, as hideous as that may be to contemplate. Bile rose quickly and Alex bent over, spewing up his last hospital meal. He heaved until there was nothing left inside.

Alex could sense that people were behind him, but it wasn't until Ellen's half-stifled "Oh, God" that he began to respond. His body was shaking uncontrollably, but he managed to turn. He'd pulled the glasses from his face to allow the tears free passage, but also so he couldn't see this abomination any longer.

Both Ellen and James were there, although she was the only one staring. James had already seen his fill.

After a time, and when he could force himself to wipe his eyes with his sleeve, Alex said to them, "Somebody fetch me a fucking blanket so I can cover up my wife."

— x —

They sat in the living room, trying not to look at the blanket, trying not to think about what was underneath it. All thoughts of who might be following or what might happen next had deserted them until Alex spoke up. It was his right after all; it was his wife that had been killed and mutilated.

"We can't stay here much longer," he said. And with that he got up and went into the bedroom. Ellen and James watched him go.

"What are you doing, Alex?" Ellen called after him. There was no reply.

This was all suddenly much more serious that it had been even a couple of hours ago. Back then it was "just" an assault inflicted on the staff back at Ellen's hospital. Now it was different, and they had all the more reason to run.

When he came back in, he was still stuffing items into a holdall, and he'd changed into a T-shirt and jeans.

"Alex, we need to talk about this," Ellen said as he wandered into the living room and dropped the holdall on the couch.

"Talk about what? How my wife's got flowers growing where… How she's strung up like some kind of…some kind of…" He was choking back the sobs again and balled his hands into fists.

"Look, I've even brought flowers."

"We need to report what's happened here," Ellen said. "We're not just looking at some petty crime stuff now. This is murder."

"You think I don't know that!" screamed Alex. "That's Beverly under that sheet. My fucking Beverly!"

"Whoever did this is sick," she continued, ignoring his rage.

"Is that your expert opinion, Ellen? Is that—"

"I already called the police."

They both looked over at James and said almost in unison: "What?"

"I said I already called the police. From here; I had to plug it back in. My…my mobile's broken. They came, they even looked right at her. Then they left again."

Alex's jaw dropped open. "What are you talking about?"

"It was as if they couldn't see her. As if they weren't meant to."

"What do you mean they couldn't see her? She's right there!" said Alex. Ellen said nothing, she just nodded her head.

"I don't know, I can't explain it. They wouldn't even listen to me."

"I-I don't understand," Alex confessed.

But you do, don't you, thought Ellen to herself. *You know what's happened here. You know exactly what's happened.*

"I'm sorry," said James. "I tried not to give them the address when they showed up at college, but…"

Alex shook his head. "It wasn't your fault, James."

"Who are they, what do they want?"

"They want me," he told his friend.

"But why?" James looked even more confused.

"That's the million dollar question, isn't it?"

"And who are you?" he nodded at Ellen.

Alex closed his eyes, then slowly opened them again. "I'm sorry, I would have made the introductions but it wasn't exactly a good time. Still isn't."

"I'm Dr. Ellen Hayward," she said rising.

"*You're* a doctor?"

"Psychiatrist. Alex has been under my care since last Thursday."

"Hold on. This is all too much."

Alex clasped him on the shoulder. "Welcome to my world, James. And you are *definitely* welcome to it."

"What are they going to do when they find you?"

"I don't know," said Alex honestly. "Which is why you need to get as far away from me as you can. Both of you."

Ellen marched over to him. "I'm not leaving you alone."

"You've seen what happens to the people around me, Ellen. I don't want you, either of you, anywhere near when these psychos finally catch up with me."

"Alex, you're still my patient—"

"Stop saying that! None of that bullshit matters anymore, can't you see?"

"It matters to me," she said, hurt.

"I'm not leaving you," said James.

Ellen echoed him. "Neither am I."

Alex looked like he was about to argue with them, then simply nodded. "Okay, okay, but let's just get out of here as soon as possible. I need to get away from here."

The decision made, they all traipsed back through the living room towards the hall. "Wait," said Alex. "I almost forgot."

He went back into the living room and opened a desk drawer. Taking out a white oblong, he folded it into the holdall now hanging over his shoulder. "Right," he said, trying purposely not to look over at the blanketed wall. "Now we can leave."

NINETEEN

– i –

THEY WERE LUCKY, VERY LUCKY.

Lucas thought The Infinity would react differently when he found out. He assumed they'd all end up at each other's throats—literally—or even just blinked out of existence altogether for their incompetence. But The Infinity obviously still had use for them.

What he had done was vent his spleen elsewhere. Burdened with the knowledge that his prey had escaped again, The Infinity shut his eyes tight and ushered the men away. The next minute he was walking purposefully across the car park, targeting a figure dressed in blue scrubs, standing outside the hospital entrance smoking a cigarette. When the figure acknowledged The Infinity, Lucas could see that it was a young woman—a very attractive one, despite the asexual clothes doing their best to mask it. At any other time Lucas might have considered her a candidate for his art: not a rough sketch like the one he'd done back at Webber's flat, but the masterpiece he'd been striving to create all his life.

However, that was not to be her fate.

The Infinity spoke; she smiled and nodded as if it was the soundest thing anybody had ever imparted. Possibly it was, Lucas had no way of knowing. Then his boss had returned, motioning them all to get back in their cars. Lucas lingered just long enough to watch the woman put out her cigarette then go back inside the hospital. Something had been set in motion, that was for sure.

They sat in silence as the vehicles piled out of the car park one by one, the black BMW following last. The traffic lights turned green for them on approach. It crossed Lucas' mind to ask The Infinity what was happening then. But his nerve went long before he could form the words.

Anyway, his question was already answered when, halfway up the main road, he heard the first loud explosion.

– ii –

Pauline Ramsey kept on telling herself she should quit.

Somebody in her profession, still a slave to nicotine? Well, it just didn't look good. She was positive that was the reason why she'd been passed over for one or two of the major surgical positions at Kirkwell General. It was true that no matter how hard you scrubbed before an operation, the yellow stains wouldn't come off your fingers. And that was also the case when she went for interviews; not to mention the stench of it on her clothes.

It wasn't as if she hadn't tried to stop. She had, many times. She'd tried everything: gum, patches, bloody e-cigs. The last time she'd even joined a support group which met periodically. Bunch of sad prats. Just being there in that room made her want a fag.

And if she heard the old joke about acupuncture and smoking one more time she'd stick pins in somebody else's eyes, see how they liked it!

At first people were encouraging. They'd understand when she became a bitch from hell, snapping without good reason. But after a couple of weeks, friends, colleagues and even family, were so sick of it they'd purposely turn a blind eye when she slipped away for five minutes and came back reeking of smoke. It was worth it just to have the old Pauline back again.

It had hampered her love life, too. Several of the men she'd been out with in recent years had been put off by it. They'd said they didn't mind to begin with when she had to pop outside at restaurants or slipped out of bed at 4:30 to have a crafty puff. But in the end all the non-smokers she'd known had given her the elbow, because of the ciggies. What else could it be? She was young, had a good job, had a nice face and body, a caring disposition—as long as she was supplied with her daily intake of nicotine. It was a vicious circle.

Pauline even half-joked that if she ever got married, which at the moment did seem fairly unlikely, she'd have a cigarette going under the veil as she walked up the aisle.

She'd make the excuse that smoking had been a part of her life since she was an adolescent. While most kids had been exploring each other behind the bike sheds, Pauline was becoming more and more intimate with Benson and Hedges, Marlboro and Superkings. To her it was much more satisfying than a tongue sandwich or a fumbling hand up the blouse. But the reason she'd started, she still couldn't remember to this day. Neither of her parents had smoked, although her grandad was happy to report he'd lit up virtually every day of his life until those cows at that home had taken them away from him as he approached his nineties. "When I was young, they even used to smoke in hospitals like yours," he once told her. "Said it was healthy, good for you. Killed the germs!"

No, it was a complete mystery to her why and even *how* she'd started. But she had, and she'd continued to smoke into her late twenties with no end in sight. Even today, in between helping out on a cartilage op and an appendix—not the most riveting of days—she was outside, in plain view of patients and staff alike, having a long, much-needed drag on a Silk Cut.

Her first thought as the man walked up to her was, *He's going to give me a bloody lecture about how I should be setting a good example, being a doctor and all. About how these things will kill me. Well, I'll tell you what, he can just piss off right now if that's*—

"Hello, Pauline," he said.

That threw her, the fact that he knew her name, yet it seemed the most natural thing. Perhaps he was an ex-patient?

Pauline sucked on the cigarette, drawing more smoke into her lungs and expelling it out of the side of her mouth. "Have we met?"

"We have now," was his reply. "I feel very fortunate to have found you here today."

"Oh?" It wasn't a particularly good chat-up line, but then Pauline wasn't all that fussy, not when she was at work and looked like this. He was attractive, kind of, although it was more the way he carried himself that was sexy. The way he could wear that suit in this heat and not even break into a sweat.

"Yes, very fortunate. Let me explain."

And he did, but not in words as such. Then he walked away again. Pauline stubbed out what was left of her cigarette on the wall. She went back into the hospital, everything so clear to her now. She was very excited, like a child again, like the first time she'd seen it, over twenty years ago.

Her parents had spent a long time preparing it, building the wood up, cooking food—sausage rolls, chicken drumsticks, hot jacket potatoes, the works. People had gathered in their backyard as the night grew dark. Pauline remembered everyone wearing jumpers and coats because it was very cold outside on that early November evening.

The bonfire was huge and it was lit at precisely eight o'clock. Her dad did it with a piece of wood. It didn't take long to catch. Pauline had watched the fire intently, the reds, oranges and yellows. Each individual flame dancing their own little dance, but at the same time somehow in unison; made for each other. Pauline was mesmerised.

That was before the firework display had even begun. Once it had, she was in her element. She gaped at the rockets shooting up into space, bursting open and spraying the blackness with purples and pinks. It was all so beautiful, even the trails of fire and smoke they left in their wake. The sparklers that the children waved, that she waved. The lighted sticks some of the adults were puffing away on nearby; adults who could do whatever they wanted, not have to be in bed by a certain time and miss the end of the display.

It was a long-lost memory, the first and last time they'd had a bonfire at their home, before her father had left them for a supermarket checkout bimbo. She remembered now, thinking how much fun they looked. To have a bright orange spark at the end of your fingertips, to watch the wisps of smoke as they wafted into the air. It explained why, when one of the older kids had offered her a cigarette one break-time as a laugh a few years later, she'd accepted. It would make her look older, more adult, able to do whatever she wanted. Also, it would be fun!

Pauline relived these moments as she walked through the hospital entranceway, past the No Smoking signs, through the double doors that would take her back to theatre. Hers was empty at the moment, and she crossed the room, opening the valves on all the gas and oxygen tanks.

We have a lot in common, you and I.

She stood in the middle of the room, listening to the loud hissing.

You've been waiting, haven't you? Just like me.

She coughed, much harder than she ever had after a smoke.

Waiting for the time to come around.

One of her colleagues noticed her in there when he arrived to scrub up. He ran inside, the smell overpowering.

Would you like to see another display, just like that one? Another blaze?

Pauline grinned at him, then took her cigarette lighter out of her pocket.

Only better?

The other doctor rushed towards her, screaming, more people in scrubs now behind him.

Then what are you waiting for? You have the power right there, at your fingertips.

She flicked at the lighter with her thumb. Once, twice...

I'm so fortunate to have found someone who understands.

Pauline Ramsey barely heard the whoosh as the metal finally sparked in her hand.

All she knew was that she was now a part of that brightness, a part of the explosion, a part of the secret dance. It felt as good as he said it would. For a fraction of a second.

Then it changed, became the worst thing she'd ever experienced in her relatively short life: her flesh frying, eyeballs melting in their sockets, hair and clothes sticking to her.

It should only have been a fleeting thing, but for Pauline touching this flame seemed like an eternity. Time meant very little in the midst of the inferno she'd created. An inferno that was to spread far quicker and with more force than it should ever have done.

And the man's last unspoken words were still going around and around in her head.

As an old acquaintance of mine once put it in song:

"C'mon baby, won't you light my fire?"

– iii –

In Casualty, Ben—on painkillers and tired of trying to tell his story to people who just wouldn't listen—was having his arm set. He wasn't nuts, he'd actually seen the things that he'd seen before the other nurses and security staff had dragged him out of there. Yes, that was right, the man just blew up like a beach ball, then popped. It was the guy with the flowers who'd done it, the one who'd been after Alex. He realised how it sounded, he was talking like one of the patients in his care. Ben didn't really understand it himself.

"All right, all right, I'll handle this," young Dr. Goddard had said. He'd asked Ben about what had happened, about the connection to Webber. He'd seemed very interested, especially when Dr. Hayward's name was mentioned.

"Ellen? Is she all right?" asked Goddard. Ben could see concern and, yes, guilt as well for some reason.

Then out of the blue Ben heard someone mention how hot it was. It shouldn't be in here, there was air conditioning; unless it had broken again? But Ben could feel it, and he knew Goddard could too. This wasn't a normal kind of warmth.

Everything flashed white, and he felt heat that was so intense it was practically cold when it washed over him, like being in icy water.

Or in death's freezing embrace.

* * *

In his office, consultant neurologist Dr. Vikram Nidra was listening to *The Planets Suite* as he finished up a little paperwork.

For some reason a patient of his from the previous week was still on his mind. He'd had a message to say Ellen Hayward had taken over the case, so that should have been that. Ellen was one of the best, Mr. Alex Webber was in good hands. So why was he at the forefront of Nidra's thoughts?

Usually he could keep his emotions at bay when it came to work, but there was something that wouldn't let him rest. He made a mental note to either ring Ellen and check on her progress, or go and visit Alex himself—just to see how he was doing.

As it was he never got the chance. The whole building started to shake, accompanied by the very stirring music of Holst's "Mars" arrangement. Dr. Nidra got up, leaving his desk, where he always kept a picture of his wife and son, who he loved more than anything in this world, and ran to the door. The orchestra blared away, but was drowned out by the sound of another almighty boom.

He just had time to make it to the doorway before the whole of that level of the hospital disintegrated beneath him. As he was engulfed by the conflagration, Dr. Nidra's thoughts were not of his family, they were still with Alex Webber, as they had been now for well over a week. He even found himself saying a little prayer in Hindu for the man's safety, although for the life of him he could not work out why.

* * *

The first sign that anything was wrong was when Wynn noticed patients walking down the corridor on their own. They were wandering about in the hallway, crying and holding their heads. Sam joined him at the door, tapping the frame systematically. Some of the patients he recognised, some he didn't. But they were all shit-scared of something, and it didn't take a genius to work out it involved the angry-looking men they'd just seen.

Sam and Wynn had gone out to question the patients—those not curled up in balls on the ground—but couldn't make head nor tail of what they were saying. One word did stand out and that was "fight." There'd obviously been some unpleasantness in the psychiatric department. Perhaps the family of one of the patients wasn't too pleased with the way a relative had been treated and sent in the heavies?

They'd decided that the best course of action was to all stay where they were. Somebody would be along at some point and they'd sort everything out. They always did.

The second sign that something was wrong came some time after that. It was a fireball that shot up the corridor and engulfed the side of the rec room wall.

Sam dived down behind his beloved pool table, which shielded him from the explosion. But Wynn and most of the others weren't so fortunate. The blast knocked Sam's erstwhile pool opponent clean across the room, pieces of wood sticking in him like a hedgehog's spines.

Another wave was hot on the heels of that one. Sam could feel its scorching power from under the table where he was now flat on his stomach, tapping his palms with his fingers.

He wondered how this had started, but even if he'd had a million guesses he never would have come up with the correct one.

However, he too thought about Alex and how he'd probably never get that game now, never find out what happened to him, or how he was.

Although something told Sam that he wasn't here anymore, that he'd escaped this. That he was safe, probably with Ellen, and would stay that way.

At least for now.

* * *

Dolan Higgins sat in one of the hospital's many labyrinthine corridors, crying.

He knew that his gran was dead. They'd taken her away, his last sight of her drenched in blood from her own red tears.

But what he didn't know was that he would soon be joining her.

Dolan rubbed away the moisture from his cheeks, recounting her last moments. He kept returning to the incident in the lift with the man. What she'd said to him:

"I can see you. The scales have been lifted."

He'd dismissed it as the ramblings of senility, but she'd been trying to tell him something, hadn't she? She'd been trying to tell them all something about the man with the flowers. Dolan understood now.

He clenched his fist, vowing there and then to look for the man and ask him exactly what he'd whispered, exactly what could have caused her to haemorrhage like that.

"I see Death."

But he knew as soon as the doors to the right of him flew off their hinges, knew when he saw the walls bubbling with heat, that he'd never get the chance. Never be able to make the man pay.

"Death and destruction."

But perhaps someone out there might.

Perhaps someone who'd never even met his gran would avenge her.

It was a thought that gave him a small amount of comfort as his body was totally engulfed in flames.

* * *

Something certainly had been set in motion, a chain of events far larger than those played out here today, but no less ruinous or destructive.

The fire spread, the explosions reaching every part of the hospital and consuming it, through pipes in the walls, along ceilings and floors. There wasn't an area that escaped its wrath, the flammable substances in Kirkwell General feeding its ravenous hunger.

For a good few miles the sounds could be heard, mistaken by many for the first rumblings of a summer storm which never arrived. One which might have broken the heat and cooled everything down.

There was precious little chance of that.

The sunset was that much brighter along the horizon of the town where the hospital blazed away. Fire engines arrived, and firemen tried in vain to dampen down its ardour but it took them almost till midnight to put it out completely.

Even then, wisps of smoke curled and danced in the night air like the trails of fireworks rockets or the remains of a dying bonfire.

Or even the last gasps of a shrinking cigarette before it is put out.

– iv –

He got her to pull over at the nearest off license and bought two bottles of 40-proof vodka which came with their own plastic shot glasses on the top. He paid with cash he'd brought from the flat.

"As your doctor I'd advise you against drinking any of that," said Ellen when he got back into the Freelander.

"What about as my friend?" Alex fired back at her.

"As your friend I'd say you could probably use it. Him too." Ellen singled out James in the back. "And me as well, if I wasn't driving." They'd decided to stay together in the bigger vehicle, leaving the two cars and James' bike.

"Let's just go, Ellen."

"Where to?"

"It doesn't matter. Anywhere away from here."

She took them on the road out of Kirkwell, drove on through Griffield and out the other side, down country lanes as the sun set—the beauty a complete contrast to the sickening sight of Beverly Webber. But by that time, Alex had already downed a couple of vodkas and was in no mood to fully appreciate the scenery.

She drove on till about eleven, when she pulled into a side road and parked up. Ahead of them was nothing but black fields and forests. "We should be okay here," she said. *Long enough to get some rest or to figure things out,* she told herself. She put on the light inside the car.

James had taken her advice and the sip of alcohol seemed to have steadied his nerves. He still had the unique look of a man who'd found his best friend's wife cut up and hanging from a wall, but then she probably had that look as well.

"To mental health!" Alex said raising his cup and knocking back another full measure of the alcohol. His eyelids were drooping.

"Why don't you try and get some sleep?" she suggested.

He wobbled in the seat. "You think I can sleep after *that*?"

She knew he was on his way already. Sometimes the body's only defence against psychological harm was to shut itself down. Ellen took the cup and bottle away from him and placed her hand on his chest. She pushed him back into the seat; there was very little resistance.

"Good night, Alex."

His eyelids lost the battle they were fighting and closed. He mumbled something that she didn't catch at all. A moment or two later he was breathing deeply.

Ellen leaned over and focused on James. "How are you doing?"

"I've been better."

"I think we all have."

"So..." said James, leaving as long a gap as he felt he could, "what's really going on here, Dr. Hayward?"

"Ellen, please. Everyone calls me Ellen."

"All right, what's going on, Ellen?"

She told him what she knew, how she'd come to be involved and how the mysterious person from Alex's subconscious had turned out to be very real indeed.

"I know, I met him," said James, telling her about what had happened at college. "I don't know how he got that information out of me. It wasn't by threatening me, because that nutcase he was with could have done anything he liked before I'd have given Alex and Beverly up to him."

"Is that what you meant before, when you said all this was your fault?"

James nodded slowly. "But it was almost like he was getting inside my head, do you know what I mean?"

Ellen knew exactly what he meant, but said nothing. Up until now she could dismiss it as her own imagination, but here was someone who'd experienced exactly the same thing. How could she gloss over it now?

"I tried to resist, but...well, I guess I wasn't strong enough. Not like..." He shook his head. James was talking about Beverly; they'd done that to her because she hadn't just given Alex up. "Back there, you didn't seem all that surprised about the police. Why?"

She told him about the car park, about how the cops had just turned around and gone back again without a fuss. "I did wonder whether he used some form of mass suggestion."

"Now you're not so sure."

"I don't think any of this can be explained away that easily," she said. "I'm starting to realise that."

James massaged the back of his neck. "Ellen, did you say you still had the recorder with you?"

"It's only got the last session on it, the one before we were...interrupted. I downloaded the rest. But I've got the notes I've been making on the others here. Thought it might be important to bring them."

"Would you mind if I had a look?"

Ellen shook her head and reached around on the floor below Alex. She handed the notebook and recorder to him.

"Thanks."

She watched as James read through her notes. His demeanour marked him out as a gentle person; the way he was handling her property—with respect, lightly turning the pages and scanning her handwriting. The way he'd stop and examine certain pages gave him a look of intelligence. And, like Alex, this was not a man who was used to violence or arguments. The closest he ever came to losing his cool with anyone was probably getting slightly miffed if his coffee cup was used in the staffroom. Even then she doubted whether he'd tackle the culprit. What had happened at college must have been difficult for him, though not quite as hard as dealing with what followed.

"You've written here that you think Alex has been grafting scenes from films over his fears, in an effort to deal with something that happened to him?"

"Yes," said Ellen.

"But how do you explain the historical bits?"

"I did think maybe he'd gotten some of that from you," she admitted.

"Me?" James' eyebrows slid up his forehead. "He can't stand me talking about that stuff. Half the time my students can't even... My students, God, they're taking their exams soon. What if we can't figure this out by then? What if we *never* figure it out?"

"I know what you mean. I've left a wing full of patients behind tonight, Heaven knows what they're going through."

"But we can't risk going back, can we?"

Ellen shook her head again. "Not after what we've seen. Not now we know what these men are capable of." *I think we're only just beginning to discover that.*

James picked up the recorder and rewound it. He pressed play and listened for a minute or two. "That's not someone who's making this stuff up," he said, speaking over the sound of Alex's voice. "That's someone who believes what they're saying. He knew they were coming for him."

She nodded, her eyes drawn to the passenger on her left, still sleeping. It seemed wrong to talk about it right in front of him.

"I think maybe—"

Ellen held up a hand.

"What is it?"

"Wait, run back that last bit again. The end of the sentence, I missed what he said."

James did as he was told, rewinding it. He played the line again.

Alex: "Have to…Have to…"

Ellen: "Snap out of it, Alex."

Alex: "Have to…"

Ellen: "What?"

Alex: "Break…break the cir…"

Ellen: "What did you just say?"

Alex: "Break the circ—"

There was nothing after this point but the sound of feet and banging. Then white noise.

Something about what he'd just said struck a chord with her, then and now. Circles within circles, wheels set in motion. Hadn't Alex talked about seeing a circle in his dream? There had even been circles used in the death of Beverly Webber.

But it was that particular phrase: "Break the circle." Ellen cursed her stupidity. Where had she heard it before?

"Ellen? Are you okay?"

"Hmmm…what? Oh yes, just thinking."

"I think we need to talk to Alex again," said James.

"Maybe, tomorrow," said Ellen, looking at the clock and aware that it already was tomorrow.

"I'm serious, perhaps I can help."

"James, it isn't something I'd recommend trying outside of a hospital environment."

"I really believe I could."

Ellen reached over and took back the notebook and recorder. "And I really believe you need to get some sleep."

He began to speak, but could see the determination in her. Wearily, he accepted her wisdom.

"We'll look at things afresh in the morning," she promised as he settled back in his own seat.

She did the same, but couldn't resist rewinding again. Lowering the volume she placed it to her ear and played the same bit several times.

"Break the circ—" Alex said, over and over like a stuttering rapper trying to find a rhyme to his next line. "Break the circ…Break the circ… Break the circ—"

— v —

He was back in the circle.

Alex hadn't thought he'd sleep at all tonight, not after seeing his wife carved up like a Sunday roast. But the combination of vodka and exhaustion, both mental and physical, finally caught up with him.

If he thought that meant he wouldn't dream, he was sadly mistaken. Now he had returned to the place where only the previous night—and a lifetime ago—he'd looked upon the face of his pursuer—and vice versa. If he hadn't slept last night, if that son of a bitch hadn't seen him clearly, maybe Beverly would still be alive. Maybe they'd still be back in the relatively safe environment of the hospital.

But what was done was done.

The ghost people were all gathered once more—the ones that he recognised, the others not so well defined. They stood on the outskirts of the circle, hanging their heads as if aware of his loss. One of the newer figures was almost there, features slipping in and out of this reality, constantly wiped and redrawn like words written on a whiteboard in marker pen. He stepped forward out of the crowd and began walking towards Alex.

"He will find you again," said the smudged man. Alex tried to place his accent. He'd heard it before, but like so many other things he'd seen and heard over the last half a month, it was just out of reach.

"I know," Alex found himself saying. He couldn't go on running. Even if he did, the things that had destroyed his life would just keep on running after him.

"There has to be a reckoning."

"What will happen when he finds me?" Alex was still attempting to focus on the man, with little success.

"You know the answer to that. You've always known, all your life. It is the outcome that is uncertain."

"What do you mean?"

"This is who he is."

He took Alex's hand. A succession of images were transferred to him instantly, quick snatches, but enough. He saw men being executed, shot in the head at close range so that their brains splattered the walls; he saw dirt and filth, loud explosions; people being herded like cattle, tortured; bullets riddling bodies; throats being slit, and jets of blood shooting out; huge metal monsters raking the earth and firing shells from their cannons; then this was opened up on a grander scale, fire all-consuming; scientists in labs, then bunkers; buildings being blown away; millions turning to ash as a huge mushroom cloud formed on the horizon. Was this the end of the world he was seeing? Alex broke free of the man's grasp, panting.

"Why are you showing me these things? What can *I* do?" he asked.

"You know what to do."

"Can I fight him?"

The man shook his head. "No."

"Then tell me what I *can* do," pleaded Alex.

"Nothing!" This wasn't the man's voice; it had been replaced by one he did know all too well. The black figure invaded the circle, smothering the person who'd been talking to Alex, erasing him completely from the whiteboard. "Hello, Alex Webber," it said. "Anyone would think you were trying to avoid me."

Alex shivered.

"Was it something I said?"

He didn't know how to respond. Here was the thing responsible for killing his Beverly, and so much more besides—so much more *to come*. Just what did you say to a mass murderer? In the end he asked the most obvious question:

"What do you want with me?"

The thing in front of him thought for a moment. "That," it said, "is a very complicated issue, and not something we have time to go into here."

"You want to kill me, like you did Beverly?"

It pulled an expression of mock disbelief. "I didn't kill your wife. My... associate got carried away. If she'd simply answered our questions to begin with, then—"

"You bastard," spat Alex.

It sneered. "I warn you not to make me angry. You've already tried my patience far too much today." Coming closer, it continued. "Her blood is on your hands, Alex Webber. As is the blood of those people at the hospital."

"What are you talking about?"

"Oh, haven't you heard?" The creature waved his hand and Alex saw more pictures, this time of the hospital—the explosions, the flames. The images faded again. "Such a shame. I doubt there were many survivors."

Tears welled in Alex's eyes again. "You're lying."

It grinned. "I never lie."

"Ellen—"

"Ah yes, best not to mention this to your doctor friend. She'll only blame you. It will be our little secret." The figure tapped its nose conspiratorially. "But if you want to prevent more of the same you know what to do."

"Don't listen to him." Another voice; not the entity's, nor the smudged man he'd been talking to originally. This one was altogether softer.

Ignoring it, the dark thing carried on. "Give yourself up to me. Make it easy on yourself and those you love. We will meet again anyway. Why postpone the inevitable?"

"Don't listen. More will die if you do." Alex felt another presence that moved alongside, joining him. "You're not alone, Alex. You know that, don't you?"

"If you don't submit, there are other ways of getting to you." The thing showed him snaps of his mother, of Steve, of other members of his family.

"Leave them out of this!" shouted Alex.

"You're not alone," said the reassuring presence. "Remember." A hand slid around his, fingers intertwining.

Alex turned, comforted and—in a strange way—strengthened. He recognised the touch, the embrace from a previous dream. That time the face of his companion had been obscured, but not now. Now Alex could see it in all its glory.

Beverly looked at him with her wide, marbled eyes. Completely white, her face was drained of all its blood, shoulders dislocated and sticking out. "You're not alone," she repeated.

Alex screamed.

– vi –

"Alex! Alex, wake up!"

He was still screaming as Ellen started slapping his face, as he opened his eyes and looked at her in dawn's early light. He wasn't quite seeing her yet, still seeing something else: a residual from the dream.

"Alex, please!"

He jerked bolt upright in the seat and she thought he was about to push her away. But his arms folded around her and he began crying into her shoulder.

"That's okay," she said patting his back. "It was just a bad dream."

Alex lifted his head slightly. "That's just the thing," he said through the tears. "It wasn't. That's what you keep telling me. That's what Beverly, what the nurses said. Just dreams, just hallucinations. But they're not, Ellen. They're real."

"Alex?" This was James from the back, who'd also woken.

"That twisted shit was talking to me *through* my dreams." Alex swung around so he could face her. "Talking to me just like I'm talking to you right now."

Ellen didn't know what to say.

"And he was threatening my family, Ellen. I've got to do something to warn them. I've got to ring mum."

"You've got a mobile?"

He showed her the one he'd packed—an old Pay As You Go that looked like it should have been traded in years ago, or put out of its misery.

"That it?" she said.

Alex shrugged. "Never seen the point of getting anything more elaborate. Besides, I've seen how smartphones suck up my students' time."

"Shame, because I think I know what we have to do next."

It was his turn to look surprised.

"If that had access to the Internet then…" she said, pointing to the ancient phone, and shaking her head. "Never mind. I need to get my hands on a computer. A cyber café would do."

It was his turn to shake his head. "What's all this about?"

"Alex, if I'm right I can take us to someone who can help. Someone who's come across this kind of thing before."

He waited for an explanation, but Ellen didn't provide one. Instead, she reached up and wiped away the moisture from his cheek. "We're going to sort this out, Alex. Don't worry."

"Ellen…" he began, then broke off. How could he tell her, how could he form the words to let her know that everyone she worked with, all her patients at the hospital were probably dead. Because of him, because of whatever that monster wanted. It was bad enough that she'd become entangled in this at all.

"What is it?"

"Nothing," he said. "Just wanted to say thanks."

She smiled, letting go of him. "You're welcome. Now if you'll pass me the map out of the glove compartment, I'm going to try and work out where exactly we are," she said, "and where the nearest hint of civilisation can be found."

PART FOUR
LOST AND FOUND

TWENTY

Ridgeton: Fifty miles south of Griffield

– i –

The nearest hint of civilisation was a small town that didn't look like it had changed since Churchill was a boy.

Dry stone walls flanked the Freelander as it approached, up over a bridge which found them on a one-way system, then into the middle of this quaint little locality. The high street seemed to consist of a hardware store, the obligatory supermarket—a tenth of the size of those in any other town or city—a hairdressers and a small café. It was the latter that interested Ellen, although as James pointed out when they drove past there didn't appear to be any computers inside.

"Let's find somewhere to stop anyway," she said.

There was a small car park in the centre of town, with enough room for eight vehicles. Luckily it wasn't exactly heaving at 9:00 a.m. on a Wednesday morning. James was the only one with any change, so was sent off to the ticket machine.

"What shall I get, an hour?"

"Make it two," said Ellen. "Just to be on the safe side. It might take that long to find any technology at all in this place."

When James returned, Alex told them he was going to try and contact his mum. He fished around again for his mobile.

"You don't think that…" James began.

"What?" asked Ellen.

James frowned. "That, well, maybe they might be able to trace your calls?"

"Seriously?" Alex asked, then sighed and said he'd make it really quick, just in case. "Like they do in the movies."

"Okay, I'll go and have a look around, see what I can find out," said Ellen. "You stay here and keep an eye on Alex."

James nodded.

"I don't need a babysitter," Alex protested. "I'm feeling much better. Apart from a bit of a headache."

Ellen stood next to the Freelander with her hands on her hips. "Neat vodka will do that to you. I'll see if they sell aspirin at the local store."

"Thanks."

She coughed and held out her hand. "Money?"

"Right." Alex gave her some notes. He felt bad that Ellen had left the hospital yesterday without any cash or her cards, or anything else for that matter, while he'd been able to pack a few essentials—plus whatever money was in the flat. But they just couldn't risk going to her place, not after what they'd found at his. That had been a stupid move as it was; anything could have happened to them. Now he had to rely on ringing people to warn them. Christ, what if something had already happened to his mother? He'd never be able to live with himself.

Ellen took the money and set off into the town, promising to be back as quick as she could.

"I still can't get my head around it," said Alex when she'd gone. "I keep thinking that this is the nightmare and I'm going to wake up from it any minute now, find Beverly beside me."

"I'm really sorry," James said to him from the back.

Alex pivoted in the seat. "I keep telling you, it's not your fault, mate."

"But if I'd got a taxi instead of taking the bike—"

"You might have been even slower getting there. It's *not* your fault," Alex said more firmly. "There was nothing you could have done, even if you'd been there. In fact I might be sat here mourning the death of my friend as well as my wife. But I tell you one thing." He picked up the phone and punched in a number. "He's not going to get to any more of my family if I can help it."

– ii –

After asking the few people who were around that morning, Ellen discovered that the local library was her best bet as their computers had Internet access. *Welcome to the 21st Century*, she thought as she located the place—a converted chapel by the looks of things—down a side street off the main drag.

As she opened the door, the sole librarian—a tall, thin woman with jet-black hair—looked up from her desk and eyed this stranger with suspicion. "Computers?" Ellen asked, conscious of the echo. She thought the woman was going to tell her to shush, in spite of the fact there was nobody else in the place, but instead she simply pointed over to the corner of the library where Ellen eventually located a table with three battered old machines resting on top.

She settled herself down behind one and grabbed the mouse, hovering it over the browser icon. Clicking on it, she let out a long moan when she heard the distinctive sound of a dial-up connection being made.

– iii –

"Can you hear me? It's a very bad connection." Alex cupped his hand over the receiver. "I think we're about ten miles too far away from the nearest mobile phone mast," he said to James.

"Alex, is that you?" the line crackled back.

"Yes, Mum, it's me."

"I've been so worried about you. I've been calling all the time. I haven't been able to get through to anyone."

"It's okay. You're talking to me now."

There was a pause. "Are you all right? Beverly wouldn't tell me a thing."

"Yes, I'm fine," he lied.

"You sound tired. And you sound upset."

Even on a dodgy mobile line miles away from home, she can still tell how I'm feeling. "Listen, Mum, I haven't got long. But I want you to do something for me. I want you to go and stay with Uncle Gerry and Aunty Joan for a few days."

"Didn't quite catch that," she said.

Alex repeated his request. "Don't worry about the cost, just do it. Get a taxi, or get Duncan next door to take you."

"What's all this about, Alexander?"

"Do you trust me?"

"You know I do."

"Then you won't ask, because I can't tell you. I just need you to do this for me, please."

"All right, love, whatever you say. I just need to know one thing?"

"Yes, Mum."

"Are you in trouble?"

He wanted to tell her right then. God yes, was he in trouble. The kind you can't really understand, but you know isn't going to end well. But it wouldn't be fair. This was one problem she couldn't sort out, one battle she couldn't fight for him.

"Just look after yourself, and tell the rest of the family to do the same."

"Alexander, does this have something to do with your brother?"

That question he wasn't expecting. "Look, I'll be in touch when I can. I love you."

"Love you too," she said, then he pressed the red cut-off button.

He didn't know how much good it would do to send her to Uncle Gerry's. After all, if the police weren't up to stopping that bastard from the hospital, what chance did his dad's brother stand? But he had to do something. Had to hold on to the illusion that she was safe, that they all were. Perhaps they'd uncover the reason for all this soon if Ellen was on to something.

Alex hoped and prayed she was, for all their sakes.

– iv –

"Here," said Ellen as she climbed in, handing Alex some dot-matrix printouts.

"You managed to find somewhere then?" James stuck his head between the seats to see what was written on the paper.

"Only took travelling back in time about fifteen years," she told him, then waved a hand to say it wasn't important. "I got supplies from the shop, too." She passed James a bag of sandwiches and crisps, but not before taking out aspirins and a bottle of water for Alex, who accepted them gladly. When he was done, she handed him his change.

"You get through to your family?"

"I got through to my mum."

"That's good. You mind if I use that to try the hospital?"

Alex hesitated, then handed it over. Ellen dialled the number a couple of times, but got nothing.

"Signal's not great out here," Alex explained with a slight tremor in his voice. He pointed at the papers. "What am I looking at here again?"

"Hmm…?" said Ellen, lowering the phone. "Oh, that." She tapped the top of the page. "Could be a clue about what's happening to you."

"'The Mystery of Johann,'" Alex read aloud. "'By Dr. Patrick Vaughn, Psychiatry Department Wittenberg Hospital.' This is well over thirty years old. You mind if I wait for the film to come out?"

"Actually, I do. Carry on reading."

Alex did as he was told, still reading out loud.

"*Acknowledgements: This paper should have been written jointly with my good friend and colleague Dr. Andreas Lehrer, who spent a great deal of time with the subject before I even encountered him. However, the Doctor's sad and untimely passing has meant that I am left to tell the story alone. With kind permission, the hospital and Dr. Lehrer's family have allowed me to make full use of notes he made during his time spent with this patient, and for that I am extremely grateful.*

"'*The story of Johann is a tragic one. But more importantly it is a mystery that continues to intrigue me, and I feel will do so for many years to come. I won't go so far as to say that this case is my white whale, but it is always there at the back of my mind and probably always will be. I don't know if I will ever find the answers to my questions, but I live in hope that one day everything will fall into place and I will gain a greater understanding of what troubled Johann and what brought about the seizure that cost him his life.'"*

"Well, I can certainly relate to that," said Alex. "I'm hoping everything's going to fall into place too."

"Just carry on reading," said Ellen. "But we'll do it as we drive." She put her seatbelt on and started the Freelander's engine.

"Where are we going?" asked James.

"When you get to the end of that piece, you'll know." Ellen promised them.

— v —

Much of what he read, with James doing the same over his shoulder, Alex didn't really comprehend.

It was written in such a way that, without a decent grounding in psychiatry or psychology, you could easily get lost. But Alex grasped the basics. It was all about a patient in Germany who had been discovered wandering down some train tracks and had spent years in an institution in Berlin before being transferred to a facility in Wittenberg. The derelict had been named Johann, after Johann Bach, because the composer's music was the only thing that could get through to him, and even then it was only gauged in nods of the head.

Alex read details of therapy sessions with Johann, about Lehrer trying to get through to the man using every technique in the book. It brought back what he'd experienced himself in the past week. There were definite parallels: something Johann had been through—something he'd seen—had shocked him into silence for all those years, just like something had buried itself in Alex's brain. He might have ended up like that if it weren't for Ellen. Might still, if they couldn't stop the dreams, the lapses.

Then Patrick Vaughn had come along and spent time with Johann. Vaughn described how he'd almost got him to talk once or twice, and explained his reaction to certain picture cards with images from the outside world—a world from which Johann had long since become disassociated. There was something about the way the doctor wrote about his patient that turned this dry article into a touching recollection of events. It was obvious Vaughn had cared a great deal about his charge and would have given anything to help him, to cure him. That same dedication and compassion Ellen had in abundance. And in Alex, in his disorder, perhaps she had found her own white whale.

But it was the telling of the final few hours of Johann's life that really got to Alex. The patient had apparently attacked a nurse and begun to mumble words, incoherent nonsense that meant nothing to anyone, only himself. Lehrer maintained that he was beginning to remember things from his past. And while he sat with the patient, Vaughn had a brief conversation of sorts with him.

Although he was still having trouble articulating himself, Johann was attempting to tell me something. That somebody, something was coming for him, something bad. I have often wondered if he meant death himself here, as some patients quite near the end have reported seeing figures approaching. They seem to know when the end is near, as it was for Johann. But he also told me he could see the demise of many people, that this "person" showed him these deaths.

Alex shivered when he read this passage.

He then went on to speak about someone he loved, who was now gone. I pressed him about who this was but could glean no further details.

Beverly. The comparison was becoming all the more apparent with each line he read.

The sense of urgency in his voice was incredible. Johann insisted that there wasn't much time left, that the bad person was coming for him. He said we must prevent this at all costs. His next words were: "Break the Circle." A pattern perhaps, or cycle of events that he was trying to tell me about.

Alex put the paper down. He knew all about the circle. It was where he ended up each time he dreamt of the shadow man. The dark thing that maybe this man saw as well all those years ago?

"Where have you got to?" Ellen looked over, only taking her eyes off the road long enough to register his shock.

"Johann's on his death bed," said Alex. "He's just told Vaughn that to stop the bad thing coming they have to—"

"Break the circle," Ellen finished for him. "Alex, that was the last thing you said, just before the disturbance at the hospital. It's on the recording, you said we had to 'break the circle.'"

"Christ. I have no idea where that came from."

"Now do you see why I needed to get hold of this? It's been a long time since I read it. I had to be sure."

Alex picked it up and read on to the end, about how Johann became even more lucid, just when they thought they'd lost him for good. And about how he'd begged Vaughn to let him go, out of some kind of sense of guilt.

He told me that his punishment was over and that he had been granted his peace. I can only assume he meant the eternal rest of the dead. Whatever the sense, Johann's wish came true seconds later, and he would no longer be trapped inside a body that wouldn't function at his command.

"It's not quite my story, but it's close," said Alex finally.

"And instead of retreating into yourself like Johann, you started to see things," James chipped in.

Ellen concurred. "So I'm guessing we're all in agreement that he saw something similar to you at some point. Had someone chasing him—just like you do. There are too many coincidences to ignore."

"What's this?" Alex ran a finger down to the base of the page. "You've underlined something."

"That's Dr. Patrick Vaughn's bio, and it looks like it's fairly up to date. The article was only posted on the net a couple of years ago anyway."

"He eventually took over as head of the psychiatry department at Wittenberg then?" Alex was impressed.

"Looks like."

"Then he came back to this country to do more research work and teach part time. A psychiatrist and a teacher…"

The corners of Ellen's mouth curved into a smile. "He's retired now, though."

"Currently residing in Armitage Bay, on the coast, with his wife Marina."

"Nice lady," whispered Ellen.

"Sorry?"

"Nothing. Take a look on the next page, I dug that out as well."

Alex read an address and phone number aloud. "Ellen, you're a star."

"I took a chance that he'd still be there. You can track almost anyone down if you have a general location." She realised the implications of what she'd just said and apologised.

"It's perfectly true," said Alex.

"I'm sure your family will be fine."

"Just like Beverly was?" Alex turned to her. "Just like we will be?"

The awkward pause that followed was broken only when James asked Ellen how she'd come across this case study.

"I was doing an essay for my MSc based on unsolved psychiatric histories. I was directed towards it by an old friend."

"An old friend?" asked Alex.

"Yes. Well, more of a mentor really than a friend. He did a lot for me and it's partly down to him that I'm sitting here with you today. He encouraged me to carry on, showed me that, above all else, our profession is about helping people."

Alex had already guessed. "Ah, I get it."

Ellen's smile broadened. "That's right. The author put me on to it himself, one of the best tutors I've ever had, Dr. Patrick Vaughn."

– vi –

"Fuck me, is this your idea of keeping a low profile?"

The TV in the back room at Yazmin's was throwing back pictures of a burnt-out Kirkwell General. A local news reporter was standing in the car park speaking into his mic and telling the audience that authorities were not yet sure what had happened but a full enquiry would soon be underway. The reporter then brought one of the fire chiefs in to talk about the possible causes.

"This is my fucking town, this is my fucking *city!*" growled Nick Metcalf.

"I'm aware of that," said Lucas Peck, making sure to speak slowly and deliberately, careful not to lose his cool.

"And my men were there! You take them on some sort of day trip then you blow a fucking hospital up! Just tell me again, what planet are you and your Mr. Finn from, Peck? Because it fucking well isn't this one!" A vein was bulging on his temple, thick and purple.

Peck let out a breath. "If you'll calm down, we can talk about this rationally."

Metcalf got up out of his leather chair and came round the side of his desk. "*Rationally?* We're going to have half the fucking police force in the country looking for us, you do realise that. I mean, as if it wasn't bad enough you have them beating up patients in a psychiatric wing. Yeah, Peck, Terry and Frank have already told me what happened there. But you do *this* as well? No amount of snow is worth this kind of heat."

Lucas remained where he was, leaning against the office door. "The hospital was an accident. That's what they'll discover. There will be no comeback for the fight there or the explosion."

Metcalf clearly couldn't believe the casual way Peck was talking about all those dead people, as if it was a necessary side effect of their business transaction. But, in essence, that's all it had been. "So where's Finn, why isn't he telling me all this himself? Can't he be arsed?"

"Mr. Finn is at his hotel, resting. The last few days have taken a lot out of him."

Metcalf let out a sarcastic "*Hah!*"

"He said to say that he will be speaking to you presently. He'll be needing your men to begin the search again as soon as—"

"*Begin again!*" Metcalf made his way over to Peck. "You've got to be fucking joking me. They aren't going anywhere with you two anymore."

Peck held Metcalf's stare again. "Perhaps you ought to ask *them* about that. It's their decision at the end of the day."

"I don't need to ask them shit!" Metcalf screamed into his face. "They take orders from me. Not from you, and definitely not from your Mr. Finn."

"Nonetheless, they will be needed."

Metcalf was obviously getting to the end of his tether. "You listen to me: No. Fucking. Way!" He jabbed Peck in the chest with each word just to emphasise them.

Lucas Peck nodded, seemingly taking the man's argument on board. Then he grabbed Metcalf's finger and snapped it back. The man screamed now for a different reason. He backed off, holding his left hand with his right. "That's it," he hissed through clenched teeth.

Metcalf brought up his right fist, swinging it in an arc. But unlike the night when he'd caught Lucas on the temple, his opponent was fully prepared. Peck blocked the punch, returning the favour with one of his own. His fist connected with Metcalf's jaw, sending him sprawling onto the carpet. There he lay, dazed and shaking his head, with Peck standing over him, triumphant.

Metcalf touched his chin and winced. At least it had taken his mind off his broken finger. "Get out!" he yelled. "Go on, get out of here and don't come back!"

Peck was in two minds. All he really wanted to do was bend down and throttle the life out of this wannabe Godfather, but he knew his orders didn't extend to that. If he pushed the boundaries of his purview, then who knows what the repercussions might be. The Infinity's patience had worn thin, and he was still surprised any of them had escaped with their lives after yesterday's fiasco. It just was not worth it. So he decided to leave Metcalf be.

"That's right, you fuck off and never show your face again." Metcalf said this as if he was the one who'd come out best in the brawl.

Lucas Peck walked out through the door without saying another word. *Just not worth it*, he reminded himself again as he went, before he changed his mind.

– vii –

"You could let me drive for a bit, you know. I'm not completely incapable."

Ellen didn't react, she just continued to let the grey streak of motorway pass beneath her gaze, and pass beneath the Freelander. "Alex, this time yesterday we were in the psychiatric ward at Kirkwell. You'd been through a lot then, but you've been through even more since. Most people would have been—"

"Basket cases?" suggested Alex.

She groaned. "Most people wouldn't have handled any of this half as well as you. It takes quite a bit of strength to cope with situations like these."

"Situations like these? You make it sound like something that happens every day."

"I didn't mean to," said Ellen. "Because it certainly doesn't."

Alex turned his head to the right. "James, you're quiet back there."

His friend was poring over Ellen's notes and the new material she'd printed off the Internet. "Oh, I'm just reading through this stuff again. It's fascinating."

"Glad it's keeping you occupied," said Alex.

"James raised his head. "I'm sorry, I didn't mean it like that."

"I know."

A stopover at the service station gave them a chance to stretch their legs. They could also refuel, both the Freelander and themselves. Alex hadn't wanted much to eat so far, but Ellen insisted that he have something, even if it was only a cheeseburger or some fries at the fast food joint. Placing the map out on the table Ellen drew a line in the direction they would have to take after the motorway. It was mainly off the beaten track from there, but Armitage Bay was a popular holiday resort and it was easy enough to find. While they waited for James to get back from the toilet she could see a question bubbling away under the surface that finally made its way out into the open.

"So, what's he like, this Dr. Vaughn?" asked Alex as she forced him to put another chip in his mouth.

"I haven't seen him in nearly a decade. He *was* a very nice, genuine man. A good teacher and a good example. Well, you've read the article. You can see that he cares."

"But is he going to care in the right way?"

Ellen took a surreptitious sip from the bottle of water she'd smuggled in. "How do you mean?"

"When we just turn up on his doorstep like this. He might not like it; might not even be there."

Ellen conceded that he had a point. "I'll try calling him if you like, give him a heads up."

"You think he'll remember you?"

Ellen laughed quietly. "He ought to do."

Another question, building up momentum. Alex's nose twitched.

"Go on, spit it out," she said.

"I was just going to ask… Well, were you and he…?"

Ellen moved her head back, eyes opening wide. "That's a bit of a personal one, isn't it?"

Embarrassed, he looked down and played with another chip.

"But to answer it, no. No we weren't." Ellen's attention also turned to the fascinating tabletop. "I won't deny I had a bit of a crush on him when I was his student, although if you ever tell anyone about that I'll jam those fries up your nose."

He smiled. "Sorry, it's none of my business."

"That's okay. I don't mind. It was a long time ago and I was in the first flushes of youth, more or less, hard as that is to believe."

Alex laughed. They both raised their eyes at the same time, then looked away from each other.

"Haven't any of your students ever had crushes on you?" she asked him.

Alex half-shrugged.

"I bet they have."

"They're just good kids," he told her.

"I'm sure they are, but it doesn't mean they don't have *those* sorts of thoughts. Trust me."

"And you had those sorts of thoughts about this Dr. Vaughn?"

Ellen pouted. "*Touché.*"

"I don't know, it just feels like I've told you everything about myself—"

"Hardly everything."

"Enough. But I don't know anything about you, your past. Who you are."

"I don't think that would've been appropriate, do you? You're still…" She caught herself before she said "my patient" and changed it swiftly to, "in my care."

He pulled a sour face. "You can't keep playing that card, Ellen. As you said yourself, a lot's happened since yesterday… I don't think it's asking too much to get to know the person whose care I'm in."

Ellen thought about this, then opened her mouth to speak just as James returned to the table. He looked at them both in turn. "Everything all right?"

"Everything's fine," said Ellen. "I was just about to go and freshen up. Eat the rest of your fries, Alex."

She rose and started to walk away, but still caught the next exchange.

"Everything's not fine, is it?" said James.

"No, it is not! Everything's about as far from fine as you can get," Alex replied. "My life's screwed up, the people I love are either dead or in danger, and I'm about to put my trust in a man I've never even met…

"All things considered," Ellen heard him conclude, "I've had much better days."

Twenty-One

Armitage Bay: 2:30 pm

– i –

Picturesque was the only way to describe it.

The smell of sea air was the first sign they were nearing the coast. It hit them some miles before they even saw the ocean, the sight of seagulls further evidence still. They drove along the backwater roads that Ellen had marked off, hardly encountering any traffic. If this had been a weekend, those same narrow lanes would have been choked with cars and caravans, equipment squashed into the back leaving barely enough room for passengers. But even so, it still brought back memories: of holidays spent camping for Alex and James; of school day trips for Ellen ("My folks didn't really do the whole seaside thing."). There might not have been any sea, but the nostalgia flooded back, wave upon wave of it.

Then suddenly they seemed to be driving parallel to the blue expanse of water. It was James who spotted this first, and the others turned in unison. They could see cliff-tops now, tufts of grass leading up towards ragged edges with perilous drops. The road dipped occasionally, giving them the impression that they were driving through valleys, but on the next rise all would become clear again. Dotted here and there were colourful houses perched precariously on the pinnacles.

The Freelander passed through a handful of small villages to get to the Bay, all about the same size as Ridgeton, but completely different in character. That had been middle England, while this was definitely on the outskirts. Peak District rock was eventually replaced by limestone and rock you could eat, striped pink and on sale outside knick-knack shops with postcards and inflatable water wings in the windows. If the roads had been quiet, then the villages made up for this: tourists rubbed shoulders with locals, and holidaying children rode through the streets on bikes. The strangers attracted some stares from passers-by, but most took no notice. The 4x4 was perfect camouflage, a holiday vehicle that was actually more out of place in Kirkwell and Griffield than here.

They left these villages behind with their whitewashed, sun-drenched houses and drew nearer to the Bay. Ellen pulled over and asked an old man walking his dog about the address she had for Vaughn. His manners left a lot to be desired, but he did put them right about where they could find the house—cresting the next ridge, overlooking the bay area itself, which consisted of a road running down to a beach and pier; all flanked by cliffs.

As the Freelander crept closer, they all felt the nerves. Ellen had been unable to reach anyone on the phone, though whether that was down to signal or not was hard to tell, so even if he was in, Vaughn still had no idea they were coming—nor why. As he'd done all day, Alex worried what the retired psychiatrist would say when, or if, he saw them. Old acquaintances very rarely turned up at your house uninvited. But this particular face from his past was also bringing with her two men he'd never clapped eyes on before, as well as a whole heap of trouble. He might well be the only person on this planet who could help Alex, who could finally solve this puzzle. Yet Vaughn might also be putting his own life at risk by doing so. Just how he'd react to that, none of them knew.

"Here it is," said Ellen, slowing the car to read the numbers on letterboxes—real letterboxes at the end of pathways. "Number 11." Vaughn's house was part of a scattered clump of cottages lifted straight from the front of a souvenir tea towel. It was far enough away from the others to be secluded, providing privacy when needed, but there were also neighbours on hand. The best of both worlds. It was the kind of place Alex always thought he'd end up when he retired, a sanctuary away from the busy stresses of life. Now it might serve as their actual sanctuary for the time being.

The Freelander ground to a halt outside the house. Nobody moved.

"I suppose we should get out," said Ellen.

Alex felt his stomach muscles tightening. "After you."

The noise the car door made as she opened it was magnified in that quiet environment. The slam as Ellen shut it was even worse. Alex waited until she came round the front before getting out himself. James was the last to disembark. The brown gate squeaked when Ellen lifted the latch and pushed. The path was a tanned beige colour, and the thought occurred to Alex as they were walking up it that this was the Yellow Brick Road. Ellen was Dorothy, whisked away from her life by a veritable tornado of violence and deposited into a warped version of Oz. James was like the cowardly Lion, trying to claw back some courage. And Alex? He was just a tin man looking for his heart.

They were all off to see the wizard, searching for explanations. But would they pull back the curtain only to be disappointed?

There was one way to find out.

The door was brown as well, and freshly painted. Like the rest of the house, it was well cared for. The kind of attention only someone with a lot of time on their hands could give. There was no knocker, so Ellen had to rap on the wood with her knuckles. She gave two taps and waited. No one came. She looked silently around at Alex and James, then gave a louder knock.

"I don't think anyone's home," said Alex, more wishful thinking than anything.

Ellen listened at the door. "I can't hear anyone inside."

"So what now?" This was James.

"Now, I guess we wait a while," said Ellen.

"A while" turned out to be about an hour, and Alex was the first person to spot the man walking up the road. They all got out of the car together this time, and the fellow came over to greet them, removing his Panama hat as he did so but leaving his sunglasses on.

"Hello," he called. "Can I help you?" He was almost completely bald, but wore it well, and what little hair he did have at his temples was snow white. There were deep lines at the corners of the glasses, but only a few other wrinkles on his face and neck. He looked at least ten or fifteen years younger than his age would suggest and he dressed this way too, in a light pastel shirt with cut-off sleeves and chinos.

"Yes," said Ellen, smiling. "Yes, you can."

The process of recognition took a bit longer for him. Alex could picture Vaughn going through faces in his mind, matching them up, trying to place who these people were on his doorstep. He gave up on two temporarily, but the third came to him, along with a name.

"Ellen? *Ellen Hayward?* Is that you?"

"Certainly is."

He shook his head in disbelief. "Elle! My dear, sweet Elle." Holding out his arms she walked gladly into them. The hug was of the bone-crushingly tight variety people reserve for family and close friends—perhaps very close friends. Somehow Alex couldn't see Vaughn turning this woman away, although what he'd make of her travelling companions was yet to be seen. Alex shuffled his feet beside her and gave a small cough.

The pair broke apart, but not before Vaughn had planted a kiss on Ellen's cheek. "I can't believe it. I haven't seen you in—"

"It's been fifteen years at least," she completed for him.

"Doesn't time just fly by?"

"I sent Christmas cards, letters for a while. But you know how busy things can be in our line of work."

Suddenly Alex felt like even more of an outsider.

"I know how it *used* to be," he said with a chuckle. "Well, well, I never thought I'd… And look at you. Just look at you, Miss Ellen Hayward. Oh, here I am assuming you're still a Miss." His eyes flicked over first at James, then Alex.

Ellen held up her left hand, wiggling a finger to show him she had no ring.

"Nobody's managed to tie you down yet, then? But not short of male attention by the looks of things. Two gentlemen escorts no less."

She tucked her chin into her shoulder, shyly.

"So who do we have here?" asked Vaughn with a genuine curiosity.

Ellen waved her hand back now. "These are two *friends* of mine, James…" She suddenly realised that she didn't have a second name. But it didn't matter anyway, Vaughn was already shaking his hand. "And this is Al—"

"I know you, don't I?" said Vaughn. He was going through the faces again, Alex could see it. "You're in the profession."

"No, not to my knowledge. Alex Webber." He took the doctor's free-floating hand and shook it just the once.

Vaughn regarded him oddly. "No? That's strange... Never mind, any friends of Elle's are welcome here." He led them up the Yellow Brick Road again, then opened the door.

"Please, all of you, come inside."

– ii –

Vaughn showed them through to the living room and insisted they make themselves comfortable on the couch.

He removed his sunglasses. "Have you been waiting long?"

"Not really," said Ellen.

"It seemed such a nice day I thought I'd go for a walk down into the bay area this morning. Time got a little away from me, though. Mixed blessing, not having transportation. Would anybody like something to drink?" Vaughn enquired. "I have some cider in the fridge, or some barley water if you prefer?"

Ellen opted for the latter, James and Alex the cider. While Vaughn was in the kitchen they had a chance to take in his décor. The walls of the cottage were just as bright on the inside as they were the outside—probably down to the patio doors leading to the garden. But apart from the big, comfortable chairs and settee there was a noticeable absence of furniture. No sideboards, no pictures, not even shelves with ornaments on. No television, either. What the room did have in abundance was bookcases. Two stood on either side of the fireplace—which was thankfully unlit—like loaded-up sentries on guard. Alex adjusted his glasses, reading some of the titles: *Maps of the Mind, Psychoanalysis and the Human Animal, The Complete Case Studies of Freud* alongside *New Age Therapy, Crystal Healing* and *Psychic Phenomena*. As for fiction, he spotted several Agatha Christies including *Murder on the Orient Express* and *The Body in the Library*. This man liked his mysteries; that was a good thing.

Vaughn brought back the drinks on a tray and handed them out before sitting down in a chair next to a wooden chess set. He cradled a barley water himself, taking a sip as he eased back into the cushions. There was small talk for a short while, mainly Vaughn enquiring about what Ellen was up to these days.

"It sounds as if you're doing sterling work," Vaughn commented when she was finished. "I always knew you'd do well. Ellen was my star pupil, you know," he told the men.

Ellen's cheeks filled with blood. "That's quite a compliment coming from you." Alex drank back half the glass of cider. It didn't go unnoticed. "So how's your wife?" Ellen asked Vaughn.

The change in his face was marked. His eyebrow twitched and there was a tremble of the lip. "I-I'm afraid Marina passed on about a year and a half ago. Alzheimer's."

Ellen put her hand to her mouth. "Oh God, Patrick, I'm so sorry. I didn't know."

"How could you?"

Alex felt guilty. Here he was making snap judgements, based on assumptions about Vaughn and Ellen's past, about their relationship. *His wife is dead, just like yours. And he probably loved her just as much. You can see it in his eyes. The pain. You know what that's like. You knew what it was like even before Beverly died, Alex. The pain of loss.*

"She'd been suffering for a long time. In fact it was diagnosed not long after I last saw you. In the end it was a relief for her. She didn't know where she was, who I was."

"I only met her a couple of times, but for what it's worth I thought she was lovely."

Vaughn breathed out slowly, controlling the emotions this conversation had stirred up. "Thank you, Elle, it means a lot. All my training, everything I've ever been through and I couldn't do a thing for her except say goodbye. That was one of the reasons we came here, you know. Thought the surroundings might do some good. And they did, I think. At first." It was Vaughn who took a long draught of his drink now. "That was a bad time."

"I can imagine." Ellen reached over and covered Vaughn's hand with her own. "Why didn't you let me know? I could have helped, come to the funeral or something."

He attempted a smile, but it crumbled. "Elle, I hadn't seen or heard from you in ages. It might feel like hardly any time has gone by sitting here, talking to each other, but it has. Life moves on. People drift in and out of it; old friends lose touch. Things change."

"I'm really sorry," she repeated.

"There's no need. What could you have done?"

"That makes me feel even worse, coming here today for help."

Vaughn put his glass down and placed his other hand over hers so that they were sandwiched together. "Nonsense. Anytime you need my help, you've got it. You know that."

Ellen fixed him with an intense gaze. "Actually, I think it might be of help to you, as well."

"What are you talking about?"

"I don't really know where to start," she said.

He patted her hand. "Why don't you start at the beginning. That's where stories usually start."

– iii –

This was going to take some time, so Ellen began by introducing Alex and James properly. She told Vaughn who they were, where they worked and how she'd come into contact with them.

"I came across Alex as a patient some days ago. He'd been having episodes—"

"You're travelling with a patient?" Vaughn interrupted, clearly worried.

"It's okay, Patrick, honestly. Let me explain."

Ellen related the incidents at college, the restaurant and home, culminating in the cuts he received in the bathroom. Alex held up his arms where the scars could still be seen quite clearly. This did nothing to persuade Vaughn that everything was okay.

"I know it looks bad, and at first I thought he might be doing this to himself, too, but I've seen enough to know that's not the case."

"Any history of paranoid schizophrenia?" asked Vaughn.

"None. An MRI scan the previous week had picked up nothing. No reports of mental disorders prior to this, except for some nerves during his school and college years."

"If that counted as a mental disease, then I would've had to treat ninety-five percent of my students when I was teaching. Including you."

Ellen went on to tell Vaughn about her sessions with Alex, and about his dreams.

"In them, Alex fears that he's being chased by something. Something very bad. My initial diagnosis was that all this was connected. That the hallucinations, the dreams, even the thing he's running from were parts of something in his past he was trying to hide from himself. That he was grafting them onto actual occurrences in his own life—for argument's sake, let's say a fire, as this is a recurring symbol. And the figure represented that which he couldn't face, buried deep in his own subconscious."

Vaughn nodded. "That probably would have been my line of thinking. But there's more, isn't there?"

"Yesterday, during our last session…" Ellen didn't know quite how to phrase the next bit, so just came right out with it. "Some people came looking for Alex. They walked right through the hospital and came marching up the wing to his room, scaring half the patients to death in the process."

"What kind of people?"

"The kind you wouldn't like to meet on a dark night down an alleyway—or even in daylight."

"Did they hurt you, Elle?"

"Not me personally. But they beat up one of my nurses. There was a fight between them and the security staff. I don't know how it ended because I got Alex out of there as quickly as possible."

"Under the circumstances, you did the right thing," Vaughn assured her.

"Then we went to Alex's flat to warn his wife."

"Not so good."

"She was…" Ellen shook her head. "We were too late."

Vaughn looked at Alex, who was biting the side of one finger.

"They found out where she was from me," James said quietly.

"Good God. Have you notified the authorities?"

"We have, but that's another story. These men, Patrick…they have influence."

"Influence? You can't just waltz into a hospital beating up nurses and security guards, and you certainly can't— Who are these people, does Alex know?"

"We think one of them might be the figure in the dream he's so scared of."

"So Alex has come across him before?"

"Possibly. He can't remember. I think it might also have something to do with his brother." Alex shot her a look, but said nothing.

The more she went on, the more bizarre all this sounded, even to her—and she'd witnessed most of it.

"His brother now? Just what have you got yourself mixed up in here, Elle?"

"I don't know," she said honestly.

"I don't think Steve is a part of this," said Alex in his defence. "You know when you said Steve's visit could have been a trigger for my hallucinations?"

Ellen nodded.

"Well, it can't have been. Steve didn't show up till lunchtime and the incident with Tim Brailes happened in the morning."

"But you did say he used to hang around with some rough company, Alex."

"Never anything like this. There's no way he'd put me or Beverly in such danger."

James leaned back on the couch. "Not intentionally. But it might have been out of his control, Alex."

"Whatever the case," said Vaughn stepping in, "it occurs to me that the reason they're looking for you, the reason you were having the hallucinations, is all to be found in here." He tapped his head.

"You haven't heard the rest of it yet." Ellen got up off the couch. "I'll be right back."

While she was gone no one uttered a word. Vaughn was mulling over the information. He got up and paced a little in front of the fireplace. Alex had no idea what he thought of him; probably hated him for involving Elle in all this. She seemed to take an eternity, during which Alex had never missed anyone so much in his life. When she came back in he let out a noticeable sigh.

She was clutching the recorder, notebook and printout. She held up the first object. "I want you to listen to this, Patrick."

Ellen pressed the PLAY button and her last session with Alex filled the silence. Vaughn followed it with interest, but when he heard the last line before the cut-off he looked like he could hardly catch his breath.

"'Break the circle,'" Ellen mimicked. "The same phrase Johann spoke, the same phrase you've been trying to discover the meaning of all these years. Alex repeated it yesterday morning. Now can you see why we're here?"

Vaughn walked towards the seated Alex, drawn to him as though answering an invisible summons. "Yes, now I know. After all this waiting... I can't quite... Elle, this is incredible."

"Patrick?" Ellen was baffled.

"Don't you see? It all slots into place now. Everything you've told me. It all makes sense. I never thought I'd get another chance but it's here, thanks to you, Elle. " He crouched down next to Alex, who tried to shuffle backwards. "Hello again, Johann. It's been a long time."

– iv –

"What's he talking about?" demanded Alex.

But Ellen was just as startled by Vaughn's words. "Patrick, you aren't seriously suggesting—"

"I am. And I've never been so serious in my life." Vaughn rose and sat down on the couch in the space Ellen had left. "I knew it as soon as I saw you—deep down. You don't look into a person's eyes as they're dying and not see something of who they really are."

Alex pushed him away and stood up. "Right, now you're freaking me out!" He went to stand beside Ellen. "I'm not Johann. My name's Alex Webber. I'm a college lecturer with a home, a wife..."

Except he wasn't. He was none of those things anymore. However, that just made him all the more determined to hang on to his true identity.

"That's who you are now, yes. It's not who you used to be."

"Oh please, Patrick. We didn't come here for this," said Ellen. "We need to find out why they both uttered the same phrase, what the link is between Alex and Johann and—"

"I've just told you what the link is, Elle."

"I can't accept that."

"No, that's because you never did have an open mind about such things."

"And yours, right now, is a little too open, Patrick."

"What are you all talking about?" Alex asked, more loudly than he'd intended.

Vaughn followed him again. "This is why you came here, isn't it? To find the answer?"

"An answer, not some tenuous theory about past lives," Ellen replied.

"Past lives?" Alex ran a hand through his hair. "Wait a second, hold on."

"What if these hallucinations haven't really been hallucinations at all, but memories," ventured Vaughn. "What if you've been remembering things not just from your past, but your *pasts*?"

Alex wobbled slightly. Ellen was right, they'd come here for explanations, not insanity.

"No, it's not easy to take in, and it goes against everything we've ever been taught in the field of psychiatry, but past lives are recognised by a lot of professionals."

"By people in robes selling scented candles," said Ellen.

Vaughn grimaced. "That's quite a generalisation. It helps to think that the soul goes on when the body dies."

"I'm worried you might be projecting what you want onto this situation. I know how you feel about Johann, I should do, but—"

"I know you credit me with more sense than that, Elle. Sometimes you have to listen to what *this* is telling you, too." He patted his chest.

She pulled a face. "Sometimes that can be wrong as well."

Both Vaughn and Alex looked at her when she said those words.

James, who'd stayed quiet during most of this conversation, now felt the need to speak up. "We can't just stand around here arguing about it. Isn't there a way to find out for sure?"

"Yes," said Vaughn, "there is."

Ellen shook her head. "You're not thinking of—"

"With Alex's permission, I'd like to regress him. Use hypnotherapy to try and unlock what's really happening."

"No," said Ellen flatly. "I won't allow it."

"It would only be an extension of your own sessions with Alex. That's why his episodes have slowed down, because you were starting to control the remembrances."

"It's a completely different thing, Patrick!"

"Hypnotism is a widely used tool in our profession. Has been for—"

"No!" she repeated, more firmly.

"But when all is said and done," Vaughn looked at Alex, "isn't that his decision to make? If he ever wants to find out the truth. If any of us do."

Ellen was looking at the clock. Time was playing tricks again, just as it had since she met Alex: speeding up at certain points, slowing down to a crawl at others. Today it was racing. "It's getting late, and it's been a long day," she said. "If we're going to find somewhere to stay we ought to be making tracks."

"You're not going anywhere," said Vaughn, too quickly for Alex's liking. "I wouldn't dream of it, not when I've got two beds upstairs, a couch and a sleeping bag."

"We've already put you out enough for one day."

"Elle, I don't want you—any of you—wandering around out there with those people on the loose. You're much safer here for the time being. Besides which, you're not going to find a hotel or boarding house with a vacancy for love nor money. They all booked up solid once the heatwave hit. And it has to be better than spending another night in that thing you've got parked outside."

He was right on both counts, they could all see that.

"You're staying here and that's final. Now, when was the last time any of you had anything decent to eat?"

— v —

The Infinity was used to disappointment on his quest.

But to have come so close, only to miss out, that was much, much worse. For almost a day, The Infinity had been locked away in his hotel room, reliving the scene in the corridor again and again. The psychiatrist shielding Webber, their brief exchange, falling, then losing them. Close, *so close* he could have reached out and touched... But he'd wanted to savour the moment, after waiting so long, wanted to enjoy every second of it. Now his chance was gone and time was running out.

Already because of *her* Webber was beginning to order his thoughts. To protect them. The randomness was ending, he was starting to remember who he really was, which meant the window of opportunity was fast closing. If The Infinity was to reach him and regain his advantage it had to be soon. Before the whole thing moved to the next stage.

But what could he do about it? A retreat to his bolthole reflected more than a need to lick his metaphorical wounds. It had been necessary so that he could now marshal his own thoughts and prepare.

Lucas, his men, they all believed he would mete out some form of punishment—and it had crossed his mind to take each, in turn, and fuck them up so badly they'd wish their fathers and mothers had never met. Yet the truth was they would all play an integral part in this, come the ending. Though it pained him to admit it, he needed them as much as they would eventually need him.

So he had directed his anger towards the place where he had lost them, at the people important to the psychiatrist. It was only another move in the game to him, but he did admit to feeling a certain satisfaction at hearing the first of the screams. The deaths had energised him, reminded him what this was all about—and what would come after the inevitable confrontation.

The ethereal contact last night had given him an insight into who Webber was. There was something different this time, something The Infinity couldn't quite put his finger on. He'd known right from the start that there might be more of a struggle. That's why he'd tried harder, searched longer than ever before. There had even been a flash of... What? Fear? Doubt? It was a transient feeling, as he was talking to Webber in the circle. He could not let him remember fully, not yet! Not until it was too late to do anything about it.

The Infinity sat on the bed again, cross-legged. He'd left word that under no circumstances should he be disturbed—by hotel staff, by Lucas, by *anybody*. He desired no repeat performance of what had happened with the maid. There were choices to be made, he had options—some of which he'd disclosed to Webber, others that would be a total surprise to the man. But for now he would watch and wait impatiently.

For Webber to show himself again.

– **vi** –

Patrick Vaughn's culinary skills had improved dramatically in the years since Marina became incapable of cooking herself. Before this, she'd always been the one who'd bought the food in, thrown it together and produced meals so mouthwatering they could have been served up at any high-class restaurant in London without complaint. Not only that, she made it all look so easy. Which of course it wasn't, as Patrick discovered himself when he took over the mantle of head chef. But he steadily improved. Soon he was dishing up plates of *salmon en croûte, boeuf bourguignon* and stir-fry. He quite enjoyed it, really, feeling that he was giving something back at last. He was looking after Marina, just like she'd taken care of him for so long.

But he was most grateful for the fact that he'd learned how to whip up a meal out of virtually nothing. Leftovers and ingredients verging on going out of date could be transformed pretty easily into delicious dinners. Something that came in very handy when she had to be admitted to the hospital.

And something that was equally useful when you had unexpected visitors.

Vaughn busied himself in the kitchen, pulling things out of the fridge, clanking pots and pans around, doing all of this on automatic pilot. His mind was whirling with what had happened today.

It wasn't just Ellen, bringing with her memories of happier times. He'd watched her mature, been with her when she saw her first patients, made her first diagnoses. At times he'd even thought of her as an equal rather than a student. It was very rewarding to see how she'd grown up and how seriously she took her responsibilities. It was lovely to see her again, that was true.

But for Patrick, this had soon been eclipsed by the case, the *patient* she'd brought with her.

He peered through the gap in the kitchen door, saw Webber talking to Ellen, his friend James still sitting on the couch. Patrick had scared the man quite badly by calling him Johann; that was stupid. But his excitement had got the better of him. He'd resigned himself to the fact that he'd never find out what Johann had been trying to tell him, what had happened in those final few minutes of his life. He thought he'd go to the grave without knowing.

He was wrong.

The fat sizzling in the pan broke his concentration. Patrick returned to the stove and tipped in chopped up meat and vegetables. He stirred them with a wooden spoon, losing himself in his thoughts again. When they were ready to serve, he got plates out of the cupboard, then knives and forks out of the drawer.

"Anything I can do to help?" Ellen appeared in the doorway where he'd been only moments before.

Patrick smiled. "You can take some plates in if you like."

"Smells fantastic," she said.

"Thank you. Not just a pretty face, you see."

"You never were."

"Elle, can I ask you something?"

She came over and stood beside him. "Sure."

"Why are you so against this whole past life theory?"

Ellen ran a finger around one of the plates. "I just don't believe in looking for solutions there, when they can probably be found in the here and now. In more rational explanations."

"It's not a very rational world, Elle. When you get to my age you'll see that for yourself."

"You talk as if you're a hundred," she said with a laugh, but there was no humour in it.

"I feel it sometimes."

"I really am sorry about Marina."

"I know you are. And I know what you're thinking, too."

"Oh?"

"That this has got something to do with her. That if reincarnation exists, it means she hasn't really gone, right?"

"No, I—"

"Be honest, Elle. It'd crossed your mind."

She couldn't deny it.

Vaughn kept his eyes fixed on the sizzling pan. "But this has more to do with just the theory itself, doesn't it?"

"What do you mean?"

"You think it's dangerous. Sending him back, confronting him with whatever might be waiting." Patrick spooned the first lot of stir-fry onto a plate. "And you care about him, don't you?" He looked up and they locked eyes.

"Who, Alex? Of course I do. I wouldn't be here if I didn't. I made him a promise."

"Right." He put a hand on her shoulder. "We'll figure this out, you know. One way or another. It'll be just like old times."

"That's what I'm afraid of," Ellen said with a half-smile.

He piled food onto a second plate and she took them both into the living room.

Just like old times.

– vii –

It had been good to eat a decent meal.

Alex didn't think he'd be able to touch it, but in the end the hunger proved too much for him. He ate as heartily as the rest of his companions, almost inhaling the food and finishing first.

Before Vaughn took the plates away he broached the subject of who was sleeping where. "Elle, you can take my bed if you like," he offered. "I'll have the sleeping bag. Alex and James can toss up for the other bed and couch."

"I'm not taking your bed away from you," protested Ellen.

"I don't mind sleeping down here," said James, adding to the debate. "You can take the other bed, Ellen."

"If it helps, I'm not planning on sleeping much anyway," said Alex. They were his first words since Vaughn had mentioned Johann. "I'll stay down here in one of the chairs."

"You need to get some rest," Vaughn told him. "You look worn out."

"I'll be fine in the chair," he restated.

"Then, James, you take the other bed. I'll keep Alex company." There was a finality to Ellen's statement that ended all further arguments. So, with the hour growing late, James excused himself to go and wash. After leaving the plates in the kitchen, Vaughn told them he was retiring to read Ellen's notes and listen to the whole of her recording.

"But before I go, I think there's something the pair of you should listen to as well." Vaughn disappeared for five minutes and they could hear him pottering around upstairs. When he came down he was carrying a small portable CD player in one hand and a disc in the other. "I had this transferred some years ago from the original tapes we made. Did it electronically so you can hear everything. And a translation that I recorded follows it in English. Anyway, I'll leave it with you. I think you might find it interesting."

He said goodnight, leaving Ellen turning the silver circle over in her hands, but came back in seconds later. "Oh, and while you're listening to it, bear this one small fact in mind. The recording was made on May fifteenth."

"The day I was born," said Alex quietly.

Vaughn nodded and this time departed for good.

Ellen looked at her reflection in the CD, tilting it so that it picked up Alex beside her on the couch.

"Are you going to play it?" he asked.

"Do you want me to?"

She took his silence as a yes and placed the CD in the machine. Ellen pressed PLAY. They sat together, experiencing the last audio highlights of Johann's life. The article had prepared Alex for what was on the recording, but it was very different actually hearing Johann speak, or try to, even if it was in German. The inflections in his voice—the fear there—was universal: you could hear it in any language.

"*Kkkkkeine Z-z-z-zeit. Bee-bee-before. Keine...keine...nicht genug Zeit be...*"

And Vaughn's calm tones becoming more concerned as the questioning continued: "*Über wen redest Du, Johann? Hat Dir jemand etwas getan?*"

"*B-B-Böse.*"

"*Etwas Böses?*"

"*Er... Er ist, der Anf-anfan... Und das...das En...*"

Then towards the climax, Johann's frantic pleas, "*Nnnein, hö... Hör mirrr zu! Keine Zeit mehr. Ich habe keine Zeit. Du mußt es beenden. Tu es nicht... Es kann nicht nochmal passieren! Nicht nochmal...*"

Vaughn's translation lost much in terms of impact, but cleared up what Johann was saying. All the concerns about someone coming for him: "*U-U-Um Himmels Willen, hör 'zu. Er... Er kommt zu mir... Kommt zu mir wa-wa-wa—*" The guilt about people he loved: "*Unser Fehler... I-I-Ich... Liebe...*" And the phrase: "*Durchbrich den kreis.*"

"*Break the circle.*"

When the CD spun to a stop, they both looked at each other.

"What do you think?" said Ellen first.

"I don't know. It's a guy in pain, in torment about something. As I said in the car on the way here, I can relate."

"Sympathise, or empathise?" Ellen left the question hanging, its implication doing the same.

"If you're asking whether the man on that recording is me, then the answer is still no. If you're asking whether parts of this sent a chill down my spine as if maybe I'd heard it before, then..."

"Yes?"

He shuffled around to face her. "Ellen, how seriously do you take what your Doctor Vaughn's saying?"

"Firstly, he's not *my* Doctor Vaughn," corrected Ellen. "And you heard my reaction earlier."

"How about now?"

Her eyes softened. "Now, I still think the mind is more complicated than we could ever hope to understand. I believe in the concept of trace memories, that have been handed down through lines for years and years—even collective memories at a push, because we pass on other traits in our genes. But I do have a problem with believing that we come back time and time again as different people. If we did, why would we make such a mess of our lives over and over? You'd think we'd get it right if we'd done it so many times in the past."

"Lord knows you're right in my case. But that's not true of yours, is it? If anything I've made a mess of it for you."

She shook her head. "I don't think what's happening is your fault. Not entirely."

"Your life was screwed up before I came along, is that what you're saying?"

"Alex, don't."

"Nobody's tied you down yet, that's what Vaughn said. And it got me thinking… You've spent the better part of a week at the hospital, with me. Isn't there anybody who's going to be worrying about you? Anybody waiting?"

The muscle in her cheek twitched. "No," she stated eventually.

"But there was once."

"I thought *I* was the psychiatrist here."

"I'm right, aren't I? What happened?"

Ellen heard that beep of the answering machine in her head, the sigh down the phone. "I really don't want to get into this."

"Was it the work, didn't he like what you did for a living?"

"Alex…"

He was like a dog with a bone; even though he could see it was upsetting her, he had to know. "Was he a jealous person? What?"

"If you have to know, he cheated on me. Okay? He lied and he cheated and I found out. End of my perfect life; end of everything." She put quite a bit of space between them. "Are you happy now? You know something about me. Damn it, you know *everything*."

And he did. Suddenly Alex knew all he'd ever need to know about this woman. That she'd thought her life was one way, only to wake up and find it wasn't. She was just as lost as him. "Sorry, Ellen," he said, but somehow it wasn't enough. It couldn't make amends for the intrusion into her private life.

"Doesn't matter." He could see the beginning of tears.

"Yes it does. For what it's worth he must have been an idiot."

Ellen dabbed at her eyes with the back of her hand. "I was the idiot."

The only way he could see to fix this was to talk about himself. Level things out again. "You know that Beverly came to see me the night before she was killed?"

"No," said Ellen, shocked. "No, I didn't."

"I wasn't sure why, or even how she managed it at the time. But I think now I know. She wanted to tell me that it was over—for good. We'd been having problems for a long time as you know."

Ellen gave a small nod.

"Even though she still cared about me and worried about what was happening, she couldn't pretend anymore. She didn't want to."

It was Ellen who said she was sorry this time.

"I think she came to say goodbye that night. But I had no idea it would be so final. I guess I was hoping when all this was over and I went home, we could at least try, or I could do something… But you can't make someone want you. They either do or they don't."

"And you still wanted her?" Ellen dipped her head, then lifted it just as suddenly. "Force of habit. You don't have to answer that, Alex."

"That's okay," he assured her. "It's difficult. If you'd asked me that a few days ago, if you'd asked me before she came to see me, my answer would have been yes, definitely. One hundred percent. Then what happened, happened, and I still don't think I've come to terms with the fact I won't see her again." He shook his head. "I just can't reconcile what I saw with the person I knew."

"Understandable. I'm surprised that any of us are keeping it together right now. Maybe we'll all tip over the edge by the time this is finished."

"Or maybe there's so much death in the world that the loss of one person's life, no matter how close you were to them, sinks without a trace."

She reached out, bridging the gap, and put a hand on his arm. "Or perhaps that makes it even more significant."

Alex looked down at her hand, felt the weight of it. Could feel the warmth on his bare skin, Ellen's pulse in her fingertips. He knew she was aware of it too and suddenly took the hand away, drawing it back into herself. He missed it once it was gone. Alex turned his head to the right, and the first thing he saw was Vaughn's chessboard.

"You sometimes get the feeling we're like that?"

"Like what?"

Alex gestured towards the board. "Pieces in some sort of massive game, being moved around the board. Being sacrificed when necessary."

Ellen leaned back on the couch and crossed her legs. "Very deep. But who are the pawns and who are the major players?"

"Who will win?" said Alex.

"Who'll lose?"

"Who is playing with us?"

Ellen looked at him, a worried frown spoiling her face. "And who'll be left on the board at the end of the game?"

– viii –

Inside the circle.

It was home, a place between worlds. A place of contrasts: a place of great brightness and darkness, pure love and pure hate, warmth and cold, life and death. There were so many figures here: ghosts—some now had faces, others were waiting to be remembered, for their stories to be told.

But it wouldn't be long now, they knew that.

There was a new face tonight, with a new voice. A voice that spoke in German. It was an old face, etched with the experiences of life, with the burden of a million woes. Repeating his deathbed words ad infinitum.

And on the outskirts something watched and waited, circling like the predator it was, hoping for an opportunity.

Hoping to discover where his prey was hiding.

– ix –

Alex snapped his eyes open with a start.

No, he hadn't fallen asleep—he'd only shut his eyes for a moment, just for a moment. He'd promised himself he wasn't going to sleep tonight. He didn't want to dream. If he did then he might inadvertently give away his position to his enemy, tied as he was to him; worse than any kind of phone trace.

And if *he* found them…

What? Alex had no idea, but like Johann he was terrified of it. He was aware of another person next to him, their head resting against his shoulder. When he looked down he saw Ellen with her eyes closed, pressed up against him on the couch. Her breathing was heavy, sucking in air through her nose and expelling it from her mouth. Alex shifted position slightly, freeing his arm from underneath her. She moved slightly and he froze, frightened of waking her. But she just lolled against him again, leaving him no option but to drape an arm around her. It should have felt uncomfortable, but it didn't. He was glad of the company; the closeness of another human being.

With his free hand he reached down the side of the couch to find the holdall he'd brought in from the car. He unzipped it as quietly as he could, one tooth at a time, and slid his hand inside. His fingers touched the edges of the square envelope he'd packed at the very last minute. Clipping it between his fingertips, he fished it out and placed it on his knee. One-handed, he took the card out of the envelope; the smutty picture on the front and the joke inside didn't make him laugh this time either. Nor did the piece of paper with the telephone number on it. He tapped it against his mouth, lost in his thoughts. Wondering whether Steve actually did have anything to do with all this, whether he should have contacted him at the same time as his mum. Wasn't that why he'd brought the card with him, to try and get some answers?

But would the real answers come if he let himself be hypnotised by Vaughn? It might at least settle things once and for all.

Alex knew that he had some tough decisions to make, and very little time in which to make them. Nobody could help him; this was something he had to decide on his own.

Twenty-Two

– i –

ELLEN SAID NOTHING WHEN SHE AWOKE the next morning, she just got up off the couch leaving Alex there bleary-eyed, in the region between waking and sleeping.

They'd talked off and on until the early hours, when she must have dozed off—despite the silent pledge she'd made to keep a watchful eye on Alex. These last few nights with little or no sleep had finally caught up with her, and if she hadn't heard the seagulls squawking outside she might have lay there peacefully the rest of the morning; possibly into the afternoon.

"Ellen?" she heard him call after her, but pretended she hadn't. She walked into the kitchen and, yawning, filled up the kettle. But it wasn't so much falling asleep that troubled her, as the position she'd found herself in when she woke. Head resting on Alex's chest, his arm around her. For fleeting moments it was like she'd gone back in time herself and had fallen asleep in front of the telly, snuggled up with Graham. Then the memories returned; she remembered what had happened in the last five days—who she was really with—and why it was oh-so-bad to be waking up in that position.

But how could she be responsible for what she'd done in her sleep? It could have been anyone sitting there—James, Patrick—and she'd probably have done the same. Only it hadn't been any of them: it had been Alex. And for one split second when she realised that, she'd been glad. This man, whose wife was barely cold, whose life had been turned upside down and who'd done the same to hers, was here, right now, with her—and she liked it. God help her she actually liked it! In that split second she also wondered what it would be like to wake up every morning with her head on his chest and—

Ellen dug her fingernails into her palms.

Now where would Patrick keep the coffee? She opened a couple of cupboards before she found the jar, lined up next to a box of tea bags and bag of sugar. But the act of making a coffee was too mundane to keep the thoughts at bay.

You saw how he was when he thought you'd had a thing with Patrick. Saw how uncomfortable it made him when you hugged the guy, when you put your hand over his. How he'd wanted to know last night whether there was anybody—

"Are you happy now? You know something about me, you know everything."

"For what it's worth he must have been an idiot."

"I was the idiot."

And you haven't changed a bit, Ellen. Stop this, stop it right now.

But you can't deny that—

"Ellen?"

She dropped the cup she was holding. It smashed on the tiled floor, a splinter ricocheting off the fridge. "Damn and blast!"

"I'm sorry," said Alex coming further into the kitchen. "Didn't mean to scare you."

"You didn't," said Ellen, bending to pick up the pieces of crockery. "You really didn't."

"Okay. Here, let me help you." But as Alex stooped to pick up bits of broken cup, she straightened and took a step back. He looked up. "Are you all right this morning?"

"I'm fine," she said, wishing she sounded it.

"You sure?"

"I'm sure."

"How'd you sleep?" he asked, standing up.

"Okay, I guess." She was thankful he didn't press the issue. Alex held out an open hand and she gaped at it; he looked like Fred Astaire asking Ginger Rogers to dance. "What?"

"The cup," he reminded her.

"Oh, yes." She handed him the segments she'd collected and he popped the lid on the bin, dumping them all inside. "I'll get Patrick a new one sometime."

"You're making coffee," said Alex, motioning towards the jar.

"I was."

"Enough water in the kettle for two?"

"Should be. Not sure how we're doing for mugs, though."

He smiled; the smile of a person fit to drop. Someone she'd been looking at for nearly a week but hadn't really *seen* until now. He didn't need her to go to pieces on him as well.

"Alex, listen, I—"

There was somebody else at the kitchen door. James was standing there with ruffled hair, in a dressing gown he must have borrowed from their host. "Thought I heard someone walking around down here. What was that noise?"

"Cup," said Ellen. "My fault."

"Ah." He turned to Alex. "You look terrible."

"Thanks." Alex rubbed his face, perhaps to coax it into a more appealing shape.

It didn't work; James was still looking at the man like his head was going to start spinning. "You get *any* sleep last night?"

"No. You?"

"Not much. Every time I shut my eyes I kept seeing... Well, you know."

"Yeah." Alex exchanged glances with Ellen. "I know."

"So..." said James. "Have you given it any thought? About what you're going to do?"

"I've done nothing but that most of the night. Ellen's not very keen on it, and I can't say I'm ecstatic about the idea. But I figure I haven't had much control over my life for a while now. If it could help me to uncover the answers I'm looking for..."

"You're making the right choice, Alex," said a final voice at the kitchen entrance. If Ellen had been holding another cup, that too might have ended up smashed. James made way for Patrick Vaughn. "We'll get started as soon as we've all had some breakfast."

– ii –

The sun was shining again, so Vaughn thought it would be a good idea if they conducted the first session in the garden. It was the best idea he could have had because Alex was in his element as soon as he saw the expanse of grass, the trickling water feature, the arrangements of flowers. It was exactly the kind of garden he'd always wanted, and took his mind off what they were about to do to him.

"This is beautiful," Alex said to him.

"I always used to enjoy my walks through the gardens at Wittenberg," Vaughn explained. "When I returned to England, I suppose I wanted to bring a little bit of the place back with me. I've had gardens like these in the last three houses I've owned."

He brought out enough chairs for them all to sit on. Vaughn suggested they move underneath the awning at the back if the sun got too hot. There were still some of Marina's old clothes upstairs—he hadn't got around to giving them away to charity yet—and Vaughn told Ellen to help herself. Reluctant at first, she finally chose a light summer dress with straps, turquoise in colour with a white spotted pattern. Though he offered to lend James and Alex clothes, they preferred to remain as they were.

Vaughn sat Alex down opposite him, while Ellen and James hung back out of the way. "Now I can see you're still worried about all this, Alex. But it isn't like you see on TV. I'm not going to make you bark like a dog or get you to stand on one leg patting your head and rubbing your stomach."

"I should hope not," said Ellen.

"I'm not going to swing a watch in front of you and say, 'you are getting sleepy.' I'm just going to put you into a very relaxed state."

"How many times have you done this?" asked Alex.

"Enough. All right, are you ready?"

Alex settled into his seat. "Let's do it before I change my mind."

Vaughn told Alex he was going to put him under but he wouldn't necessarily be aware of it happening. Then he held up a pen and told Alex to concentrate on it. No "Look into my eyes…" No "You will fall into a deep, deep sleep!" Just the pen and the sound of Vaughn's soothing voice. "I want you to focus on the pen, Alex. You're not aware of anything else, just the pen. Now breathe, in and out, in and out. Listen to the rhythm of your own breathing."

Alex closed his eyes, inhaled and exhaled. The constant in and out that was keeping him alive. He felt at peace.

"Now whenever I say the word, 'Return,' you will be back here with us. No matter where you are, what you're doing. This will be your anchor, Alex—do you understand?

"Yes," he told Vaughn.

"You've already remembered some of this, but we need to know more. I want you to tell me about that day at college a couple of weeks ago. The day when you were teaching and you looked up to see your student's face change. Can you see him?"

"Yes. Timothy Brailes."

"But it's not Timothy anymore. Alex, you told Ellen that you thought you recognised that person. Who is it, can you remember?"

He bent forwards, as if trying to get a better look. "That's right: I do know who this is."

"Okay. Where have you seen this before? Was it in a film?"

Alex shook his head. "No, not in a film. I know that face because—"

"Yes?"

"Because the man I'm looking at is my father."

– iii –

"His father?" Ellen couldn't hide the amazement in her voice.

Patrick put a finger to his lips. She sank back in her chair and mouthed a silent apology.

"Alex," said Vaughn, "you're telling me the person you saw that day was your father?"

"Yes, that's how I know him," he insisted.

"Ellen, Alex's father is dead. He died of a stroke," James said to her.

"No stroke," said Alex, overhearing. "He was killed while he slept."

Vaughn did a slight double take. "Killed?"

"Shot dead."

Ellen put a hand to her mouth.

"He was shot? Who shot him, Alex?"

He started to speak in another language; Vaughn asked him to talk in English so they could understand. "The soldiers. They came during the night. Cowards! The bastards were cowards!" Alex shouted the last bit, anger and hatred in every word.

Soldiers? thought Ellen.

Vaughn carried on. "Why did they do it? What reason—"

"Because he was different to them; because they wanted our land!" The enmity was still there—if anything it had increased.

"I don't understand. Help me to understand."

But he apparently couldn't hear Vaughn. Alex was picturing something else, they could see his eyeballs moving around under their lids. "Where are you now?"

"Sat around the fire. There is dancing and singing. It is a celebration."

"That's the scene he described to me back at the hospital," whispered Ellen.

"Why are you celebrating?" asked Vaughn.

"The hunt has gone well today," said Alex when prompted. We will eat and our women and children will be warm." The change from third to first person didn't go unnoticed by Ellen.

"The hunt? What were you hunting, Alex?"

Alex said one word: "*Tatonka*."

"I'm sorry," said Vaughn, "I didn't catch that."

"*Tatonka*… Buffalo."

"So you were out hunting buffalo?"

"Yes. We sent out rider scouts to pick up the trail and the village moved to follow them. This was the first hunt since then and it went well."

"So your father is pleased?"

"Yes, very pleased. Fighting Bear is proud of his son today. But soon the white man will come and shoot the herd for sport. I will have to prove myself as a warrior as well as a hunter. To wear the eagle feather and paint my horse with the markings that my father's bore."

"I see. Can you tell me the significance of the name Broken Tree. Is it someone you know, someone who has spoken to you?"

"Broken Tree," repeated Alex. It sounded sad, the way he said it. "That is the name I have been given."

"Oh my God," said Ellen.

Vaughn just took it in his stride. "Broken Tree, tell me how you feel. Are you worried about the white man coming?"

"About them coming for the people I love."

"Are you scared of failing those who've put their trust in you?"

"I'm scared, yes." Then he added, "For my tribe will all die."

"How do you know that?"

Alex gritted his teeth, rocking in his chair. "Because I have seen it. I saw it when I returned."

"From where?"

"They are all dancing; it is a good time." Alex was retreating back to the memory of the celebration, but Vaughn wouldn't let him. "Stay with me, Broken Tree. Tell me where you returned from."

Alex didn't answer, so Vaughn tried a different approach. "Was that the last celebration the tribe enjoyed?"

"Yes."

"Where were you when they were all killed, Broken Tree? Where were you when Fighting Bear was murdered?"

Alex's face contorted with fear. "I should have been with them. They should have killed me too."

"Go back, Broken Tree. Remember."

"*Wakishni!*"

"Where were you?"

"*Wakishni!*" Alex was shaking, his hands clapped around himself, fingers trembling.

"Is that a name?" Vaughn looked at Ellen but she gave a shrug. "Relax, Broken Tree. Relax."

"It was true, what he showed me. Everything was *true!*"

"What who showed you?"

"The Holy Man. My dreams, I could see a bird—a huge black bird. And a ring of fire. He said I would have to face that which sought me out, through valleys and down rivers."

"The white man?"

Alex shook his head. "I see him. What he lets me see of him. My skills as a hunter are good, but his are better. He rides like the wind for me."

"Where are you now? Where are you seeing these things?"

"Through the rising smoke. He's passing the pipe to me."

"Where are you?"

"Inside the Holy Man's tent. His daughter is there; she is watching me. I can feel her eyes on me. She will be a powerful Shaman one day... perhaps. But her father is trying to warn me about what is to come. I am frightened. I do not want to listen. If only I'd listened..."

"What happened then?" asked Ellen.

"I ran. I was afraid. The Holy Man's words scared me more than the thought of any white man. I wanted to believe that my spirit guide would protect me, lead me to the right choice. But my faith was not strong."

"And when you returned you found everyone dead," Vaughn mused. "What happened to you after you ran away?"

Alex straightened in the chair.

"Broken Tree? What happened after you left the Holy Man's tent?"

"I-I rode my horse—as far away from the tribe as I could."

"Then what?"

Alex began shaking violently. "I...I..."

"Broken Tree? What happened?"

He sprang from the chair and gripped Vaughn by the shoulders—his eyes snapped open; they were wild and fierce. Alex was screaming, tears flowing down his face.

Ellen stepped forward, but it wasn't necessary. "Alex, return. Return to your anchor," Vaughn told him.

Alex's eyes closed. His arms slackened, his whole body flopped and Ellen helped him back into the chair.

"Good," said Vaughn. He looked over at the others. "I'd call that progress, wouldn't you?"

The progress continued.

Ellen voiced her concerns about what happened towards the end, but let Vaughn carry on sifting through the episodes Alex had experienced. He took them in the order that they'd happened, starting with the fire at the restaurant.

Eyes closed, chin resting on his chest, Alex said, "It is not a restaurant, I'm in my favourite hostelry. I always visit when I travel from Southwark into the city."

"I understand. Can you tell me about the events leading up to this? What were you doing in the hostelry?"

"Talking with three gentlemen. We've been conducting our business and joking with the comely lass who brought our drinks. Her name's Wendy. I see her every time I call; I think she has the eye for me." Alex smiled. "But the hour has grown late, well past my usual turning in time. I should retire for the evening, for my room awaits me upstairs."

"And who am I talking to right now?" Vaughn asked.

"Why, my name is William Croker, my dear fellow. Have you not heard of me, or my reputation?"

"I'm sorry to say I haven't, William. Are you well known in these parts?"

"Aye, my good man, that I am. When I'm not travelling I'm easy enough to find."

"So…you've retired to bed—"

"Not that I shall sleep well, even with the amount I've flapped my lips and drunk tonight. I have been restless these past weeks, it is true."

"What about the fire, William—where did you see the fire?"

Alex held up his hand. "I do not wish to—"

"Please, William. It's important."

This seemed to do the trick. "It is the early hours of the morning and my bladder is aching fit to burst. That is what stirs me, but once I am wakened I can smell the smoke. It is coming in through the window, thick and black."

"What happened next?"

"I rush out of my door and there are the other people staying here, some are dressed, even wearing their hats and wigs. Some only have their undergarments on. There's the owner—a rotund fellow by the name of Jacob Hooke—and the serving maid, Wendy. She's regarding me in a strange fashion. We make for the stairs but find that the lower floor is ablaze. Fire is lapping at the wooden walls and bar, the spirits there causing it to spread. Then I hear the first of the screams." Alex began to writhe in his chair, fists clenched. "One of the guests is on fire. He had tried to make it to the door but could not reach it in time. The place is a veritable inferno. Someone has brought a blanket down with them from upstairs. He tries to cover himself, but the fire still reaches him. I can see his skin bubbling and blistering. I am going to die in here; I am going to die tonight."

"I know it's difficult, William, but you have to continue. Tell me more. Tell me what you see."

Alex grimaced. "There's someone else there in the flames. I think he is here to help us escape. I can only just make him out against the fire. Oh, but it is scorching my face, I am holding up my arms to protect myself but it is no use. Water…I pray to the Lord in Heaven that this man has brought water." Alex was clawing at his cheeks, slapping down the imaginary flames.

"What then?" pressed Vaughn, cautious of the response but desperate to know.

"No! It cannot be. It cannot!" cried Alex. "Stay back, stay away!"

"What is it? Tell me what you can see."

"I cannot—it is…it is not real. I thought it only a nightmare. He is…." Alex pitched forwards, so hard the back legs of the chair lifted off the ground. Then he jerked backwards again. "I am outside, but I can hardly breathe. "

Vaughn frowned. "Wait a minute. William, how did you get outside? What happened after you saw the man?"

Alex was ignoring him, carrying on with his tale. "The people, running around, distracted, howling out with lamentation for lost loved ones or for their own safety."

"How did you get out of the hostelry, William?" Vaughn asked again, but Alex wouldn't answer him.

"The fire is leaping from house to house, as if it somehow has a will of its own—and, aye, I think it does at that." His voice was soft and low, and there were tears in Alex's eyes. "The wood is burning, I wonder what will be left after this. If there will be anything at all.

"In the street, oh my heavens, there's Wendy. She is on the floor and the people are trampling her in their rush to flee. Fighting my way through the bodies, I struggle to reach her, and at last I do. She is horribly burned, like myself. Her arms, face. I reach out for her hand, but she is too terrified to take it. In the end I pull her to her feet, force her to move, half carrying the woman along. The noise is deafening above us; the cracking of timber, the roar of impetuous flames. I happen to look up, just once, and see the sky has taken on a fiery aspect as well—it is as red as blood. Some will say that this is a cleansing, after the plague of the year afore. I know differently; I know, as I help Wendy through the streets, towards the Thames. I remember and it will haunt my waking existence evermore."

"The Thames," said James. "Al— William, what year is this?"

"Why, it is the year of our Lord, sixteen sixty-six."

— v —

"I, Agami, go this night to the Imperial Palace, at the insistence of the Princess Yuko, daughter of the Emperor Toshiyaku. There is to be an entertainment in the court that will last the whole of the night. As official messenger and aide to the governor of Musashi, I am here by royal decree. There are many people at the palace, within and without, and the princess—as beautiful as the spring—is attended to by some of her loyal handmaidens. I have heard tales that they are only visited by their fathers and lovers, of which it is said there are many. I have only ever desired one true beauty to satisfy me. And I feel I might have found it here, miles from the place of my birth. My enquiries have uncovered that she travelled with her family when she was very young, to stay here at the Royal City. She was chosen personally because of this family bond by the princess to attend her: Cho, my butterfly.

"I have written poetry and asked that it should be passed on to her. *What intensity of memory clings to your heart?* I asked her, but she has not yet replied. Though I search with my eyes, I cannot see her. Perhaps it is a fool's errand for I do not know how she feels about me, and she may have a number of suitors already. But there is another amongst the guests that I recognise—not from any waking meeting, but from somewhere else. His clothes, his fine silks and sash, denote him to be of noble birth. His men all refer to him as Sama: their Lord. His eyes are the strangest of colours, like none I have ever seen before. Everyone appears to know of him as he walks among the visitors; but all the time, like myself, he is searching and looking for something—or someone. It occurs to me that this might be one of Cho's lovers. As his eyes are directed towards me, I am certain that he must have read my poetry, intercepted it somehow, and is bent on revenge. If so, this cannot be settled here—it must be done in the honourable tradition.

"By the sword.

"I am trained in the arts of war—my father was a great samurai warrior—and I am not frightened of engaging any man. Except this one. For some reason his presence scares me more than anything in this world, even the thought that I may have lost Cho to him."

* * *

"I was born and raised in a remote province called Eboe, in the valley named Effaka. I had never heard of white men or travellers or of the seas. My father, one of the elders of the village, styled Embrence, his head marked—the highest distinction—never spoke about such things to me. My days spent there seem like a dream, the dance and music, the public rejoicing after the men returned from a triumphant battle. I was the youngest of all his sons, the greatest favourite with my mother. Until the day the men came...

"I was taken as a young boy, sold on to those who took me across my beloved Africa. On my journey I was hearing many languages, not much different to Europeans as I later learned. In all the places where I was the soil was exceedingly rich; the eadas, plantains and yams were in great supply, and of incredible size. There were also vast quantities of different gums, though not used for any purpose, and much tobacco and cotton.

"Until eventually I came to the coast. The first thing which I saw was the blue sea, and on it a ship, waiting for its cargo. I was now sure that I had found myself amongst a world of bad spirits, and that the crew were going to kill me. Their complexions were different, lighter. I was cast into the bowels of the ship where there were more of my countrymen, all chained together. I knew I would never see my home again and before the journey was over I would wish myself dead more times than once.

"Shipped off to a strange land, I was eventually sold on to a planta-tion owner where I worked long hours and was whipped and beaten by a brutal manager. Once, I was left bleeding and half unconscious. Were it not for the attentions of Alice, one of the maids from the house, I would not have survived. Her name before she was called Alice was Gzifa. She doesn't remember much before she was taken and sold, either. We have talked about our homeland and how we miss it. She tended to my cuts and bathed my bruises; if she had been found we would both have been punished. We had come to know each other because my master had sum-moned me once to the big house to fan him on a hot day and she had been serving him food.

"Two days later my master received a gentleman at the house calling on business. As Alice described him to me, I felt terrible afeared. 'Blue eyes,' she said. 'As blue as the sea.' I thought about how blue the seas had been that day when they threw me into the ship, that same blue I have been dreaming about, and I knew that it meant danger, but I didn't know how or why. Then my master came to me the next day saying he was sell-ing some of his slaves on to this man. I knew I couldn't let it happen, that I didn't want to be that man's slave.

"Even a thousand beatings would be better than that."

* * *

"Kept in the darkness I've lost all sense of time here. All I've had to eat are bits of mouldy bread, and to drink: stale water. I can hear the scuttling of the rats at night, feel cockroaches and spiders crawling all over me. I do not even know what I have been charged with; they have not told me. The Inquisition do not need to tell anyone their business. They only answer to Torquémada himself, and to God. I have attempted to tell them I am innocent of whatever they think I have done. I am no more a heretic than the Pope himself! I have always tried to live a good, honest life. My trade is in wood. I carve: tables, chairs, ornaments. My hands are skilled, or at least they were before the men who took me stamped on them, before they set upon me down here with their knives: those first few times they held me down and cut me.

"But perhaps the most heinous of torture devices is that of time. The waiting is agonising. Waiting to find out what they will do with me; what will happen the next time they come. And the dreams. My Lord, what nightmares they be! What imaginings my fevered mind has produced. I have seen demons in them, and perhaps they are right to think I consent with such, but it is against my will I tell you! I have not made mention of this, as it will lead to my certain death, but before they are done with me I might be glad of that anyway.

"At long last hooded men come for me again. Two of them drag me through the stone corridors into a larger room—one I haven't seen before. Not far away, an old man is on a rack shaped like a wheel; he has been left there for some time, by the looks of it. On the wall two figures hang in chains. One naked man is nothing but skin and bones, his body bruised and beaten. A woman is the other, long hair hanging down over her face, head lolling forward. Her clothes are filthy, no more than rags.

"'Shall we see to the witch first?' asks one of the men. I am not sure whether he is talking to the friars present, but then I see he is consulting another man—the Inquisitor who asked me question upon question when I first arrived. He shakes his head and points to the other prisoner, who is removed from the chains, dragged across to a strange device, and strapped into it by his arms and legs. I take his place on the wall. 'Confess your sins—for the last time, confess them!' shouts the Inquisitor. I knew then by the look of him that he didn't care one way or the other. For he was enjoying this, actually enjoying the pain and suffering of the gaunt man, who could not answer him; who did not even have enough breath left to scream when they placed heavy weights on the ends of attached ropes, raising him and then releasing the ropes so that he was stretched painfully and suddenly—the opposite of the man on the rack. The cords in his neck stand out and his eyes are so round and wide and full of terror I cannot not bear to look at them. Then it is over. The man drops forward, and they can torture him no more.

"The 'witch,' as they'd called her, raises her head and I see tears on her cheeks. I have no idea or way of knowing if she knew the man, or if she is crying because she faces the same, or much worse, but I feel like crying with her.

"Then the Inquisitor has his men show her the instruments they will use to extract her confession. Irons are heated, her head pulled back by the hair, and the glowing end brought nearer to her face. She is promised leniency if she co-operates, freedom if she tells them the names they so obviously wish to hear. But a death sentence will mean she'd be burned alive as an *auto de fé*. To her credit she shows no fear, even as they hang her in the middle of the room by her arms. They open and close hot pinchers in front of her. One of the hooded men rips open her already torn clothes and threatens to clamp a nipple hard if she does not talk. He brings the pincers closer as one of the holy men reads from his Bible, and I want to shout that this is madness, that we have done nothing wrong.

"Before anything can happen, the grilled door to the chamber opens and a man in robes appears. He must be a bishop I think, but he is not alone. There is another fellow with him and he is hooded like those who brought me here, but definitely not a servant. The bishop allows the hooded man inside, head bowed. He stands there for a moment, and removes the cowl.

"It is then that I realise that these tortures, these instruments are nothing compared to some."

* * *

On and on, backwards and forwards through time, through more lives: being in the cheering crowd at an execution in Revolutionary France; an Aztec just before Spaniards marched on Tenochtitlán; a nobleman in the Middle Ages attending the jousts; a Viking freeman and member of the Thing, a law court held once a year...

They worked on through lunch—nobody seemed that hungry—and well into the afternoon. Vaughn spent time delving into some of the stories Alex had to tell, but skimming over a lot. He had to, there were simply too many. Alex took them to Arabia during the rise of Islam, described what it was like to be a slave in the year fire devastated Rome, gave them a guided tour of Mycenaean civilisation. He even took them back to when the first known tools were made by man.

"My God," said James, "the cave paintings, the fire. It's got to be the Palaeolithic ages!"

In each one the main highlight would be an encounter with a mysterious figure that Vaughn couldn't get him to speak about. He would simply shut down, even under hypnosis.

But the doctor saved what was most important to him until last.

– vi –

Lucas Peck sat on the bench, looking at the painting in front of him. An abstract by a little known northern artist called Habersitch.

The bright colours swished and swirled, folding into each other like a kaleidoscope of shapes. He could appreciate what Habersitch had done, and like all the other pieces he'd seen in this local gallery—seconds away from the Olympia if the call should come—he admired what it was trying to say. In this instance, that life is a confusion of sights: what we see every day is such a blur to us, that to try and make sense of it would be impossible. That's why he liked art, he thought to himself, because you knew where you stood with it. Most artists were only trying to express themselves. All their work had some kind of meaning, was making some sort of point: good or bad. Whereas life was what it was—generally meaning*less* and point*less*. Spent doing and saying things that ultimately would have no impact on anything at all.

If The Infinity had shown him anything it was that.

These people went about their daily routines, doing the same things they'd always done—day in, day out—unaware that they affected nothing. That in the grand scheme of things they were bugs. No, lower: microscopic organisms that didn't have a hope of understanding what was going on around them.

Not that Lucas did either. If he could then he wouldn't be a man anymore, he would be something else. Something more like The Infinity.

He wondered if his art would ever find a home in a place like this.

Probably not. It wasn't worth exhibiting anyway, just dry runs for the perfect piece to come. No artist was ever truly satisfied with their work, and Lucas was no exception. He craved flawlessness, the moment when he could stand back and say: "Yes, this is it. This is the one." It hadn't happened yet, not with all the others he'd worked on, those living—those *dead* pieces of sculpture and painting. Certainly not with his most recent daub.

But he had purpose. He knew what his own life was all about, even if he couldn't exactly recall where he'd come from or how The Infinity had found him all that time ago. It made him more than them, more than the materials he used. He was doing them a favour actually. He was giving them *meaning*.

Just as The Infinity would give this whole world meaning before he was done. Instead of simply playing at it, the serious stuff would begin. And that day, Lucas knew whose side he wished to be on. The side that had a vision, had purpose. Not that of the hunted, the weak, the exposed.

There would be no contest.

There never had been.

– vii –

"You've told us about so many things today, Alex. Now I want you to tell me about Johann," said the former psychiatrist at last.

With eyes still closed, Alex tilted his head. "Johann?"

"Yes. Do you recognise that name?"

"It was mentioned in a paper written by Dr. Patrick Vaughn, he was one of his patients—"

"Anything else?"

Alex shook his head.

Vaughn was puzzled, then remembered that Johann was the name they'd christened him with *after* he was found. It wasn't the man's real name. "Take me back and tell me about the person you were before Alex Webber," he clarified. "Can you do that?"

Alex nodded.

"What was your name."

"Klein. Lars Klein."

Even after all the times she'd heard this today, Ellen still let out a gasp. It was weird to listen to somebody you knew talk about being another person—and so casually.

"When were you born, Lars?"

"In 1895 in Dresden."

"What are your earliest memories?"

Alex concentrated hard. "Of sitting on my father's lap and him reading to me. It is a story about a little bird migrating when the cold weather comes. There is music in the background. My mother is listening to Bach."

"Very good. And later…?"

Born into a working class family, Lars went on to tell them he had attended school where he had excelled in literature and mathematics. Then, when the Great War came, he'd signed up to fight for his country. "I have seen some awful things in the trenches. We have been stationed at Ypres, where the Allied troops are trying to gain ground. Myself and my comrades are going over the top to meet them head-on today. The sentry on duty is raising his head over the parapet, ready to give the signal. Then up and over into No Man's Land, over our own barbed wire. Some of the men are caught on this before they even get a chance to fight. Then the bullets come, to the left and right." Alex began to dodge the imaginary fire, raising an invisible rifle. "The dead still litter the ground where our gas has done its worst. No one should have to see those faces, bulging yellow and purple. There are men coming towards us, charging with bayonets."

Alex screamed.

"What is it?" asked Vaughn.

"An explosion, it knocks me off my feet. I lay very still on the muddy ground, my fallen friends not far away. Another body lands on top of me; it's heavy, pins me down. I blink away the blood but don't move. Out of the corner of my eye I see our enemy still running past. Another wave of explosions will stop them before they get to our trenches, and then I will be able to crawl back under the cover of darkness. But…"

"Yes?"

"But there is someone else out here too. Someone walking over No Man's Land. He wears a British officer's peaked cap and holds a pistol. There's something about the way he's moving from one dead man to the other, as if he's examining them. I see him empty a bullet into one wounded soldier. I cannot tell for certain but I think it might even be one of his own. A mercy killing. No—he's smiling. I can see those bright blue eyes from here; I can see that he *enjoyed* it. I know it's important to remain very, very still. I cannot let him see me. He stands and surveys the scene of destruction and I can tell he feels at home. He has sent his men to their deaths, now he's standing and watching as they're torn to pieces. What kind of a world is this?"

"What happened then, Lars?"

"I think I must have lost consciousness because he's gone when I wake up. Everything is still and quiet. Quiet as a... The first time I move it feels like I've seized up, but I manage to shrug off the corpse covering me, and begin the return journey to our trench."

"Well, that would certainly account for why Joha— Lars ended up as he did," said Ellen.

"Wait," Vaughn told her, "there's more."

Alex continued his tale, telling them what happened when Lars returned home, how his family lost most of their money in the depression of the following decade. "There were many who did not agree with the direction our country was going in. I, myself and my wife, suffered during the hard times a few years ago after Wall Street. And although I did not lose my employment, I saw families devastated by the slump in the economy. A slump that saw millions of Germans turning to another source of inspiration."

Vaughn, Ellen and James all looked at each other.

"Hitler's party has been gaining momentum. It is the largest political party in the Reichstag. Vice Chancellor von Papen is losing support and it cannot be long before another challenge comes. So we meet: myself and some of my friends—political activists mostly—to see what can be done to turn back the tide...if it is not already too late. If Hitler, God forbid, comes into power then I fear that he will turn this country into a slave race following his bidding. The army is already with him, and I know of people who have been threatened because of their opposition to the man. My most precious Rita has begged me to stop attending. 'What good can only a small number of people do?' she tells me. But if we don't do something then I think that the dreams I have been having will become a reality."

"What dreams, Lars?" asked Vaughn.

"In them, I see people dying, screaming. I see fire and guns and explosions. At first I thought I was reliving my time in the trenches, as I often did when I returned from the War. But the dreams are subtly different. More hellish than even I could have imagined. He is there, the man with blue eyes—laughing."

"Again," said Ellen.

"Let me ask you one thing," said Vaughn. "When did you start having the dreams? When did you start dreaming about the circle?"

"Just after my birthday," Alex stated matter of factly.

"And when did the man in the dreams catch up with you?"

"At one of the meetings they are waiting for us. Men in long, dark coats pulled around them, concealing their pistols. They know that only a small number can become more, that one day we might stand against them. Uwe, Rüdiger and Marius are shot as they leave the building, in the head and chest. The bullets make no sound. 'God in Heaven, no! Stop—these are good men! They have families, they have wives and children!' We are running about, panicking, trying to hide. It is then, as they approach, that I see he is with them. The man from my dream, from the battlefield years ago. He has Rita. As the rest of the men are killed, my friends and comrades, she is all I can see, her beautiful face in the light from the street."

"What happened, Lars?" Vaughn asked in a quiet voice.

Once more Alex became agitated, just as he always did when it came to describing a meeting with the man. "I-I can't—"

"It's extremely important."

Alex was shaking. "He wants me. This is all because of me. 'No, keep back—you stay away from me!'"

Ellen rose again. "Patrick?"

Alex was practically convulsing. "No….nmmmmnnnnnnnoooo!"

"Patrick, help him," ordered Ellen, now at Vaughn's side. "Bring him out of it."

"Yes, yes of course. Return to your anchor, Alex. Return—"

But he was too far gone to listen. Alex fell from the chair, curling up into a ball on the floor. His body went rigid.

Vaughn stood back, open-mouthed.

Ellen was down on the floor, holding Alex's shoulders. "Do something!" she shouted at Vaughn.

"I'm bringing you out of there. Can you hear me?"

If he could, he didn't show any signs of it.

"Hurry, for God's sake," said Ellen.

"I can't do it as quickly as that," Vaughn told her. "It could be harmful."

"More harmful than *this*?" Ellen snapped, crouching down and taking Alex's hand in her own.

"All right, I'm going to count down from five. When I get to five you will wake up, but you will remember everything. Okay, five…four…three…two…*one!*"

As soon as Vaughn said the last number, Alex stopped shaking. He opened his eyes, saw Ellen down on the floor next to him and reached up with both hands. She took him in her arms.

There they stayed for a good ten minutes, with the others standing watching, not knowing what to do next.

– viii –

Alex lay on the couch, resting, while Ellen dabbed at his forehead with a damp cloth. James and Vaughn were both standing, wondering who was going to start the conversation they so desperately needed to have.

In the end it was Vaughn who broke the silence. "How's he feeling?"

"How's he…" Ellen was furious. "I warned you something like this would happen."

"I'm sorry. It won't the next time we—"

"There isn't going to *be* a next time," she informed him. "I think he's been through enough, don't you?"

"We've only just scratched the surface," said Vaughn.

"James?" Ellen was looking to him, as Alex's friend, for backup.

"The historical details certainly sounded genuine enough. But I'll have to do some checking: the references, his descriptions of life in those different historical periods." He shook his head. "I just don't see how he could be making all that up; there was stuff that even surprised me."

"You're welcome to use my computer to verify any facts you like," Vaughn announced. "But I wholeheartedly believe that Alex has been remembering his past lives, just as I said." He waited for Ellen to say something, but she dabbed at Alex's brow. "We still don't know the significance of the figure from the dream, though." Vaughn leaned on the mantelpiece. "The person who crops up in every single past life Alex has lived, the man who is apparently chasing him in this one."

"So what, you think they're reliving some past life experience as well?" said James. "That those are the blue-eyed man's previous incarnations?"

"Makes perfect sense. We tend to repeat the same cycles over and over in our lives, past and present. In documentation on past lives people claim to have known each other in many different times, whether it be as friends, relatives, mothers, daughters, husbands, brothers. It doesn't matter, they still seem to find each other."

"Except here one wants to kill the other," said James.

"He doesn't want to kill me," said Alex from the couch.

All eyes turned towards him at once.

He tried to sit up and Ellen placed a hand on his chest. "Take it slowly."

"I'm okay," he promised. "Really."

"That's rubbish and you know it."

"Let him speak," said Vaughn, which earned him another stern look. He ignored it. "What *does* he want, Alex?"

"I can't remember," said Alex. "Every time I try it's like there are red-hot needles in my brain. But whatever it is, it isn't good."

"And it sent Johann, I mean Lars, completely insane," Vaughn reminded them. "He met the blue-eyed man in the 1930s, and was picked up on the train tracks decades later. But what happened in between?"

"That's been blotted out as well," said Alex.

"If we can discover that, we might just solve our puzzle," said Vaughn.

Ellen couldn't let that slide. "Or you might send Alex the same way as Johann, then we get nothing anyway."

"I do know one thing," said Alex. "He's not going to stop looking for me until he gets whatever it is he wants. We're connected, and he'll find me the same way he did last time. He'll also kill anyone else who gets in his way. Beverly was only the beginning." He looked at them gravely. "The longer I stay here, the more chance there is that you'll all join her."

– ix –

The place was a dive, but he called it home. For now.

It was all he could afford, low-rent accommodation for a lowlife. He laughed to himself as he read the OUT OF ORDER sign on the lift for the third time that week.

The job hunting wasn't going well either. Who wanted to employ someone with a criminal record? Steve Webber couldn't even get a job as a pizza delivery guy in Syria right now. His silver tongue could only earn him so much grace from the landlord of this fine establishment, and once the two month's rent in advance ran out, he could kiss the whole kit and caboodle goodbye.

He'd considered making use of his only other talent, apart from being able to pick a lock in under thirty seconds. With all the women he'd slept with in the past, you could more or less call him a gigolo anyway. He'd been called worse. What was the harm in getting paid for it? But that wasn't really an option since *she'd* come back into his life. He hadn't been expecting to hear from her at all, not after the way they'd left it. All that time apart. But like the rest of 'em, once they'd had a taste of the good stuff there was no turning back. Seems like he'd been on her mind since he went away. Just like she'd been on his.

But there were...complications. He'd tried not to fall for her, told himself it would only end in tears. But the chemistry! When they went to bed the Earth moved all right—the whole universe in fact! That wasn't the problem. Never had been with him. She was mixed up, in a strange place right now, and he had to admit he'd felt guilty about taking advantage. When they'd met again it had been great—like they were the only two people on the planet. But they weren't. And it had been days now since he'd heard from her.

Steve made his way up the stairs with his groceries, which represented the last of his petty cash: a loan. She'd given him money before in the past and he'd felt bad about taking it this time. But she could see the situation he was in. *And a guy's gotta eat.*

A loaf of bread, some milk, tea and cheese. He'd dine like a king tonight. It was better than the shit they served up in stir, anyway. Standing in line, waiting for some Hairy Mary to slop beans and powdered mash on your tray. If he ever saw another plate of boiled fish, Steve thought he might just throw up on the spot. Compared with that, cheese on toast was like a four course fucking banquet.

Don't worry, something'll turn up—it usually does.

The only thing was it always turned out to be highly illegal. He'd made a promise he would definitely go straight this time. That's why he was keeping a low profile. A low profile for a lowlife.

When he finally reached his level, Steve jammed the key into his flat door and turned it. He surveyed the kingdom in which he was going to prepare his royal feast. The faded carpets and curdled-cream curtains, the ripped sofa with stuffing coming out of the side. When he'd first seen this he'd said to the landlord, "Who was your last tenant, Wolverine?"

The battered TV, which was even more battered now, due to Steve's repeated bangs on the top to get it to work properly, stood in one corner. He switched it on and heard the first bars of a cop show theme. Steve hit it again, just for good measure. "That's all I need," he muttered under his breath. The snow on screen obscured his vision, but that wasn't necessarily a bad thing.

He took his food into the kitchen. There was no toaster, but there was a grill in the oven. Steve turned on the gas and searched around for a match, finding a Swan Vesta on the verge of disappearing down a crack on the work surface. "Got ya!" Now all he needed was something to strike it on. Steve opted for the wall, as it was rougher than any sandpaper he'd ever come across. The grill lit, he let it heat up while he took a knife out of the drawer and cut some cheese. He placed two slices of bread inside to begin toasting.

Just as he was about to check it, the phone rang.

"Oh, shit!" *Leave it,* he thought. *If it's important, they'll ring back. Just think about your royal dining appointment, the cheese that would soon be bubbling under the grill.*

The ring persisted. *No, it might be her—she might be free, or might need him. He couldn't just let it ring off.*

Steve went back into the living room and homed in on the phone, a black model from the 1970s complete with dial. He flipped the receiver with one hand and caught it with the other. "Y'ello," he said.

"Steve?" Instead of the female voice he'd been expecting, it was a man's. "Steve, is that you?"

He hesitated before answering. "Who wants to know?"

"Steve, stop messing about. I haven't got time."

Who the hell did they think they were, talking to him like—

"Steve, it's your brother."

"Alex?" Steve's voice cracked when he said the name. Of all people it might be, his sibling was the last one he'd been expecting. "How you been, bruv?"

"Terrible."

"Oh, right." Steve slid down into a tatty armchair. "Anything wrong in particular?"

"I wouldn't know where to start. Steve, my whole world's imploding."

"Alex, look—"

"Steve, I haven't got long. You remember my birthday?"

"Seems like a lifetime ago."

"Several at least," said Alex.

"What?"

"Doesn't matter."

"You'll have to speak up—I can hardly hear you, bruv."

"Steve, shut up and listen! You said that if I ever needed anything I should ask. Well, I'm in trouble. Big trouble."

"What are you talking about?"

"Someone's looking for me."

"You mean like an angry parent or something? What *have* you been up to?"

"Steve, I'm serious."

And he was, Steve knew what that tone meant. "Go on, bruv, I'm listening."

"At first I thought it might have something to do with you. Like that time when—"

"I told you, I'm legit now. Or tryin' to be."

"Doesn't mean there aren't people looking for you, Steve."

He had a point.

"But I know the truth now," Alex said. "This guy's looking for *me*."

"What's he want?"

There was a gap before Alex replied, "I haven't got a clue."

"So, why don't you just tell the fuzz." As if to emphasise his point, the cop music played again as the programme went to a commercial break.

"Doesn't work like that; this guy's connected."

"And what's… Beverly have to say about all this?"

Another gap, longer this time. "Beverly's dead, Steve. They killed her."

Steve nearly dropped the phone. "What?"

"You heard me."

"She can't be… How?" He let his head fall back on the chair.

"They… Steve, Steve? Are you still there?"

"Yeah, bruv, I'm here." He fought hard to control his voice.

"So you see, I'm in real trouble."

"Yeah, I see. Does Mum know?"

A pause. "No, and I don't want her to. Got it?"

This wasn't the time for point scoring. "But what if he comes after—"

"I told her to go away for a little while," Alex cut in. "She should be all right, it's me the guy wants."

"Okay, what do you want me to do?"

"I need to disappear. Any ideas?"

Steve whistled. "What—you mean like skip the country?"

"That might be a good start. Where would I be able to get my hands on a fake ID, or passport?"

He wasn't used to his brother talking about things like this. Alex was as straight as they came, never so much as stole a chocolate bar. "You're talking about some serious cash to pull that off."

"But could it be done?"

"Yeah, I suppose. I know some people. A few of them owe me favours. It'd mean surfacing again, though."

"I don't want you getting involved any more than you have to. Is there anywhere I could go to around here? Anybody I could see?"

"What, in Kirkwell you mean?"

The third pause. "I'm not in Kirkwell. Sorry, forgot to mention that."

"Then where the bloody hell are you?"

"At…a friend's house. On the coast."

"On the coast? What—"

"He's helping me."

"How do you mean?"

"He's a…well, he *was* a psychiatrist," Alex explained.

"Oh, right. It all makes perfect sense now."

"He's an old friend of a friend."

"And who's that then?"

"She's a psychiatrist as well. James is here with us and—"

"Fucking hell, mate," said Steve. "I'm gonna need a minute here."

"You know me, Steve. I'm not crazy, even though I've had my doubts about that recently. I'm just in trouble and need to know whether I can count on you. I don't know who else to turn to."

Now it was Steve who took a time out from the conversation before answering. "Yeah, you can count on me. I'll sort you out. But you need to tell me where you are, *exactly* where you are."

Silence.

"Tell me where," said Steve. "Or don't you trust me?"

"I'm staying with a Dr. Patrick Vaughn, in a place called Armitage Bay."

"Armitage Bay, got it."

"Look, I've got to go."

Before he did, Steve asked him for his mobile number. "Don't worry, bruv, I'll sort everything. And… I'm sorry about Beverly."

"Thanks. Listen, watch your back, okay?"

"I always do."

Alex said goodbye and clicked off the phone. Steve got up and placed the receiver back on its cradle. The decrepit smoke alarm woke up, doing its best to alert him to the fact there was smoke coming from the kitchen. He ran in and pulled out the toast from under the grill, coughing as he did. Steve dumped the whole thing in the sink and ran the tap over it. It was burnt to a crisp.

"Shit," he said.

He returned to the living room, wafting the smoke away until the alarm gave up the ghost, and rubbed his chin. Then he picked up the phone again and started to make some calls.

— x —

"Everything okay?"

Alex started when he heard Ellen's voice behind him. He was standing in the hallway, next to the phone table. "What?"

"I was worried about you. You know, after…"

"I was just on my way back," said Alex.

She leaned against the wall opposite. "When are you going to learn that you can't pull the wool over my eyes, Alex Webber."

"What do you mean?"

"I heard you talking on the phone."

"Ellen, listen—"

"You don't have to sneak away to call your mum, you know."

Alex let out a breath. "I know… I withheld the number," he added.

Ellen nodded. "I've been trying to get through to the hospital myself, but nothing still…"

Alex fidgeted about awkwardly. He knew Ellen thought those men had covered up the whole incident at the hospital, the ruckus in the psychiatric department, but that was only the half of it.

"So how is she?"

"Hmm?"

"Your mum."

"Oh, right. She's okay."

"She sounds nice; I hope I get to meet her sometime."

"I hope so, too."

Ellen looked down. "I wish I had that kind of relationship with my mother. I sometimes think she only had me because she felt obliged. An accessory to the marriage; the handbag to match the shoes. Can't even be in the same country when I need her."

"I'm sure it's not as bad as that."

"You don't know my parents."

Alex stepped closer. "No, but I'd be very proud if I had a daughter like you. Someone with principles, someone who cares about people."

She looked at him. "Sometimes you can care too much."

"Not all men are like…well, like *him*. One day you'll meet someone and it'll wipe all the pain away. You'll know when it's right. Both of you. And he'll realise just what a lucky guy he is."

"Flatterer," she said, smiling.

"I mean it."

Breaking eye contact, she said: "Did you mean it when you said you were going to run away?"

"I don't know. I just don't want anyone else to get hurt because of me."

"But is that the answer? You said yourself this guy's not going to stop looking for you. Isn't it better to try and work out a way to stop him? To stop running and make a stand?" She pushed herself off the wall and drifted across to him.

"But I don't know if he *can* be stopped."

"We're all in this now," said Ellen. "We can find a way together."

Alex faced front and looked past the Freelander to the edge of the bay. The sun had just begun its descent into a red sky. It looked as if it would boil the ocean when it finally sank. The heat of the day was giving way to mugginess.

"We'll find a way together," she reiterated, then kissed him softly on the cheek.

TWENTY-THREE

– i –

"ARE YOU SURE IT'LL WORK?" ASKED ALEX.

Vaughn rubbed the back of his neck. "It should do. The suggestion I planted while you were under should stop you from dreaming—at least about him. Block out the nightmares."

"And stop him from reaching me?"

That was the main thing; if his pursuer could get to him through his dreams, he might find out where they all were.

"We'll have to take the risk," said Ellen. "You need to get some sleep." She was right; he'd never felt this drained in his life. Even so, he'd resisted sleep as long as possible. James insisted Ellen took the bed upstairs, so he took her place downstairs with Alex. They talked about old times, nights out and college life, steering the conversation away from anything to do with the last few days, the last couple of weeks, until gradually and inevitably, Alex had closed his eyes and they'd stayed closed. Sheer mental and physical exhaustion took him and didn't let go until about midday on Friday.

He woke to find the room empty and sunlight streaming in through the window. But rather than making him feel better, the lay-in made him feel like he'd been run over by a truck. His legs and arms were stiff when he tried to move, and his head was pounding again, all without the aid of booze. Dragging those memories out must have taken its toll and was worse than any hangover he'd ever had.

He heard the mumble of voices coming from the garden. He got up and walked towards the open window so he could hear better, standing behind the curtain so he wouldn't be seen.

"...do him irreparable harm, Patrick." That was Ellen speaking.

"I know what I'm doing; I'll be careful. We need to find out what all this is really about," said Vaughn.

"I'm not your student anymore. You can't just dismiss my concerns with a flick of your wrist. I'm beginning to wish I'd never brought him here. Perhaps I could have found a way myself to—"

He missed a bit, then heard, "...doing such a good job. Disjointed information, half remembered scenes and cuts on his arm—"

"That happened before I even met him!"

"Ellen, Dr. Vaughn, this isn't helping." James' voice. "We're all curious about what this means, and we're all in danger. But it's Alex this man is after. It's up to him what we do next, don't you think?"

"Is he in any fit state to decide?" said Vaughn.

"Of course he is," Ellen argued.

Alex missed the rest because his mobile started vibrating in his pocket; he'd been keeping it on him just in case. Alex crept away from the window and took it out.

"Hello?"

"Yeah, hello bruv...." The line crackled badly. "...news...someone who might...able to..."

"Could you say that again, Steve? The signal's lousy."

"I said I think I can sort you out. Had a word with a few people and it's doable." The volume was low but he could just about hear him.

"Okay," said Alex. "Thanks."

"And you're cool about changing your name?" asked Steve.

"I don't think that really matters anymore; I've had so many already."

"Say again, bruv."

"It's okay with me. So how's this going to work?"

"We're...going to...up."

"You went again, can you repeat that?"

"Going to have to meet up," said Steve again.

Alex didn't say anything.

"Did you hear me, bruv?"

"Yes, I heard," he said at last. "I can't come back home, Steve."

"…know…over…you…"

"What?"

"Said I'll come over to you. I'm not exactly busy—and I could use a holiday." Alex pictured him smirking at the other end of the line.

"Okay, when?"

"I can make it by tonight, say half-seven. That suit you?"

"That's fine."

"Whereabouts?"

Alex thought about it for a moment. They couldn't meet here, and he didn't really know this area well enough to give another location. "We can hook up in the bay bit of the town," he said at last.

They said their goodbyes, Alex thanked him again and switched off the phone. He sat down on the couch, clutching his head in his hands, Ellen's words from last night going through his mind. *"Isn't it better to try and work out a way to stop him? To stop running and make a stand? We'll find a way together."*

But then he saw Beverly's lifeless eyes gazing back at him, and for an instant they became Ellen's.

He couldn't let that happen. He had to lure this thing away from them. Away from her.

– ii –

Steve put the phone down.

He stared at the receiver hard, his hand stuck to it like flypaper.

"Everything all right?" said a voice from behind.

"Yeah, it's all set up. I'm meeting him tonight, at Armitage Bay." Steve finally took his hand off the phone.

"Good boy."

"I don't like this at all," said Steve, turning to look at the other man in the room.

"What's the matter, don't you trust me?"

"I hardly know you."

"Yes you do—you know me, Steve. We're very much alike you and I. Very much. Your former boss in Liverpool speaks very highly of you. He was impressed by the way you took that dive. So was I. That took guts."

Steve could barely look at him.

"I'm helping you out. That's what you wanted isn't it? Steve Webber?" The man took out one of his famous slimline cigars, his finger bandaged.

"Yeah, that's what I wanted," said Steve.

"Exactly." Nicholas Metcalf stuck the cigar in his mouth, still sore from where Lucas Peck had punched him, and lit up. "I'm glad we understand each other. After all, you're a part of the family now, and that's what family's all about. Isn't it?"

– iii –

"He's not going under again, and that's final," said Ellen.

"Not quite."

She turned to see Alex at the patio door. "You're awake."

"Yes, and I've decided to let him try one more time. We need to find out who this blue-eyed bastard is, what he wants from me."

"Alex, you can't."

He walked across to join her. "I have to know what all this has been about, what Beverly died for."

"But you don't know what it might do to you."

"It might be my last chance. I owe it to myself. I owe it to him," said Alex, pointing at Vaughn.

The older man gave a single nod of the head. "If there's even a hint of trouble, I'll pull you out."

"What, like yesterday?" Ellen protested.

But it was useless to argue. Alex was already taking up his position in the chair. "If we're going to do it, let's do it," he said.

— iv —

"How long will it take to round up my men?" asked The Infinity.

"About half an hour," said Lucas. They were standing in the lobby of the Olympia Hotel, cases packed, ready to check out. It wasn't unusual for them to leave a place at a moment's notice.

"I still don't understand how you were able to locate him." Lucas directed one of the hotel staff to take the cases to the BMW. "Did the signal increase?"

"No, in fact I'm being blocked," said The Infinity. "But I have other sources that are coming through loud and clear."

"So this is it, this time? I mean really *it*?"

"That would seem to be the case, Lucas. They will not escape me in Armitage Bay. The place where this will draw to its close, where events will play out to their ultimate conclusion." The porter carrying their suitcases glanced over at The Infinity as if he was insane.

"Finally," said Lucas.

"Yes, finally."

They stepped out into the brilliant sunshine, the glaring light illuminating them both. "I have the distinct feeling," said The Infinity, "that it is going to be a very beautiful day. And as for what will come tomorrow." Lucas opened the back door for him. "Let's just say I have plans."

— v —

"Can you see him? Can you see the man?"

Alex nodded at Vaughn's question. He could see the man all right. The vision of him walking towards Alex was generic. In all the lives he'd lived, the man with the penetrating blue eyes had been there, searching for him, wanting something from him. The sight made Alex shudder.

"What is he saying to you?"

"He's saying hello. He's saying that he's waited for this moment for a long time. And that he is happy it has come around again."

"What's he doing now?" asked Vaughn.

"He's almost here, almost in front of me. No! No, stay away!" Alex's voice was rising, just as it always did when he reached this point.

"You're perfectly safe. I won't let anything or anyone harm you. These are just memories."

But Alex was bucking, hands clenched into fists, tendons standing proud on his wrists.

"Alex, can you hear me? Nothing can hurt you."

"*He* can," said Alex simply, plainly. The certainty of those two words even caused Vaughn to take a mental step back. "He can hurt you in ways you can't begin to imagine. And now he's coming. Oh sweet Jesus Christ, he's coming for me."

"Who is he?"

"He… He…*ahhhhh!*"

Vaughn put a hand on his shoulder to steady him. "Listen to my voice, can you hear it? Listen and focus only on that. Detach yourself from what's happening. Tell me what you can see."

Alex seemed to calm down a little, enough to describe the man and what he was doing: reaching out to touch Alex. "He's inside my mind—in my head. He can see your thoughts, he knows what you are, what you've been, what you will be. Oh no, oh no—look what he's doing. Ah…AH-HHH!" Alex's wail caused the stunned ex-psychiatrist to let go, and clap his hands to his ears.

He could hear Ellen asking, demanding to know what was wrong.

"Pull back. Tell me where you are."

His head rocked and he let out an agonising howl. "Gaaahhhhh!"

"Patrick," said Ellen, "what are you doing to him?" She was about to go to Alex but James held her back. He could see now what Vaughn was attempting.

"Wait, let him finish."

"Alex, you're safe. Remember, you're watching this. It isn't happening to you."

"Gmnnnn. But it *is!*" Spittle was flying out of his mouth as he twisted and turned.

"Tell me where you are. Can you do that?"

"NNnnnnnmmm… The ssssccccirrrle!"

"He's in the circle from his dreams," said Ellen.

"Is the man there with you?"

Alex nodded so hard, he used his entire body.

"Who is he? Who is the man?"

"Eif…Eif…Eif…"

Vaughn blinked hard. They were the same noises Johann had made before he died.

"Eif…Eif…Infini…."

James strained to hear. "What did he say? It sounded like—"

"Infinity," Ellen completed for him.

"Eee…eee…He…" Alex spoke through a wall of teeth. "Heee is… the…beginning…and…and…the end…" Alex snapped his eyes open and lunged at Vaughn, knocking him off his chair. "The beginning and the end. *The beginning and the end!*" he screamed into the man's face.

Ellen broke free of James' grasp and went to help them. James was seconds behind. "Pull Alex off him!" she ordered.

They separated the two men and Vaughn scrambled to his feet, smoothing down his clothes. Alex was staring wide-eyed at nothing. Ellen brushed the hair out of his face and looked back up at the person who'd done this to him. "Are you satisfied now?"

"Alex, when I count back from five you'll be back here with us." Vaughn reeled off the numbers, just as he'd done the day before.

Alex didn't move, barely even seemed to be breathing.

"Come back to us," said Ellen, still running her hand through his hair. She took his head in her hands. "Please."

There was a single loud breath, followed by another, then two more. Alex exercised his cheekbone, squinting, and grimacing.

Ellen smiled when she saw the movement—at least it meant he wasn't catatonic. He coughed, bringing up a hand to rub his sore throat.

"Somebody get him a drink," said Ellen.

James went to the kitchen and came back with a glass of water. Alex grabbed it and started to gulp it down.

Ellen clasped her hand around the glass, easing it back. "Slowly, sip it." When he was done she said. "Are you all right?"

"Not really." he croaked. "But I'll live."

She hugged him. "You gave me a scare, Alex. Frightened us all."

"I frightened myself."

"It was worth it, though," said Vaughn. "We know more now than we did before."

"We don't know anything," said Alex.

"Alex," asked James, broaching the subject that they were all shying away from. "What is an Infinity?"

He didn't look at his friend when he replied, just gazed into Ellen's eyes. "Not an Infinity. *The* Infinity. It's the thing that's been after me all this time."

– **vi** –

"So what are we dealing with here?" said James. "A guy who's been around, what, centuries?"

"Try millennia," said Alex, now back on the sofa with Ellen next to him.

"There has to be some other explanation," she said.

Vaughn was pacing again, up and down the carpet. "He's the beginning and the end."

"The Infinity," said James. "And what, he can't die?"

"I don't think so," said Alex.

"Which means he was never reincarnated, he doesn't have past lives? The man all those other *yous* encountered was the same person, every time—he was just waiting for you to come back again after you died?" James had to sit down.

"Pretty much."

"But we still don't know what he wants," said Vaughn. "Are you quite sure you can't remember?"

"He's told you he can't, Patrick," Ellen held up a finger. "And there really is no way you're putting him under again to find out. We almost didn't get him back this time."

Vaughn smiled, his eyes filled with apology. "You're right. I'm sorry, Elle. Alex. But at least a few more bits of information have come to light."

"What does it mean, 'The Infinity'?" asked James.

"Dictionary definition," said Vaughn, "would suggest that it is the state of being infinite. Something that is boundless, colossal, incalculable."

"Eternal," offered Alex.

James stood back up again. "Wait a minute, isn't the symbol of infinity a figure eight?"

"What's that got to do with anything?" asked Ellen.

James shrugged. "Probably nothing... But an eight is basically two circles put together, isn't it."

"My God!" Vaughn was rubbing his head. "I've just remembered something."

"What? Don't keep us in suspense, Patrick. It seems to be the week for remembering things." Ellen didn't even bother to hide the sarcasm in her voice.

He went over to the bookshelves and began rooting through them. "They'll be here somewhere. Ah, yes..." Vaughn pulled out a box, no more than about an inch wide. "When I was first attempting to get through to Johann...Lars, the only success I ever had was during a session with these." Opening up the box he took out some picture cards. Kneeling down, he spread them out on the floor. Oversized and faded, they had simple illustrations on the front: houses, people—doing different jobs, such as a sailor or a farmer. "I got some sort of reaction when I showed him this one," said Vaughn, pointing to a man in uniform. "Which is understandable, given what he must have been through in the trenches. But the most interesting thing was when I showed him the animals." He fanned out the picture cards wider, to show representations of pigs, dogs, sheep. "He became extremely agitated when it came to this one."

Vaughn picked up a card. It had an earthworm on it, crawling around in the soil. "I never connected it until now, until James said that."

"I still don't understand," said Ellen.

"If someone was showing you these cards, and your perception of things was not, how to put it, as good as it might be, wouldn't you say that looked a lot like a snake?"

"So?" asked Ellen.

"The *symbol* for infinity might well be a continuous figure eight, two circles," Patrick said. "But the Ouroboros has also been said to have a meaning of *infinity* or wholeness."

Alex frowned. "The Ouroboros?"

Patrick rooted through the books on his shelves, found one, then flicked through the pages. "Ah, here we go," he said, holding up a picture of the thing in question. "A snake eating its own tail. A perfect circle. Something coming around again, constantly re-creating itself. Cycles beginning anew as soon as they end."

The three of them said nothing, just gazed at the picture.

It was Ellen who eventually broke the silence. "You're reaching, Patrick. You're seeing patterns in the static."

"Maybe, but the patterns have to be there in the first place."

"You know as well as I do that our minds create links. Three dots in the right place and you have a triangle."

"So, this Infinity's a monster—is that what you're saying?" said James.

Ellen rankled. "I think we know that already. Look at what he's done in the last few days. Perhaps Johann was just very scared of snakes?"

"The snake is also a symbol of evil," said Vaughn. "Of what we all fear most."

Alex was loathe to agree with him, but he was right. "He's using it. He messes with your mind, can make you see what he wants you to see. He's the ultimate hypnotist if you like."

Ellen thought back to the encounter with him in the hospital, the incident with the police. But how was that possible—how was any of this possible? She was just about coming to terms with the notion that Alex might have been here before, that he could have been the man Patrick Vaughn called Johann. But to believe there was this immortal thing chasing him down through the ages. That took a serious leap.

"So what do we do?" asked James. "We're still no further with that one."

"We need more time to work on it." Vaughn gathered up all the cards, but used the one with the worm as a bookmark, before placing the tome on his mantelpiece.

"Time we don't really have," said the history lecturer.

"If it's okay with you, I'm going to go and have a rest upstairs." Alex rose, still shaky on his feet; Ellen placed a hand on his back to steady him.

"I think that's a very good idea," she said.

Ellen walked with Alex to the living room door, then he told her he'd be okay. The expression on her face said that she didn't believe it for a second, but she let him go anyway.

"I think this is bigger than any of us first thought," said Vaughn once Alex was out of the room.

James was still trying to process it all. "You're telling me."

"That might be true, but Alex is the only person I'm concerned about right now," said Ellen. "No matter how big this is, he's still my responsibility."

"Are you quite sure that's all he is?" asked Vaughn.

She closed her eyes slowly, then opened them again. "Go to Hell," she said, and made to walk through into the kitchen to get herself a drink.

"We might all be going," Vaughn said after her. "And sooner than you think."

– vii –

He lay there on the bed in the spare room, tossing and turning.

So much for rest.

Alex had one eye on the clock anyway, as it crept around to half-past five, then six. He'd pretended to be asleep when he heard someone approach the door and open it. Ellen had brought him a sandwich, which she left on the bedside table. He ate it when she'd gone, looking longingly at the space where she'd stood just moments before. What was he doing, what was he contemplating doing? He should stay with her, with the others—so they could work out what to do.

We're going to see this through to the end, together.

But every time such thoughts came, they found themselves locked in a battle with invading forces. He was doing this for them, for *her*. Draw The Infinity away, just as he'd done with his family; it would follow Alex wherever he went, would find him somehow, probably through his dreams. When that happened he didn't want anybody he cared about in the neighbourhood. *Anyone.*

His feelings were still bothering him; should you be having them for someone so soon after your wife had died? After the way she'd died?

Should you be having them at all about someone who'd been—who technically still was—your doctor? Your psychiatrist for pity's sake! Wasn't that some kind of syndrome, named after Florence Nightingale? But they were there, and no matter how much he denied them, they kept coming back. When he looked at Ellen, he felt something he hadn't felt since those early days with Beverly. Something that had been completely missing during their last year or more together. Totally inappropriate, totally wrong. And bad timing, because he was going to have to say goodbye to her forever.

He probably wouldn't even get the chance to say goodbye, if he was sneaking out of the cottage to meet up with Steve. He might not get an opportunity to return. Alex had no idea how this would work; he'd never absconded before. Would it be wise to come back anyway? He'd already put Ellen through so much disruption, dragged her into this craziness, it wasn't fair he should let it continue. She could go back to her life—or what was left of it now—and get on with things. Try to forget about everything that had happened this week. Try to forget about him.

Because as weird as he knew it was, Alex felt sure that his feelings were reciprocated. Her feelings for him were growing stronger too. It was nothing she could help, nothing either of them could avoid, but this would nip the whole thing in the bud before it got a chance to bloom.

The time now was climbing up to seven. He'd tried to keep track of who was where by listening out for movement. James, he suspected, was upstairs too—in Vaughn's study doing some Internet research. He'd heard him talking to Vaughn earlier, telling him the dates and historical facts all checked out. Alex got off the bed, distributing his weight evenly; he could just see the edges of two chairs out on the back through the window, and a pair of feet accompanying them: definitely Vaughn's. That only left one person unaccounted for, the person he was most worried about bumping into again. He tip-toed very carefully over to the door, when the thought suddenly struck him.

If he was going to borrow—all right, take—the Freelander, he was going to need Ellen's keys. She wouldn't still have them on her, because there were no pockets that he could see on the summer dress. Which meant they had to be in the pocket of the trousers she'd been wearing when they arrived. He looked around the spare room he was in and couldn't see them. Perhaps she'd put them in the wardrobe? No, they weren't in there either. They had to be in Vaughn's room: that's where she'd changed into his late wife's things.

Alex opened the door a crack and peeked out. Vaughn's bedroom was just across the hall, but his study was down the other end towards the front of the cottage. Its door was open and Alex could see James sitting with his back to him, engrossed in something on the computer. As quietly as he could, he crept across the hall to Vaughn's room. There was a nervous moment when the floorboards creaked and he thought James was going to look up and around. He didn't; he was too absorbed in his work. Feeling like a cat burglar sneaking into a museum, Alex opened the door to Vaughn's room. Aware that anyone could hear him from downstairs if he made too much noise, he was even more careful in here. He saw what he'd been searching for almost right away: Ellen's clothes folded neatly and placed on a chair in the corner. He rummaged around inside the pockets—feeling like he was violating the woman herself—until he heard the jangle of keys.

He took them out. Turning, he spotted Ellen's notepad on Vaughn's bedside table. He picked it up, flipping through the pages: a document chronicling his time spent with her at the hospital. He couldn't just go without saying anything. Alex contemplated leaving a note, but to whom? To all of them, or just Ellen? How could he ever possibly fit in everything he wished to say? In the end he tore off a sheet and wrote the words THANK YOU, then signed it. Even to him that didn't seem much, but it would have to do. Hopefully Ellen would read between the lines, if it was possible to do that in a one-line note, and understand what he was trying to say. He left it on the bed where he knew they would find it.

Just as he was about to open the door again, he heard someone coming up the stairs. The footfalls were too light to be Vaughn; it had to be Ellen. He held his breath and waited to see what she would do. She paused at the top of the stairs, standing in the hall between the spare room and Vaughn's.

Please don't go into the spare room, Ellen. Please don't come into Vaughn's room either for that matter.

He could hear her breathing, slow and shallow. She was thinking about knocking on the spare room door, he just knew she was.

But she passed by and he heard her opening the bathroom door, then closing it again. Now was his chance. Alex came out of Vaughn's room and crept down the stairs to the front door. A backwards glance through the living room told him that Vaughn was still outside, so he twisted the Yale knob on the front door. It wouldn't open. Alex tried again. It was stuck fast.

Upstairs he could hear the toilet flushing; water running.

He noticed that the catch was still on the lock. Flicking it up with one hand, he simultaneously turned the knob with the other. The door opened—

Then he remembered his bag. It was still in the living room down the side of the sofa. Should he go back for it? It only had a few changes of clothes in it.

And what was left of his money, his cards. *Damn!* Alex hadn't really thought this getaway through, and now it was all falling apart.

Imploding…

He ran into the living room and bent over the couch. The bag was gone.

Think! What did you do with it?

Muffled voices upstairs. Ellen must be talking to James. Alex prayed that Vaughn wouldn't turn around in his seat outside and see him.

Over by the other chair. It was where he'd dumped it after rooting around for his phone. Alex snatched up the holdall, but running back to the living room door he heard the thumping of feet on the stairs.

It was Ellen.

Quickly, he hid behind the door and waited for her to enter.

She walked across the room, and even though he wanted to see her face so much one final time, he willed her not to look around. She didn't. Instead, Ellen headed out through the patio doors and sat down next to Vaughn on a chair.

Letting out the breath he'd been holding, Alex slid through the door and into the hallway. He'd almost made it when a voice said: "Where are you going?"

Alex looked up to see James at the top of the stairway. He tried to think of an excuse good enough to let him get away, but there wasn't one. He had a holdall, he had the keys to the Freelander in his hand, and he was heading for the front door.

"You're bailing?" said James, coming down the stairs.

Alex shushed him. "The longer I stay here, the more danger I'm placing you all in. That thing's never going to stop searching for me, you know that."

James' expression was a mixture of disappointment and sadness. "I can't let you do it."

Alex put a hand on his shoulder. "You can and you will. This is for the best, James. We both know it."

"What about Ellen?"

"I…" Again he was at a loss for words. "She'll understand."

"No, I don't think she will. She's put a lot on the line for you."

"I know, you too. But I can't let you both go on doing that. This is between him and me."

"Where will you go?"

"To the bay area first, then who knows?"

"The bay?"

But Alex wasn't about to tell him any more; he'd already said too much.

James looked like he was going to say something else, but didn't. He just hugged his friend and let him go.

Alex took one last look over his shoulder and went out through the front door, shutting it behind him. The Freelander was dead ahead.

The car beeped when he pressed the lock on the key fob and stupidly he found himself shushing that too. Climbing inside, he slung his bag on the passenger seat. He'd never driven anything this high up before and never in a million years thought he'd be doing it now, but Alex started the engine and put her into first.

Taking one last look up at the cottage, he slipped off the handbrake and drove away down the road.

Twenty-Four

– i –

The sun had lost none of its power as the day wore on. If anything, it was growing even hotter—which just confirmed what Vaughn had said to the group a few hours ago. If they weren't careful they'd all be going to Hell. Actually, he wouldn't be surprised if they were there already.

"I shouldn't have snapped like that earlier," Ellen said to Vaughn on the patio. "It's just after everything we've been through this past week—"

"There's no need to apologise." Vaughn adjusted his sunglasses. "I was the one in the wrong. You're right about one thing; when it comes to Johann I do have a tendency to lose my perspective. But I was right, wasn't I? About you and Alex? About how you feel?"

Ellen ignored the question and posed one of her own. "What do you think about this Infinity person? What do you really think's happening here?"

"What do you want me to say? We're all thinking the same thing here. James is checking out some of the dates we got from Alex yesterday. He can't be completely sure, but thinks that most of them coincide with major events in human history."

"I know, I just spoke to him."

"It can't just be a coincidence, can it? Patterns in the static?"

"Throughout history there has been one tragic event following another."

"Perhaps. Or maybe we've stumbled upon the cause of all of them."

Vaughn sat back in his chair, feeling the heat of the sun on his face. "If that's true, then what happens the next time Alex meets up with his 'friend'?"

– ii –

Lucas pressed his accelerator down as much as he dared.

The needle swept past 90 as he led the procession of cars down the motorway. He was pushing it at this. Obviously they wouldn't have to worry if they were stopped by the police, but it would be a delay, an annoyance. He checked to see the other cars were there, counted them. Yes, they were: even the convertible with the Brothers Dim inside.

"Can you smell that, Lucas?" said The Infinity from the back seat.

The only thing he could smell was the exhaust from the trucks in front of them—that and just the faintest hint of salt air. "No," he said, honestly. "What is it?"

"It's getting stronger with each mile we cover. Can you really not discern it?"

"No," repeated Lucas.

"It is the smell of victory, of a long journey coming to an end. That is why things didn't go as well as they might have done back at the hospital. There wasn't the *smell*. It was not meant to happen there, not like that."

"There was quite a smell when you left the hospital though, wasn't there?" Lucas risked the joke; The Infinity was in a fine mood today. Peck's judgement was good.

"Indeed there was, Lucas," said the man, snorting. "But this one is much sweeter. It has a distinct bouquet; I only wish you could share it with me."

"I wish I could as well."

A car on his left attempted to pull over into the fast lane, but Lucas wouldn't let it. The way ahead was clear and he wasn't going to have someone in front, bringing the whole convoy down to a snail's pace. Lucas increased his speed again, causing the man in the car to stick up his middle finger. If he'd had the time and inclination—and hadn't been carrying

The Infinity in the back—he might have swung over and driven that prick right off the road.

But he just left the other driver behind in his wake.

"Onward," The Infinity said, waving to the man as they passed him. "Ever onward, Lucas."

– iii –

"What do you mean he's gone?" spluttered Vaughn. "He can't be."

"Can't he?" Ellen said. "Well he's not in the spare room and my car's vanished. I can't think of any other explanation. And he left this upstairs in your room when he took my keys." She held out the piece of paper for Vaughn to read.

James said nothing.

"Is that it? 'Thank you'?" said Vaughn.

"Looks like." Ellen slapped her hand to her head. "He's not thinking clearly, what happened this afternoon must have—"

"He's trying to protect us. Protect you," said James in his defence.

Ellen eyed him suspiciously. "You know something about this, don't you?"

James did his best to look hurt, and failed. "No," he lied.

"If you know where he is, you'd better tell me right now."

"I can't, he doesn't want you to go after him."

Ellen glared at James. "Tell me."

"He's trying to draw this thing away from us, Ellen."

"And you let him go!" she shouted.

"I couldn't do much to stop him. It was what he wanted; I owe him."

"How could you be so stupid?"

Vaughn stepped between the pair of them before the tension increased. "This won't get us anywhere."

"We've got to try and find him."

"But where would we start looking?" said Vaughn.

"He can't have got far."

"Yes, but Elle, we don't have any transport."

She'd forgotten Patrick didn't drive. Ellen threw her hands up in the air. "Oh, well that's just great. Fantastic!" She surprised herself with the intensity of her outburst, but the next words she meant with all her heart. "You'd just better hope and pray he's all right, James, because if anything happens to him…I don't know what I'll do."

– iv –

He sat in the Freelander at the mouth of the road that led down into the bay area; the vehicle itself tucked into one of the parking spaces there. The angle was too acute for it to be seen from Vaughn's cottage, but Alex stayed back a bit anyway, just in case. He rested his arms on the steering wheel, looking out towards the pier, the funfair, beach and sea. A wind had appeared from somewhere and was stoking the waves, making them crash against the legs of the pier, but the sun was still out, scorching everything in sight. The lights of the big wheel, the giant tea-cup ride and dodgems were on, and there were smatterings of people milling around. It hadn't looked like it would be this busy from up top; perhaps he should have arranged a more private place?

Like where? You don't know any places—private or otherwise—around here. The bay was the best spot, easiest to find. Nobody'll take any notice, they're all too busy having fun and enjoying their holidays; stuffing their faces and buying "kiss me quick" hats.

Alex's eyes dipped to the clock on the dash. It read twenty to eight.

Steve was late. But that was nothing new. He'd never been one for punctuality. There was only one way into the bay area so he was bound to see his brother arrive, especially in that battered Capri.

All these thoughts were going through his head when the cars finally arrived. There were three. Two dark blue, and the lead one was black. Alex was suddenly very worried. Those were the sort of cars that belonged to people you didn't want to know. They were also the sort of cars he'd seen in the car park of Kirkwell General four days ago.

He slid down behind the wheel, making himself small—he was high enough up to see them, but they couldn't see him. Fortunately, he hadn't told Steve what kind of car he'd be in, or even that he'd have a car at all.

The saloons drove past, then pulled up down at the bottom of the bay.

Alex waited, watching to see what would happen.

The back door of the first car swung open.

— v —

"We can't just sit around here doing nothing," said Ellen. "I'm going out there to look for him on foot if I have to!"

"Talk sense," Vaughn said. "Alex could be miles away by now. Let's think about this rationally."

"Let's not," she said. "If I'd been thinking rationally I wouldn't have brought him here in the first place. But I thought you could help me, Patrick. I really thought you could—"

"Ellen," not Elle this time, *Ellen*, "that's not fair, I…" She was storming off towards the front door, not listening to a word. "Look, come back. Don't just take off like this."

Ellen rounded. "Patrick, you were right about people changing." Her hand was on the Yale lock.

"Now that's enough, Ellen. That's—"

The door suddenly crashed inwards, knocking Ellen off her feet. She tumbled back into Vaughn, who cushioned her as he, too, fell. The door was swinging off its hinges, and there was a big dent in the wall where it had slammed into it. Ellen and Vaughn both looked up in unison to see two men the size and relative shape of tanks standing there, wearing sunglasses. The nearest one reached in and steadied the door, the second stepped aside to allow someone else passage.

This man was older, leaner—but no less menacing. The last time Ellen had seen him, he'd been bending one of her nurse's arms back so far it snapped like a breadstick. He walked in, treading on bits of wood and glass. He was comfortable in situations like this, she could tell; in fact she'd even go so far as to say he thrived on them. The older man looked to the side, seeing the telephone on the table; he grabbed it and pulled the lead out of the wall, then tossed the phone itself aside. Ellen was shunting

Vaughn, nudging him, trying to get him to go backwards—but he was in too much of a daze to take any notice.

She knew it wouldn't be long now before *he* came in. And suddenly there he was, the man with the blue eyes. The person who had been chasing Alex for over a fortnight—probably more. The first man held back, as if he'd only been checking it was safe for his boss, who was rapidly taking charge.

He tutted, examining the flimsy door, which wobbled in his hand.

"They don't make these the way they used to," he uttered.

"No!" was all James had to say from the living room.

Vaughn found his voice, though it wasn't the one he usually spoke with. It wasn't filled with the confidence of knowledge, with the assuredness of the psychiatrist and teacher he'd been. It was more like a frightened child in the dark, telling the bogeyman to get out of his room. "Who are you, what are you doing here?"

"What are we doing here? Hmm…I'd have thought that was perfectly obvious by now," said the blue-eyed man. "But if you need introductions, so be it. This is Mr. Lucas Peck." He held out his right hand to indicate the man who'd got rid of the phone. "Behind me are Francis and Terence, who appear to have made quite a mess of your front door. Say sorry, you two."

The big men both apologised.

"There are more outside, but we don't really need to trouble them at present. As for myself, I'm known in certain circles as Mr. Finn. But people have been known to call me—"

"The Infinity," whispered Vaughn.

"That's right. How very clever of you." He walked further inside and stood with his hands on his hips. "Now, I don't intend to trouble you for very long, but there is one thing I need to know. One tiny scrap of information that would make this journey worthwhile. We've travelled a long road, and I don't just mean down the motorway." He smiled at Ellen. "So perhaps one of you would be kind enough to point me in the direction of Alexander Webber. The sooner we can get this started, the sooner it will all be over."

– vi –

The man who got out of the black car—a Jag—was about Alex's height and weight, but looked like he could handle himself about a hundred times better. The forefinger on his left hand was strapped up, though, and the bandage reflected the sun's rays, making it much whiter than it should be. He had a cigar in his mouth, which he took out, blowing smoke in the direction the wind was heading. Alex kept low, still waiting.

Seconds later, someone else got out of the other side at the back. It was his brother, Steve, who proceeded to lean on the top of the car with hands spread apart, as if he were about to be frisked by a policeman. He struck Alex as a man at ease, not brought here against his will; hadn't been beaten up. If anything, the other man looked like he'd come off worst in a punch-up—the whole side of his mouth was the colour of radishes. There were more men in the other cars, and they were all obviously here together, but wasn't that how these sorts of people always operated? They never did anything alone, not even going to the bathroom.

Alex decided to make a move. He couldn't stay in the car all night wondering and, after all, *he'd* dragged his brother out here to Armitage Bay. If he didn't show his face, Steve might well end up looking like the guy with the busted jaw and broken finger. He couldn't do that to him.

Alex opened the door of the Freelander slowly, and eased out. He swung it shut behind, but didn't lock it—just in case he had to make a swift getaway. As he was walking gingerly towards the cars, Steve caught sight of him. His brother gave a small wave and the cigar man pivoted to see. Conscious that he was utterly exposed, Alex started to shiver, in spite of the cloying heat. Steve beckoned him with the same hand he'd used to wave.

"Alex, there you are!"

Looking left at the other cars, he nervously raised a hand to say hello. "Steve. Everything okay?"

"Everything's cool," his brother said.

Cool? He hated it when his students said that, and when his brother said it—especially when it was hot enough to fry eggs on the pavement. "Right. Who's this?"

Alex was only metres away from the other man, who stuck the cigar back in his mouth and stepped forward to extend his good hand. "Name's Nick Metcalf," he said. Alex shook it tentatively.

"When I put the feelers out, Nick here caught wind of it."

"Nothing much happens on my turf that I don't know about."

"A lot's changed since I was inside. But he's going to help you out, bruv."

"Steve here says you're looking for a way out of the country, false passports, identities, that sort of thing. I'm your man." Nick reached into his pocket and produced some documents and a passport. "I can see to it that you get away safely."

Alex looked at Steve. "It's okay, bruv."

"How much?" said Alex.

Metcalf raised an eyebrow. "Direct, isn't he?"

"I haven't got time to be anything else."

"Well, you see, for you I'd be willing to do a deal." Metcalf grinned.

Again Alex looked at his brother, but couldn't get much from his expression. "What kind of deal?"

"Information."

Alex rubbed the back of his head. "Mr. Metcalf, I don't know what Steve's told you, but I'm… The thing is I'm not in your line of work."

Metcalf's smile faded. "My line of work? What's that supposed to mean?"

"Nothing, just that I'm not sure I'd have the type of information you'd be interested in."

"Oh, I think you do. Someone who wants to get away that quickly must have done something, or must *know* something. All *I* want to know is what you know. Simple as that."

"What I know?"

Metcalf put a hand on his shoulder and squeezed. "All right, let's stop fucking around here. Someone's looking for you, Webber. And I know who it is."

Alex tried to pull away, but Metcalf wouldn't let him.

"Nick?" said Steve, coming around the side of the car. Two men appeared from nowhere—probably the driver and passenger, thought Alex—to cut him off.

"Now," said Metcalf, taking his hand down. "I can get you away, that's no problem: I've done it before when things have gone tits up with people. The thing is, I'm curious. What's so special about you?"

"Nothing," said Alex earnestly. "Nothing at all."

"Then why is Mr. Finn looking for you? Why has he muscled in on me and my operation? Why is he so desperate to get his hands on you?"

Mr. Finn? The Infinity?

"I don't know, and that's the truth," said Alex. "I swear."

Metcalf nodded, taking out the cigar again and blowing smoke in Alex's face. He waited for the man to stop coughing before he went on. "I see. But that's a shame, because I reckon you and I have a common enemy. I've come a long way to meet you and I think we can work together, if you'd just level with me."

"He wants something from me," said Alex. "But I can't remember what it is."

"Convenient. Must be something pretty important that's worth blowing up a hospital for."

"Fucking hell," said Steve. "That had something to do with you?"

Nick glanced across the car at him. "It had more to do with our mutual associate Mr. Finn. Now, all I'm wanting to know is who the fuck he is, what he wants, and how I can get rid of him."

"I don't know any of those things," said Alex. "If I did, I wouldn't be here."

"All right." Metcalf gazed about him. "Now this is a very public place. Not really conducive to 'my line of work.' I'm thinking maybe it's time you and me went for a little drive."

– vii –

"Isn't this cosy?"

They were all in the living room: Vaughn and Ellen huddled together on the couch; James in the chair; The Infinity and his men standing over them. Peck was staring at Ellen, head to one side. His eyes were all over her.

"So, who would like to go first? Perhaps you?" The Infinity pointed at Vaughn.

"I barely know the man."

The Infinity squinted. "That's not entirely true, is it? What have you been doing here with him, Dr. Vaughn?"

"Helping him."

"To remember? I really wish you hadn't done that. It only makes everything more complicated." His eyes found the book on Vaughn's mantelpiece and he opened it up at the marked page showing the Ouroboros. The Infinity shook his head. "You people really have no idea, do you."

"Maybe I ought to practise my art again," said Peck; he was still gaping at Ellen.

The Infinity tracked his vision, shutting the book and replacing it. "No," he said.

"But she's so—"

"I said no."

Ellen put a hand to her mouth, her eyes large. "Oh my God. You. You're the one who did that to Alex's wife?"

James tensed in the chair.

Peck grinned. "Did you like it? It was a rush job, not perfect by any means. But you. I could do so much with you. I—"

"Lucas!" snapped The Infinity.

"I'm sorry, it's just that she's—"

"Focus. We have things to attend to." He returned his gaze to Vaughn. "Where is he, Doctor? Where's your little Johann?" The Infinity reached out with his hand. Vaughn's eyes drooped, his mouth gaped open. "Tell me. Tell me right now."

"Mmnnnot afraid of you," slurred Vaughn.

James got up off his chair. "Leave him alone."

"Aww. Oh no... Noooo! *Marina!*" wailed Vaughn.

"I said, leave him alone!" shouted James.

Peck dragged his attention away from Ellen and fixed it on the tutor. "Sit down, friend," he said.

James remained upright. "I'm not your friend." There was pure hatred in his voice.

"*Ahhhh!*" screamed Vaughn.

"He doesn't know anything." James made a move towards the two men, but Peck was there waiting. The tutor took a clumsy swing, missing by a mile. Peck knocked him backwards with the flat of his hand. He toppled into the chess set and ended up on the floor. The whole fight was over in seconds.

The Infinity left Vaughn and walked over towards James. "He doesn't know anything, but you do, don't you?" He bent and scrutinised him with those blue eyes—trying to extract the information. James fought as hard as he could, legs kicking out. But in the end it was useless.

"There now, that wasn't so difficult was it?"

"Bastard," James murmured.

"Takes one to know one," replied The Infinity. Then he rose and stepped back, pausing to whisper something to Peck. Lucas took his place, crouching down at the side of the prone figure. He took the man's face in his hands. James tried to twist out of his grasp.

"Nothing personal," Lucas said, then snapped the man's head sideways until there was a terrible crack. James' eyes rolled back into his skull as Lucas let his head drop. Ellen let out a tiny scream.

"Francis, Terence," said The Infinity. "Escort everyone outside. It's time we were on our way."

They stared at James on the floor.

"Now," snarled The Infinity.

Frank motioned for Ellen and Vaughn to get up, while Terry waved them into the hall. None of them protested; they were all too shaken to say anything.

The Infinity was about to follow, when he stopped. He picked something up off the floor, brought it to his face. Then he placed it on the mantelpiece, on top of the book, and walked out of the room, through the hall and the wrecked front door. Lucas Peck, at the rear, gave the object a cursory glance before catching up. It was one of the chess pieces that had wound up on the floor, but he didn't have time to look closer.

If he had done, he would have seen that it was the king.

"I'm not going anywhere with you," said Alex.

"Come on, be a good boy, get in the car." Metcalf was pushing him towards the open back door of the Jag. "There are a lot of people down here, I'd rather nobody got hurt."

"Get off me." Alex wrestled with the man. Then he felt something hard and cold pressing against his back. He looked over his shoulder and down, saw the silver handgun wedged there. Metcalf was expertly blocking the sight of it with his own body.

"In the fucking car. Right now."

Alex did as he was told. Steve was shoved inside next, one of Metcalf's men following closely behind. Once the car doors were shut, he produced a gun too and pointed it in their direction. Metcalf walked around the car and climbed in the passenger side at the front. The driver was the last person to get in.

"All right, let's go."

The black Jaguar started up and the man did a rough three-point turn. The other cars waited for them to pass, then copied his lead.

"There we are," said Metcalf. "Now what was all the fuss about?"

"I swear I didn't know a thing about this," said Steve hastily.

The scarecrow, thought Alex, *looking for a brain.*

"He said I was owed, for what I'd been through, the way I'd been treated. Said he'd help."

Metcalf laughed, twisting around in his seat. "Stevie, you were used then and you've been used now. That's what separates people like you from people like me. It's the nature of things."

"And what separates you from Finn?" asked Alex.

"Right now, about a hundred or so miles."

"You're being used too, you know."

"Not anymore," Metcalf growled.

"He's been sending out the flying monkeys to do his dirty work," said Alex.

The man in the back with them stabbed the gun in Alex's direction. "Watch who you're calling a fucking monkey, mate!"

"Easy, Rory. You, Webber, ought to watch your mouth," warned Metcalf. "Before—"

"Er…boss," said the driver.

"For Christ's sakes, what is it?"

"You'd better see this. I think we've got a problem."

Metcalf faced front again. "Shit!"

– ix –

Ellen and Vaughn both rode with The Infinity, in the back of the car. Ellen was able to consider the man more closely now and realised that the coldness of those eyes extended to the rest of him. He didn't feel an ounce of remorse about any of the things he'd done. Probably wasn't even capable of feeling such an emotion as guilt.

"Your analytical skills are wasted on me, Dr. Hayward," he told her when they were a good way into their drive.

"I know," she said.

"Do they give you a sense of superiority over others?"

It was a strange question to ask, but then he was a strange kind of man. If he was even a man at all. "No."

"Not even a little bit?"

"I don't think I'm in any position to judge anyone. All I do is try to help people."

He got more comfortable on the seat. "There's that word again. Help. Why do you even bother? Can't you see you're wasting your time? That nothing you do for them in the long run will ever really *help*."

"That's your opinion."

"Yes, it is. And it just happens to be right."

Vaughn, who'd been flipping between unconsciousness and a doped form of wakefulness, finally stirred. He muttered something incomprehensible, a gibberish that only he could understand.

"What did you do to him?" asked Ellen.

"Nothing really," said The Infinity. "I simply forced him to relive his wife's demise. To look into her eyes again as she shuffled off her mortal coil."

The hatred welled inside Ellen.

"Then I merely told him the thing he most wanted to know."

"What?"

"Why all this is happening. I showed him, I explained it to him. It's not my fault if he can't process the information."

"Grrhnaaamuplll," said Vaughn, dribbling out of the side of his mouth.

Ellen wiped it away with the edge of her dress. When she'd finished, she turned to The Infinity. "How can you do the things you do? Who are you?" she asked him. "I mean, who are you really?"

"I…" he began.

"We're here," said Lucas from the driver's seat.

— x —

"Shit! Fuck!" barked Metcalf.

Slap bang in front of them was a van with surfboards loaded on top, and behind it a trailer with a canvas covering. It was parked at an angle across the narrow road, blocking their exit. A man and woman, dressed in DayGlo wetsuits, were standing looking at the van. The man was scratching his head and the woman had her hands on her hips.

"I think they've broken down," the driver speculated.

"I'll fucking break them down in a minute," Metcalf said, puffing on his cigar.

"Shall we get out and help them?"

"Yeah, and take some of the other boys with you. If you can't do anything, shoot the fuckers and push the van into the bushes there."

The driver nodded.

"That was a joke," said Metcalf. "What have I been left with here, *all* the morons?"

The driver got out and made a hand signal to the other cars. In the side mirrors, Alex could see four or five large men get out, dressed in shirts and ties. They walked past the Jag and went to talk to the surfers.

"Alex, I really am sorry," said Steve for the fortieth time.

"*You're* sorry."

"He's sorry, you're sorry—we're all fucking sorry," said Metcalf. "Come on, what's the big hold up here?"

His men had lifted the bonnet and were looking inside.

Metcalf rolled down the window and stuck his head out. "What do we look like, the fucking AA or something?" The driver came back over to the Jag.

"We think it's the battery; they can't get it to start at all."

"Well, just pop the handbrake and help them roll it down to the bay. Fuck me, do I have to do all the thinking around here?"

The driver strode up to the man and woman and said something. They both nodded, smiled, then the surfer man kicked the driver in the balls. As he went down, the woman swung at the second man, just as he went for his gun. Within moments she'd snatched it out of his hand, pressed it against his head, and let off a round. The driver's head exploded all over the road like a ripe watermelon.

"What the fuck?" said Metcalf.

She was already turning it on the other men, who were drawing their weapons. Without even taking aim, she shot one in the shoulder and another in the gut. One of Metcalf's men returned fire, hitting her in the knee. She went down instantly.

Her partner was just about to pick up a gun when he was shot in the chest.

Below, in the bay area itself, people were screaming. Crowds were gathering.

"This is not good; this is *so* not good. You wanna explain to me what's going on here?" said Metcalf to no one in particular. "What the fuck was all that about?"

"He's here," Alex told them.

"Who?" asked Steve.

"The Infinity."

"Finn?" said Metcalf, tossing his cigar out of the window and drawing his gun. "What's he doing here?"

"He's come for me."

Metcalf's remaining men were retreating, amazed at what had just taken place.

Then they spotted the men swarming around the van. Metcalf's men; the ones Finn had commandeered nearly a week ago. Their guns were drawn too, except these were sawn-off shotguns and Scorpion Vz 61 machine pistols. There was no point getting out and trying to reason with them; they were working for Finn now, heart and soul. Metcalf slid over into the driver's position and gunned the engine. A shot webbed the windscreen. He backed up into one of his own cars.

It threw them all forward, and the man who'd objected to being called a monkey dropped his gun. Steve reached down and there was a scramble for the weapon.

"Ah-ah-ah," said Metcalf leaning over and jamming his own gun against Steve's head. "Let him pick it up."

Monkey-man Rory snatched up his weapon, then hit Steve with the butt of it.

"Ow!"

More men were getting out of the cars from behind, Alex could see them in the side mirrors. The noise of gunfire was deafening. Casualties were falling on either side. For a heartbeat he was somewhere else again, in No Man's Land with the explosions and bullets all around him, over the wire, in the mud, waiting to be found. But this was no flashback to an earlier life—this was real.

There was a shout of "Ceasefire!" from somewhere that could have been mistaken for a military order. Though it took a few seconds to sink in, the men on both sides complied. It held such an air of authority they had no choice.

"If he's been harmed in any way," Alex heard the same voice shout, "there won't be words to describe the agony you will all feel. Metcalf, show yourself."

One person was standing in the space between the vehicles. A person about medium height and build, wearing an indigo suit and tie. Alex could see the man's blue eyes from here: they shone from his head like lighthouse beams. It was The Infinity.

"You have something I want. Hand him over, and you can walk away from this right now."

The crime lord opened his door. "Fuck you!" came the reply.

"That isn't very productive," The Infinity called back.

"Those are all my men—they're my own fucking men!"

The Infinity looked around, there weren't that many left. Most were lying bleeding on the floor, some had simply run off. There were just a handful on his side and even less on Metcalf's. "I think you'll find they're my men now," he said. "In fact, why don't the rest of you boys all come over here and join us."

The men still loyal to Metcalf looked at each other. It might have been that they realised they were on the losing side, just like they had when Metcalf took over the nightclub, or it might have been something to do with the inflection of those words—none of them were as strong-willed as their boss—but they suddenly decided to switch their allegiance. Alex watched as those stragglers now flocked to The Infinity; he welcomed them with a smile of greeting. Men who'd been shooting at each other seconds earlier were closing ranks, leaving Metcalf alone.

"You lousy shits! Come back," he whined.

Rory shifted about in the back of the Jag and Metcalf swung round with the gun again. "Going somewhere?"

"No, boss."

"Now," said The Infinity, "would you care to negotiate?"

There was a short gap where nothing happened. Then Metcalf opened his door wider. He got out of the Jag and walked around the front. Through the smashed up windscreen, Alex saw him raise his hands in the air—which was sensible, given that there were a number of guns trained on him—but the silver pistol was clearly visible, tucked into the back of Metcalf's trousers.

The crime lord began walking slowly towards The Infinity.

"So," Alex heard him say, "let's talk."

– xi –

The man who'd been introduced to her as Lucas Peck seemed obsessed.

They were in the back of the BMW, Vaughn on her right, Peck now on her left. It didn't leave her any room. The Infinity had told Peck to stay here and keep an eye on them while he went to speak to a couple on their way down to the bay, their van loaded with surfing equipment. Ellen watched as he banged on their door, getting them to step out of the vehicle. One short chat later, and they were nodding and smiling, getting back into the van and driving a short way down the road—where they parked diagonally across it. The Infinity then came back up and motioned for his other men to get out of the cars behind. He shook his head at the convertible containing Frank and Terry, though.

Then the group had marched down the road, keeping to the side out of sight. It was obvious they were setting a trap for somebody—and Ellen knew exactly who it must be. What on earth was Alex doing here? She'd assumed he was long gone.

"Could you stop doing that?" she said eventually, when she found the nerve.

He refused to look away. "I'm sorry, but you're so… You're perfect," he told her.

"I'm not perfect," she said, increasingly uncomfortable.

"Yes, you are."

Ellen's eyes narrowed. "And Beverly? Was she perfect too?"

"Beverly?"

"Alex's wife. You murdered her."

Lucas sneered. "I tried to make her more beautiful. I didn't have long; it wasn't my finest piece. That's yet to come."

The way he said that made her think he'd already chosen his subject matter. He was examining it right now. Ellen closed her eyes tight, tried not to picture herself strung up on a wall, flaps of skin dangling, limbs severed. A judder ran through the whole of her body. When she opened her eyes, Peck was still there, eyes boring into her—his head obviously buzzing with ideas.

"You've done it before?"

"Many times. Some came close. But most, like the one back at the flat, were simple renderings: sketches, studies."

He can't bring himself to say her name, Beverly. Because that would make her human, less like material for his art. You can use that, make him think of you as a person, make him understand what he's going to do. What he's going to take away from you.

"My name is Ellen. Ellen Hayward," she said.

"I know."

"My favourite music is R&B, I love salmon lasagne. I live in an apartment just outside of Kirkwell. I work at Kirkwell General—"

"You used to," said Peck.

"What do you mean?"

"Nothing."

"Tell me." But she already knew. It was the reason she hadn't been able to get through on the phone—there was nothing at the end of the line. In her heart of hearts she'd known that something was very wrong. That was probably the real reason why she'd been in no hurry to check the news. It hadn't just slipped her mind because of everything else that was going on—she didn't want to know *for sure*. Didn't want to see their calling card. That way there was still a slim chance she could go back home, return to normal life, whatever the hell that was.

"Doesn't exist anymore." Peck made a *POOF* noise and opened his hand.

"You're lying," she said, but knew he wasn't.

"It's gone. So you can relax now. Nobody's waiting for you to get back, no hassles with patients or your superiors. Think of this as a long, enforced vacation."

Ellen felt saltwater gathering at the corners of her eyes, but didn't want to give this scum the satisfaction of seeing her cry. The effort was too much, though: all those faces, work colleagues, patients like Sam. A single tear tracked down her left cheek. Lucas Peck brought a finger up to her face and caught it. Then he licked at it like a dog with a water bowl. The action made Ellen feel sick.

Suddenly his hand was brushing her hair, feeling the gloss and texture. She slapped it away, but he brought a hand up and clamped it around her throat. He didn't squeeze too tightly—didn't want to damage his masterpiece before he'd even begun—but it was enough to stop her struggling. She'd seen this man in action, twice, and in spite of his age she wouldn't stand any chance against him if it came to a fight. None of her psychiatrist's tricks would work with this maniac, either. "Don't," he warned her.

Ellen shook as his other hand glided over her skin, brushing her exposed shoulders with the back of his fingers. Then it went lower; he pawed at the light material of the summer dress and Ellen wished she'd never changed into it. At least her old clothes would have provided some kind of barrier. Now there was just a filmy covering of material between his hand and her skin, and when he finally cupped a breast she sucked in air. He squeezed hard, massaging.

Disgusted, she tried to turn her head away from his face, but the light pressure he applied at her neck prevented her. "Look at me," he said. "I want you to look at me."

His hand was reaching lower.

"Gmmmhhhlll." The noise was coming from Vaughn at the side of her.

"Please," whispered Ellen.

"I don't think he'll mind. He's a vegetable."

His hand was on her stomach, then she felt his fingertips probing, inching their way down. It had always been a fear of hers when dealing with an unstable patient, that they might break free, overcome the nurse and—

She'd never once had that fear with Alex. Never once had she felt threatened or at risk, regardless of his unpredictable behaviour. There was always something telling her that she'd be okay. Now that something was telling her she'd be far from fine.

When his fingers finally found her, she squirmed—not because he was so close to such an intimate part of her, but because she found his probing repugnant.

"Keep still," he warned her.

Ellen's movements increased.

"I said…" The knife was out and in front of her face in seconds. "Keep still."

She went rigid when she saw the blade. It was quite thin and only about four or five inches long. Not the biggest knife in the world, but in the hands of a craftsman like Peck it could do some serious damage.

He released her neck and started to trace patterns there with the tip of the knife. Her skin was slick with sweat, and he bent to lick at this once or twice. Ellen fought back the bile rising in her throat. The knife was following the curve of her left breast now, around the outside, the flat side smooth against the roundness of the flesh.

Come on then—get on with it if you're going to do it, just get on with it! What she couldn't stand was the way he was playing with her; the wait, not knowing what he was going to do and whether it would be worse than what had happened to Beverly, if that was possible.

The first gunshot took them all by surprise. Lucas turned, caught off-guard for a moment. When he whipped his head back again he was struck on the temple by a pair of clasped hands. He hadn't been expecting an attack from the side. From the front perhaps, which he could handle, but not from the mumbling gooseberry whose mind had been so obviously bent by The Infinity. Lucas fell against the back of the passenger seat. Another blow, and another. Vaughn rained them down on him, leaning across Ellen. Peck couldn't bring his hands up in time to shield himself.

That was when Ellen made a move for the knife. She grabbed the hand clasping it, brought it closer, then bit it. Lucas cried out, letting go of the weapon, and Ellen seized it. But he was lunging for her again, swinging to strike Vaughn. In the cramped confines of the back of the BMW, though, his manoeuvrability was limited and his combat skills greatly decreased. Ellen arced the knife, catching him across the bridge of the nose. Then she started to plunge it downwards, stabbing like Norman Bates in drag. The first couple of hits only broke the surface of his skin, but the third she pounded in hard at a point where his shoulder connected with his chest. The knife slid in up to the hilt and she lost her grip on it. Peck was rolling around in the space between the dip at her feet. She reached past Vaughn to open the door. Ellen pushed him out, hoping he could still walk, then clambered after. Below, past the van and trailer, there were more gunshots. She wanted to run down that slope and stop the men, but her more immediate worry was Peck.

Dragging Vaughn, she slid into the foliage that flanked the road.

– xii –

"Did you see that?" said Frank in the driver's seat.

"Yeah," said Terry.

"What do you think we should do?"

They'd just witnessed a woman and man tumble from the back of the BMW in front and stagger into the bushes.

Terry threw the question back at him: "What do *you* think we should do?"

"Fuck it," said Frank, shrugging.

– xiii –

With each step he took, Metcalf could feel the force of Finn's vision. Those eyes were even bluer than he remembered. But this felt better, one-on-one. Maybe there was a way to salvage something out of this? And if not…

"Listen, shouldn't we be getting out of here, Finn? We've caused a bit of a fucking stir." Metcalf's eyes roamed from body to body, then looked back to see the people gathered below, watching. "I don't really want to be around when the Old Bill gets here, know what I mean?"

"That won't be a problem." Whether he meant the police wouldn't be an issue or Metcalf wouldn't be around when they arrived wasn't entirely clear. "I thought we were going to talk."

"We are talking—that's what this means when you open your mouth and fucking words come out." Metcalf slowly started to lower his arms. "You mind?"

The Infinity shook his head.

"Okay, it's like this. You want Webber? I've got him. And his brother."

"I'm not interested in his brother. Just him," said The Infinity.

Metcalf frowned. "I've gotta ask this again, because he don't seem to know himself—either that or he's not talking. But what the fuck do you want him for anyway?"

"That's my affair, as I think I told you once before."

"Oh come on, you go to all this trouble… You pay me off, take my men, go traipsing all over the country after this boy. What did he do, screw your old woman or something?"

The Infinity gave a polite smile.

"What?"

"The last person I told now wishes I hadn't."

"Is it about money? Information? Power?"

"It is about all of these things, Metcalf, and about none of them."

"Stop talking in fucking riddles!"

"Then stop asking me them."

Metcalf shook his head. "You know, when you first came to my club and barged your way inside, yeah I was pissed off. But I thought we could do business together."

"We did," The Infinity told him.

"I mean real fucking business, not just you walking all over me."

"This was none of your concern. You shouldn't even be here today. If you had stayed out of the way, there wouldn't have been a stir, however temporary an amusement it afforded."

"Come again?"

"I fucking *enjoy* stirring," The Infinity clarified for him in words he could understand. "But the time has come for me to complete what I set out to do. So I'd be grateful if you would hand over Webber immediately."

"Oh, would you now?"

"Or we'll have to take him by force."

"Oh, will you now?" Metcalf called back to the Jag. "Rory, get them out of the car."

Behind him, the Jaguar's rear door opened up and Alex Webber and his brother were ushered out. The Infinity flinched slightly when he saw the man with the gun get out next. Rory straightened his pistol arm, the Beretta 92F aiming directly at Alex's head.

"If I were you, I'd advise your man to not even breathe," said The Infinity.

Metcalf smirked, feeling comfortable enough to fish his pack of cigars and lighter out of his pocket. "Now doesn't this put a slightly different spin on things, *Mr.* Finn? And no talking to Rory, neither. None of that fancy come on over to our gang shit. He knows which side his bread's buttered."

"Very well. It would appear we have a stalemate. What would you like to happen next?"

Metcalf didn't care for the way Finn was staring even harder at him now, still trying to break his spirit. "I… What's going to happen is…" He was losing his train of thought. No, what he wanted was to find out the importance of all this, and whether he could gain anything from it.

Yes, that was right—he was going to… The Infinity was blurring, his features muddied. He was becoming someone else, taking on that person's appearance.

"I said, what would you like to happen next, Nicky?" said the bloated corpse of his old boss Eddie King. "Maybe we should all go for a little drive?"

"No," said Metcalf. "You're dead. You—"

King looked down at his grey skin. "So I am. Well would you look at that, Nicky boy!"

He *was* looking at it, couldn't exactly do anything else. "You're… No, I killed you. This isn't real."

"Isn't it? Only about as real as whacking me over the head and then taking me out to the middle of nowhere to dump my body. Do you have any idea how cold it is at the bottom of that river, Nick? Do ya? Would you like to find out?"

"You keep the fuck away from me!"

"How could you? I treated you like a son and this is how you repaid me!" King took a step closer and Metcalf drew his gun. He levelled the silver Colt Double Eagle at the ghost.

"Put that thing away, Nick. How ya gonna kill me when I'm already dead?"

"I-I don't…" Metcalf's gun hand was shaking.

"Tell you what. Call Rory off back there and I promise to disappear forever. How's that sound? You don't hafta have the nightmares anymore where you see my face, just before you cave my skull in. You don't hafta think about me every time you set foot in that office of yours, every time you open the boot of a car. How's that sound, Nicky boy? Sounds good, don't it?"

Metcalf nodded. It sounded like a deal he could live with, which was more than could be said for King. "Rory. Put down your gun."

"But, boss—" shouted Rory.

"Do it!"

Rory lowered his Beretta.

"Good boy," said King. It was a catchphrase he used all the time, and one which Metcalf had inherited after his death. King pushed Metcalf's gun away from him, so that it pointed in the other direction. Then he plucked the cigars and lighter from his other hand. "You mind? It's been so long since I had a decent one of these." King took out one of the slim-lines and lit up; he blew smoke rings into the air. "*Ahhh!* That's better. Okay, now get Rory to bring them over."

"Rory," shouted Metcalf, "bring—"

But that was all he managed before his chest exploded, knocking him back and over. King turned to see which one of his men had fired, disobeying a direct order. But the shot had come lower down, from the ground.

The girl wearing the DayGlo wetsuit was grinning insanely, smoking pistol in her hand.

– xiv –

She'd done it.

Seventeen-year-old Jeanie Newfield had zapped another one. Still woozy from the loss of blood and hardly able to move because her knee-cap had been blown away, she'd valiantly raised her laser pistol and had taken out another one of the alien invaders—just like in their favourite computer game. Her and her brother Russ were always playing it, when they weren't out surfing as they'd planned to do today. Where exactly was Russ, anyway? They hadn't got him, had they?

It had all made so much sense, you see, once the man with blue eyes had explained it. They'll be in disguise as humans, and they'll be trying to get you to move your van, but you have to resist them. The president's life is at stake, President Webber.

But they'd got off a lucky shot, putting her out of the game for a while. Once she'd come to and seen the freak standing there, waving his gun in the face of the man with blue eyes, she had to do something. He was the only hope for humanity, he was the only one who could save them all from this terrible threat.

She'd done good, hadn't she? Saved him—probably saved them all. So why was he walking over to her now, the blue-eyed man, an angry expression on his face? And why was everything going black all of a sudden? Why did she feel so cold?

Jeanie had no idea. But the only thing on her mind when she lost consciousness again was that Earth was in such danger, and only a few people knew about it.

– **xv** –

It was all the distraction Steve needed.

When the gun went off, killing Metcalf, he leaped across and pounced on Rory. The bigger man went down easily, Steve pummelling him with his fists first, then elbowing him in the face to make sure he stayed down. He picked up the gun, but tossed it quickly aside.

"Not my style," he said. "Come on, let's get out of here!"

"Make for the Freelander," shouted Alex.

Just as they were about to run for it, someone shouted his name from the undergrowth. "Wait." Alex tried to pinpoint where it was coming from and saw Ellen, struggling, half-carrying Vaughn. Putting his confusion aside, Alex went over to them.

"Ellen?" he said. "How did—"

"We'll talk later, if there *is* a later," she said.

"And James?"

Ellen shook her head.

Biting his lip, Alex slung Vaughn's arm over his shoulder and between them they carried him across the road. Steve stood waving them on.

"Get a bloody move on, bruv. They'll be after us any second."

Ellen looked over at Alex. "Your brother, I take it?"

"Steve, Ellen. Ellen, Steve."

Steve gave a wave of acknowledgement. "This must be the shrink, then? No offence," he said at her look of annoyance. "Toss me the keys, bruv."

Alex threw him the keys to the Freelander and Steve ran off ahead. "It's not locked," Alex called after him.

Looking over his shoulder, he saw The Infinity massing the troops he had left.

Steve was at the car, in the driver's seat, starting her up. He pulled out of the parking space, swinging the vehicle around to pick them up. They climbed inside, Ellen and Vaughn in the back, Alex in the front.

"Okay, so now what?" said Alex.

"We can't get out that way," Ellen told them. "Apart from the van and trailer, he's got about five or six cars parked up there. More men, and the guy who killed Beverly."

Alex shot her a grave look.

"What's that rattling sound?" asked Steve. "Down by the bottom of your feet."

Alex lowered his eyes and saw the bottles of vodka still there. One was half empty, but the other was full. He held them up, exchanged a look with his brother and smiled. "Are you thinking what I'm thinking?"

"Well, it is Russian vodka," said Steve.

Ellen tapped Alex on the shoulder. "What's that supposed to mean?"

"Just that it's very good for making cocktails," Alex replied. Untucking his shirt he began ripping it at the corner. At the same time Steve pushed in the cigarette lighter.

"And," Alex went on, "that you were right. Sometimes you do have to make a stand. Sometimes you have to fight fire with fire."

– xvi –

The Infinity had no sooner given the order for his men to pursue and bring back Webber, than he saw the Freelander charging up the slope directly towards them.

He knew that somehow Ellen and Vaughn had gotten away from Lucas—and would deal with that in time. He also knew it wouldn't be long before all this was finished. What he didn't know was why these people were hurtling towards him, why they should want to end this as quickly as he did. Why they wanted to come to him, just as Metcalf's men had done.

Until it was too late.

"*Fall back!*" ordered The Infinity as the Freelander braked, smoke rising from screeching tyres. Through the open window, Alex lobbed a bottle of alcohol at Metcalf's Jaguar, a flaming rag in the end. When it hit, the liquid bathed the car in a layer of fire. A second bottle followed—and this landed in the space between the vehicles, streaking up towards the van.

The Freelander reversed, backing off just as the first car exploded.

It was a domino effect; just like Kirkwell General.

By the time the third car exploded—and the van not long afterwards—all that could be seen of the gangster's battlefield were glowing, flickering plumes of yellow and red.

TWENTY-FIVE

Armitage Bay: Friday, 8:45 pm

– i –

THEY WATCHED FROM A SAFE DISTANCE.

The crowds that had simultaneously gathered and fled when the gun-fight started, had returned to witness this new spectacle. When they'd booked their holidays they hadn't expected this much excitement. All they'd really banked on were fish and chip suppers and boat rides around the bay.

The people who had just caused this watched too. They got out of their 4x4 and stood regarding the flames. Nobody approached them, nobody went over to ask what in the name of all that was holy they thought they were doing. It didn't seem wise after they'd seen them escape a bloodbath and napalm several cars. Which suited the instigators just fine. It would have been a tough one to explain to a bystander anyway.

"Nobody could have got out of that alive," said Steve, finally, to break the agonising silence that had descended. "I'm right, aren't I? This is over?"

Neither Ellen nor Alex answered him. Only Vaughn, propped up against the side of the Freelander, mumbled something.

"What happened to him?" asked Alex.

"The Infinity happened to him," Ellen said. "Told him why he was looking for you, and it blew his mind."

"Terrific. And…did he do that to James, too?"

"No," said Ellen. "That was the other man, Peck." She wanted to carry on, say "That was the guy who tried to rape me back there in the car, and all because you decided to do a vanishing act on us!" but bit it back.

As they watched, the fire appeared to die down slightly, revealing a figure, walking through the flames towards them: two eyes, as blue as the sea not far away, capturing the four of them in his glare.

Ellen recalled Alex's description of the fire in London, when William had encountered this man. The timber, the smell of burning, the cries of the crowd… She was pretty sure Alex would be doing the same.

When The Infinity passed through the flames, he held out his hands as if patting a faithful canine. They died down even more, curls of black smoke taking their place. Here and there, fires continued to rage, but where he'd walked was clear. It was almost like he'd parted the fire so he could pass through, and from behind came three of the men closest to him who'd survived the blast—guns still in their hands. Except one had a big hole in his chest, the flesh on his face and arms ravaged by the blaze.

Then the smoke seemed to come alive, moulding itself into shiny metal. The black BMW nosed its way down through the devastation, its front dented in where it had done the same to the remains of the van to shift it out of the way. It shunted the smouldering wreckage of the Jag and the other cars off the road, its own tyres on fire, flames whirling around and around.

"Jesus H., Mary and Joseph," gasped Steve.

"Get back in the car," Alex told them. "Right now."

"But this can't be happening, bruv. It can't be him."

"That's what I've been telling myself all along—but it is."

Ellen helped Vaughn back inside the Freelander, while Steve and Alex got into their respective seats. "Where to?" asked Ellen.

Alex kept his eyes on what was unfolding. "We don't have many options. Down there? Maybe there's another way out of here."

The BMW was virtually clear, a phoenix riding through the ashes. It stopped to pick up The Infinity and his men. As it pulled away from the fire, another car followed: a convertible with its top up.

Steve put the car in gear and drove past the assembled holidaymakers. The road was even tighter the further down into the bay area they went, and Steve didn't want to risk doing more than thirty in case they met something coming in the opposite direction.

"They following?" Alex enquired.

Ellen, who was looking out through the back window said: "What do you think?"

Vaughn was shaking his head in the back. "Nnmmnooo."

Alex turned around. "What's he saying?"

"I think he might be trying to tell us that this is a dead end." Ellen pointed to the sea wall not far away.

"Fuck!" said Steve. "All right, what now?"

On the left-hand side were a few scattered shops selling ice cream, cheap knick-knacks and souvenirs, plus one very sheer cliff-face. On the right, not far away, was the funfair on a platform. It was small, but there had to be places in there to hide. "From here," Alex said, "I guess we're on foot."

They left the Freelander where it was. There was a metal barrier surrounding the funfair with a turnstile attached and a small wooden booth where someone was taking money for admittance.

"Hurry!" shouted Alex, checking the road for the approaching cars. They didn't have much time left. He and Steve carried Vaughn between them, but the man was virtually a dead weight, dragging his feet on the floor.

The dumpy woman at the booth observed their approach with interest. The carnival music was very loud, which had masked the sound of the gunfight and the explosions at the other end of the bay, but like everyone else down here she could see the smoke rising into the sky. She didn't like the looks of that, nor for that matter the looks of these people. The eldest appeared to be on drugs, and at his age—should know better. She wasn't about to let these four in, no way. It was bad for business.

"Sorry," she said to them. "No admittance."

"Please," Ellen begged her. "We have to get inside."

The woman, who'd positioned her large electric fan just centimetres away to get the full benefit, didn't like the way this lady kept looking over her shoulder down the road either. Sort of twitchy.

"No admittance," she repeated.

"Look," said Ellen, "my uncle here is very sick and we promised to take him to the fair before we leave. It's important to him."

Vaughn's head lolled to one side and he made a raspberry noise. "No admittance."

Steve took Vaughn's arm from around his shoulder and glanced down at the gate. There was a padlock on it, holding the metal barrier together. He took something out of his pocket and started to pick the lock.

"Hey! What're you sodding well doing?" shouted the woman. "You can't do that!"

The lock sprang open and Steve pushed the barrier aside.

Ellen smiled. "Looks like he can."

The woman stood up inside her booth. "Wait! Hey, you come back!" But it was too late; they were already inside and there was nothing she could do to stop them. Seconds later, they'd disappeared from sight.

– ii –

The BMW pulled up before it got to the Freelander. The convertible tucked in behind.

From the driver's side, Lucas Peck got out, clutching his shoulder. He opened the back door for The Infinity. He hadn't said anything about how Lucas had let the girl and the old man escape. Hadn't needed to; it was all in his blue eyes.

But now he did say something, except it wasn't in words. He grabbed Lucas by the shoulder and dug his thumb into the relatively fresh knife wound, pressing hard against the makeshift handkerchief bandage inside his shirt. Lucas showed his teeth, the pain excruciating. The Infinity let him go and he fell against the side of the car, just as Metcalf was getting out, barely recognisable as the man he'd been before—his skin puckered and blistering, his melted shirt stuck to a chest that sported a large gunshot wound. He'd retrieved his pistol from the floor and was holding it like a trophy. Lucas knew the gangster had been revived just to piss him—and probably Metcalf himself—off. He was followed by two other men: needle-nosed Hamilton and another Lucas didn't recognise.

The Infinity went over to the convertible. "Out, you two! Right now!"

Terry and Frank did as they were told.

Lucas stood upright, eyes red but determined not to show his discomfort in front of the foot soldiers. He made his way round to the boot and undid it. Then he opened his case inside, letting his hands roam over the assorted weapons within. He finally plumped for the curved blade, his hand-held scythe.

When the group was gathered, The Infinity led them to the booth and turnstile. They found the gate open and were about to enter when the woman inside started mouthing off.

"You can't come in! No admittance! No. Sodding. Admittance!" she spat, still on her feet. Then she spotted the guns, Peck's curved blade, the size of the two guys wearing sunglasses, not to mention the burnt man with the hole in his chest, and she sat back down again.

"We can do whatever we like, Eileen," The Infinity told her. "Now, why don't you stick your face in that big fan of yours. It's such a hot day; you need to cool off."

Eileen nodded. Apparently that sounded like a great idea. She undid the clasps on the side, pulling off the protective mesh on the front. Then she took hold of the fan with both hands, pushing her face into the whipping blades.

As The Infinity and his men entered the funfair, the sound of her screams could be heard even above the carnival music.

– iii –

It was an easy place to get lost in, which was good.

To their right were the spinning cups, to the left dodgems, and in front an alley full of stalls and games, such as hoop tossing and smashing pink furry animals over the head with a squeaky hammer. There was a Test Your Strength machine—which one youth was beating to death—a shooting gallery and a fortune-teller's tent.

But they wouldn't need anyone to tell them their future if they didn't find somewhere to hide—and quick.

"Through here," said Alex, helping Vaughn over the steps. Families waiting at the candyfloss machine looked at them oddly, but it was nothing the four of them weren't used to. They pushed through a queue of people, out into an open space.

"Perhaps we might be better off splitting up," suggested Steve.

Ellen shook her head. "How are we going to find each other again?"

"We could arrange to meet. Wait it out somewhere in the meantime."

"The Infinity has been waiting to catch up with me for this long," said Alex. "I don't think he's going anywhere till this is settled."

"That what this guy's calling himself? The Infinity?"

Alex realised his brother still didn't know half the story. He had no idea about what had happened over the past couple of weeks, over the past week. "Yeah."

"Heard Metcalf mention something about a Mr. Finn when he was talking to you. Must be like his nickname?"

"Something like that."

Steve grinned. "I'd have gone for The Terminator, personally."

In spite of himself, Alex chuckled. If nothing else, his brother had always been able to make him laugh. Usually in times of most stress, and usually after situations he had caused.

"Look, maybe I can slow them down at least," Steve said. "Buy you guys some time to find a bolthole. I know how these kind of people operate. I know what makes them tick."

Somehow I doubt that very much, Steve, thought Alex.

"I still don't think we should split up," said Ellen.

"I may have bollocksed up a lot of things in my time, including tonight," Steve told his brother, a serious expression on his face. "But it's like I said before, I want to see you right. Metcalf was spot on about one thing—that's what families are all about." He gave Alex a hug. "This is something I've got to do. I don't care if he is fireproof."

Alex grabbed him by the arm before he could go. "Steve—"

"It's okay." He winked. "I know what I'm doing. I can take care of myself."

Then he was running off, around the back of one of the rides.

"Be careful," Alex called after him, but he had no idea if Steve heard.

– iv –

The Infinity and his group had no such qualms about spreading out.

They split into three teams: Hamilton and Metcalf's other man, who they referred to as Fisher; Terry, Frank and Metcalf; Lucas and his master. The first group headed up the stall alley, the second went right past the spinning cups, and the third went left—The Infinity walking *through* the dodgems, none of which hit him, naturally.

The people down the alleyway fled when they saw Hamilton and Fisher approaching, guns still drawn. Some part of the hired hands' minds knew this was wrong and they would never be doing it normally, but that was swamped by the voice telling them how vital it was they find Webber. How anyone who got in their way must be disposed of. It was the same voice that had toned down the severity of what they'd been through back on Lower Armitage Road. It was giving them *carte blanche* to act like the hoods they'd always known they were.

Fisher tucked his sawn-off shotgun under his arm and walked over to one of the stalls. He picked up a rubber hammer and began whacking the furry creatures bobbing up and down. *Squeak-whack! Squeak-whack!*

"Shoot three of the targets and get a cuddly toy!" the apple-cheeked barker at the shooting gallery was proclaiming. Hamilton turned in his direction, smiled, and raised his Scorpion machine pistol. The owner just had time to duck before the bullets dotted the metal targets, sawing a couple in half then riddling the selection of stuffed giraffes, elephants and bears he was using as prizes. Ignoring the yells of terrified people nearby, he leaned over to pick up one of the animals: a smoking ginger cat.

"You ready?" Fisher said, tugging his arm.

"Am now," replied Hamilton.

Fisher went on ahead, walking down the remainder of the alley and turning the corner. He never saw the Test Your Strength mallet which smacked him in the face. There was no squeak this time, but a hell of a *WHACK.* He fell sideways into a laughing policeman box, his shotgun going off in the process. Hamilton dropped the stuffed toy and let off another volley of bullets, but missed the man who'd ducked around the corner.

"I heard Metcalf's men were all pussies," came a cry.

When Hamilton got there the man had gone. He returned to Fisher, whose face was so much mulch; nose splattered and eyes completely white. The policeman in the box was laughing so hard he was in danger of falling from his perch. Hamilton picked up Fisher's shotgun and blew the copper's head off.

Then he went in search of the person who'd done this.

* * *

Terry and Frank ended up outside the ghost train ride, Metcalf shambling along beside them. "One of us ought to check it out," said Frank.

Terry pulled down his shades and examined the pictures on the side: hideous and luminous fiends with green faces, deathly white spectres with big black holes for eyes. "You fucking go then," he said.

"What are you, scared?"

"No," said Terry.

"Then *you* go in," Frank told him. "No, wait. Who do you think should go in, Mr. Metcalf?" He pulled the man up by his arm. Nick Metcalf stared vacantly at him.

"You know something," said Terry. "He doesn't look so good. I think he might need a doctor or somethin'."

"Never mind about that, who's going in?" asked Frank "You do it, go on. I dare you."

Terry rolled his head on his shoulders to loosen up the muscles in his neck. "All right then, I will. Watch him."

Terry got on the ride, taking up two seats. The gears ground as it started up, working hard to transport this enormous man inside. Kangarooing, he finally made it through the black curtain and Frank heard a haunting "Oooeeeeooooh" coming from inside.

"Wuss," said Frank.

Someone tapped him on the shoulder. "Want to buy a balloon, big fella?"

Frank turned, ready to take this seller's balloons and burst them one by one, saving the last to shove up his arse. "No, I don't want to buy a fuckin—"

He couldn't believe what he was seeing. There, right in front of him, holding a bunch of silver helium balloons with the faces of cartoon characters on them, was a man dressed as a clown. His baggy yellow and blue costume had big red buttons up the front, a bit like miniature pom-poms. He was wearing long, floppy shoes that were four or five sizes too big, and white magician's gloves covered his hands. His face was alabaster, a huge smile painted over his lips. Black eyebrows that were too high touched the fringe of his curly, green hair—and the whole thing was set off by his big, red nose.

Frank let go of Metcalf's arm. He backed away. The clown took a step towards him.

"Keep away. Keep away!"

"What's the matter?" said the clown. "Don't you wanna play?"

Frank ran—and for a man of his size, his speed was impressive. Metcalf frowned, eyes trailing his former hired gun.

The clown now turned to him. "What's the matter with your mate? I was only having a laugh." Then the balloon seller frowned as he took in the bullet wound and the gun.

Metcalf gazed at the clown, then wandered off, bumping into railings as he went.

There was a clanking noise as the train came back through. "Piece of piss," said the big man stuffed into the car. "I even decked one of the vampires when it tried to bite me."

He stopped talking when he saw the balloon man. Then looked in both directions.

The clown gave a shrug and walked off.

* * *

On the other side of the dodgems, Lucas was struggling to keep up with The Infinity. He'd deserved his punishment—and probably more besides. He'd let both his guard slip and his charges get away. It was unforgivable. There was no excuse. Apart from, of course, how that woman made him feel, how crazy she'd sent him: ironic given her profession. In his eyes she was perfect, the woman he'd been looking for all this time. But he'd be lucky if The Infinity gave her to him after this. He'd be lucky if all he got by the end of the day was a knife wound to the shoulder. First the mess at the hospital, then this. The Infinity wouldn't forget.

The only way he might make this better would be if he could find Webber first. That may just save his skin. Who knows, The Infinity might be so grateful he'd give Lucas the woman as a reward. Had to pick his moment, though. Slip away quietly. He doubted whether The Infinity would miss him lagging behind anyway—the man was in a world of his own. Lost in the chase.

Lucas dodged sideways and cut through behind a go-carting track. Children, old and small, were racing around the circuit, which was only the length of a small garden. Yes, if he could just find them, it might make up for a lot of things.

If he could just find them first.

— v —

"We can't carry him much further," said Ellen.

She was right; lugging Vaughn around was wearing them out.

"Look, we can rest over there." Alex guided them over to some boxes beside the platform rail. They laid him down. Alex looked over the rail; the sea beneath this part of the pier was churning and frothing.

"Why did you take off like that?"

Ellen's question took him by surprise. "I-I thought it would be for the best."

"For the best? Alex, didn't we say we were going to see this through… together?"

"You said that, yes. But I didn't want you to get hurt."

Ellen reacted as if she'd been slapped. "So you just left. After everything… God, if you only knew what I'd been through back there."

He couldn't look her in the eye. "I'm sorry, Ellen."

"I thought that was it. Thought I was never going to see you again."

Alex's heart was racing. "Why would that bother you?"

"Why would it…?" She closed the gap between them. "Why do you think? Don't tell me you don't know."

"Ellen, I—"

Vaughn sat bolt upright on the bench. "Grrggnnnnah."

They both turned at the same time. Ellen came around the boxes and got down beside the man. "Patrick? Patrick…"

"Ennllllleeenn," he murmured.

"He said your name." Alex joined them.

"Enllnlne…Johnhhhbnbb"

"Johann? He's gone, don't you remember? Oh, please *try* to remember." It was devastating for her to see him like this. It struck her that this must have been what he'd gone through with Marina towards the end, and how much worse it would be going through it with someone you loved.

Vaughn tapped her hand, so she opened it. "What is it, Patrick? What are you trying to tell me?"

He took his finger and drew a circle in her palm. It tickled, but she kept her hand still. Vaughn looked into her eyes, trying to transmit the information. He drew another circle. Then he made a fist and brought it down on her palm until it slapped against the flesh.

"Break the circle," said Alex. "He's telling us to break the circle."

Vaughn gave a hard nod of his head and grunted.

"Patrick, what's the circle? What do you want us to do?"

He brought his fist down again.

"The same thing you said in the hospital. The same thing Johann… Lars said." Ellen cocked back her head. "But what does it mean?"

"You said The Infinity told him what all this was about," said Alex.

"Uh-huh."

"Well, maybe he's figured out the way to defeat him. Maybe that's what they've been trying to tell me all along. Johann and the others. Maybe that's what the dreams have been about, Ellen."

"The circle."

"Warnings, ways of communicating. I don't know."

"And if we could just figure it out—"

"We could stop this Infinity thing right in its tracks," finished Alex.

– vi –

The little boy was on his own; lost.

He'd become separated from his parents when the big bangs had started near the hoopla stall. Somehow he'd wandered through the fair and wound up here, the sound of crying like a beacon. He was clutching the balloon his mum had bought from the clown, and it had guided him to the man sat crying behind the tent.

"Hello," said the little boy.

The man started, petrified. When he saw the balloon he let out a yell.

"Why're you crying? Are you lost?"

The man nodded.

"I'm lost too." He held out his balloon for the man to take. "It's okay, someone will find us soon."

The crying man hesitated, as if he wasn't going to accept the balloon at all—then he reached out and pinched the string. He looked up at the funny cartoon character painted on the front.

"It's Froggy," said the little boy. "He's a frog."

The man stopped crying, and smiled.

Then he got up and took the boy's hand.

"Where are we going? To find Mummy and Daddy?"

The man nodded his head. "Yeah," he said.

"My name's Martin," said the little boy. "What's yours?"

"Frank," the man told him, drying his eyes. "My name's Frank."

– vii –

Steve ducked back behind the waltzers.

It was okay, nobody had seen him come this way, nobody was following him. He gripped the Test Your Strength mallet with both hands. The handle was slippery, the end still slick with blood.

S'alright. S'cool. Nothing you didn't have to deal with when you were inside. There were bullies in there as well, but they left you alone if they knew you could handle yourself. Only difference was they didn't have guns, did they Steve? They weren't Nick Metcalf's fucking henchmen.

How the shitting hellfire had his brother got tangled up with them? And how had he got tangled up with that Finn bloke? The one who'd taken over Metcalf's outfit. They'd *all* be on the run for the rest of their lives at this rate. But that was in the future…if they had one. Deal with the here and now for starters. Shouldn't be too difficult for someone who spent most of his time living in it.

What he wouldn't give to be with his lover right now. But that was impossible.

Steve closed his eyes and tried not to think about that. It hurt too much.

He walked backwards, keeping his eyes and ears open, alert for anything…apart from the person he bumped into, who was also walking backwards.

Steve turned; the other person turned.

Shit! thought Steve and swung the mallet.

– viii –

"Ghnnhaaammm."

No use, they didn't catch that one. So far, apart from that nugget about the circle, which they'd pretty much guessed anyway, Alex and Ellen had got nothing out of Vaughn.

"He's becoming more coherent," said Ellen.

"Yeah?" Alex didn't know if he meant it sarcastically or not, or whether it would be taken that way. It wasn't.

"Yes, I can see the signs. His eyes are clearer, he's using his hands more. Given time he might be able to tell us what we need to know."

"Given time? Ellen, I don't think we have much more of that. Steve's out there doing his John McClane thing."

"Who?"

"Doesn't matter," said Alex. "The point is I'm worried about him; I'm worried about *us*. I have no idea how all this is going to work out and it scares me, Ellen."

"You don't think I'm frightened too? I have been since this whole thing began." She took his hand and he felt how it was shaking. But it also felt natural; fit so well. He gave it a small squeeze.

Now, do it now—you may not get another chance, thought Alex.

He leaned across and looked into her eyes. "If I don't do this I'll regret it for the rest of my life," Alex said.

"Just shut up and kiss me."

Alex pressed his lips against hers. That seemed right too. In spite of everything that was going on around them, everything that had happened and the way they'd met, this felt like it was meant to be. He couldn't explain it and he doubted Ellen could either. No one ever really could explain these sorts of things.

The kiss was soft and tender, there was no urgency to it, nothing animalistic about it. As Alex's lips brushed against hers, she parted her mouth slightly and gave a little moan. Both their eyes were closed or they might have spotted the approaching figure. And if they hadn't been so lost in each other, they might have heard the noise of his footsteps.

"Ahh," he said, when he saw them. "Isn't that just precious."

– ix –

"There he is, that's him."

Martin pointed to the guy not far away. "That's the horrible man who made all the noise. That's why I'm lost, Frank."

The man was carrying two guns, one a sawn-off, one a machine-pistol.

"Hamilton," said Frank.

Frank told Martin to wait there while he had a word with the man.

Walking over to Hamilton, holding his Froggy balloon, Frank was well aware that he must have looked quite peculiar. But he didn't care what Hamilton thought. The guy was a headcase of the highest order, and he'd caused Martin to become separated from his parents. That was inexcusable.

"Oi, got a minute?" he said to Hamilton.

The needle-nosed man regarded his erstwhile colleague coolly. "Not really."

"You been shooting the place up, Hamilton?"

He nodded.

"You been scaring the kids and that ain't nice."

"Fuck 'em," said Hamilton.

"What did you say?"

"You heard."

Frank pushed him. Hamilton raised the machine pistol.

"I'll give you five seconds to put that down," Frank warned him.

Hamilton shrugged casually.

"Four…three…two…"

Hamilton brought his shotgun up and pulled the trigger. Frank's balloon was blown into a million pieces, the bang tremendous. Hamilton raised the Scorpion to Frank's head.

"Who's the big man now?" Hamilton said.

He felt a hand on his shoulder, a large hand that spun him completely around. The guns were slapped out of his grasp before he could fire and he was hoisted off his feet.

"Having a bit of trouble, Frank?" asked Terry.

Frank was looking at the string in his hand. "Nothing I couldn't handle. Put him down, Terry."

The colossal man did as his friend had requested.

Frank bent down and picked up the guns. Hamilton swallowed hard, the Adam's apple in his throat bobbing up and down. Frank raised both weapons and pointed them at the needle-nosed man's head. Then he gathered them both together in one hand, walked past Hamilton, and dropped them in the nearest bin.

Hamilton breathed a sigh of relief.

On his way back, Frank put on his dark glasses again.

"So, what do we do with him?" asked Terry, clamping a hand down on Hamilton's shoulder again.

"His name's not on the list," said Frank. "So we show him the door." He motioned over towards the railing not far away.

Hamilton swallowed hard.

"For your sake," Terry told him as he took him by the arm, "I hope you can swim."

Frank grinned and took the other arm.

– x –

"Come on out from behind there," said Peck.

Ellen and Alex broke off their kiss, startled by his sudden appearance. In one hand he was holding what appeared to be a scythe—and there was blood dripping from it. In the other he was holding Steve by the scruff of the neck, unconscious. Both men looked like they'd just come from a hard day's grind at a butcher's shop: their clothes and faces stained red. Peck touched Steve's neck with the point of the scythe. "I said come on out here into the open. *Now!*"

Ellen moved to pick up Vaughn's arm, but Peck told her to leave him. He backed out into an open space on the platform, and motioned with the scythe for them to do the same.

"If you've hurt him…" said Alex.

"You'll what?"

Alex said nothing.

"Don't believe we've met properly, Webber." Peck dropped Steve on the floor. "But Ellen and I have been formerly introduced. I'm disappointed that you ran out on me back there, sweetheart—just when we were starting to get to know each other better."

Alex looked from Peck to Ellen, who was seething with contempt.

"She's my muse, you see," he explained. "The inspiration for my next… my *finest* piece."

It all suddenly clicked into place for Alex. "Beverly." He took a step forward, but Ellen's hand was on his arm.

"She was good, but as I explained to your new girlfriend—easy come, easy go, eh?—I was in a hurry." He returned Ellen's gaze, though his was a mixture of awe and excitement. "I'm going to take my time with *her*."

"You touch Ellen and I swear to God I'll—"

"I've got to admit I admire your tastes, Webber. They're very similar to mine. You know something special when you see it, and so do I."

"We've got nothing in common, you sick bastard."

"Sick? At least she's not my doctor—and getting it on just days after your wife's…untimely passing. Now that's positively perverse, isn't it?"

"It's not like that," Alex countered, but his defence was a weak one.

"Pity I have to split up the happy couple, but…well, The Infinity's waiting to have a bit of a chat with you, Webber. And then, *oh then*." He stuck out his tongue and licked the scythe.

That was it. Alex, pulled his arm away from Ellen and charged at Peck. "Alex, no! He'll kill you."

Peck easily sidestepped Alex, whipping his arm around to thump him on the back. Alex crashed into another set of boxes on the far side of the platform, skidding along the floor.

"You should listen to her," Peck told him. "She talks a lot of sense."

Alex got to his feet, throwing himself at his opponent again. This time Peck kicked him in the stomach on approach. Alex doubled up and dropped to his knees, his glasses falling from his face.

"Stay down, this time."

But Alex was up again in moments. Peck was a blur, but he reached out and grabbed him around the waist. He pushed the pair of them back against a post, winding Peck. "*Ahgh!*"

"His shoulder," called out Ellen. "Where I stabbed him!"

Alex punched him there. For the first punch he'd ever thrown in his life, it wasn't half bad, and it had the desired effect. Peck screamed.

But Alex didn't have long to feel proud. Peck swung the scythe, catching his arm. A cut opened at the bicep, and blood poured from the injury. Alex took baby steps backwards, clutching the wound.

Peck's next kick got him squarely in the chest. Alex went flying head over heels, landing awkwardly on the wooden platform, flopping to the ground…

Peck walked over to Alex, scythe raised. All thoughts about The Infinity and his mission were forgotten; the only thing he could see was the enemy, an attacker he needed—*wanted*—to wipe out.

Peck drew the blade back.

And felt two hands preventing him from bringing it down again. He turned and saw Ellen's face centimetres away from his own—a determined scowl on her face. Peck dragged her around, then shook her off.

"Wait your turn," he told her.

She kicked him hard in the side. If he felt it, he didn't show it. Peck hooked her round the back of the neck with the scythe, drawing her to him, sealing his mouth over hers. He shoved his tongue inside, worming it around, in a kiss the antithesis of the one she'd shared with Alex.

She scratched his face, right down the cheek.

"Bitch!" shouted Peck, and shoved her so that she lost her footing and fell over. He touched the scratch but there was so much blood there already it was impossible to tell which was fresh anymore.

"Now, where was I?" he said, twisting around and hefting the scythe. As he did, there was movement in the periphery of his vision, weaving from side to side. It was slow, but it had something in its raised hand. He heard the shot at the same time as the bullet ricocheted off the handle of the scythe, causing him to drop it; then the thing was on him, a punch to the jaw sending Peck sprawling backwards. He looked over and saw Metcalf grinning, teeth white against the red and black ruin of his face.

Peck, dizzy but still standing, staggered, attempting to make his way back towards his victim, when a voice stopped him.

"Lucas. That's enough." Peck turned to see who was speaking, as if there had ever been any doubt. The Infinity was standing at the base of the big Ferris wheel.

"It would seem I've arrived just in time," he said, blue eyes twinkling against the ever-darkening sky.

Twenty-Six

– i –

"Lucas, to me! Now!"

Like a dog trained to heel, Peck scampered as best he could towards the sound of his master's voice. Ellen crawled along the floor and found Alex again. They put their arms around each other. The Infinity saw the blood where Peck had cut Alex, saw Steve lying on the platform, unconscious. Saw Metcalf raising his gun again.

"Rest," said The Infinity, pointing at Metcalf. The former gangland boss stopped grinning, blinked once, twice, then fell sideways onto the wooden boards.

Peck was almost there, cowering in front of The Infinity. "I-I've found them," he whimpered.

The Infinity closed his eyes slowly, then opened them again. "Yes, you did—and look at the damage you have caused."

"Don't be angry," Peck pleaded with him.

"You were about to kill Alex Webber. How could you be so foolish! After all these years of searching, after all this time, you could have ended it here with one blow of that toy of yours." The Infinity's tone was like that of a headmaster having to berate one of his favourite students: hard and disappointed. "It would all have been wasted, all have been in vain. Because of you, Lucas. Because of you!"

Peck's head was bowed.

"Look at me," said The Infinity.

He was shaking, but complied. "I've served you faithfully," Peck whispered.

"Yes," said The Infinity, lifting Peck's chin with his hand. "You have. But the time has come to say goodbye, Lucas."

"No. Please…"

"I created you, and now I must also destroy you—my only son."

"Son?" Peck looked confused.

The Infinity's eyes glowed blue; the bluest anyone had ever seen them. They became more than just eyes, they took up half of his head, growing bigger and bigger. Those watching had to shield their own from the intensity.

Peck brought his hands up, the light from those eyes unbearable. He shrieked at the top of his lungs, but it didn't stop what happened next. His body began deconstructing itself, flesh on the cheekbones melting, fingernails falling off and hair falling out. His trousers and shirt fell away as his frame contracted, legs and arms drawing into themselves, withering away.

Soon Peck was just molecules, and even these were dissipating, cells decreasing instead of multiplying, returning to nothing. There was one last brilliant flash of light, and The Infinity was standing there. Alone. His eyes returned to their normal shade, but even this had a disquieting effect.

He appeared to be deep in thought, contemplating what he had just done. But this was transient and soon he had refocused his attention on his prey.

* * *

With arms still wrapped around each other, Ellen and Alex rose. Ellen looked around, searching for an escape route.

The Infinity walked towards them.

They were trapped. There was no door this time, no set of stairs, no security guard to distract him while they made their getaway. The game of hide-and-seek was over, and The Infinity had won.

"You've led me a merry dance this time," he said, footsteps pounding on the platform slats. "I'll give you that much."

Alex hid Ellen behind him. "You can do what you want with me, but let Ellen and the others go." It helped that he could barely see his enemy because he'd lost his glasses; it gave his words strength.

The Infinity laughed a tired laugh. "You are in no position to be making demands. What I want I shall take. In this world at any rate."

"That's it, isn't it? That's what this is all about—you get off on doing whatever you want. Doesn't matter what the consequences are, or who gets hurt."

"How little you know about any of this. Which benefits me no end."

"Promise me you'll leave them out of this." He reached around behind and took Ellen's hand.

"We're wasting time," said The Infinity, metres away and narrowing the margin.

"Promise me!"

"Them, yes." He waved his hand to indicate Steve and Vaughn. "But her…" The Infinity was suddenly standing next to him. "Her I cannot."

"What are you talking about?"

In an instant The Infinity had reached out with both of his hands, left and right: he took Alex's free hand in one, and Ellen's in the other.

"She's the one who delivered you to me," said The Infinity.

Then they all collapsed on the platform deck.

– ii –

To be back again was bizarre. Alex hadn't visited the circle since the night they'd fled the hospital—not really, not that he could remember.

Now here he was again, a place so familiar yet so alien. The ghostly shapes were appearing once more, showing themselves to him. Slowly they became clear—there was no need for glasses now—the people he had been in previous lives. He put faces to names, knew histories where before he knew nothing. They were all him and he was all of them.

It was different now that he was aware of this. But they were watching him, as if expecting him to do something. Alex had no idea what.

He was aware of the presence of someone else, close to him. Someone beside him, with her hand in his. "Ellen?" he said.

She was there, with him just as she had been all this week—just as she always had been. He recognised her touch, the warmth she spread in this place. She didn't seem in the least bit alarmed by any of it. How could they be sharing the same dream? How could they be dreaming anyway, with The Infinity about to—

Was that it, were they both dead? Was this the afterlife?

"Alex," she said. "Alex, you have to try and remember."

What was she talking about? "Ellen, why did The Infinity say that you'd led him to me?"

She shook her head. "Concentrate; we don't have much time. You have to help me."

You have to help me.

How?

By remembering.

"Ellen, how can it have been you?"

"Please, Alex, think! This isn't the first time you've been here."

No, he'd been here quite a few times in the last couple of weeks, although he hadn't really understood at first what was happening—or why.

There were more ghosts appearing, just as they had before. These were blank, formless, non-existent. But that couldn't be—he'd remembered the people he had been. Patrick Vaughn had done that much for him. What else did they want, and how could there be any more?

Ellen returned the squeeze he'd given her hand back in the waking world. All of a sudden he understood. He could see the faces, knew what Ellen had been getting at: the medicine man's daughter; William's barmaid; Cho, the samurai's butterfly; the witch in the torture chamber; Alice, Lars' wife; even the woman he'd bumped into in the market in Egypt. He hadn't been the only person who'd lived these past lives; in every single one he'd found her somehow. Call it fate or whatever, sooner or later he'd met up with Ellen in a different guise. And she'd been here in the circle, all those times he'd dreamt about it, even before he'd met her at the hospital; encouraging him to remember, trying to get him to help her, and by extension help himself. But why didn't she say anything, why didn't she tell him in any of her sessions? Why now, here at the end?

"Because she wouldn't acknowledge it, not even to herself," said a voice Alex recognised only too well. Darkness had fallen on the circle, just as it had in the real world. But this darkness had a shape, a name. A purpose. The thing with the blue eyes was everywhere and nowhere. A part of this place, just as they were. It was his home as well as theirs. Alex was aware of that, only he didn't know how. It also had a projection of substance, like them, and was walking around the pair. Circling them.

"Here, *she* remembers more than you. But she didn't start to dream the dream with you until this week. Until two days ago to be precise. Until her birthday."

"I'm sorry," Ellen told him. "I didn't know…my parents never told me."

"Told you what?" asked Alex.

"That she was adopted," said The Infinity, laughing. "That her birthday isn't really in November at all. When she started to dream, I had a new source to focus on. One year and two weeks younger than you."

"So it wasn't through Metcalf at all," said Alex. "The Infinity found us through your dreams—he tracked us down through *you*."

"Ah, the first of many deceptions. On both sides." The Infinity cupped his hands and an image appeared, growing until it was as big as a small TV screen—then bigger still, like a film being projected. Its edges wavered and flickered, more dreamlike than the actual dream. It showed them a picture of Kirkwell General.

"I don't want to see this," she said, but couldn't look away.

As they watched the entire building exploded, engulfed in a fireball that couldn't possibly be natural, or even man-made—possibly it had started that way, but as always The Infinity had fanned the flames. Images of the people inside and what they had suffered appeared, horrific deaths that nobody deserved. Ellen started to cry and buried her head in Alex's shoulder.

"What's the matter, Alexander? You don't looked shocked at all," said The Infinity. "Could it be because you already knew about this and kept it from her?"

Ellen pulled her head away. "Alex?"

"He knew and didn't tell you. He let you go on thinking that everything was all right, that you'd be able to go back there after all this was over and done with."

"Alex, is that true? Did you know?"

"He showed me that night in the car. I didn't know whether to believe him or not, and I didn't want to upset you if it was wrong."

"But it wasn't wrong, was it?" said The Infinity. "And deep down you *did* know that. You just didn't want Ellen to blame you for it. You knew, in spite of the fact it wasn't really your fault, that she would. She'd hate you because you came into her life, bringing all this torment and heartache and—"

"Shut up!" shouted Alex.

The Infinity smiled. "Temper, temper."

Ellen shifted her body, angling it away from Alex. He felt her stiffen, but wouldn't let go of her. "I-I didn't know how to—"

"I wouldn't have blamed you, Alex. You should have told me."

"After all, she wasn't in any rush to check on those people, was she?" The Infinity broke in. "Too preoccupied with thoughts of you."

It was Ellen who told him to shut up now.

"I think a big part of you might have blamed me," Alex told her.

"No. But a massive part of me hates being lied to, and some of the worst lies are told by keeping your mouth shut. Do you know how I found out about this?"

Alex shook his head.

"That bastard who slaughtered your wife told me." The Infinity raised an eyebrow at the word bastard. "While he was trying to rape me."

Alex didn't know what to say; he felt like crying himself.

"And don't forget," added The Infinity, "he ran off and left you alone to face all that. Took off to meet his brother, to arrange his escape."

"That's bullshit," said Alex, stabbing a finger at his accuser. "I was trying to keep her safe, trying to steer *you* away from her. From them all. I knew it was me you were after, and I'd put them through enough."

"Not nearly enough by the looks of things," came the reply.

Ellen didn't say a word in Alex's defence.

"You're forgetting one thing," Alex fired back at both of them. "*He* would have found us anyway, because you let him know where you were. I realise you didn't mean to do it, but all the time I was trying to avoid contact in this place, you were here, telling him what he needed to know."

"It took a couple of nights, but I got a picture of the place, got Vaughn's name," admitted The Infinity, proud of himself. "You were a much harder nut to crack than her. If you'll pardon the pun."

It was still hard for Alex to believe; Ellen was strong-willed, focused and clear of mind.

"Ah, but she was so wrapped up in the whole idea of trying to explain me away, it was easy to use that to my advantage." Alex had forgotten that in here, his thoughts were far from private. There were no boundaries and The Infinity could now see through him like glass. "Why would she believe that she was giving away secrets to me in her dreams, when she didn't even believe you were? Everything has to have a rational explanation. Even now, even after all she's seen tonight, she's fighting against it. Aren't you?"

Ellen held her silence.

"You're here, you're a part of this, yet you're still dismissing it as some form of illusion. That world, the one you know so well and cling to—*that* is the illusion. This is your reality; the only one you've truly known."

"No, I—"

Alex squeezed her hand more tightly. "Ellen, listen to me, you remember when we were in the hospital? You were the only thing I was holding on to. You got through to me at a time when I thought I was losing my mind. Now, trust me, hold on to me." He put his arms around her. "Can't you see what he's doing? He's trying to divide us, split us up. He needs to keep us confused." He brushed a hair away from her face and she looked at him. "It doesn't matter how we got here, what you believe or what you don't believe. We need to stick together—remember? Together to the end of this?"

"Yes," she said. "You're right."

"I know why it was pointless trying to ignore my feelings. Look around you." She took in the faces—the pairs of faces—ghost men and women from different ages. "We've been together so many times. My soul knows you even if my mind doesn't remember. And I think you feel it too."

She nodded, then she kissed him.

"Nice speech," said The Infinity. "Touching."

"I don't know what you want, but whatever it is you're not going to get it this time. Not as long as we're here, together," said Alex, adamant.

"You think?"

"I know."

"You know nothing," The Infinity assured him.

"We know that you're evil, that you manipulate," said Ellen. "You kill, you destroy."

"Yes, I do all that—but your definition of evil differs so much from mine. It's all about perspective."

"Perspective?" Alex could hardly get the word out. "How can shooting someone in the head be a question of interpretation?"

The Infinity opened his blue eyes wider. "You do not see the bigger picture. Without my 'manipulation' there would be no progress. You were there when I gave them this." He drew a circle in the air. "You might not have understood as you were at the time, but you did when you returned here. To the inspiration for it."

"James said that at every point you'd both met, there followed an event of devastating proportions," said Ellen. "Like the Great Fire of London, the decimation of the Native Americans. He checked what dates he could through the Internet and—"

The Infinity snorted. "The Internet. A useful invention; all it took was a few words in the right ears."

A sudden realisation smacked Alex in the face. "What you showed me that night I fell asleep in the car, it happened didn't it? You were showing me what you showed Lars. But it wasn't the future for me, it was the past. You were showing me the Second World War."

"Without which there would not have been half the technological advances there have been in the western world," The Infinity maintained.

"And nowhere near as many deaths," said Ellen.

"The yin to its yang. For every action there is an equal and opposite reaction."

"Bullshit," said Alex. "You're not doing any of this for some greater good. You're doing it because you enjoy it."

"As I say, you know nothing about this. Nothing about *me*."

"But we do, don't we," said Alex; it wasn't a question. "We do know who you are, the same as you know us. It's just that we're having trouble remembering."

The Infinity stared him out. "So who do you think I am?"

"I can make an educated guess."

The thing with blue eyes laughed again, loud and long: a hearty belly laugh. He shook with the force of it, shoulders jiggling up and down. When it had subsided, he said: "Oh, that's a good one. The irony is that you could only say it in your present ignorant state."

"What does he mean?" Ellen asked Alex.

"That I think he's the Devil."

"Lucifer, Beelzebub, the Dark Prince, The Fallen One. Ring any bells?" The Infinity said to her.

Ellen gasped.

"Think about it, the fire, the snake. It all fits into place."

"If that's what you believe, then perhaps this would be more of a fitting environment." The Infinity waved his hand and the circle began to transform itself, shrubbery cropping up, trees and foliage everywhere. Alex looked down to see he was wearing no clothes, and neither was Ellen. It was the first time he'd seen her naked and he couldn't help staring; she was even more beautiful than he'd imagined. He noticed that she was looking at him too, a hand now on his chest as she held him. At that moment he wanted nothing more than to just lay her down and make love to her, to cover that body in kisses, to be inside her. He'd never wanted anyone as much; even Beverly when they'd first met and hormones had been running wild. More than that, he knew what it would feel like—trace memories of being with her so many times. Even here, in the circle.

"Now, now, let's try and control ourselves, shall we." The voice was coming from a huge black serpent with blue eyes, curling around a tree with a single, solitary apple hanging from it. The fruit looked about as perfect as could be, succulent and ripe; it probably tasted delicious. "Go on then, take it," said The Infinity. "That's what you're supposed to do: taste the forbidden."

Alex and Ellen stood in wonderment at the scene in front of them, even more confused.

"God created the world in seven days, then he created you—Alex— then took one of his ribs to create you, Ellen. Isn't that right? Isn't that how you remember it?"

"What...?"

"Take the fruit. Go on, see what happens."

"No," Ellen replied, steel in her voice.

"No?" The snake suddenly grew legs and arms, but its head was still reptilian, forked tongue darting in and out. It plucked the apple from the tree and approached them with it. "Here, take a bite."

Alex could feel Ellen's body trembling. "She said no."

"Spoilsport." The serpent's features contorted, transforming into The Infinity's face again. "I am no more the Devil than you are Adam and

Eve," he guffawed. "According to Greek myth, chaos came first and the Earth and the Heavens came from the splitting of an egg. Norse mythology says that in the beginning there was nothing but a bottomless deep known as Ginnungagap and a land of mist called Niflheim, from which twelve rivers flowed; the water from this froze, and was turned into vapour by the fire from the south. And from this came the giant Ymir, whose body became the Earth and whose blood became the seas, his bones making mountains and his hair becoming trees. Babylonians celebrated the victory of the god Marduk over the monster Tiamat. Marduk would then be free to marry the goddess Ishtar…"

With each tale, the surroundings changed to reflect what The Infinity explained: Alex and Ellen witnessed the birth of creation as these different cultures had pictured it. Then, finally, they were standing on a beach by the sea: not unlike the one in Armitage Bay itself.

"The Japanese, like your good friend Agami, tell of a primeval oily ocean, from which emerged a reed-like substance. This became a powerful deity. At the same time two more divine creatures followed, a male and a female. But little is known about the trio other than they produced generations of gods and goddesses in their celestial land—including Izanagi and Izanami, who came down from Heaven to the oily mass on a rainbow bridge and created an island from which mankind supposedly flowed. Scientists, however, talk about a big bang out of which the universe was created, and say that human beings emerged from the seas. So which one of them is right?"

Ellen put a hand to her head, exasperated. "What's this got to do with us? Why are you showing us these things?"

The Infinity gave an apologetic tip of the head. "It's in my nature to be theatrical," he said. "In a sense it's irrelevant, but I couldn't help myself. This species has such a vivid imagination, don't you think? That's what makes them so much fun."

"What do you want?" asked Ellen.

"He needs us to yield," Alex suddenly exclaimed. "Don't you?"

"Starting to come back to you a little, is it?"

"I know that each time you've caught up with me—caught up with us—in the past, something has happened. Something terrible."

"I thought we'd been through all that," said The Infinity. "Good, bad: it all depends on how you look at it."

"But you can't go ahead until we agree, can you?"

That wiped the smile from The Infinity's face.

"It's what sent Lars mad. The guilt, the knowledge that he was indirectly responsible for so much devastation."

"You've given in every single time and you will do so again."

Alex shook his head vehemently.

"Let me show you something of the people you're trying to protect," said The Infinity.

"More Hollywood theatrics," said Alex.

"I would have thought you'd enjoy that? But no, just what you would call reality."

Another scene shift and they were seeing the world in all its glory. In a bed-sit somewhere an anonymous junky was shoving a needle into his vein and jacking up. His face was white, red track marks flowing down his arms. Somewhere else a woman was being attacked by the side of the road for her money, and nobody was stopping to help—nobody wanted to get involved. They were shown people on the streets, begging for cash, sleeping rough. In nightclubs across the country, just like Yazmin's, bodies heaving and thrashing around, strangers colliding together, unaware that later they'd be passing on deadly viruses through their bodily fluids: or maybe they just didn't care. In a home somewhere, a girl of about ten listened for the creak on the landing that signified her mother's boyfriend was going to steal into her room again—but she mustn't tell, she mustn't breathe a word. On estates, gangs of youths were terrorising old people, hanging around on street corners smoking, throwing bricks through people's windows and pissing in telephone boxes. In some foreign country, terrorists were breaking into a hotel room to take an innocent man hostage; if his country didn't agree to their demands, then he would be beheaded within twenty-four hours.

"How dare you!" shouted Alex. "How dare you stand there and show us these things, after everything you've done. After all the things you've affected and tampered with."

"I have nothing to do with any of these things," The Infinity insisted. "They are happening on a day-to-day basis. *I* guide events on a grander scale."

"Which has a knock-on effect for what happens lower down," Ellen contended. "You help a drug dealer get their product on the street and you get junkies. Cause and effect."

"They don't have to *buy* the product, though." The Infinity spread his arms wide. "You're missing the point. I wouldn't be able to do the things I do if this race wasn't inherently rotten to the core. Just as it's in my nature to do the things I do, it's in theirs to cause their own suffering and misery. To be fundamentally greedy and selfish. To be power hungry, even though they know nothing of what power truly is."

"And you're missing something, too," said Alex. "What about love? What about the power of helping others, what about caring and the support of friends and family?"

The Infinity had apparently been waiting for this to come up. "The same old discussion, repeated ad...infinitum." He tittered. "You would both know something of families and friends, wouldn't you?"

Alex narrowed his eyes. "I know I would give my life for mine."

"Your life? Your life?" The Infinity found this concept amusing. "Not quite there yet, are you?" He turned his blue eyes on Ellen. "And you, you'd give your '*life*' for yours? Hmm? Where are your '*mother*' and '*father*,' Ellen? Where are they right now? Are they worried about you?" He showed her exactly where they were, playing tennis on the court of the cruise liner, not a care in the world. "How about Graham? Did he care about you? You loved him so much and how did he repay you?" A picture of the man in question appeared, and the corner of Alex's mouth twitched.

"He knows what he did was wrong," said Ellen. "It'll haunt him forever."

"Will it?" The Infinity smiled that cheeky smile again. "I think not. Take a look at where he is now: engaged, happy." He showed her Graham walking hand in hand with a tall red-headed woman through a park. "They're expecting their first child next year."

Ellen's mouth was wide open.

"You have this image of him sat at home pining for you; thinking about what might have been, just as you do. But the truth is, Ellen, he hardly ever thinks about you *at all* anymore. He's moved on, as you should have done. Those calls you keep getting are from two men trying to work out whether you're at home or not, so they can come and steal from you. In fact, they've already done it—they did it the first night you spent in your car." The Infinity showed her a picture of her flat, ransacked, clothes everywhere, TV and stereo gone, a photo album on the floor, the pages ripped, the pictures torn out; a small jewellery box open, the contents—a pair of pearl earrings and a diamond necklace Graham had once given her—gone. Ellen was crying again. "Of course, if you had any friends outside of work colleagues you could have asked them to keep an eye on the place for you. But nobody really wants to know you, do they Ellen?"

"You cruel son of a bitch," said Alex.

"Ah, but the best is yet to come." The Infinity tapped his nose. "Let's talk about *your* family, shall we? "To start with, your Uncle Gerry, that nice affable man you so wish your dad had been like: what a good sport he is, what a laugh. Did you know that he once put your Aunty Joan in hospital? Punched her so hard in the stomach she miscarried their second child. She bled internally, Alex. They never had any more children after Kevin—couldn't, because of the damage done. Joan still can't look at her three grandchildren without thinking about that night and what her un-born child might have become. Kevin? Well, now, he thinks you're the world's biggest bore. The arty farty intellectual teaching at college, who his wife secretly wishes he was more like. Better hope the children have got her genes and not his, eh? Your Aunt Sylvia's quite a character too. She put Judy down so much when she was growing up, telling her how ugly she was, that she developed an eating disorder and used to cut her arms in her bedroom with a razorblade. She's taken these insecurities with her into the modelling world and they're going to cost her that precious TV career Sylvia keeps harping on about, just to prove to her sister that her daugh-ter's done better than you and Steve." As with Ellen, pictures of the family members flashed up for them to see as The Infinity listed their faults.

"Stop it," bawled Alex. "*Stop it!*"

"We're just getting to the good part. Ever wondered why your dad was so low all the time? Why he'd snap and snarl, why you could never do anything right—and why you could never make him proud of you? He was jealous, Alex. Jealous of the attention your mother gave to you. Saw you as a threat, and there were times when it even crossed his mind when you were little, to just put a pillow over your face and get rid of you once and for all. Didn't help that his wife wasn't having sex with him anymore, either, which forced him to visit a big Polish woman on Staley Crescent two times a week who gave him oral pleasure and indulged in his fetish for leather underwear. To put it simply, Alex, he hated you."

Alex's face was turning crimson, his breathing erratic.

"It wasn't Steve who caused his death, it was you. He didn't give a damn about what Steve was doing or what he wasn't doing, but he got very wound up every time your mum paid you any attention—bought you something with money that *he'd* earned. Didn't you also think to yourself what it would be like to be the master of that household, with your father and brother out of the way? And when it came true, when you had your chance, you let her down. Moved out and left her alone when she wasn't any use to you anymore. Classic Oedipus, wouldn't you say Dr. Hayward?"

"Stop it!"

But The Infinity had already brought up another picture. This one was of a bedroom. The moans and sighs were as loud as thunder inside the circle, as the couple thrashed about in bed. The sheets rose and fell with each thrust, springs squeaking, headboard banging against the wall. Followed by a close-up of Beverly's face, eyes closed, lips pulled back over her teeth—crying out with pleasure as the man on top of her pounded away faster and faster.

Ellen stopped crying for a moment and watched them, feeling the same way Alex had when he saw Graham. To see Beverly and Alex together like that when she now had feelings for him…

But when she looked closer, she realised it wasn't Alex at all. The hair was different, shoulders more angular.

"Take a good look," said The Infinity. "This was what your wife was doing while you were being assessed for psychiatric treatment. Oh, but don't blame yourself; she stopped loving you in that way long before this started."

Alex's body was tensing.

"You think she's enjoying it more than she used to do with you? Looks like she is, doesn't it? But here's the stinger, Alex. Recognise the person who's about to spread his seed inside her?" The man was speeding up, head over Beverly's, tongue in her mouth.

"God! It's Steve, isn't it," said Ellen.

There was a close-up as the man pulled his head away and she realised just how wrong she was. There was James, from the point of view of Beverly underneath him. His eyes were screwed up tight as he gave one last thrust and slumped down on top of her.

"That's right. Your friend, Alex. Your *best* friend." The Infinity stood back, folding his arms smugly. His work was done and the expression on Alex's face said it all. He was mortified.

"James… James and Beverly…"

"Screwing," said The Infinity. "And you've been wracked with guilt about her…" He nodded at Ellen. "…sleeping with her head on your shoulder. Not really any comparison, is there?"

Alex refocused on this creature who'd shown him a vision of his worst nightmare. His hatred couldn't be measured.

"So, how do you feel about the milk of human kindness now?"

Alex broke into a run, lunging at The Infinity. As she'd done with Peck, Ellen attempted to hold him back—but she couldn't. He took a swing; The Infinity didn't move. The blow struck him on the chin and his face turned to the right. Alex hit him again, this time his head flipped the other way. When The Infinity straightened and faced front, his eyes were glowing a vibrant blue. "You see, a natural human reaction. Now it's my turn."

The Infinity seemed to grow, filling the space around him with blackness. Pure evil, if there was ever such a thing, couldn't have been more terrifying than this—his temperament and character reflected a million fold. This was what The Infinity truly was, indescribable and horrifying. He wasn't solid anymore, if he'd been solid at all in the circle, but rather broke himself down into a nebulous substance which coiled around Alex, blue and black. It entered him through his ears, up his nose, in through his eyes. Alex yelled, clutching his head. He dropped to his knees, swatting at his face as if a swarm of angry bees were after him.

Ellen came over, placing a hand on his shoulder. "Alex, speak to me— are you all right?"

He lifted his head, calmly, slowly, eyes closed. "I've never felt better." His eyelids snapped open and she was overwhelmed by their blueness. Alex stood and grabbed her by the shoulders, shaking her. "If neither of you will listen to reason, then perhaps this is the only method left to me." It was The Infinity's voice. He slapped her. Then he gripped her head, fingers spread over cheeks, cupping just behind the ears—thumbs inching up towards her eyes.

"Do you yield?" he said to Ellen, increasing the pressure. In spite of this she shook her head.

"N-Never."

"Then how about you?" the voice asked itself. "Could you live with the knowledge that you'd murdered the woman you care about so much? Are *they* worth that?"

The thing masquerading as Alex squeezed her mouth to open it and put his own close to hers, allowing the blue-blackness to flow from one host to the other. When it was done, Ellen's eyes were burning with cerulean brightness. She backed away from Alex.

"Ellen," Alex said, his eyes returning to normal.

She grabbed her own neck, digging her nails in. "I could rip out her throat right here, right now. How would you like that?" Then she stuck out one arm, placing a nail at the wrist. "Or slash these open and make you watch her bleed to death slowly."

The anguish was etched on Alex's face, but there was also a look of enlightenment there. "Why not? You've already killed your own son—destroyed the being you created because you were so lonely. Why not kill another member of your family, now that you've systematically pulled apart the ones that we had. In fact, come on!" Alex put his hand around his own throat. "Let's all go together, shall we?"

Ellen froze, nail hovering over her wrist.

"Except we can't, can we? There's no way that can possibly happen."

"You know the truth then," she said. It wasn't a question, more a statement of fact.

"Yes," said Alex. "I know enough. And so does she."

"Of course—what you know, she does soon afterwards. It doesn't really change anything."

"Oh, I think it does. And I know what you have planned, why it was so important for you to find us before we remembered this time. That would have suited you just fine, wouldn't it?"

The blue-black substance seeped out of Ellen and coalesced beside her.

"You think you've proved your point?" said Alex. "You think you've had your revenge?

The shape quickly morphed into The Infinity. "I think I have made a reasonable case. As for revenge, that's not what this is about."

"No? Loneliness, betrayal, jealousy. I can see all of that in you."

Ellen caught her breath, still recovering. "If I were to analyse you, I'd be here for years."

"Go ahead, we have the time," said Alex. "We're not going anywhere until this is settled, are we?"

Behind them the picture shifted again: it showed a future world where humans were advancing technologically in leaps and bounds; where the marvels of modern science could hardly keep up anymore and each new day brought another development. At the same time, weaponry was increasing in sophistication and efficiency to destroy. The genetically engineered bioweapons of today out of control, new power sources backfiring and scorching the earth, where handfuls of mutated survivors roamed in packs, people starved, and killed and foraged for what scraps of clothes or food they could find, The water, poisoned; predators preying on the weak. It was beyond the vision of any prophet or doomsayer, a world so bent and twisted that cannibals were rife and babies taken from their mother's arms so they could be thrown in pots and boiled alive. It showed a future vision where The Infinity watched as humanity wiped itself out. Then, finally, he would be satisfied.

"Total control over it all. The ability to end everything. You're asking us to do that to our own children?"

"Again, you misunderstand. I wouldn't be controlling anything, I never have. 'Man shall destroy himself.' It says that in the Bible." The Infinity smirked.

"With a few pushes in the right direction, naturally," said Ellen. "A few key words whispered in the right ears."

"As always."

"I think you were wrong," said Alex.

"How so?"

"I think you really are the Devil."

"A construct, like every other myth," answered The Infinity.

"But, like all myths, there's always a grain of truth behind them. In a sense I *am* Eve, Alex *is* Adam," Ellen said. "We were the first."

"We are *the circle!*" roared The Infinity, outraged by their blasphemy.

"All this," said Alex, "because we chose mortality. Because we chose to live and die—"

"Die? You *cannot* die, not as those idiots know it."

Alex ignored him. "Because we chose to love."

"Your 'love' had a side effect though, didn't it?"

"Humanity is not a side effect, my deluded brother," said Ellen.

"Humanity is weak; I've proven it. They are fallible."

"They haven't been given a chance!" Alex slammed his fist into his hand. "What would have happened without your interference, your manipulation, your lies?"

"They wouldn't have made it out of the caves," said The Infinity. "And neither would you, come to that."

"How do you *know*? And so what if they hadn't. Your 'progress' was only leading to one thing: their ultimate annihilation."

The Infinity looked like he was about to say something, then said something else instead. "I repeat my original question, do you yield to me?"

"Give you permission to do what you want with them?" Alex shook his head.

Ellen did the same.

"You think your knowledge makes you more powerful now. You think that can stop me from getting what I want. As you say, we have all the time we will ever need to finish this. I *will* get you to submit, one way or the other. I always do."

"You can't touch them without our consent. They are of us, and we of them," Ellen reminded him.

"Yes, that is what makes them what they are. Why they will always fail."

"Our offspring were strong and kind, which is more than could be said for your son." Ellen pulled a face, remembering Peck. "You passed on all your badness to him, all your warped interpretations of the world. Who'd be normal after that? He wasn't even born of a woman because you didn't want him to be tainted by our line. He was a plaything for you, a doll you could order around because, after all this time, you were sick to death of your own company."

"I am really going to enjoy making you suffer, little sister."

"I don't think so," said Alex. "Not this time."

The picture flickered and changed again. On it was the universe; vast, circular, almost like a molecule. And zooming in, the solar system, past other planets, Uranus, Jupiter, Mars, to get to the Earth: blue and white… and round. Another extreme close-up, past clouds, travelling along the sea, skimming the ocean to Armitage Bay and coming to rest above the three of them at the funfair, on the platform.

"It's taken us generations to pass on the information," said Alex, "but we finally fathomed it out."

There lay The Infinity, Ellen and Alex, holding hands. Their prone bodies formed a circle.

"We've finally found a way to stop you," said Ellen.

"Oh?" The Infinity didn't look too bothered.

"Yes."

As they watched, Ellen's arm moved in the waking world. She opened her hand, wrestling it out of the grip of The Infinity. At the other side, Alex was doing the same.

"No, wait. You can't do that until we've finished," he said, making himself large again, making himself more intimidating, distributing his blackness.

"You don't scare us anymore big brother," said Alex. "You may have been the first, but we are not the circle anymore."

"Wait. You don't know what you're doing. It's *dangerous!*"

On the platform they both let go of The Infinity.

The circle was broken.

Inside the otherscape, the circle began to crumble too—the confines billowed and cracked. The pure energy buzzed, fizzling out. Their home was toppling down around their ears, The Infinity filled with fear for the first time since the two of them abandoned him at the dawn of everything.

"*NOOOO!*" he screeched.

But it was already too late. The circle exploded, the ghosts of Alex and Ellen's former lives were set free, streaking off into who knows where...

* * *

On the platform, Steve opened one eye in time to see a blue light cover the whole of The Infinity's body, working its way out from inside—then witness it erupt into the heavens in a special effect beyond any Hollywood CGI expert's capabilities. He also felt a thump in the pit of his stomach similar to when bass is played very loudly and you're too close to the speaker.

That seen, that experienced, he drifted back into unconsciousness, unaware that the fate of the entire planet had been decided.

By his little brother, and his little brother's shrink.

– iii –

The first drops of rain woke them.

Alex first, then Ellen. They were still holding hands, though their free hands were empty. They looked to the space were The Infinity had been. He was gone, just like Peck had vanished before they entered the circle.

Alex blinked water out of his eyes. His glasses lay where they'd fallen, but he could see clearly now; more clearly than he ever had in his life. "Are you all right?" he asked Ellen

She said that she was.

Shakily, he got to his feet, helping her up too. They hugged each other as the light shower sprinkled them with water. They kissed again, to reinforce that they were still here, still alive and together.

There was a groan coming from the ground not far away. Alex went over to Steve and lifted him up, slapping him lightly on the cheek. "Steve, talk to me. Steve?"

The rain was washing away the blood from his face and Alex could see how swelled up it was, a black eye flowering, bruising at his jaw. He came round again but was still groggy. "You look like shit, bruv," he said.

Alex laughed. "You're not exactly Chris Hemsworth yourself at the moment."

Steve started coughing, a laugh in there somewhere.

"Come on, let's get you out of here."

Ellen helped Vaughn up as well, and they all began to make their way through the funfair in the hopes they'd find the exit soon. The place seemed deserted, most people fleeing after the trouble had started. The rain was coming down more heavily, and there was a definite chill to the air, so anybody who was still around would be looking for shelter anyway.

Which just left the four of them walking past rides that had now shut down, lights and electrical systems failing.

Alex couldn't resist one last look back over his shoulder at the giant wheel. Standing there like a monument to what had happened beneath its gaze. To the outcome of this final conclusive battle of physical and mental strength. A meeting of wills from which they had emerged victorious.

Strangely, it gave him no satisfaction. There was just a sense of loss, of deep sadness that it should have come to this. That their kin couldn't have left them and their offspring alone. And a sense of nervousness now that the human race was on its own—free to make its own mistakes and forge its own future. Alex couldn't help wondering if The Infinity had been right, that they would still head towards disaster anyway, that it was in their nature to do so.

But then he thought of his students back at college, the hopes and dreams of their futures, and knew that all was not lost.

– iv –

"There they are!"

Martin pointed across to the stalls where his mum and dad were sheltering against the rain, frantic with worry. There was a third person with them and Frank shuddered when he saw who it was. "There's no need to be frightened anymore," Martin told him. "We've both been found, haven't we?"

He went over, leaving Frank and Terry for a moment. His parents hugged the boy and made a fuss of him, and he pointed back to indicate who had found him and brought him back to them. Then he spoke to the clown standing alongside, who gave him another of his silver balloons.

Martin ran over to Frank with it. "I told him about how you'd found me and he said to give you this." The clown offered a small wave. "Thank you, Frank," said Martin, and returned to his folks.

Frank looked at the picture on the balloon—it was another Froggy to replace the one that had been shot. He waved back to Martin, his parents *and* the clown.

"Soppy git," said Terry.

The rain was pounding down, but neither were in any hurry to leave. They stood there for some time, not really saying anything—just thinking. Wondering what had happened to the rest of the people they'd come with, and who else had been lost and found today.

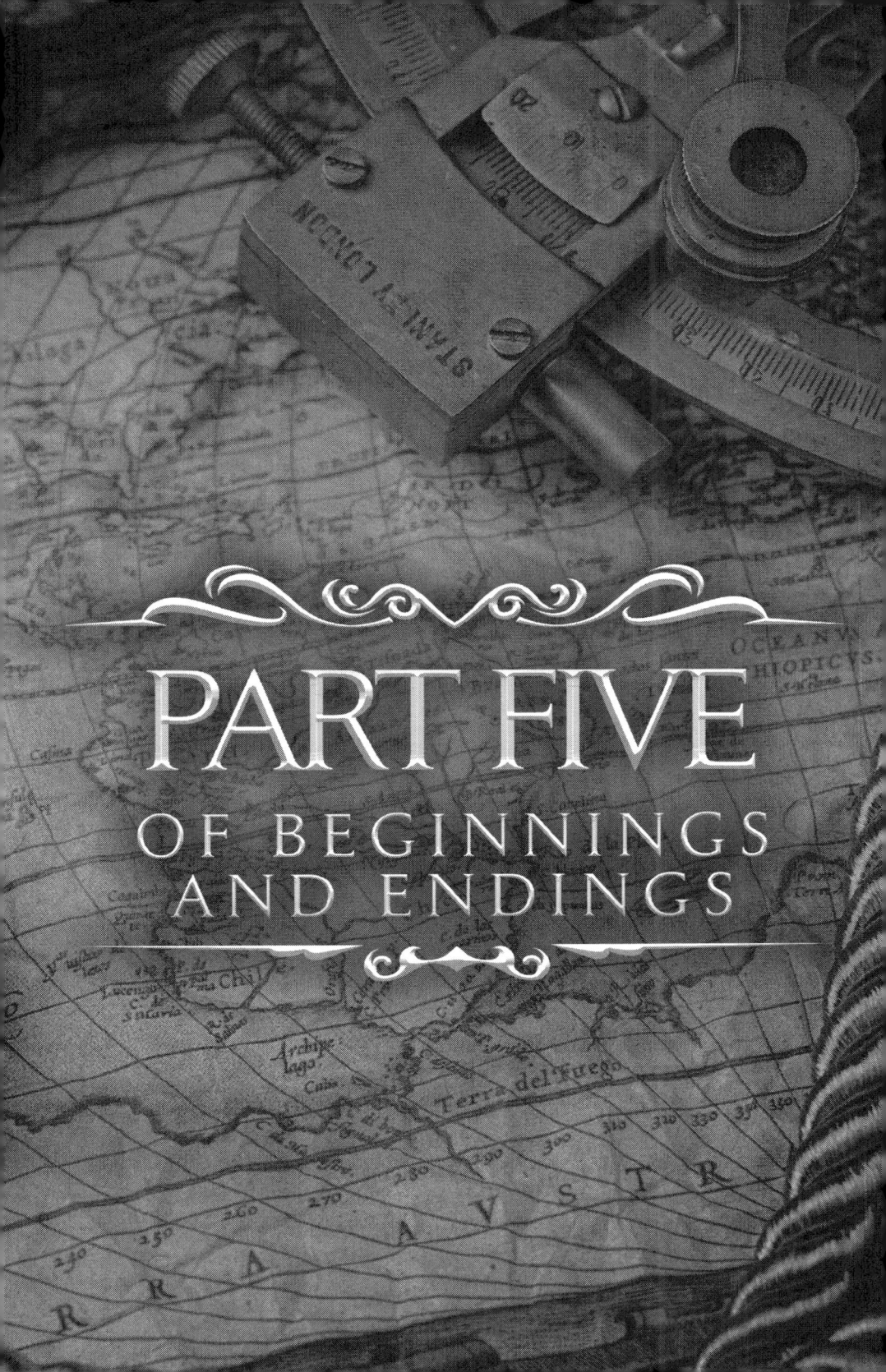

PART FIVE

OF BEGINNINGS
AND ENDINGS

Twenty-Seven

Yazmin's Nightclub, Five Months Later

– i –

They'd never really been nightclub people.

Even when they were younger they'd shied away from nights on the town, from the loud music and drink. It wasn't their scene at all. But they'd come tonight to show their support, to wish Steve well, and to check out their new investment. The bank had put most of the money into it, but Alex and Ellen both had significant stakes in the place. Ellen had taken some convincing, but she trusted Alex implicitly and knew his brother was trying his hardest to get back on his feet.

"He really has gone legit," Alex assured her. "And the 'word on the street' as they say, is that Yazmin's is a place to stay away from if you're up to no good."

Steve had vowed to turn the place around, to take what had been Nicky Metcalf's undercity HQ and weed out all the lowlifes. "What better bloke to spot them than somebody who used to be one," he'd told them.

After the police had finally investigated Metcalf, they'd put a lot of his operations out of commission anyway. Not one of his contacts was daring to raise his head above the parapet in case someone hit it with a baton. What the cops had been unable to get to the bottom of, though, was the gunfight at Armitage Bay and why Metcalf had been there in the first place. They suspected it might have something to do with a drugs shipment coming in illegally from abroad. That Metcalf had been there to oversee the drop—a considerable amount of coke had been found in his safe back home, in a case brought in from Amsterdam. But something must have gone spectacularly wrong, and as a consequence there had been a bloodbath down in the bay area. Reports of the shootings were patchy, as if none of the eyewitnesses could quite put their finger on what they'd seen, and the violence had extended to the funfair where two bodies were found: one of them Metcalf's. Of the surviving gangsters, the one called Fisher had been hospitalised and claimed he had no memory of anything due to the blows he'd received; the other—a man called Hamilton—had been found washed up on shore a few miles down the coast ranting and raving, and had been taken into custody. He was currently undergoing psychiatric evaluation.

"So, what can I get you both?" said the new manager of Yazmin's as they sat down at the bar. "And please don't say vodka."

Alex smiled and thought about it. "Just a lager for me, I'm a man of simple tastes."

"Gin and tonic," Ellen told Steve.

"On the house, naturally," he informed them.

Alex watched his big brother fix the drinks. He preferred the hands-on approach to running this place and hardly ever used the back room. Besides, he seemed right at home behind the bar, laughing and joking with staff and punters—he was a natural. It was good to see him so together and sorted out. He'd even introduced them to his girlfriend, who'd been promoted from semi-serious to serious. "Caroline had her doubts about me," he told them, "and I can't say I blame her, but we're going to give it a go. She's doing an accountancy course part-time, so she'll even be able to help out with the books for this place."

Alex nodded. "Just so long as you hang on to her a bit longer than the others."

"Don't worry, I've learnt my lesson," said Steve, winking. "I'm even taking her round to see Mum at the weekend."

Alex had encouraged the two of them to put their differences aside more lately, and things were tentatively moving forward. It was too early for Alex to introduce her to Ellen, however, so this would take the heat off him for a while. The distraction would be good because things were still a bit up in the air as far as their own lives were concerned. There was a lot to work out, including what direction their careers would move in. Ellen had been in talks with some of the people at Griffield Royal where she'd brought Patrick Vaughn to recuperate, where the survivors from Kirkwell had ended up—including Sam, who'd been over the moon to see her. He'd also spent an afternoon beating Alex at pool. The hospital were very impressed with her credentials and the way she was getting through to her patients, slowly but surely—which had more than a little to do with some newly remembered talents she'd brought back with her from the circle.

"I only use them when absolutely necessary, Alex," she'd said to him one night in bed at her redecorated flat.

And those talents had been more than necessary when it came to convincing the authorities about Beverly and James. Both Ellen and Alex respectively found that they'd been able to convince the police that they'd died of natural causes. It was tricky, but not impossible. No worse than some of the things The Infinity had persuaded people of. Both had been given decent funerals.

"Will you ever be able to forgive them?" Ellen had asked afterwards.

And he'd replied: "There's nothing to forgive. They needed each other. In a strange sort of way I understand." But there was still a great deal to work through, and that was one of the reasons he'd taken a break from teaching. The other was to do with what had happened to him back in May.

"The college wouldn't hold it against you, honestly," Ellen promised him. "At least, not after I'm finished with them."

"I don't know, I just feel like a complete change. Maybe take on some university work. If you do end up at Griffield, we could be nearer to each other," he said to Ellen.

But that was all ahead of them, in a world where they knew they would be able to live in peace…for now. Where at least there would be no outside forces tinkering with major developments. What happened would happen of its own accord. And they planned to still be around then to see it, if not in those bodies, then the next ones.

They'd thought about manipulating the memories of those closest to them, just to stop the occasional question that kept cropping up about what had occurred those few weeks last summer. But they found that after a while people stopped asking anyway. Their recollections adjusted, glossing over certain incidents and events. Ellen called it the mind's way of coping. Alex thought maybe it was a delayed mind-wipe initiated by The Infinity.

"Nobody's meant to know what all this is about. Only us."

"All the other times our compliance has sent us mad with guilt," Ellen mused. "It's what drove Lars and his wife apart after they'd visited the circle."

"Then a year after his death, she'd died too, alone. At the end I…he was still thinking about her…I mean, you… God it gets so confusing sometimes, all of this past life business."

"Tell me about it."

"Anyway, Lars was still thinking about her at the end of his life. She was the one he was talking about on that tape. The person he loved."

"I know." Ellen smiled. "I have a feeling she was thinking about him too, even though they weren't together. I know I would have been thinking about you."

The DJ in the club was cranking up the music, and the lights were dimming. Alex looked round at the young people in there, and wondered what their lives would be like; what was in store for them.

"Doesn't it make you want to be young again?" Ellen asked him, taking hold of his hand.

"You're only as old as you feel," Alex replied. "Which in our case—"

"Don't even go there," Ellen warned him.

"Here you are." Steve placed the drinks in front of them and they thanked him.

"Lively crowd tonight," Alex said to his brother. "You're sure everything's under control?"

Steve knew exactly what he meant. "Everything's cool, bruv. This place is strictly off limits to a certain clientele now; nothing dodgy. If they don't get the message, then I'm sure our security staff would be happy to deliver it to them personally." He waved across the room at two men, as big and wide as tower blocks, both wearing sunglasses. Frank and Terry waved back. "They know exactly who—and what—to look for."

"I'm sure they do," said Ellen, who was the only one of the three who still had doubts about them, having witnessed their performances in the hospital and at Vaughn's house. But, if this had taught them anything, it was that people are not all bad and not all good. There were grey areas, but as long as there was balance then that was the best anyone could ever really hope for.

"Okay, then," said Alex, raising his glass. "What shall we drink to?"

"How about the future," Steve suggested.

Ellen nodded. "I'll definitely drink to that."

Alex clinked his lager glass with her gin and tonic.

"The future," said Ellen.

"The future," Alex echoed, and took a sip.

Just outside the Arctic Circle—Sometime in The Future

– ii –

Nobody ever put a bet on whether it would snow for Christmas around here.

It was a running joke amongst the members of the exploration team. "How much are you going to put on it, then?" Sanders had said the other day.

"There aren't enough bucks in the whole world," Temple had replied. He'd much rather save his cash for the poker evenings they were used to having around eight every night. They'd got quite a good school going here and as a sideline he'd won himself about fifty dollars this week. Who knows, by the time he was finished here, he'd probably have amassed a nice little pot to take home to Tanya, which might make up for the fact that he was absent again at Yuletide.

He could just imagine her and his teenage daughter Deana making preparations for the festive season, putting up the tree, hanging the stockings on the wall, buying presents. He'd left theirs at home, but they'd have to wait until the New Year before they could return the favour. It was a complete pain in the butt, he knew, especially for them.

"What's still left for people to explore out there?" Deana wanted to know.

"Plenty," he'd told her. "For example, we're still trying to work out the effects of global warming in those regions, honey. You see, the Department of Geology and Planetary Science at the university—"

"Whatever," his daughter had said.

But he wasn't prepared for what they had seen a little over a week ago, five days out from the research station. Strange lights in the sky, flashes of white and red and purple, just like the Northern lights. Some of the team had even joked that it was extraterrestrial activity.

"Come on," Sanders said when they were back inside the tents, "why would they fly all the way to Earth just to land in the Arctic? Hell, I'm not even sure what I'm doing out here, apart from freezing my balls off."

"Might've crash landed," Milhouse offered, his face stern. "Like in that movie, *It's Alive*." An expert in sedimentology, paleolimnology and climate change and he still didn't know his Sci-Fi.

"That was *The Thing*," Temple corrected him. "*It's Alive* is about a mutant baby."

"You sure?" said Milhouse. "Cos I thought *It's Alive* was about aliens."

"You're thinking of *They Live*, with that wrestler guy. Same director made it I think." Temple pulled back his hood and wiped off the sweat.

"So what's *The Thing* about?"

"Kurt Russell's in the Arctic and they come across this killer dog that turns into like an octopus or something," said Sanders. "That's right, isn't it? Turns out it was a shape-shifting alien that crashed here."

"Basically," said Temple. "But you're no Roger Ebert."

"Anyways, it picks off the research team at this station. It can look like anyone y'see, it can look human." Sanders grabbed Milhouse by the arm and the man jumped.

"Cut that out."

Sanders was laughing fit to burst. They didn't get much in the way of amusement in the Arctic at Christmas time.

But he wasn't laughing a few days later when they found the footprint in the snow. Sanders had come across it first and shouted for the others.

"Just look at that," Temple had said.

"Some of them look like they've been covered over by fresh snowfalls, but I'd say they were heading in that direction." Sanders pointed over the rise with his gloved finger.

Temple got down to examine the print. "What would you say made it?"

"I don't know—it's only small though. Couldn't have been a bear. Chris..." Temple knew he was in trouble when the guy used his first name. "I'm not sure about it, but this looks...well it looks like it was made by a man. And it looks like he was barefoot."

That had sent a shiver down their spines. It wasn't beyond the realms of possibility that there was another research team out here at the same time. They hadn't heard anything, but maybe the British had sent some of their people to this sector? What was damned bizarre was the fact that they were dancing around with their boots off in temperatures where you kept them on if you were attached to all your toes.

Milhouse was the most freaked out by it. He looked paler than usual, and that was saying something. "H-How could there be anyone out here making these?"

"Only one way to find out," said Temple.

They followed the tracks for about a day, losing them at one point, then picking them up again a few klicks away. Then the tracks stopped completely.

Because they found the thing that had been making them, curled up and unconscious.

Sanders had been right; they'd been made by a man, with bare feet. With bare everything in fact. Lying there, in the snow, they found an average-sized guy, approximately average weight, completely naked.

"How's he survived out here?" asked Milhouse.

"*Is* he alive?" asked Sanders.

Again, there was only one way to find out. Temple got down, pulled off his glove and pressed his fingers against the man's neck.

"Don't touch him," shouted Milhouse. "He might shoot tentacles out at you or something."

"Shut up," Sanders said.

Temple shook his head. "No pulse. He's dead as a—"

The man opened his eyes. Bright blue, cobalt eyes. He regarded the team, looking from one person to the other.

"Jesus," said Sanders.

"See!" Milhouse was hopping up and down in the snow. "He's one of them—he's a fucking alien!"

"Milhouse, will you calm yourself." Temple bent over the man. "Hi." He couldn't think of anything else to say.

Sanders stepped forward. "Ask him if he can speak English."

The man nodded. He attempted to move, propping himself up on one elbow.

"Easy now," said Temple, helping him.

The man opened his mouth, but nothing came out at first.

"Where am I?" he croaked eventually.

"Where are you? It sure ain't Miami Beach, fella," said Sanders.

"What happened to you?" Temple enquired. "Where are your clothes?"

The man told them that he couldn't remember. "I've…I've been… somewhere… But…" He shook his head, unable to dredge the information up.

"Never mind, it'll come. Probably exposure." Temple was getting out some blankets from his pack and wrapping them around him. They'd set up camp again in a minute and get him in out of the elements, get him some warm food; maybe get some answers. The man surprised them all then by getting up, and standing—albeit shakily.

Sanders averted his eyes from his nakedness. Milhouse just stared. "Guy's got no belly button," he whispered. "I'm telling you, there's something not right here."

"Do you have a name?" asked Temple.

The man thought about this. "I-I don't… Wait, wait. I think…I think I'm called Finn. Where did you say I was again?"

"The Arctic Circle, buddy," Sanders told him bluntly.

"The circle." This seemed to strike a chord with him. "I must…I have to go somewhere… I have something I must do."

"You're not going anywhere until we get you heated up some."

"No, you will take me now!" said the man. His blue eyes flashed brightly, and for a moment Temple almost forgot where he was, what he was doing, and obeyed him. But he shrugged off the feeling, clearing his head in seconds.

"We'll set up camp here tonight," he told his men. "First food and heat for you, Finn. Then we'll head back to the station before the next severe storm hits, talk about what to do next."

* * *

Finn nodded wearily at the man's suggestion. He didn't have the strength to argue, and the offer of warmth did sound good to him.

He just wished he could remember who he was, what he was doing here. He had a feeling he'd been away for quite some time. But now he was back, and in time he would find out. In time.

But he did remember this much: a beginning and an end.

I wonder what that means, he thought.

No, not *a* beginning; *The* beginning.

The beginning and—

The End.

Acknowledgements

My heartfelt gratitude to Anthony Rivera at Grey Matter Press for having such faith in this story, and totally getting where I was coming from with it—and to Dean Samed for the brilliant cover. Thanks guys for taking my suggestions on board, and for working at the eleventh hour so we could get that piece in about the book to *Horrorville* magazine!

A novel as huge as this one doesn't happen without the support of a great many people, beginning with my late Mum, Dad & Nan; I couldn't have started this or even continued it without them and I owe all three so, so much; I wish they'd been around to see it come out.

As always, hugs and massive thank yous to all my friends in the writing and film/TV world for their continual help and faith in me. A very special thank you, though, to people like Clive Barker, Neil Gaiman, Mandy Slater, Stephen Jones, Amanda Foubister, Peter Atkins and Dana Middleton, Christopher Fowler, RC Matheson, Stephen Volk, Sarah Pinborough, Mike Marshall Smith and Paula Grainger, Alexandra Benedict, Tim Lebbon, Mike Carey, Barbie Wilde, Pete & Nicky Crowther, Simon Clark, Jason Arnopp and oh so many more. You're all stars!

Last, but never, ever least, a big words are not enough thank you to my incredible family and my darling wife Marie, who is my rock. Love you ever so much.

ABOUT THE AUTHOR

PAUL KANE IS AN AWARD-WINNING writer and editor based in Derby-shire, UK. His short story collections include *Alone (In the Dark)*, *Touching the Flame*, *FunnyBones*, *Peripheral Visions*, *Shadow Writer*, *The Adventures of Dalton Quayle*, *The Butterfly Man and Other Stories*, *The Spaces Between*, *Ghosts*, *Monsters* and *Nailbiters*. His novellas include *The Lazarus Condition*, *RED* and *Pain Cages*. He is the author of such novels as *Of Darkness and Light*, *The Gemini Factor* and the bestselling *Arrowhead* trilogy (*Arrowhead*, *Broken Arrow* and *Arrowland*, gathered together in the sellout omnibus edition *Hooded Man*), a post-apocalyptic reworking of the Robin Hood mythology. His latest novels are *Lunar* (which is set to be turned into a feature film), *Sleeper(s)* (a modern, horror version of *Sleeping Beauty*), the short Y.A. novel *The Rainbow Man* (as P.B. Kane), the sequel to *RED—Blood RED*—and the critically-acclaimed award-winning hit *Sherlock Holmes and the Servants of Hell* from Solaris.

He has also written for comics, most notably for the *Dead Roots* zombie anthology alongside writers such as James Moran (*Torchwood*, *Cockneys vs. Zombies*) and Jason Arnopp (*Friday The 13th*, *The Last Days of Jack Sparks*) and as part of the team turning *Clive Barker's Books of Blood* into motion comics for Seraphim/MadeFire. Paul is co-editor of the anthology *Hellbound Hearts* (Simon & Schuster)—stories based around the mythology that spawned *Hellraiser—The Mammoth Book of Body Horror* (Constable & Robinson/Running Press), featuring the likes of Stephen King and James Herbert, *A Carnivàle of Horror* (PS) featuring Ray Bradbury and Joe Hill, and *Beyond Rue Morgue* from Titan, stories based around Poe's detective, Dupin.

His non-fiction books are *The Hellraiser Films and Their Legacy*, *Voices in the Dark* and *Shadow Writer—The Non-Fiction. Vol. 1: Reviews* and *Vol. 2: Articles and Essays*, plus his genre journalism has appeared in the likes of *SFX*, *Fangoria*, *Dreamwatch*, *Gorezone*, *Rue Morgue* and *DeathRay*. He has been a guest at Alt.Fiction five times, was a guest at the first SFX Weekender, at Thought Bubble in 2011, Derbyshire Literary Festival, Off the Shelf in 2012, Monster Mash and Event Horizon in 2013, Edge-Lit in 2014, HorrorCon, HorrorFest and Grimm Up North in 2015, The Dublin Ghost Story Festival and Sledge-Lit in 2016, plus IMATS Olympia in 2017, as well as being a panellist at FantasyCon and the World Fantasy Convention, and a fiction judge at Sci-Fi London. He is a former Special Publications Editor of the British Fantasy Society and is currently serving as co-chair of the UK arm of the Horror Writers Association.

His work has been optioned for film and television, and his zombie story "Dead Time" was turned into an episode of the Lionsgate/NBC TV series *Fear Itself*, adapted by Steve Niles (*30 Days of Night*) and directed by Darren Lynn Bousman (*SAW II-IV*). He also scripted *The Opportunity*, which premiered at the Cannes Film Festival, *Wind Chimes* (directed by Brad "*7th Dimension*" Watson and which sold to TV) and *The Weeping Woman*—filmed by award-winning director Mark Steensland and starring Tony-nominated actor Stephen Geoffreys (*Fright Night*). You can find out more at his website www.shadow-writer.co.uk which has featured Guest Writers such as Dean Koontz, Robert Kirkman, Charlaine Harris and Guillermo del Toro.

OTHER BOOKS BY PAUL KANE

NOVELS

Arrowhead

Broken Arrow

Arrowland

Hooded Man (Omnibus)

The Gemini Factor

Of Darkness and Light

Lunar

Sleeper(s)

The Rainbow Man (as P.B. Kane)

Blood RED

Sherlock Holmes and the Servants of Hell

Before

Forthcoming: Deep RED

NOVELLAS & NOVELETTES

Signs of Life

The Lazarus Condition

Dalton Quayle Rides Out

RED

Pain Cages

Creakers (chapbook)

Flaming Arrow

The Bric-a-Brac Man

The P.I.'s Tale

Snow

The Rot

Forthcoming: Coming of Age

COLLECTIONS

Alone (In the Dark)

Touching the Flame

FunnyBones

The Shadows Trilogy (ebook)

Peripheral Visions

The Adventures of Dalton Quayle

Shadow Writer

The Butterfly Man and Other Stories

The Spaces Between
Ghosts
Monsters
The Dead Trilogy (ebook)
Shadow Casting
The Spirits of Christmas
Nailbiters
Disexistence
Death

EDITOR & CO-EDITOR
Shadow Writers Vol. 1 & 2
Terror Tales #1-4
Top International Horror
Albions Alptraume: Zombies
The British Fantasy Society: A Celebration
Hellbound Hearts
The Mammoth Book of Body Horror
A Carnivàle of Horror: Dark Tales from the Fairground
Beyond Rue Morgue
Forthcoming: Dark Mirages

NON-FICTION
Contemporary North American Film Directors: A Wallflower Critical Guide
(Major Contributor)
Cinema Macabre (Contributor)
The Hellraiser Films And Their Legacy
Voices in the Dark
Shadow Writer – The Non-Fiction. Vol. 1: Reviews
Shadow Writer – The Non-Fiction. Vol. 2: Articles & Essays

MORE DARK FICTION FROM
GREY MATTER PRESS

"Grey Matter Press has managed to establish itself as one of the premiere purveyors of horror fiction currently in existence via both a series of killer anthologies — *SPLATTERLANDS, OMINOUS REALITIES, EQUILIBRIUM OVERTURNED* — and John F.D. Taff's harrowing novella collection *THE END IN ALL BEGINNINGS.*"

- *FANGORIA Magazine*

GREY MATTER
P R E S S

THE **REAL MONSTERS** ARE IN YOUR MIRROR

PEEL BACK THE SKIN

FROM BRAM STOKER AWARD® NOMINATED EDITORS

ANTHONY
RIVERA

SHARON
LAWSON

PEEL BACK THE SKIN
ANTHOLOGY OF HORROR

They are among us.

They live down the street. In the apartment next door. And even in our own homes.

They're the real monsters. And they stare back at us from our bathroom mirrors.

Peel Back the Skin is a powerhouse new anthology of terror that strips away the mask from the real monsters of our time – mankind.

Featuring all-new fiction from a star-studded cast of award-winning authors from the horror, dark fantasy, speculative, transgressive, extreme horror and thriller genres, *Peel Back the Skin* is the next game-changing release from Bram Stoker Award-nominated editors Anthony Rivera and Sharon Lawson.

FEATURING:

Jonathan Maberry	James Lowder
Ray Garton	Lucy Taylor
Tim Lebbon	Joe McKinney
Ed Kurtz	Erik Williams
William Meikle	Charles Austin Muir
Yvonne Navarro	John McCallum Swain
Durand Sheng Welsh	Nancy A. Collins

Graham Masterton

GREY MATTER
P R E S S

greymatterpress.com

EVEN MONSTERS CAN LOVE

SEEING
DOUBLE

KAREN RUNGE

SEEING DOUBLE
BY KAREN RUNGE

A trio of expats living in Asia form a tenuous bond based on mutual attraction, sexual obsession and the insatiable desire to experience the deadliest of thrills.

As their relationship matures, the dangerous love triangle in which they've become entwined quickly escalates into a series of brutal sexual conquests as they struggle to deal with lives spinning out of control and the debilitating psychological effects mental and physical abuse.

Known for her distinctive brand of unsettling fiction, author Karen Runge is at the top of the modern horror game in this, her premiere novel. Seeing Double is a beautifully evocative and stunningly dark coming-of-age exploration of human sexuality and the roles of masculinity and feminism, polyamorous relationships, social and psychological isolation, and the humiliation of ultimate betrayal.

———————————

Karen Runge is an artist and horror writer whoe teaches adults English as a second language. Her fiction has appeared in *Pseudopod*, *Something Wicked*, *Pantheon* Magazine and *Structo*.

Her story with editor and author Simon Dewar, "High Art." is featured in the Grey Matter Press anthology *Death's Realm*. Runge's short story "Good Help," which appears in *Shock Totem 9*, prompted horror icon Jack Ketchum to tell her, "Karen, you scare me."

———————————

GREY MATTER
P R E S S

greymatterpress.com

A DARK THRILLER

MISTER WHITE

THE NOVEL

DO NOT SPEAK HIS NAME

JOHN C. FOSTER

MISTER WHITE
BY JOHN C. FOSTER

In the shadowy world of international espionage and governmental black ops, when a group of American spies go bad and inadvertently unleash an ancient malevolent force that feeds on the fears of mankind, a young family finds themselves in the crosshairs of a frantic supernatural mystery of global proportions with only one man to turn to for their salvation.

Combine the intricate, plot-driven stylings of suspense masters Tom Clancy and Robert Ludlum, add a healthy dose of Clive Barker's dark and brooding occult horror themes, and you get a glimpse into the supernatural world of international espionage that the chilling new horror novel *Mister White* is about to reveal.

John C. Foster's *Mister White* is a terrifying genre-busting suspense shocker that, once and for all, answer the question you dare not ask: "Who is Mister White?"

"*Mister White* is a potent and hypnotic brew that blends horror, espionage and mystery. Foster has written the kind of book that keeps the genre fresh and alive and will make fans cheer. Books like this are the reason I love horror fiction." – RAY GARTON, Grand Master of Horror and Bram Stoker Award®-nominated author of *Live Girls* and *Scissors*.

"*Mister White* is like Stephen King's *The Stand* meets Ian Fleming's James Bond with Graham Masterton's *The Manitou* thrown in for good measure. It's frenetically paced, spectacularly gory and eerie as hell. Highly recommended!" – JOHN F.D. TAFF, Bram Stoker Award®-nominated author of *The End in All Beginnings*

GREY MATTER
P R E S S

greymatterpress.com

BRAM STOKER AWARD® NOMINATED
THE END IN ALL BEGINNINGS
"CHILLING"
- Kealan Patrick Burke
"THE BEST NOVELLA COLLECTION IN YEARS!"
- Jack Ketchum
JOHN F.D. TAFF
MODERN HORROR'S KING OF PAIN

THE END IN ALL BEGINNINGS
BY JOHN F.D. TAFF

The Bram Stoker Award-nominated *The End in All Beginnings* is a tour de force through the emotional pain and anguish of the human condition. Hailed as one of the best volumes of heartfelt and gut-wrenching horror in recent history, *The End in All Beginnings* is a disturbing trip through the ages exploring the painful tragedies of life, love and loss.

Exploring complex themes that run the gamut from loss of childhood innocence, to the dreadful reality of survival after everything we hold dear is gone, to some of the most profound aspects of human tragedy, author John F.D. Taff takes readers on a skillfully balanced emotional journey through everyday terrors that are uncomfortably real over the course of the human lifetime. Taff's highly nuanced writing style is at times darkly comedic, often deeply poetic and always devastatingly accurate in the most terrifying of ways.

Evoking the literary styles of horror legends Mary Shelley, Edgar Allen Poe and Bram Stoker, *The End in All Beginnings* pays homage to modern masters Stephen King, Ramsey Campbell, Ray Bradbury and Clive Barker.

"*The End in All Beginnings* is accomplished stuff, complex and heartfelt. It's one of the best novella collections I've read in years!" – JACK KETCHUM, Bram Stoker Award®-winning author of *The Box, Closing Time* and *Peaceable Kingdom*

"Taff brings the pain in five damaged and disturbing tales of love gone horribly wrong. This collection is like a knife in the heart. Highly recommended!" – JONATHAN MABERRY, *New York Times* bestselling author of *Code Zero* and *Fall of Night*

GREY MATTER
P R E S S

greymatterpress.com

COMING SOON
FROM GREY MATTER PRESS

Little Black Spots by John F.D. Taff

Little Deaths: 5th Anniversary Edition by John F.D. Taff

The Madness of Crowds: The Ladies Bristol Occult Adventures #2 by Rhoads Brazos

MORE TITLES
FROM GREY MATTER PRESS

Before by Paul Kane

The Devil's Trill: The Ladies Bristol Occult Adventures #1 by Rhoads Brazos

Dark Visions: A Collection of Modern Horror - Volume One

Dark Visions: A Collection of Modern Horror - Volume Two

Death's Realm: The Anthology

Dread: The Best of Grey Matter Press - Volume One

The End in All Beginnings by John F.D. Taff

Equilibrium Overturned: A Volume of Apocalyptic Horrors

I Can Taste the Blood

Mister White: The Novel by John C. Foster

The Night Marchers and Other Strange Tales by Daniel Braum

Ominous Realities

Peel Back the Skin: Anthology of Horror

Savage Beasts

Secrets of the Weird by Chad Stroup

Seeing Double by Karen Runge

Splatterlands

RETURNING IN 2017
FROM GREY MATTER PRESS

The Bell Witch by John F.D. Taff

Kill/ Off by John F.D. Taff

23198151R00298

Printed in Great Britain
by Amazon